ALSO BY MATT JAMES

THE JACK REILLY ADVENTURES
The Forgotten Fortune
The Roosevelt Conspiracy
The Dorado Deception
The Undying Kingdom
The Venetian Pursuit (2023)

THE ZAHRA KANE THRILLERS with Nick Thacker
Empire Lost
Anubis Plague

THE UNSEEN (Previously published as DEAD MOON)
Origin (2022)
Desolation (2022)
Perseverance (2023)
Inferno (2023)
Abomination (New/2023)

ADVENTURES IN THE DANE MADDOCK UNIVERSE with David Wood
Berserk
Skin and Bones
Venom
Lost City

STAND-ALONE NOVELS
The Dragon
Dark Island
Sub-Zero
Cradle of Death

THE HANK BOYD ADVENTURES
Blood and Sand
Mayan Darkness
Babel Found
Elixir of Life

OTHER TITLES
The Cursed Pharaoh
Broken Glass
Plague
Evolve

PRAISE FOR MATT JAMES

"The words of a Matt James story flow like the best rivers. Smooth and subtle at times, interrupted by danger and thrills at every churn of whitewater. This guy is the real deal!"
—Ernest Dempsey, *USA Today* bestselling author of WHERE HORIZONS END

"Matt James is my go-to guy for heart-stopping adventure and bone-chilling suspense!"
—Greig Beck, bestselling author of TO THE CENTER OF THE EARTH

"If you enjoy globetrotting adventures jampacked with over-the-top action, then you'll love Matt James' work!"
—Nick Thacker, *USA Today* bestselling author of THE ENIGMA STRAIN

"If you're looking for a fast-moving tale with action to spare, give Matt James a try!"
—David Wood, *USA Today* bestselling author of SERPENT

"Searching for relentless action and harrowing adventure in dangerous locales? Look no further than Matt James!"
—Michael McBride, international bestselling author of SUBHUMAN

"Matt James is a must-read! The thrilling action, unexpected turns, and rip-roaring chases across the globe are fantastic adventures every time! You won't be disappointed."
—Andrew Clawson, bestselling author of THE ARTHURIAN RELIC

"Matt James reminds devotees of Indiana Jones and Nathan Drake why their love for rock-solid action-adventure springs eternal!"
—Rick Chesler, international bestselling author of ATLANTIS GOLD

"Matt's novels need a pause button. They do not stop!"
—Lee Murray, *Bram Stoker Award* winning author of INTO THE MIST

"A talent voice in the action-thriller genre!"
—Richard Bard, *Wall Street Journal* bestselling author of BRAINRUSH

"If you like thrills, chills, and nonstop action, then Matt James may just be your next favorite author!"
—John Sneeden, bestselling author of THE SIGNAL

"Matt James has proven that true adventure is found in the fine line between myth and reality. James walks that tightrope with a master's touch."
—J.M. LeDuc, bestselling author of SIN

"Matt James has cemented his place among the finest talents!"
—SUSPENSE MAGAZINE

THE UNDYING KINGDOM: AN ARCHAEOLOGICAL THRILLER
(THE JACK REILLY ADVENTURES - BOOK 4)
BY MATT JAMES

SEVEREDPRESS

THE UNDYING KINGDOM

THE UNDYING KINGDOM
THE JACK REILLY ADVENTURES - BOOK 4

BY MATT JAMES

PROLOGUE

Kantipur Hospital
Kathmandu, Nepal

Binsa hustled to the emergency entrance to help receive their new transfer. She'd been clued into the interesting nature of the man beforehand. Apparently, he was delusional, possibly dehydrated from his climb. The patient had been found in the foothills of the mountains directly to the north, gasping for breath and in pain.

She waved in one of the ambulance's EMTs, who met her halfway. "What's his name again?"

The EMT flipped to the second page on his clipboard. "He says it's Dhonu Thapa, but he has no identification of any kind. No driver's license, credit card, or insurance information, either."

Two other men wheeled Binsa's new patient in on a stretcher. She walked next to it while they headed for the elevator. "Sir," she said softly, "what's your date of birth?"

Thapa looked up at her. His eyes were deep and intense.

"Six…" he muttered. "Sixty…five."

The EMT snickered. "1965? There's no way this guy was born in 1965. He has to be twenty or thirty years older than that!"

"No!" Thapa shouted, grabbing Binsa's arm. The EMT dove at her arm to remove the elderly man's hand. But he couldn't. Thapa's grip was impossibly strong. His heavy breaths turned into gasps. The EMT stopped in his attempt when the patient spoke again.

"1865." His hand fell away. The man's strength faded, as did his consciousness. "Beware…" He coughed. "The valley—beware! Beware the curse!"

"What valley?" Binsa asked.

"Did he say 'curse?'" the EMT asked.

"The valley?" Binsa asked, patting his hand. "What valley?"

"The valley—" he broke out in a fit of coughs. Thapa took a deep breath and shouted, "Shangri-La!" Then, he passed out.

Binsa checked for a pulse and was surprised by how strong it was.

What's going on with this guy?

"1865?" the EMT asked. "That would make him, what—?"

"157 years old," Binsa finished, doing the math.

The young EMT shook his head and pressed the up arrow on the wall next to the elevator. "Just the ramblings of an old fool."

"And what about Shangri-La?" Binsa asked.

The EMT snorted. "Nothing more than a child's fantasy."

BIOfinity Genetics Group
Shanghai, China

He walked in a blur. His world had just been torn away, thrown to the ground, and trampled. At forty-nine years of age, David Cho had everything he could ever want. His company made billions, held lucrative military contracts, and was in the middle of its largest expansion. Still, at this moment, the biotech CEO didn't care.

He was dying.

Cancer... Six months. I'm sorry.

It was all he could recall from the doctor's appointment. David had already scheduled an appointment to get a second opinion, but something told him it wouldn't matter. His fate had been sealed.

"Mr. Cho," his assistant said. "Sir, are you alright?"

David ignored him and continued into his office. If Li knew what was best for him, he wouldn't follow. David needed to be alone. He needed to get some things in order. BIOfinity Genetics Group was going to need a replacement at the top. David had been its CEO since its rise to glory. No one had been more responsible for the company's launch into stardom than him. It had been him who had negotiated the company's first government contract. A prideful moment, for sure. He was a nationalist at heart, and it meant the world to him to be helping his country. And since then, David hadn't been able to keep up with all the money pouring in.

"Can't take it with you," he mumbled, plopping into his expensive office chair.

He gazed at the abstract painting on his wall, forgetting who had produced it. All he remembered was that it had been created over a century ago and had cost him a fortune.

Well, it had cost the company a fortune. Office expenses, blah, blah, blah.

David didn't care. Money wasn't a problem. He had thought it looked nice and would shock those who entered his domain. His office was decorated with several priceless historical artifacts, as well. He didn't know anything about those either, except that they had come from one of the ancient dynasties.

"That's right, 157 years old!"

David's eyes rolled over to the seventy-inch flatscreen. The TV was on low, but it was still loud enough for him to hear bits and pieces of the news story. A climber had been rescued from the base of the Himalayas, rambling on about Shangri-La. The man's detailed account was what interested David the most. The reports indicated that the climber's incident had occurred over a week ago and since then he had been slipping in and out of consciousness due to a diminished immune system.

This also piqued David's interest. His company had been working on a little concoction to boost a human's immunities tenfold. But, alas, the project had seen more failures than successes.

Project: Eternity.

The idea behind the project was to cheat death, eventually, but that was impossible. Nothing suggested that living forever was possible, not unless a digital option was considered. The project team had yet to delve into the science fiction of downloading a living creature's consciousness, but recent research had showed promise. It was still light years away, though. However, David knew it would only be a matter of time before he got his company involved with it.

Time... He didn't have time.

"The man claims to be a missing Sherpa named Dhonu Thapa. We had to do some digging, but our investigation suggests that Thapa was last seen over a century ago!" The reporter chuckled. "Regardless of who he really is, our weary traveler is resting comfortably at Kantipur Hospital in Nepal."

"Li!" David shouted, slamming his finger down on his intercom.

His assistant rushed in. "Yes, sir?"

David sat forward. He knew what he had to do. "Get me Shenlong."

Li's eyes opened wide, and he nodded emphatically. He knew that if David wanted to speak with Shenlong, then the situation was dire. The last time Shenlong and his compatriots had gotten involved, many people had died. Luckily, nothing had been traced back to BIOfinity Genetics.

Li bowed and backed out of David's office, shutting the door.

David glanced at his phone. He needed to contact someone else, and he would make the call himself. No one, except for maybe his trusted assistant, could know *he* was involved. This wasn't going to be a typical partnership. Everything from here on out would be done in secret and from the shadows.

Ministry of State Security
Beijing, China

Everything Jin Zhao could see belonged to him. It was a part of the job that he loved. The power he wielded as the Minister of State Security was unfathomable. Zhao was China, and China was Zhao. Few held his authority.

The MSS specialized in fields such as civilian intelligence and cyber espionage. But where they excelled was the use of homegrown foot soldiers— spies. Zhao had eyes everywhere and ears everywhere else. The whole of Asia was scrutinized twenty-four-seven, as were rival superpowers around the globe. No one was off limits. Information was key, and Zhao wanted it all for himself and, of course, his homeland. But if he was being honest, it was more for his own gain.

Eventually, Zhao and China would be one in the same.

"Excuse me, Minister Zhao?"

He didn't respond to the interruption. He just continued to stare out his window.

"I think you should see this."

He sighed and turned. He didn't speak unless what he had to say was worthwhile. Long ago, Zhao had been taught that the foolish typically opened their mouths the most.

His assistant cautiously entered, holding a plain manila envelope to her chest. Their exchange was nonverbal. She held out the offering with a slight tremble. Zhao took it, knowing it was important enough for her to interrupt him.

She left immediately.

Zhao faced his window and opened the envelope. Inside was a single printout. The information it contained was vague, yet it spoke volumes. He pulled his cell phone from his pocket and dialed. The person on the other end didn't verbally acknowledge him.

"I need you in Nepal. More information inbound."

He hung up and pocketed the device, but it quickly began to vibrate. He removed it again and looked at the screen. He recognized the number, crossed his office, and locked the door.

Cho?

He answered the call. "Yes?"

"Greetings, Minister. I have a proposition for you."

1

Yellowstone National Park
Wyoming, USA

Being on call twenty-four-seven sucked. Jack could be tossed onto a transcontinental flight at the drop of a hat. It was a tough way to exist, though it also had its benefits. Like now, instead of sitting at home and twiddling his thumbs, Jack had decided to enjoy the in-between moments. Jack wished the animal trotting beneath him had gotten the message. It had been a long time since Jack had ridden a horse.

Feels like it too, he thought. Jack desperately tried to ignore the discomfort in both his groin and lower back.

His companions seemed to be faring much better. Then again, they had grown up riding. Jack had ridden quite a bit over the years, but not recently. He was out of practice. Saddle tolerance wasn't his friend.

The valley's morning mist was a sight to behold. Even though Jack had worked in Yellowstone for nearly five years, the park's natural enchantment still hit him hard. It took his breath away. He'd sometimes find himself staring off into the distance, not looking at anything in particular.

"Holy crap, Jack!" Hawk said, eyes wide. "You found El Dorado?"

Jack could still envision the massive Titanoboa slithering up the side of the marooned German U-boat, *U-590.*

Holy crap, indeed.

Jack wasn't supposed to tell anyone about his wild escapades. Director Raegor wouldn't appreciate him spilling all of TAC's beans. The Tactical Archaeological Command worked deep in the shadows for a reason. There was an untold fortune out there, and plenty of people were willing to pillage and plunder those discoveries. That's where Jack and his employers came into play. It was essentially a series of "not on my watch" scenarios, not that Jack ever planned to stand in front of a speeding locomotive filled with loot and scream, "You shall not pass!"

Jack wasn't a fan of heavy wizard cloaks, either.

"Yes, very impressive." Bull was just as excited as his nephew, but as always, he emoted himself very differently.

It was good to be in the presence of the Durhams. On his left was Bull, Jack's closest friend. Hawk was to his right and had become a reliable source of laughter, whether it was on purpose or not. The latter had a way about him that made Jack smile, reminding Jack of a younger version of himself. Hawk was full of piss and vinegar, and he had a good heart.

At the request of Bull, Hawk had been hired on as his uncle's trainee with the National Park Service (NPS). He had proven himself time and time again during their heavily classified romp over in Cascade. It also helped that a mysterious benefactor—Solomon Raegor—had advised the NPS to give the elder Durham whatever he wanted in terms of help after they had dropped a sizeable donation in the agency's lap. Besides a pay raise for his fellow Yellowstone rangers and an upgrade in essential equipment, Bull had calmly demanded that Hawk be hired.

No one argued once they had seen all the zeros on the check.

Jack's horse hit a dip in the trail, jarring Jack's lower back. He readjusted his position, but it took no pressure off his spine.

"Tell me again why we're out here?" Jack asked.

Hawk happily relayed the information. "Montana PD has reason to believe that four gunmen are hiding in the park. Last week, they hit two banks, wounding a teller."

"Four days ago," Bull added, "the men were spotted fleeing into Yellowstone before vanishing from sight."

"Definitely locals," Jack said. Both Durhams stared at him. Jack explained his hypothesis. "No outsider would be dumb enough to run off into the park without knowing exactly where they were going."

"Are we even sure they're still in the park?" Hawk asked.

Bull shrugged. "I don't know. Police have set up roadblocks at all the major roads in and out of Yellowstone along its northern and western borders, yet there has still been no sign of them leaving."

"And the horses?" Jack asked.

Hawk snorted out a laugh. "You see any roads out here?"

Good point. Even the most offroad-worthy four-by-four would struggle on this terrain.

Jack sighed. "And here I thought I was going to get a peaceful reunion back home. Nope! Instead, I'm out here huntin' varmint!"

Hawk rolled his eyes. "Drama queen."

Jack grinned.

Bull didn't seem to hear any of their banter. He was too busy studying the landscape. He was an expert tracker, after all. He was easily four steps ahead of Mother Nature, already contemplating tomorrow's activities. It was getting dark, and the trio would need to stop for the night and pitch camp.

Camping at night in Yellowstone without a car nearby. What could go wrong?

They were headed to Lava Creek Tuff, a secluded area surrounding Gardner River in the park's northwest corner. Jack's most fun fact about Lava Creek was that its eruption had formed the famed Yellowstone Caldera—a subterranean super volcano powerful enough to destroy all life on Planet Earth. Neat.

Jack imagined the park going BOOM!

Heat. Lots of heat.

They headed for the water. At least, they tried to. Jack's horse wasn't having any of it. Dandelion was as stubborn as a mule. Jack guessed it was because he resented his name and probably his rider.

"His name is Dandelion?" Jack had asked, looking back and forth between the horse and Bull.

Bull nodded.

Hawk held back a laugh.

Dandelion softly neighed and bumped Jack with the top of his head. Jack reached out and gently patted and rubbed the horse's nose.

"Good boy, Danny," he said, deciding on a new-ish name. "Shh, shh, I know, I know, it's not your fault. It's a terrible name."

Just then, Danny reared up and threw Jack to the ground. Something had spooked the animal into tossing him. Jack landed hard, jamming his left shoulder a little. But the pain in his joint wasn't what Jack was worried about. The rising crescendo of a maraca alarmed both man and beast.

A creature slithered out from beneath a low shrub, beelining straight for Jack. He instantly recognized the four-foot-long asshole as *Crotalus v. viridis*, the prairie rattlesnake. It was the most dangerous snake in the park, one that would fight to the death if it felt its home was in danger.

Jack and Danny had, evidently, pissed it off enough for it to feel threatened. Jack figured there must've been a nest nearby. The rattler took the quickest path to Jack, veering toward the horse in the process.

Danny didn't take kindly to it.

As he had done moments earlier, Danny reared up, lifting the front half of his thick, muscular body off the ground. But instead of tossing his rider to the ground, the 1,000-pound animal brought his hoofs down atop the serpent.

The snake never knew what hit it.

With a bone-crunching force, Danny pounded the snake into oblivion, only stopping once Bull got close enough to snag his reins. Hawk dismounted and helped Jack to his feet. The rattlesnake now looked like pummeled jerky rather than a dangerous predator.

With Danny under control, Bull climbed off his horse and unsheathed his large utility knife. He got down to one knee and, with a swift jerk of his hand, removed the small, corncob-looking rattle from the end of the snake's tail. He turned and lobbed it to Jack.

"Um, thanks?" Jack said, pocketing the spoils. He then faced Danny and gently stroked the horse's forehead. "You, too."

Danny snorted and nodded his head as if he understood Jack.

"You two besties now?" Hawk asked, motioning between Jack and Danny.

"Totally!" Jack climbed back onto his steed in shining hide and pretended to toss back his hair. "We're going to stay up all night and talk about the cute mares back at HQ and braid each other's manes."

"Quiet."

Bull's steady, unemotional voice silenced the jovial pair of Jack and Hawk. The elder tracker looked west, but Jack couldn't see anything of note, even from the higher vantage atop Danny. Hawk didn't see anything either.

"What is it, Uncle?" Hawk asked, guiding his horse up next to Bull. Jack joined them and waited for Bull to reply. Jack had never seen someone so in-tune with nature. It was spooky sometimes how much Bull could learn from nothing more than a gentle breeze and a broken twig.

"Breathe deep," Bull advised. "Concentrate, and you will see as I do."

Jack trusted his friend and closed his eyes, shutting down everything else except his sense of smell. Whatever Bull had picked up on, he thought Jack and Hawk would be able to identify it too if they focused hard enough. Even now, Bull was still teaching Jack a thing or two.

He tried and failed. So did Hawk. Both men opened their eyes for guidance.

Bull's eyes were intense. He stayed quiet, per usual. Jack took a deep breath and let it out slowly while he shut his eyes again. His inhalations and exhalations were smooth and steady. When he was about to give up, he noticed something that hadn't been there a moment before. Jack locked in on the invasive odor and pondered its existence and its origin.

A soft breeze swooped through the valley, beginning at Lava Creek's highest point. They were downwind of it, giving away the smell's directional location.

"North," Jack said, confident. He zoned in on the smell. "Smoke."

"I smell it too," Hawk said, excited. "A fire?"

Both men opened their eyes and found a proud Bull smiling at them.

"Well done. If I were a betting man—"

"Please, Uncle, no more casinos." Hawk's face paled, and Jack knew why. He had a rotten history with them as of late.

"Yes, well, I believe our bank robbers have set up camp in the trees at the foot of that elevation." Bull pointed at a mountainous hill.

They were too far away to see any proof of a campfire, but Jack, like he always did, trusted Bull's judgment. He led the way. Jack and Hawk followed closely. They kept their speech to a minimum, hoping their presence would go unnoticed. Jack doubted the men in question would see a threesome on horseback coming to take them down.

"Are we really just going to call this in and wait?" Jack asked in hushed tones.

Bull glanced at him. "Either way, we do need to call the police." A small smirk formed on his face. "Whether these criminals sit idly by and wait to be arrested is entirely up to them."

Right, Jack thought, *looks like we're doing this the hard way.*

2

Their approach was slow and methodical. The horses were perfectly syncopated, trotting steadily along. It took them time to get close enough to see anything at all. The sun was nearly gone, and soon, there would be no natural light to see by, except what they could see by starlight.

Bull held up his fist. Jack eased back on Danny's reins, and they came to a stop with a grunt—the horse, not Jack. For good measure, Danny snapped his head around and bit the tip of Jack's boot. Jack didn't feel it through his steel-toe footwear, and he paid the ornery animal no attention.

They stood still and waited. Jack could see flickering firelight just inside the tree line, although it was creating a fudgy aura around something dark and rectangular.

What the hell?

He quietly slid out a small pair of binoculars from inside a saddlebag and held them up to his eyes. The object wasn't easy to distinguish against the darkened forest, but Jack was pretty sure he saw an SUV of some kind. The fire had been built behind the bulbous vehicle. It was used to shield the flickering light.

Clever.

Jack relayed what he saw.

"Huh," Hawk said, "I guess you can get a truck out here."

Jack inspected the front of the SUV, seeing something he liked. The vehicle was leaning terribly to the right. "Yeah, but you won't be getting it back." He brought the binoculars back down and looked at Hawk. "The front axle is busted."

They sat in silence for a moment.

"Head right," Jack said, tipping his chin in that direction. "Give them some space. I don't like this."

"What don't you like?" Hawk asked.

A gunshot echoed around them. Jack couldn't tell where it had come from, but he recognized it as a rifle round. None of them were hit. The shot hadn't been directed at them. It had been fired deeper into the woods.

"Are they hunting?" Hawk asked, hand on his holstered pistol.

"They've been out here for a couple of days." Jack shrugged. "A guy's gotta eat, right?"

Speaking of which… Jack's stomach rumbled. Lunch had been light, and dinner, so far, was nonexistent.

Jack softly spurred Danny into motion, and they moved east and looped around to the trees. There, they paused again, and Jack peered back through his binoculars. He saw nothing. The bank robbers had yet to return to their campsite. From his angle, Jack could see around the SUV. It looked like these guys had been here for a bit. In the firelight, he spotted clothes hanging on nearby branches. If it were Jack, he would've used the neighboring river for bathing.

In fact, he had.

It should be packed with fish too.

Trout, yum.

A few years back, Jack had slipped and slid down a slope, coming to rest in a pile of some unknown animal's dung. Bull had thought it was amusing, mostly because Jack's reaction was as if he had been lit on fire. He had danced around and gagged several times. The stench had been wretched, not that the river water did much to clean him up. It had removed some of the thicker, nastier, wetter clumps from his body. The smell, however, had stuck around until he could properly shower.

Bull spoke softly into his satellite phone, no doubt talking to the police. He finished up and ended the call, dismounting his single horsepower ride. Jack followed his lead. Hawk tried to do the same but was stopped by his uncle.

"No," Bull said, handing the young man the phone. "Stay here."

Jack winked at Hawk. "Don't worry, kid, we got this."

Typically, four versus two weren't good fighting odds. But they didn't know Jack—or Bull, for that matter. Believe it or not, the passive Lakotan was impressive in a fight, even though he actively avoided getting into them.

Jack, on the other hand, *always* seemed to find himself in some sort of skirmish. He blamed it on shit luck, but deep down he knew that he enjoyed it— action, that is. It's what had made him so good at his job back with Delta. He had been confident in his abilities and unafraid. But he was also a hell of a lot more reckless back then. Now, things just seemed to hurt more, and his ability to recover from injuries lagged on longer.

Like bouncing around on a horse saddle for hours on end. His ass was going to be sore for days.

Jack's vision at night was remarkably sharp, as was Bull's. It was another example of their prominent search and rescue skills, which had become legendary in the NPS community. The pair crept forward, staying just inside the tree line. The bank robbers had, indeed, set up shop here. And based on the remote location and their lack of transportation, Jack had to assume they had planned on staying put for a while. There was no other choice. It's not like they were going to leave their loot behind.

"I don't like this," Bull said, voice low.

Jack placed a hand on his friend's shoulder. "That makes two of us."

The retired Delta operator drew his sidearm, a Glock 19 with a Streamlight TLR-7A weapon light mounted beneath its barrel. Jack had recently switched back to the make and model firearm, citing that its ability to hold more bullets than his previous carry gun was a huge advantage in the field. Plus, Glock parts were more easily accessible on the open market.

Bull slid his pistol free, getting Jack's attention.

His eyes flicked back and forth between it and its handler. Bull carried a Glock 20. The variant was bigger than Jack's, and it was loaded with ten-millimeter rounds rather than the more conventional nine-millimeter. "Ten mil" was great at taking down bears and the like. Nine-millimeter bullets had a nasty habit of pissing grizzlies off, not killing them.

Jack eyed the front of the sports utility vehicle, confirming that the axle was, indeed, broken. These guys weren't going anywhere soon.

The two men stepped into the makeshift campsite, swinging their pistols left and right, careful not to muzzle one another. Once the area was clear, they lowered their weapons slightly and began their investigation. There was no sign of foul play other than a handful of obvious parking violations. Jack was half-expecting to see a pile of money bags—dollar signs and all. But there was nothing, nor was there a Scrooge McDuck-like character doing snow angels in piles of cash.

Bummer.

They spun at the sound of voices coming from deeper in the trees. Jack and Bull looked for somewhere to hide. They balked, though. Besides diving into the suspects' SUV, there wasn't anywhere to go. So, they quickly scampered around to the opposite side of the inert vehicle and ducked into the darkness.

Jack heard something dragging along the ground. He knelt and looked beneath the SUV, seeing a pair of filthy workboots pulling along the carcass of a deer. *The gunshot.* They'd wait until the men were busy preparing their meal before making their move.

Bull turned to Jack and held up his hand and shrugged. The starlight was bright enough for Jack to see the two fingers Bull was holding up. He knew what Bull was implying.

Where were the other two guys? Police reported four men, not two.

The clopping of horses filled Jack with dread. Bull nearly leaped out of cover when they spotted Hawk being led forward at gunpoint. The two missing bank robbers rode alongside him on Jack and Bull's horses. Seeing another man on top of Danny made Jack feel violated.

I'm coming, buddy. You too, Hawk.

Bull leaned in close. "Now what?"

Jack thought it over, and it came to him. Seeing Danny jogged his memory. He dug into his pocket, careful to keep the object he sought from making any noise. Jack gripped it tight and stood.

This better work.

He charged out from cover and feverously shook the dismembered snake rattle. He headed straight for the horses. They reacted instantaneously. As he had done before, Danny reared up and threw his rider. Bull's horse wildly bucked like a rodeo bronco. Hawk was an outstanding rider and kept his horse from going crazy. He directed his horse away from the action, disappearing into the dark valley.

Amid the chaos, Jack dove atop the fallen bank robber's back, pushed his face into the dirt, and slugged him in the temple three times. The last shot knocked him out cold. A pair of hooves landed mere inches from Jack's head. He looked up and, for a moment, locked eyes with Danny. The horse backed off and allowed Jack to stand. Bull had forced his horse's rider to the ground, felling him as quickly as Jack had.

"You can stop now."

They spun toward the speaker and found two rifles pointed at them.

"Guns."

Jack and Bull dropped their weapons.

The larger of the two men stepped forward, showing off his filthy, bloodied overalls. Jack guessed the blood belonged to the deer, not a human. His friend had on tattered blue jeans and a yellowed tank top. Both wore cowboy hats and boots and owned a similar sneer.

Brothers?

"Who are you?" the bigger guy asked.

Jack motioned back and forth between him and Bull. "I'm papa bear, and this is mama bear. Your friends here threatened baby bear."

"You a comedian?"

Jack shook his head. "No, it's just how I deal with stress, and it's a surefire way to distract my enemies."

The pounding of hooves came thundering back into the campsite, entering from behind the gunmen. Hawk and his horse were a blur. He directed his horse right between the pair of surprised country boys. One of them got hip checked by the horse. He went tumbling to the ground with a groan.

Bull went for that one.

The overalls guy dove out of the way.

He was now Jack's dance partner.

The rifle swung towards Jack, but he snapped his foot up and kicked it out of the kneeling man's hands. Jack then kicked at the earth, sending a miasmic cloud of dirt into the bank robber's face. The move allowed Jack to launch a knee strike into his face. It connected, but not as solidly as Jack had hoped. Both men spilled to the ground, trading blows as they rolled. Jack shoved away from his foe and stood, raising his fists. He now stood between the overalls guy and the fire. The warmth felt nice across Jack's back.

The warmth felt great on his tailbone.

Stupid horse.

Overalls guy closed in, but Jack stood his ground. He didn't have to wait long. His opponent owned zero patience and stepped forward and swung at Jack's face with a wild right. Jack ducked, reached out and grabbed one of the man's overalls straps, and pulled. Using his own momentum against him, Jack yanked the local off balance and right into the roaring fire.

Overalls guy reacted as expected. He screeched like a barn owl and rolled around like a more attractive version of him in slop. Jack casually circumnavigated the fire, walked right up to the alight man, and kicked him as hard as he could in the side of the head. His lights were immediately extinguished, and he went *night night*. But Jack wasn't done with him. He stepped up beside the unconscious man and snuffed out his leg with the thick sole of his hiking boot.

"Hawk!" Jack shouted, breathing hard. "Phone!"

"Already did it," Hawk replied, dismounting his horse. "Police are inbound as we speak."

Jack nodded and gave him a thumbs up. Then, gingerly sat, feeling his lower back protest the action. Bull looked fine, per usual. He sat next to Jack.

They didn't stay seated for long.

The noise was faint, coming in from the south. At first, Jack wasn't sure what the muddled *whupping* was. But as the sound moved closer and picked up in volume, he quickly deduced its origin.

"Dammit…"

Jack grunted and stood. There, he waited, hands on hips, none too pleased.

"That was fast," Hawk said, also facing south.

"That's not the cops," Jack said. "If it were," he stuck a thumb over his shoulder, "they'd be coming from the north."

"Who is it then?"

Jack knew. There were only two other people who knew where Jack was located. And they had promised not to bother him and keep their asses away during his time off.

A thunderous roar dropped down from directly overhead. The black aberration was difficult to spot against the equally dark sky. But Jack could see it. He hadn't been looking for *it*. Jack had been waiting for a section of the stars to vanish.

The Sikorsky UH-60 was easily one of the most recognizable military transport vehicles, thanks to movies like *Black Hawk Down*. Jack watched the four-bladed Black Hawk helicopter descend. This one was matte black and seemed to absorb the firelight. A door on the left side of the wraith-like apparition opened, and a figure stepped into view. The lowlight inside the helicopter's rear hold was just bright enough for Jack to recognize the individual's thin, feminine silhouette.

The passenger threw a line down and leaped from the hovering aircraft, landing seconds later with the fire to her back. Bull and Hawk took a step back. Jack didn't, though. He just crossed his arms and waited for the woman to speak. She removed her protective helmet. Her short blonde hair contrasted with her all-black attire.

"Hello, Jack."

"Hey, Eddy." Jack sighed. "I can't say I'm happy to see you."

The corner of Eddy's mouth curled up. "I'm sorry to hear that." She gave him a playful wink. "I'm always happy to see you."

Hawk tapped Jack's shoulder and whispered. "Who's that?"

Jack didn't yet know what Eddy was to him. Raegor was their boss, that much he understood. Eddy was still an enigma. She was Raegor's closest confidant, which would technically give her authority over TAC field operatives—people like Jack.

"She's a *friend*," Jack replied. He stepped toward Eddy. "What's this about? You know I'm on leave."

"About that," she sincerely apologized with her eyes. "Sorry, but duty calls. We need you to come in."

Jack rubbed his neck and faced the Durhams. This was the life Jack had chosen when he signed on with TAC. He knew he could be pulled away at any moment—like now.

He shook Bull and Hawk's hands. "Looks like I'm cutting out early."

"Be careful," Hawk said.

Jack gave him a sly smile. Bull returned the smile with a curt nod of his bald head.

Jack turned and stepped up next to Eddy. "How we doin' this?"

She grinned. "*You* are going to hold on tight."

Jack groaned and wrapped his arms around Eddy. One arm went over her left shoulder. The other slid beneath her right armpit. He clasped his hands around her back and squeezed, rubbing his cheek against hers.

"Don't get used to this, Jack," Eddy said, pulling on the cable.

He grinned. "I'd never think of it."

The pair was then whisked into the night sky.

3

Kathmandu, Nepal

"K-K-K-Katmandu. I think that's really where I'm going to. If I ever get out of here. I'm going to Katmandu."

Jack sat in the backseat of a beater taxi, mumbling along to the words of the Bob Seger classic. He didn't dare sing. The driver didn't deserve to have his eardrums violated. Jack also understood how cliché it was to be listening to a song named "Katmandu" while traveling through the Nepali capital, though, for whatever reason, the song title was spelled differently. It would've been just as lame for Jack to walk the streets of Manhattan while screeching the chorus to Frank Sinatra's "New York, New York." But honestly, he didn't really care. It was a damn good song, regardless of where he was.

All he had been given as far as intel was an address and a name, Wu. He was set to meet Wu at the location provided. Then, the two agents were to interview the patient in question, a Khumbu Sherpa named Dhonu Thapa. From there, it was up to Jack where the mission went. If there was enough evidence to pursue Shangri-La, he would.

Jack couldn't believe the news reports coming out of Nepal. The rescued man claimed to be someone who had disappeared over a hundred years ago. Still, as outlandish as it sounded, the news had spurred a Chinese biotech giant with massive government contracts into motion. The fact that they were even remotely interested had concerned Raegor.

"Could you imagine if the Chinese got hold of a tech that slowed down death?"

Jack scratched his head. "Yeah, that would suck."

"Indeed, it would."

"But Shangri-La?" Jack had asked. "Really?"

"I know how it sounds, Jack. But I think even you can agree that there's a lot of strange things this world has to offer."

And that was the truth.

Shangri-La was no different from El Dorado in some ways. Another nation's shrouded utopian kingdom. If El Dorado existed, then why couldn't Shangri-La? Much of the Himalayas were inhospitable. Very few had ever attempted to navigate the more remote areas of the 1,500-mile-long range. Many of those who had tried had died along the way. Mount Everest alone contained over 200 bodies, many of which were presently used as location markers along the operating trails. The fact that the Himalayas shared a border with the Chinese-governed Tibet made the region much more dangerous and difficult to explore. The Chinese Communist Party wasn't fond of border crossers, accidental or not.

As far as Wu was concerned, Raegor had sources in other agencies who had been in contact with the agent through coded messages. Wu worked deep within China's Ministry of State Security (MSS). The government agency operated similarly to the United States' CIA. Wu stated that the brass atop the MSS had gone too far in recent years. Jack was curious as to what exactly Wu was talking about. And if Shangri-La did exist, what would the Chinese government do to it if they found it first?

What Jack also found interesting was that Raegor couldn't confirm whether Wu was a man or a woman.

"It's a strategic move," Jack said. "It makes it *that much* harder to identify Wu if you couldn't narrow down the person's gender."

"I'd also gander that there's a large number of people with the same last name," Raegor added. "If that's truly Wu's last name."

"Most definitely," Jack had agreed.

"How will you know it's *your* Wu? What if you're walking into a trap?"

Jack shrugged. "No idea, but if I do get into a firefight, hopefully, Wu will be one of the people not pointing a gun at me."

It was plain to see that Jack's taxi had entered the tourist center of Kathmandu. Thamel was essentially a neighborhood-sized shopping district, sporting narrow alleys overcrowded with shops, vendors, and patrons. Literally, everything was available here. If Jack wanted pirated DVDs from twenty years ago, state-of-the-art trekking gear, decadent one-of-a-kind pastries, or simple woolen clothes, he wouldn't have to leave Thamel.

It was late, but not late enough for the people of Thamel. Things were just getting started around here. Jack wanted nothing to do with it. He was seriously jetlagged and starving. His cabbie had passed dozens of local food joints. Jack couldn't read any of the signs and was too hungry to be that picky. At this point, he'd happily order his meal by grunting and pointing at a picture.

They slowed, stopping in front of a three-story building featuring a very festive Buddha jumping and twirling above the door. The Buddha moved along three separate neon signs, each move depicting him in a different pose. It all made sense when Jack saw the English translation of the establishment's name printed beneath the Nepali name.

"The Dancing Buddha?" Jack asked rhetorically.

"Yes," the driver said through missing front teeth.

"This is the address?"

"Yes," he replied again.

Jack opened his door. "Is that the only word you know in English?"

He nodded empathically. "Yes."

Jack rolled his eyes and climbed out, stretching his six-foot-two frame. He cracked his lower back, instantly feeling some relief. The cab ride hadn't been a long one. His discomfort had come from the vehicle's rear seat. It was in desperate need of some TLC. Jack had packed light, per the usual, and threw his single duffel bag over his shoulder. He stepped away but was called out to from behind.

"Tip?"

Jack turned. *I guess 'yes' isn't the only word he knows.*

He tossed a handful of rupees through the front passenger seat window and shot the driver with a well-executed finger gun. The local was thrilled with what must've been a large tip. Jack had no idea how much he had given the guy, and nor did he care. It wasn't Jack's money, after all. He was traveling on the company's dime.

"See ya later, pal."

Obnoxious electronic music blasted from every direction. The bass notes shook Jack's pupils. The loudest of it was coming from straight ahead. Jack already hated this assignment. The last thing he wanted to do right now was go clubbing for information, especially while being unarmed. It was the worst part of the job. Jack traveled as a normal tourist and abided by the law, just like everyone else.

Minus the criminals. They always had guns.

Jack gave the doorman a nod and entered. It was easy to see that he was in the security business. His black attire, thick build, and guard dog demeanor made him stick out like a sore thumb, and that was the point sometimes. If troublemakers knew, right off the bat, that you had a large security presence on hand, then they might just avoid your place.

"Holy…shit?" The expletive came out as a question. Jack couldn't believe what he was witnessing.

As he walked in, the first thing Jack saw was that the bartop was on fire—and on purpose too. He stopped in his tracks while he watched the bartender pour booze onto the bar to keep the blaze going. Everyone loved it too. Everyone except Jack, that was. Right this second, he'd like nothing more than to be back in Yellowstone riding around on Danny. Jack couldn't believe this was the place where a Chinese government agent wanted to meet him.

He skirted around a trio of scantily clad girls. They looked young, giving Jack another reason to keep walking. He needed to find Wu, and who better to ask than the person who would know everything about anything going on here, the bartender. Jack passed beneath a large square opening, revealing the two additional levels above him. The second and third floors sported decorative railings and multiple doors, from what Jack could see.

Is this a hotel too? He recalled the three younglings. *Or a brothel?* Jack leaned more toward the latter, though both were entirely possible.

The bar area was three deep, and Jack needed to wait his turn to be served.

The barkeep wore a jovial smile and a name tag reading *Jhony.* "What can I get you, my friend?"

"You speak English?" Jack was honestly shocked. It was clipped, laced heavily with Nepali, but still very easy to understand, even with the thumping backbeat.

Jhony shrugged. "America is where the money is, yes?"

"If you say so," Jack replied. "Anyways, I'm not looking for a drink. I'm actually looking for something else…"

Jhony took a step back. "Sorry, we do not do *that* kind of business here."

Jack was confused. "And what kind of business would that be?"

Seeing that Jack wasn't looking for whatever the hell Jhony thought he was looking for, he leaned back onto the smoldering bartop and waited for Jack to continue.

"I'm looking for someone. Goes by Wu."

There was a hint of recognition. When the man didn't say anything, Jack thought it best not to push him. He couldn't risk being thrown out on his ass.

Finally, the bartender spoke up again. He poured Jack a shot and forced a smile. "Have one on the house. I have to take my break. Enjoy yourself."

Jhony muttered something to one of his coworkers and slid out from behind the bar. Once again, Jack didn't push him. He waited and watched. He could tell Jhony knew Wu, or at least where the person was. Once Jhony mounted a set of stairs at the rear of the main building, Jack grabbed his lowball, stood, and subtly followed the shady character. He slid past another group of twenty-somethings. This one looked like a group of rah-rah college kids, perhaps a fraternity taking a sabbatical.

A two-tiered fountain had been built into the middle of the room, directly under the three-story-tall courtyard. At its raised center was a life-size re-creation of the dancing Buddha from outside. His head was tilted back, and he had water streaming out of his mouth. When Jhony was halfway up the steps, he turned and looked out over the first floor. Jack knew the barkeep was looking for him.

Jack did the only thing he could think of doing. He put Buddha in between himself and Jhony, ducked his head, and paid no attention to the couple who were observing his odd behavior. If Jhony knew that Jack was on to him, then the night, and possibly the entire mission, could be a bust.

Thankfully, Jhony didn't spot him.

Jack leaned left and confirmed that the bartender had moved on. He quickly moved to the base of the stairs. He waited, giving Jhony a little extra distance. Once Jack mounted the steps, he'd have nowhere to hide. But he couldn't give his man too much time.

"Crap," Jack grumbled. He'd have to chance it.

Jack took the steps two at a time and made it up to the second floor without issue. He tried the first door and found it locked. The second one wasn't, however. Jack slipped inside and watched Jhony continue over to the other side of the floor and quickly begin to scale another flight of stairs up to the third floor. Jack waited for Jhony to disappear from view, and then he emerged, and power walked to the other side.

The bartender was gone.

Jack growled and hustled forward.

He climbed higher and then freaked when Jhony looked over the rail toward him. With nowhere to go, Jack dropped to the shadowy steps and faced the wall, just as someone else came pounding down them. The random patron couldn't have timed it any better. Did Jhony see him, or did the newcomer block his line of sight? Jack just hoped he hadn't been seen.

For good measure, Jack held up his lowball and moaned and coughed, acting like a drunk. The local person rambled something off in Nepali and smartly gave the inebriated man—Jack—some room. Jack looked over his shoulder and spied Jhony knocking on a door on the other side. After a second, it opened, and he was allowed to enter.

Once Jhony was gone, Jack sprang to his feet and hauled ass, leaving his drink on the stairs. He bounded up the steps and around to the same side of the floor as the door Jhony had just entered. He slowed and crept up to the now shut partition. Jack carefully leaned against it and listened. The door was lightweight, and he could easily hear voices speaking to one another on the other side, even over the music floating up from downstairs. They were speaking Nepali and Jack could only make out one word.

Wu.

Gotcha. If Jack couldn't convince the bartender to speak, his fist might get the job done instead.

Jack stepped away from the hollow core door, then put his foot into it, aiming three inches to the left of the deadbolt. The thin material exploded under the pressure of his kick. Jack hurried in to find Jhony standing between two very large men. The pair wore the same security outfits as the doorman Jack had seen earlier. They stood over a seated hooded figure. Jack couldn't see the individual's hands. and he was pretty sure they were bound to the chair behind the person's back.

Oops.

"Uh, sorry." He raised his hands and stepped back. "I, uh, thought this was the shitter."

A third guard appeared in the doorway behind Jack. It gave him a horrible foreboding feeling—a premonition of what was to come.

Jack was about to get into a good old-fashioned slobber knocker.

4

Jack took in the room, analyzing every detail. There wasn't much. First off, it was dark. The only light source was from a single tabletop lamp in the front, right-hand corner of the twenty-by-twenty box. A table had been moved there, missing one of its two chairs. Jack glanced back to the hooded figure and the chair Wu sat in. A razor-thin mattress sat atop a cheap metal spring frame along the rear wall, and there were two dressers off to Jack's left.

"What do you want with Wu?" Jhony asked, looking very confident.

Jack looked over his shoulder before answering. "He's an old friend. We go way back."

A sly smile crept onto the bartender's face. He knew something Jack didn't, and it bugged the crap out of Jack. "You are no friend of Wu." Jhony snapped off a string of Nepali, and his comrades closed in.

"Well, then, call off your dogs!" Jack blurted. He eyed the two guards in front of him but homed in on the footsteps of the man coming up from behind. Luckily, the building was old, and the wood floors creaked loudly with every step.

Jhony laughed. "I think not. Just because you are no friend of Wu does not mean you are a friend of mine. We will happily take our reward, and there is nothing you can do about it. Wu is worth more alive, though the reward for proof of death is still a handsome sum."

Reward? What the hell did I get in the middle of?

But he knew.

The MSS had put out a hit on their runaway agent. Jack would be hilariously deluded if he didn't think the Chinese had sleeper cells in neighboring countries. And it looked as if Jhony was in one of them, if only as a profiting informant.

The shorter bartender strutted up to Jack like a fearless peacock. Whatever he was going to say was interrupted by Jack's knuckles. He slugged Jhony in the face, spilling him to the floor. Then, Jack popped the guy on the left in the throat with a quick jab, while simultaneously kicking the other man in the crotch. Both went down like giant sacks of potatoes. Before Jack could turn his attention to the goon near the door, he was tackled from behind.

Jack was driven face-first into Wu's lap and struggled to free himself from the third guy's embrace. He had wrapped his arms around Jack in a bearhug, pinning his arms down to his side. "Oops...sorry 'bout this...buddy." Jack fought against his attacker. "Be right...with you." He slammed the back of his head into the guard's face, earning a crunch and a moan.

Wu pulled, struggling against the ropes, but made no progress. Jack would have to dispatch his foe before helping the rogue MSS agent.

The second goon recovered and ran at Jack. He sidestepped the attempt, grabbed the man's jacket, and hip tossed him to the floor. The guy's foot clipped the small table holding the lamp and knocked it off. The only light source within the room broke when it hit. Now, the only illumination was coming from outside the door. And it wasn't much.

Jack got sucker punched from behind, but the glancing blow did very little damage. Jack spun and lifted his fist. Jhony covered his face like a coward but peeked through his hands when Jack didn't hit him again.

Then, Jack hit him again.

Jhony stumbled and then fell back, colliding with Wu and tipping the bound agent over. The bartender landed hard and hit his head on the nearby bedframe, rendering him unconscious.

Jack's second assailant was still on the floor holding his junk, and it didn't look like he was going to recover any time soon. The third one was already advancing on Jack once again. Jack stood his ground and allowed him to attack first. He blocked the wild punch, then kicked him inside the left knee. The guy limped back. There was concern slathered on his face.

"You can leave if you'd like?"

He turned and looked at the door but raised his hands and faced Jack.

Jack shrugged. "Your funeral."

He didn't have time for this. Jack needed to finish this one off and then get Wu out of here. So, Jack ran at his foe, happy to see him stumble back a little. The other guy lifted his hands to protect his face. Jack, instead, leaped forward and drove his right foot into the man's chest, much like he had done to the door. The local was thrown back and crashed through the antiquated third-floor railing.

He fell.

Jack turned his attention to Wu, unconcerned about the third guard's fate. Screams tore through the first-floor bar, no doubt caused by the man plummeting from three floors up. Jack dove at Wu's hands and untied the ropes. He helped Wu up and was stunned to see just how short the jacketed MSS agent was.

Jack's body was blocking the hallway light, making the dim room that much darker. That, along with Wu's all-black attire, had made it difficult to gauge the operative's size. A commotion drew Jack back to the doorway. He crossed the room and looked, seeing nothing on their level. He turned to check on Wu and was met with a spinning side-kick to the chest. Jack nearly dodged the attack but still took a sledgehammer impact to his shoulder. He stumbled back into the doorframe, spilling to the floor just outside the door.

Jack crab-walked backward but froze in place when a hoodless Wu emerged.

And *she* was beautiful. The woman was somewhere in her mid-thirties and sported shoulder-length, raven-black hair. She also possessed a look that could kill.

He held up a hand in surrender and got to his feet. Wu never once took her eyes off him. Jack had never seen such focus. It kind of spooked him. She reminded him of one of those creepy pictures that followed you as you walked past it.

"Easy there… You must be Wu. I'm—"

She roared and jumped at Jack, kicking him in the hands. He had miraculously gotten them up in time to parry the thunderous blow. The petite woman packed a mean punch.

Uh, kick…

She pushed Jack back with a flurry of flawlessly produced kicks. Jack knew taekwondo when he saw it. He had taken a few classes years ago. It was a martial arts style that focused mostly on kicking instead of punching, though he was guessing that Wu could throw a punch just fine too.

"Stop!" Jack shouted, blocking another kick. "Ow!" His hands stung.

So far, she had yet to land anything too devastating. Jack didn't want to hit her, but he needed to fight back. He swung at her. She ducked, kneed him in the ribs, and then slid behind him. She quickly started up another wave of attacks. None of the kicks repeated themselves. He couldn't read her at all.

So many kicks!

That's when he figured out what she was doing. She snuck in another shot to Jack's ribs, teetering him back over the busted third-story railing. His heels found air, and he flailed his arms for balance, righting himself just as she rocked back her fist to punch him.

"Stop!" he cried. Her hand shot forward. "I'm Jack Reilly!"

He tipped backward but was caught by the same hand that had been bound for his nose. Wu had grabbed his shirt, holding him in place like a bloodied stump dangling above a shark tank. She could easily let him go if she decided that he was lying.

"How do I know you are really Jack Reilly? How do I know you were not sent to kill me?"

Like Jhony, Wu's English was impressive. And like Jhony, her speech contained a strong accent curtesy of her home country, in this case, China.

Um... Jack had no idea what he could say to convince the ultra-paranoid woman. She was a spy on the run, after all.

So, he cleared his throat and sang.

"K-K-K-Katmandu. I think that's really where I'm going to. If I ever get out of here. I'm going to Katmandu."

Wu's eyebrow raised. "That was…awful."

Jack shrugged and teetered. "Karaoke isn't my thing."

"I don't see how that helps your case."

"Can't hurt it, though. If I was here to harm you, would I break out in song and embarrass myself like that? This isn't an episode of *Glee*."

Jack could see that she was processing him. Admittedly, it wasn't his best idea.

An explosion followed by gunfire got Jack and Wu moving again. Jack rocked forward just as Wu released her hold on him. They both darted back into the destroyed room, and each searched a body.

Jack found what he was looking for—a pistol—a QSZ-92. It was a popular firearm within the Chinese armed forces, specifically the People's Liberation Army (PLA). He slipped the weapon free and was forced to snap it toward Wu in response to her aiming one at him. Thankfully, neither of them pulled the trigger. A heartbeat later, someone holding an assault rifle stepped through the doorway. Jack and Wu shifted their aim toward the gunman, and they each shot him once.

They swiftly refocused on one another.

Jack lowered his aim and stood. "I'm not here to hurt you." A second explosion rocked the Dancing Buddha. He pointed toward the door. "But they are."

Her aim didn't budge.

"See this?" Jack held up his pilfered pistol. "Chinese army issue. And that guy had a QBZ-95 bullpup—also Chinese army. You are being hunted by your own people, not me." Still nothing. He sighed, unsure what else he could say to convince her. More screams from below greeted them. "Innocent people are getting hurt, Wu."

She slowly dropped her sights down. Without acknowledging Jack, she slid over to Jhony. He moaned when she touched him. Wu threw a quick jab and rendered the man unconscious once more. She dug into his pockets and produced a phone. Wu pocketed the device and stood and faced Jack.

She studied him.

Jack let her.

"You are the American sent to help me?"

He grinned. "Not what you expected, huh? I'm also here to prove whether Shangri-La exists."

"Is it for you," her eyes narrowed, "or for us all?"

Jack understood what Wu was doing. She was assessing him. The Chinese government, no doubt, wanted the discovery for themselves, which meant war would come to Nepal. It meant a ton of people were going to die.

Jack shook his head. "This isn't about me."

"Good," Wu said, nodding. "Follow me."

They each took up positions just inside the door. "So, do you have a name other than Wu?"

She leaned out and looked into the hall, then she rolled back into cover and met eyes with Jack. "My name is Mayleen."

"Mayleen?"

"You don't need to sound so disappointed."

Jack blushed. "That's not what I... Sorry, you're not what I was expecting."

May's hands found her hips. "Were you expecting a man?"

"Honestly, I have no idea what I was expecting. But definitely not someone that looks like..." Jack zoned out, lost in her dark eyes. He blinked. "Never mind."

Jack needed the subject changed. "So, Mayleen, huh?"

"Or May, if you'd like?"

"Well, May..." Feet pounded up the nearby stairs. Jack stepped out and shot a pair of gunmen just as they appeared. He turned. "I'm Jack."

A third, much larger explosion nearly sent Jack plummeting into the raging fire below. May snagged the back of his jacket and pulled him to the right. She led him around to the opposite side of the floor. Instead of there being a staircase to a fourth floor, there was a simple ladder bolted to the wall. It led up to a hatch in the ceiling.

"Up we go?"

May didn't elaborate. She slid her gun into her jeans and mounted the ladder, scaling it quickly. Jack followed her, hoping it was solid enough to support the both of them. A few of the rungs creaked under his weight, but they held, nonetheless. May pushed the rooftop access lid. It didn't budge. She tried again, and there was more of nothing.

"Let me try," Jack said.

May leaned to the side and allowed Jack to scale higher. The two were impossibly close. She smelled amazing.

Lavender.

Jack pushed aside the notion of May being anything else besides a woman who had just tried to kill him and leaned to the side. May shimmied down the ladder, giving Jack the room he needed. He pushed his shoulder up into the heavy lid and climbed another rung. Jack used his legs and drove himself skyward, praying the ladder didn't give out.

The lid groaned and shifted. Slowly, it began to open. Jack climbed higher still, using his height to his advantage. He shoved harder. The lid opened more.

"Hold it there," May said, monkeying around Jack's body. Somehow, she slinked between him and the rim of the hatch and wiggled through an opening barely wide enough to fit Jack's thigh.

"Hurry!" Jack cried, feeling lightheaded. The strain was becoming unbearable.

For a moment, he thought May had left him high and dry. He breathed a breath of fresh air when her hands came into view. She gripped the edge of the lid and took some of the weight. Jack gave himself half a second to adjust his stance, and then, yet again, he drove his shoulder into the lid. Between the two of them, they got it open. May engaged a locking arm, and Jack all but fell out onto the roof, utterly exhausted. He closed his eyes and caught his breath. A soft, cool breeze washed over him. He let out a long exhalation and opened his eyes.

"What are you doing?" she asked, standing over him. "We don't have time for this."

Jack waved her off and slowly rolled onto his hands and knees. He launched to his feet as he felt the three-story structure rumble. He and May looked at one another. A second, infinitely larger tremor sent them into a mad dash for the building's edge. The first-floor explosions had done their share of damage.

The Dancing Buddha was coming down.

5

The crimson pagoda-style rooftop slanted in four directions and was slick underfoot. Right now, Jack and May were trying not to fall off any of the sides. Unfortunately, from what Jack could see, there wasn't a viable outside escape route. The only way down was back through the first-floor inferno.

No chance, Jack thought. He'd rather fall to his death than be charbroiled alive.

He pointed east toward a neighboring building. "What about that?" The tiled roof quaked again.

They stepped lightly and crept out toward the edge. One of the tiles shifted beneath his weight. The other building wasn't all that close, but it was a full floor shorter. Jack was confident they could jump to it if they could gain enough speed. Their raised position would simulate a shorter distance.

In theory.

Jack wasn't all that good with physics. What he knew for certain was that gravity was a bitch, and that the ground was typically hard, and it hurt like hell when he hit it, which had become a reoccurring problem.

"You're kidding me, right?" May asked. She looked queasy.

"Scared of heights?"

She shook her head. "Not at all. I'm just not comfortable leaping to my death."

"Better than vacationing in Salem for the summer." Jack pointed back down the glowing roof hatch.

May glanced back and forth between Jack and the open lid. "Was that an attempt at humor?"

"Yeah," Jack replied, looking down, "it sounded better in my head. But seriously, you really want to go back down there?"

The clear answer was *no*.

May stepped aside and gave Jack some room. "Well, since you seem to have done something like this before, walk me through it. How are we going about this?"

The building shuddered. Pieces broke away and fell. Some of them connected with nothing but paved road. Other, bigger chucks crushed cars.

"Jack?" May asked, her defenses whittled down to nothing.

"Move!" Jack grabbed her hand and ran.

The Dancing Buddha leaned south, over the road. Jack and May angled up the increasing incline but also kept heading east for the building next door. When they got to the edge, Jack didn't stop. Ergo, neither did May. They jumped, sailing out over nothingness. As the Dancing Buddha collapsed, bullets zipped past them. He couldn't see who was shooting at them, but Jack figured that it was probably the rifle-wielding shooter's friends.

Suddenly, Jack's mortal enemy—gravity—took its course, and they fell. But Jack's supposition had been correct. Their lower-tiered landing zone slid into view beneath their feet just as they hit.

Jack pulled May in tight, and they rolled across the flat-roofed structure. For his part, Jack took the brunt of their jarring arrival. He ended up flat on his back with May lying face down atop him. Both took a moment to catch their breath. May's head rose and fell with each of Jack's heavy inhalations.

"You okay?" she asked, lifting her head.

Jack looked at her and nodded but said, "No."

May laughed, causing Jack to laugh, which made him moan in pain. May sat up, careful not to push off Jack's chest. His ribs ached, and he tasted blood. It had only taken an hour for Kathmandu to make Jack bleed.

"Thanks, by the way."

Jack nonchalantly waved her off. "Yeah, sure…" He spat the blood away. "All in a day's work."

May got to her feet and offered him her hand. Jack gladly accepted it, and he stood. He rubbed his back, cringing when he touched it.

"Here, let me."

Jack tried to argue but May slid behind him and poked and prodded at his spine. She balled up her fist and drove it in deep and twisted. Jack felt a pop. He yelped, but the pain quickly dissipated. He bent and touched his toes, feeling worlds better.

"How?"

She smiled. "Ancient Chinese secret."

Jack massaged his back. "Says the woman employing Korean taekwondo."

May shot him a look that said it would benefit him to let it go. So, he did. If she could take the pain away, she could almost certainly return it in spades.

"We gotta get out of here," Jack said, looking around. This building was of a different design. "Bingo." Unlike the Dancing Buddha, this one had an outside access ladder down to street level.

Jack jogged over to it, leaned out, and checked to see if the coast was clear. It was. Thank God. He went first, placing his hands and feet on the outside of the metal ladder. He relaxed his grip. Jack slid, controlling the rate of his descent by altering the pressure he applied with his four points of contact. He looked up and saw that May was following his lead. She was remarkable, to say the least.

He finished his descent and turned to discover a pistol pointed at his head. Then, just like that, it was gone, as was the gunman's consciousness. May kicked away from the ladder and spun, clearing Jack's head by inches. Then, she planted her foot in the side of the gunman's head. For added effect, she landed like a cat beside a stunned Jack Reilly.

"You made that look way too easy," Jack said, shaking his head.

She dusted herself off. "You aren't doing too bad yourself."

He knelt and searched the man's coat pockets and found two spare magazines. His gun was gone. It had disappeared into the shadows somewhere over by a pair of dumpsters. Fortunately, he had been outfitted with the same pistol as Jhony's cohorts. Jack lobbed one of the mags to May, and she caught it and pocketed it.

He held up his magazine. "More Chinese army?"

She nodded. "Looks like it."

"I figured it would take longer." He sighed.

"How do you mean?"

He stood. "Usually, it takes a day or two for a nuclear power to try and kill me."

Jack could tell May was trying to decide whether to laugh or not.

He gave her a wink, relaxing her some.

May looked up and down the alley. "We need to keep moving."

"Agreed, but where do we go?"

"I have a place nearby. If we can find transportation, we should be able to slip away unnoticed."

Jack nodded, hearing people screaming and alarms blaring. "Sounds good to me." The pandemonium would mask their exodus.

They stayed in the alleyway and popped out onto the street a hundred yards further east of the now obliterated Dancing Buddha. Sirens wailed from all directions, and fires raged. Jack was about to check the surrounding area but May held him back.

"Let me. You stand out."

Jack looked down at his larger frame.

She ducked away before he could respond. She navigated the area like a ninja, using whatever she could for cover. Jack snuck a look and didn't see anyone running toward them, guns blazing. He got an idea when a young boy came riding towards them.

"Hey, kid!" Jack called. "Over here!"

He doubted the youth knew English, but he undoubtedly knew an eager customer when he saw one. May stood erect and looked at Jack as if he had an arm growing out of his ass. He was doing the exact opposite of what she had said.

"Found us a ride," Jack said, doing his best Vanna White impression while showcasing the getaway vehicle.

"A rickshaw?"

Jack shrugged. "You got a better idea?"

She didn't, and the sound of erupting gunfire spurred her into agreement. Not only had paramedics arrived on the scene, but so had the police, and they were just in time to engage some not-so-nice individuals in a firefight. May chirped at the teenager and pushed Jack into the rear seat of the bicycle-powered carriage. If the kid had been on foot, Jack would've reconsidered.

"What did you tell him?" Jack asked, not understanding a lick.

"I gave him directions to my place."

Jack was stunned. "Just like that?" Now, he was the paranoid one.

"Not everyone is trying to kill us, Jack. And if it makes you feel better, I told him the intersection, not the actual address."

They set off. May reached out and pilfered a pair of colorful scarves from a distracted garment vendor's stand. He was too busy gawking at the destruction to notice. She grinned and handed one to Jack.

"Put it on," she said, wrapping one around her own head.

"We doin' the Thelma and Louise bit now?"

May didn't understand the reference. He let it go, threw on the scarf, and sat back. It was a good idea too. From behind, the simple head covering would make them look like any other sightseeing visitor. They had, essentially, just vanished into thin air.

Hiding in plain sight.

"So," Jack said after a minute of silence, "where did you learn to fight like that?"

She didn't answer immediately. Jack hoped he hadn't struck an emotional nerve of some kind.

May sighed. "My mother."

Jack turned and faced her the best he could. "Again, not what I expected."

"When I was a girl," she explained, "my mother taught self-defense courses to the other mothers so they could protect themselves better. She had been a champion before I was born."

Jack poked at his ribs. "That explains your superhuman leg strength."

May frowned. "Did I hurt you?"

"Only my pride."

That cheered her up.

Something still didn't add up. "Out of all the martial arts disciplines to choose from, why taekwondo?"

"My mother was Korean, not Chinese. I mastered it to pay respect to her."

Was, he thought. *Dammit, Jack.*

"She died when I was very young."

"I'm sorry."

She nodded and looked off. "So am I. I miss her very much, even now."

Jack knew what it felt like to lose loved ones.

"My mom and dad died when I was a kid—plane crash in Peru." May gazed at him. "Grew up with my grandparents and joined the army right out of high school."

Jack didn't need to share any of this, but he figured it couldn't hurt. If anything, it would encourage May to trust him more.

He caught himself staring and looked away and cleared his throat. "What about your father?"

She snorted. "Chinese through and through. They never married. I was sent to him when my mother passed." Her expression quickly changed to regret. "He also works for the government."

Jack noticed her change in demeanor. "What branch?"

"The Ministry of State Security, same as me. Well, the branch I used to work for. That ship has most definitely sailed."

Oh, crap! Jack knew that May's bosses were the ones hunting her down.

She looked him in the eyes, making sure he fully grasped what she was about to say.

"My father is Minister Jin Zhao. He's the one trying to kill me."

Ministry of State Security
Beijing, China

The news of his men's failure in Kathmandu was disappointing. It infuriated Zhao. But it didn't shock him, either. His daughter was one of the best field agents he had ever seen. Add in the help she was receiving from an American operative, and she'd be almost impossible to catch. Whoever he was, he was a conundrum to Zhao.

"So," he said, staring into his whiskey glass, "we will let you roam."

Zhao was a patient man. He'd let Mayleen and her new friend guide them along, and when the time was right, he'd pounce. He checked his watch and sat at his desk. His home office was much more lavish than his work office. There, he was meant to be unemotional and intimidating. Here, Zhao preferred the typical comforts of life. His 5,000-square-foot residence was proof enough. He sipped on his thirty-year-old single malt and waited. Zhao was expecting a text from David Cho at any moment.

Bing!

He dug his phone out of his pocket and read the message.

Shenlong inbound. Pull your men back.

He'd let Cho lead the charge for now. At worst, BIOfinity Genetics Group would take the brunt of the blame for anything bad that happened. No one would even know that the MSS had been involved. The men Zhao had used hadn't been part of any active cell. They had been hired mercenaries with past military experience and nothing more. Then, as the dust settled, Zhao would seize full control of the biotech conglomerate.

"Shenlong," he whispered.

Zhao had heard of the man before, though, until now, he thought of him as more of a ghost story within the intelligence community. He was supposedly ex-military, formerly of the Falcon Commando Unit. But even Zhao didn't have the clearance to learn the man's identity. He had allegedly been killed in action a decade ago.

Apparently, not.

"How do you know him, Cho?"

It was yet another question with no answer.

Zhao knew that Shenlong was known to be especially brutal in his methods.

6

Lalitpur, Nepal

The rickshaw ride was short and sweet, which was fine by Jack. The backseat had hardly any padding, and the roads desperately needed repair. It had felt like he was back on Danny. The teenaged chauffeur dropped them off at a corner sporting four apartment buildings. Technically, they weren't in Kathmandu anymore. The city of Lalitpur began a block ago.

May waited for the "taxi" to disappear before moving again. Jack also stayed put, doing his best to look inconspicuous. It didn't work. He was at least six inches taller than anyone around him. This was exactly the reason why Special Forces guys only worked in certain areas. If you didn't look the part, you'd stick out like a sore thumb and inadvertently place a target on your back. Thankfully, Nepal wasn't a part of a current conflict that required American forces to be present. The locals would just think of Jack as a typical foreigner, not a soldier.

They entered the building on the southeast corner and paused at a pair of elevators. May pushed the arrow pointing up, and they waited, and waited, and waited. Jack had to actually check his watch.

"What's taking so long?"

"There are only two elevators in the entire building."

He looked up and around and pictured the hundreds, possibly thousands, of apartments these two lifts serviced. No wonder they were taking forever. The elevators disgorged their haul seconds later. Jack had never seen so many people be regurgitated from an elevator before, particularly at the present hour. It was like the overcrowded train cars in India, or the subway in Mexico City, although to a much lesser extent.

Jack hurried in, and as soon as May selected the floor, he repeatedly slammed home the button to close the doors. They almost made it too. One man, a portly fellow, jabbed a sausage-fingered hand inside, causing the door to rebound and open. Then, three more people followed him in. Then, another five.

Jack and May were pinned to the rear of the elevator car, standing chest to chest with one another. May was short enough that she had to crane her neck back to meet Jack's eyes. He didn't mind the view, but the extra company was a major nuisance. One after the other, the others got off. It wasn't until they were alone that Jack realized that he and May were still cuddled together.

May noticed too, and the pair separated.

Jack felt foolish and a little embarrassed.

"Uh, sorry…"

She shook her head. "No, don't be. You did nothing wrong."

Now, the empty car felt more uncomfortable than it had earlier. Thankfully, the ding of the elevator bell broke the awkward air. The door slid open, and Jack nearly ran over May as they both exited at the same time. He stepped back, but so did she.

Jack put his hands on his hips and stared at the floor, admitting defeat.

"Please, go."

His face was flushed. He couldn't look at her. But out of the corner of his eye, he saw a slight smile creep onto May's face. He followed her out, berating himself for acting like a lovesick middle schooler. May was amazing. He already knew that, but she was also the mission. Jack never mixed work and pleasure together, though he did generally have a lot of fun while working.

Except for the asskickings, the intercontinental redeye flights, the lack of decent sleep, and the shitty work schedule, of course.

They hung a left and continued to the end of the hall. May keyed open the second-to-last door on the right. The pair slipped in, unseen, and relocked the door. Jack breathed easy for the first time since arriving at the Dancing Buddha. The apartment was simple and held one room off the main living area. A quaint kitchen and a card table, and two folding chairs were all that May had on hand. No couch or TV. Jack doubted there was much in the way of furniture in the bedroom, either.

He stood in the empty living room, deep in thought.

"What are you thinking?"

He turned and faced May. "I think I need to call the office."

The office was Solomon Raegor.

Jack slid free his phone and dialed the memorized number. No useful information was ever saved on the device, just in case. It rang twice and was picked up.

"What's wrong, Jack?" Raegor knew something was up. Jack wasn't supposed to break silence unless it was absolutely necessary.

"We, uh, have a problem, sir."

Jack relayed what he knew. TAC figured the MSS would be involved, but not to this extent. The fact a kill squad had been sent after May changed everything.

"This is bad, Jack."

"Yeah," he laughed, tired, "tell me about it." He slinked to the floor and sat against the wall.

"No, Jack, this is more than you. No offense."

"I understand, sir. This is an international incident involving a global superpower. Chinese mercs on the loose in a bordering country. People dying. Buildings being destroyed."

"You destroyed a building?"

Oh. Jack may have forgotten to mention that detail.

"I was there, yes, but it wasn't my fault. Either way, this is a big-time issue."

May stepped over to Jack and sat next to him. "It doesn't have to be."

Jack pulled the phone away from his ear. He looked at May. She had something pertinent to add. "Hang on, sir. I'm putting you on speaker."

"Jack, no, I—" Raegor started, but it was too late.

"Director Raegor, I'd like you to meet Mayleen Wu, now formerly of China's Ministry of State Security and daughter of the asshole pulling all the strings."

Raegor grumbled under his breath. He was no doubt miffed at Jack for exposing him like this. "Yes, Ms. Wu, hello, you have something for me?"

"I believe I do—and thank you for your help. I was thinking... What if we release everything we know about the Ministry's involvement—and BIOfinity

Genetics?"

Jack perked up. "Send the cockroaches running, so to speak."

"Exactly."

"Won't they connect the dots?" Raegor asked.

The back of May's head clunked against the drywall. "I think that cat is already out of that bag. Plus, I still have friends on the inside I can trust. Just because they know it's me doesn't mean they can catch me."

"We could also leak it to local news companies," Jack added. "The social media sites will spread it like wildfire. Think of the headlines! *China invades Nepal*!"

"What about the patient in question, Mr. Thapa?" Raegor asked.

May leaned in closer to the phone. "I was able to visit him only once, shortly before I realized I had been compromised."

"How did you manage to see him?" Raegor asked. Jack was curious too.

May dug into her pocket and produced an ID card. "I used this."

For Raegor's sake, Jack described the item May had just produced. "A fake ID with the last name 'Thapa.' Looks legit too."

May nodded. "As I said, I still have friends I can trust." Her face saddened. "Even though, my last contact just proved me wrong."

Jack didn't connect the dots right away.

His eyes opened wide. "Jhony?"

She nodded. "The Dancing Buddha was a safehouse for us for years. I thought I'd be able to use it one more time." She sighed. "I was wrong."

"Which is why I found you, how I found you."

She nodded. "He planned to collect a large sum of money as payment for my capture."

Jack was very happy to have ruined that jackass' day.

Raegor spoke up, steering the conversation back on course. "What did you learn from Thapa, Ms. Wu?"

"Not much," she replied, "I told him that I was his great-great-granddaughter. I told his nurse the same thing. She didn't believe it, but why would I lie to her, right? Mr. Thapa genuinely believes he's a missing Sherpa from a century ago, and he's, in fact, 157 years old."

Jack cleared his throat. "And Shangri-La?"

May looked unsure, but she said, "His conviction was undeniable. Even in his weakened state, he wholeheartedly believes that's where he's been this entire time."

"If that's true, why didn't he leave decades ago?" Jack asked, needing to consider every angle.

May didn't say.

"Ms. Wu?" Raegor asked.

"He… He said there was a curse."

"A curse?" Jack asked.

"Yes," May confirmed, "a curse. It was a few hours later that I realized I was being hunted by my own people—after I was debriefed by my father."

"Minister Zhao," Raegor said.

"Yes. He said a support team was inbound and to stay put until their arrival.

The thing is, we never 'stay put.' We always keep moving. That's when I knew they were either coming to collect me and bring me back to Beijing or kill me, not 'support' me."

Jack handed his phone to May, and he stood. Sitting still wasn't helping. He needed to get up and move, even if just to pace back and forth.

"The curse," Jack said, "does Mr. Thapa know where it came from?"

May attempted to stop him. "Jack, I—"

"Hear me out. Does he know where it came from?"

May shook her head. "I don't know. We never got that far. He grew tired and was unable to go on. His nurse said that, though he is in good spirits, his health is deteriorating rapidly. They have tried everything, but his immune system and many of his organs are beyond repair."

"Cancer?" Jack asked.

"No," May replied. "At first, that was the obvious culprit, but all tests have come back negative. Something masking itself from modern medicine is killing our Sherpa. They've never seen anything like it."

Jack stopped and rubbed his stubbled chin, deep in thought. "Best guess, if his claims are true—and that's an Everest-sized if—is that this curse is some kind of illness." He held up a hand and stopped May, mouth agape. "Trust me, May, we've seen some weird shit, right, sir?"

"Correct."

May's attention darted between the phone and Jack.

"Can Shangri-La exist?" Jack asked rhetorically. "Yes, or at least, a place that inspired the lore surrounding it could. And do I think we're dealing with a real-life curse? No."

The room went silent.

"What do we do now?" May asked. "I can't just walk away. Real or not, it is a bad sign that the MSS is this involved."

"Hmmm," Raegor mumbled. "Jack, you're my lead agent here. What do you think? I can only armchair manage so much. There's not enough information for me to make any kind of decision from the other side of the globe."

May's eyes pleaded for help. They were full of loss and fear. Everything she knew in the world was now gone. If he refused to continue his investigation, she'd be on her own with the whole of China looking for her. He doubted they played nice with traitorous agents.

Jack knew what he had to do.

"I think we should trust her, sir. We owe May that much after everything she's done, you know, ruining her life and all."

May smiled.

Raegor mulled it over. Jack could hear him whispering to someone in the room. He knew it was Eddy. She'd be the only one within earshot of him.

"Okay, Jack, but be careful and get some rest—the both of you. Raegor out."

Kathmandu, Nepal

The ruins of the Dancing Buddha were a smoldering mess, and it was up to Dev and two other Nepali cops to keep watch over the scene. Firefighters had finally gotten the inferno under control a few hours earlier. Plus, a soft drizzle had started up too. Luckily, none of the neighboring buildings had caught fire, though they had experienced some heavy smoke damage and a touch of light scorching. Dev's eyes located the singe marks, and he smirked. There was nothing *light* about them. The next building's side wall was charred and black. The rest of it was off-white and dark green.

"Lousy insurance companies," he mumbled.

He knew the game. An insurance agent would show up later that morning and figure out how to fork out the least amount of money possible.

Yellow police tape blocked off all access into the devastated structure, one Dev had frequented years earlier. However, he didn't partake in that kind of lifestyle any longer. His captain had not approved of his after-hours behavior, especially when it began to impact his effectiveness while on the clock. Dev was forced to choose between the booze and the career.

"And now I'm guarding ash."

"What?" Indra asked.

Dev waved him off, looking away from his colleague as well as the remains of the Dancing Buddha. Movement behind him caught his eye. He turned to find a lone man standing across the street. Dev couldn't get a good look at him. The newcomer's face was shrouded by a hooded zip-up. The stranger's presence was an oddity, considering the time, but there were also some other stragglers out and about too. Dev was just being paranoid. He was tired and annoyed. He could've done without the rain.

Damn socks.

A car alarm went off down the street. The disturbance took Dev's attention off his new friend for a moment. When he looked back, he was stunned to see that the hooded figure was upon him. Before Dev could reach his service pistol, an Indian-made duplicate of the Browning Hi-Power, the unknown man reached out and grabbed Dev's throat. Whoever this guy was, he had just assaulted a police officer. And whoever he was, he had a grip like a vice.

Dev abandoned his sidearm and grabbed at his accoster's wrist with both hands, but he couldn't break the man's inhuman grip. He felt the brute's fingertips dig in deeper and increase the pressure around his larynx. Dev's vision warbled, and his knees weakened. He got in one good punch, but it did little besides knocking the man's hood away.

The first thing that caught Dev's attention was just how calm this guy was. This was nothing new to him based on his lax facial expression. The second thing he noticed was that he was Asiatic, possibly Chinese, and he sported a shaved head and had tattoos running down his neck. Dev was pretty sure he saw blue dragon scales. Whatever the pattern was, it disappeared beneath his collar.

Dev's knees buckled in time with his workmates noticing the incident.

"Freeze!" one cop shouted.

"Let him go!" another yelled.

Dev went down, and out of the corner of his fading vision, he saw Indra and Mukti taken out by a pair of muffled coughs. They were each hit in the chest with a subsonic projectile. Twin puffs of blood followed as the rounds exited their backs, burying themselves in the smoldering rubble of the Dancing Buddha.

The gunmen were out of sight, playing overwatch for their comrade here.

The pressure on Dev's neck loosened enough to get a breath in. He gasped for air and tried to cry for help. The former was all he could do before the bald, relaxed stranger re-tightened his grip. Once again, Dev was being choked out. Only, this time, his would-be killer leaned in close and asked him a question.

"There was a man that worked here by the name of Jhony. Where is he?"

Dev gagged but was allowed to speak.

He coughed and said, "Everyone injured… Brought to—to—hospital."

The man displayed his first emotion. Rage. He squeezed so hard that Dev thought he was going to rip out his larynx.

"Which hospital?" he growled.

Dev raised a hand and uselessly attempted to berate the man. He let Dev hit him, although it resembled little more than a toddler slapping a boulder.

The pressure lessened enough for Dev to divulge the location.

Dev's attacker smiled. "Thank you." Two other men then joined him. Each of them held scoped suppressed rifles. They must've been the snipers that had killed Indra and Mukti.

The mystery man squeezed until Dev felt a pinch. A sickening pop followed the unyielding pressure. Dev clawed at his own throat, trying to catch his breath, but instead, he drowned in his own blood.

7

Lalitpur, Nepal

Jack awoke to the sound of obnoxious neighbors. Music blasted through the drywall to his left while a couple shouted at one another to his right. He felt hungover. The headache was penetrating and irritating. The brawl with May, then Jhony's boys, combined with the immense amount of smoke inhalation, had done their job.

May.

Jack rolled to his right side and found her. She was facing away from him, sharing the same uncomfortable mattress as him. It was the only piece of furniture in the bedroom. It wasn't accompanied by any of the usual amenities either. No frame, sheets, pillows, or blanket. Nothing. Just a flat-ass mattress.

He had passed out as soon as he hit, but had woken up several times to a tossing and turning bedmate. May had struggled mightily to fall asleep. He doubted she got much rest at all. Sometime in the middle of the night, Jack had raised a hand, planning to lay it gently on her back. The purpose of the gesture was to soothe her peaked anxiety. But he held back. He didn't want her to think it was some sort of inappropriate sexual advance.

They were sharing the same bed, after all.

May roused awake. The neighbor's heated cries increased tenfold, spooking the runaway Chinese agent. She sat bolt upright and startled Jack, lifting her pistol and pointing it at the bedroom door. Her eyes were wide. Her hands shook. She was petrified and not fully awake. Jack had been in her state several times.

Night terrors.

His war-induced PTSD had lessened some since being back out in the wild as a TAC operative. Something about the awestruck experiences and shitty travel schedule had interrupted the chaotic awakenings. May was going through the same sort of thing now.

"Breathe," Jack said, keeping his voice soft. "Take a second…and breathe."

Tears rolled down May's cheeks. She blinked, sending more of them streaking down her face. Her hands, and gun tremored violently. She tried to release her air, spurting out small amounts of spit as she did. She had yet to blink since sitting up. Jack stayed on his back and slowly lifted his hand. He laid it on the slide of her pistol.

"May." She blinked and looked down at him. "Breathe." The two didn't break eye contact. "Breathe."

May took one long, deep breath. Just when Jack thought she was about to get her emotions under control, the hardened MSS agent broke down. May's walls crumbled, and she dropped the gun and fell into Jack's arms. The pair squeezed one another hard. Jack was content with staying put all day if they had to. May needed someone. Jack was happy to oblige. He knew what it was like to be alone with your worst enemy dwelling inside your own head.

Jack never had that someone, not until Bull came along.

May wept, getting it all out. Jack let her too. He didn't say a word since he had instructed her to breathe. He knew that once you got your heart rate under control, the rest would eventually fall into place. He also knew that it was immensely easier to get through the horrifying experience of waking up in fear with someone else around to help.

He'd be that for May.

This was years of pent-up emotion too. Jack could see it. May had lived a life on the road, traveling the world, doing God-knows-what for her country. Jack had done the same for years, but he liked to think his actions had been for a more noble cause. Then again, who was he to point the finger? Both he and May had blood on their hands.

"You're okay," he whispered. "It's just us."

May's sobs slowed and softened, and her grip on his body let up. She released her bearhug and pushed herself off Jack. She sat atop him, straddling his hips, looking terrible. She was exhausted. Her eyes were puffy, and her hair resembled a tangled bird's nest. Jack's assumption that she hadn't slept much the night before had been correct.

She pulled her hair back into a ponytail and took a much-needed, long inhalation. With it came some of May's resolve.

He couldn't stop staring at her.

May's hands were still wrapped around the back of her head when she noticed her counterpart's attentive gaze. She paused, looked down at their *positioning*, and rolled her eyes. May stood, doing her best to hide her embarrassment. Like Jack, it had probably been years since she had displayed this kind of vulnerability, especially to someone of the opposite sex.

Without another word, May spun and marched out of the bedroom.

Jack sighed. "So, I guess we're getting up?"

He rolled off the mattress and onto his hands and knees. It took him a second, but Jack eventually got to his feet once his bones, joints, and bruised muscles allowed it. He was sore for so many reasons he didn't know where to begin. "Oh, right." It was probably the death-defying leap from the roof of a three-story tall burning building. That had been the icing on the cake, for sure. His shoulder and ribs ached from the bruising landing.

He went to step away from the mattress but stopped. Jack bent over and reached beneath it, retrieving his pilfered pistol. "Not exactly a bedside safe," he mumbled.

Jack checked it before shoving it into the front of his pants. He left the room and found May standing and staring at the far wall, the one they had sat against the night before, while conversing with Director Raegor. Her arms were folded across her chest, and she stood with her left hip popped out to the side.

He waited for her to say something.

"Thank you." May's voice was soft. She sounded ashamed.

Jack shrugged, though she couldn't see. "No problem. Happy to help."

She faced him. May really was exhausted. "Why?"

Jack's left eyebrow rose. "Why what?"

"Why did you do that…back in there?" she tipped her chin to the bedroom.

Jack shrugged again. "Because it was the nice thing to do?" He honestly had no idea what she was getting at. Also, Jack had never really understood women. Now he was analyzing his own intentions. "You needed help."

May stepped toward him. "And just like *that*," she snapped her fingers, "you came to my rescue?"

Jack was confused. He looked behind him, confirming there was no one else in the room. "Uh, yes?"

It was plain to see that May had not experienced that type of kindness from a human in a long, long time—maybe never. Jack was just trying to console a friend.

So, he told her that.

"I've been through a lot in my life, and I did it alone. I was in bad shape a few years after I retired from the military. It was hell. Then, I met a man named Bull."

"His name is 'Bull?'"

Jack grinned. "Well, I call him Bull. He quickly became a mentor and a rock for me to lean on. He helped me get my shit together and start over."

"And now you're paying it forward?" May asked. "Is that what you're doing?"

Once more, Jack shrugged. "I guess, yeah. Look, I need you at your best for our job. But I also know what it's like to go through what you're going through up here." He tapped his temple. "The mind can tear you down."

The pair stood in silence for a moment. Jack didn't know what to do next. Standing around doing nothing after the talk they just had was killing him.

"What?"

Jack blinked hard. He hadn't realized that he'd been staring off into nothing. Unfortunately, that *nothing* was in May's direction. Now, it was his turn to feel mortified. Before she could comment, Jack asked the single most important question since they had both awoken.

"Know a good place to get some coffee?"

They cautiously exited the apartment building. The hustle wasn't bustling yet at the early hour. Even the elevator ride wasn't nearly as cramped as it was yesterday. May had mentioned that there was a small café a block away. A walk would do Jack some good and help loosen his lower half.

They hooked right and headed east along the Lalitpur-Kathmandu border. Locals were out and about. Some walked with purpose, possibly on their way to work. Others meandered about, enjoying the beautiful morning. The air was crisp but not uncomfortable. It was refreshing. May's safehouse lacked anything in the way of creature comforts, including electricity and heat. Gratefully, the quaint bedroom had trapped most of whatever heat there was.

Jack adjusted his jacket and frowned. The collar was crispy—charred—and he stunk of smoke.

"I, uh, guess I could use some new clothes." May stopped and looked him over, smiling when he showed her his collar. She started off. "But coffee first."

May rolled her eyes and picked up the pace.

Just over a block later, they arrived. The café didn't sport an English translation as the Dancing Buddha had. This place was obviously a local spot, not one that purposely attracted out-of-towners like those over in Thamel.

"This the place?" Jack asked.

May nodded, and her lips morphed into a stunning smile. Even her posture changed. Gone were her hunched shoulders and tired eyes. May had instantly transformed herself into a different person in the blink of an eye.

"Yes," she said. Even her voice was higher. "And my name is 'Ju Yang' when we're here, okay?"

Jack nodded and opened the door.

Ju?

It hit him. "Ju" was a false persona. He wondered how many fake names and personalities May owned—and memorized.

"Ju, huh?" he asked, leaning in close.

She hissed. "Shut up."

May then slung a string of Nepali throughout the room, getting a resounding cheer back from the small gathering of locals. There was a mixture of young and old, and mostly women, though a few gents dotted the space. Jack was stunned at how busy it was and a little uneasy with all the attention the big, hulking American was getting.

Jack didn't understand a lick of what was being said, but he was pretty sure it was about him.

May whispered, "I told them that you rescued me from a car accident late last night and that we haven't had a chance to change yet." She waved at an older man and spoke through a forced, toothy smile. "I said that I brought you here as a thank you."

Before Jack could comment, a shorter man burst through a squeaky door, rushing around the front counter with two small, steaming mugs. He practically threw them at Jack and May before retreating into, what Jack guessed was, the kitchen.

"Um, thanks."

"*Dhan'yavada*," May said.

"Yeah," Jack added, "Donny-vada."

His poor attempt at speaking Nepali got a laugh out of everyone. He grinned like an idiot and was pulled aside by May. She led him to a table by the front window.

Jack sniffed his coffee and smiled. He sipped it, speaking softly while he did. "So, who is Ju exactly?"

May shot him daggers. He wasn't letting it go, and she knew it. She cleared her throat and explained.

"Believe it or not, the MSS doesn't always carry out nefarious missions." Jack didn't believe her, but he didn't openly argue against it. "Ju is a businesswoman with ties to an investor who's been dumping money into this area."

That surprised Jack. The Ministry of State Security wasn't typically recognized as an agency of 'goodwill.'

A smirk formed on his face.

"What?" May asked, seeing it.

He set his mug down and sat back in his chair. "You've been funneling resources to these people behind your daddy's back, haven't you? This had nothing to do with the MSS." He leaned forward. "This is all you."

"Shhh," she hissed. A nearby couple exchanged looks with Jack and May before returning to their own conversation. She broke into a fake laugh and waved at them but spoke to Jack. "I have no idea what you're talking about."

Jack sipped his coffee and mumbled, "I'm sure you don't."

8

Kantipur Hospital
Kathmandu, Nepal

Getting clothes was easier than Jack thought it'd be. The owner of the café directed him and May to a place further up the block. Jack used his company card to make the purchases. TAC paid for May's new attire too. He went for his customary outfit: jeans, a t-shirt, and a leather jacket. May had chosen something similar, though, opted for an all-black ensemble. Both of them also selected heavy-duty hiking boots.

A rickshaw similar to the one they used to escape the mayhem surrounding the Dancing Buddha dropped them off at Kantipur Hospital. Jack's first impression of the medical facility was that it kind of looked like a hotel combined with the New York firehouse that would eventually become the Ghostbusters' headquarters. The building's most distinguishing feature was the four-story-tall window built into its front façade.

May headed through the gated entrance with Jack following closely behind her. She'd been here before. Jack would let her do her magic and get them inside without an issue. The only identification Jack had on him was his passport featuring the name Robert Seger. A pair of security guards stood outside the front doors. Neither one would be a challenge for Jack to subdue if it came to that.

May greeted them in Nepali. Jack was shocked when they did nothing else besides greet her back. She and Jack waltzed right in without so much as a question. Jack figured someone like him would've at least gotten a second look, but no. May definitely knew what she was doing.

"That was good," Jack said.

"You have to own it." May winked at him. "Plus, they were here the last time I came by to see my great-grandfather."

Jack grinned. "I thought he was your great-great-grandfather?"

May balled her fist and held it up. "Don't start. You knew what I meant."

This was the Mayleen Wu that Jack liked. She was fiery and didn't take shit from anyone. All May had needed was to get out a good cry and release some of that repressed emotion. Since then, she'd been back to normal.

May headed for the front counter and signed them into the visitor logbook. The only words Jack recognized were May's fake first name, Ju, and his bogus moniker.

The woman at the counter looked back and forth between them and said, "*mangetara*?" May nodded and repeated the word.

Jack had no idea what it meant. May thanked her and circled around the desk, heading for the nearest elevator. Jack had to move quickly to keep up.

"What does *mangetara* mean?" he asked.

May acted as if she didn't hear him. That meant Jack needed to know what it meant even more. He leaned in and asked again.

She pushed the button for the elevator. "It means *fiancé*, okay?"

Jack turned and fully faced May. "You told her we were engaged?"

"It's all I could come up with on the spot."

"Sure, I guess..." He turned back toward the elevator but stopped and faced May again. "But engaged, really?"

May didn't reply.

Jack stayed quiet until the lift arrived. When the door opened, May stepped in. Jack couldn't help himself.

"You know..." May's shoulders slumped, and she turned, clearly irritated, "May Reilly does have a nice ring to it."

Her eyes narrowed. "Please, don't make me kick your ass again." She went to turn away but stopped. "And wouldn't it be May Seger?"

They rode the elevator up to the fourth floor, exited, and went left, stopping at the fifth door on the left, 405. Dhonu Thapa had been given an outside room, giving him a westerly view of the setting sun and the nearby Bagmati River. A stocky man stood in front of Thapa's door. Unlike the two security guards downstairs, this one did not move after spotting May. He stood his ground, looking very much like an ornery English bulldog.

May dug into her pants pocket and removed her ID. She held it out for the guard to see. He read it for what seemed like an eternity before finally stepping aside. Jack prayed that the guard wasn't going to ask for his too. He couldn't imagine this guy letting in some random tourist. May must've thought the same thing because she grabbed Jack's hand and interlocked her fingers in his.

May followed it up by giving Jack a quick peck on the cheek, promoting their fake engagement for all to be seen. It worked too. The outward display of affection made the security guard visibly uncomfortable, and he opened the door, waving them both inside. Jack was yanked forward, lost in the memory of the kiss.

The hospital room had been built to handle three patients comfortably, but it currently held only one, Dhonu Thapa. The elder rested in a bed with pillows propped up under his back and head. The only word Jack could use to describe him was *peaceful*. The door clicked shut behind them, rousing Thapa from a nap. He smacked his lips together and pushed himself up, looking much healthier than Jack had expected.

This guy is 157? No friggin' way.

Until he was proven otherwise, Jack wasn't buying it. And if that were the case, then he'd be going home tonight. If he was being honest, Jack really wanted this guy to be 157. He wasn't ready to leave yet.

His eyes darted over to May.

She spoke softly to Thapa, utilizing the Nepali word for fiancé. The old man shifted his attention to Jack and held out his hand. Jack stepped over and was prepared to shake it, but instead, Thapa squeezed it with a strength belaying his age, 157 or not. Even if the guy was a phony, he'd still have to be in his eighties. He was a remarkable individual, regardless if the outcome of Jack's investigation proved he was nothing more than a shyster.

May conversed with Thapa before speaking to Jack again.

"I told him you'd like to know more about Shangri-La, or as he calls it, the Valley of Petals."

Valley of Petals? Jack had never heard Shangri-La called that before.

The most common name for the mythical Himalayan paradise, besides Shangri-La, was Shambhala. Shambhala was regarded as a utopian, spiritual kingdom in Tibetan Buddhist tradition. Ancient scriptures tell of a closely associated fabled land called Tagzig Olmo Lung Ring, a timeless realm filled with joy and harmony. Essentially, it was Eden-like or sort of like a heaven on earth.

"Yes, that's true. I'd love to hear more about it."

May translated but didn't seem to like what Thapa said next. Jack didn't either, not that he understood the man. What Jack didn't like was that Thapa only replied with a single word.

May looked at Jack. "He asks, 'why?'"

"Why what?"

"I think he wants to know why you want to know more." Thapa spoke through May again. "Yes, he wants to know what you'd do with such knowledge."

Just as Jack was skeptical of Thapa being who he said he was, the man was also wary of Jack's intentions. He believed his information was valuable enough to hide from someone like Jack, an outsider he had only just met.

So, Jack did something potentially stupid. He told the truth. Well, most of it.

He revealed who he was and who he worked for but left out TAC's name. He also described who else was coming after Shangri-La, the Valley of Petals. Jack left almost no stone unturned. He needed this man's trust. Without it, they weren't getting anywhere fast.

Thapa spoke, and May quickly translated.

"So, you're a soldier who wants treasure?"

Jack stepped forward. "Not at all. I'm just a guy who wants to protect history, and sometimes, the only way to do that is to get there first before someone with nastier intentions does. Like the Chinese government."

May slung a string of Nepali at Thapa. The man's face contorted, and he broke out into a series of wet coughs. His strength, as it seemed, was only on the outside. Jack recalled what May had said about his deteriorating health. After a half dozen hacks, Thapa's hand came away with blood on it.

"Please," Jack said, "we only want to protect Shang—the Valley of Petals. We aren't here to loot it. We aren't pirates." He pointed out the window. "But there are people out there who are, and they're on their way here, right now."

Thapa wiped his mouth with a handkerchief and then took a deep breath. He quietly conversed with May as she stepped over to a table and retrieved a cup of water. She went as far as placing her hand on his shoulder. The look in her eyes said that she believed him hook, line, and sinker.

Jack had little reason to doubt him, either. He had nothing to gain by lying like this. If anything, he could've kept his mouth shut, and no one would've found out about the potential of Shangri-La existing. But for some reason, the old guy had come down the mountain and informed humanity.

"Why did you come back?" Jack asked. He still didn't entirely believe Thapa's tall tale, and it wouldn't hurt to ask the question. "You mentioned a curse to your nurse."

If Shangri-La was, in fact, real and it was, in fact, a paradise, why on earth would someone willingly leave such a place? The world was chockful of shitty people and circumstances. Jack could only imagine the bliss of not being around any of it. He expected the old timer to stammer through some garbage on the way to a half-cocked answer. But Thapa gave him something entirely different: gut-wrenching emotion.

Tears fell from the Sherpa's eyes as he spoke.

"Because," May translated, "they killed my beloved."

Ehani was sick to death of Unnat hitting on her. The hospital orderly was nice, but Ehani had been in a stable relationship for over a year, and she wasn't about to give it up, never mind for someone she saw every day at work. Only once had Ehani been in a workplace romance. It had been miserable after they broke up. The Unnat dating rabbit hole needed to stay unexplored.

"I know, right?" she said, speaking in hushed tones with another nurse. "Unnat just can't take a hint. He—"

"Excuse me."

"Welcome to Kantipur Hospital," Ehani started, turning around and stuttering her next words. "M—may I help you?"

The newcomer was a sight. His head was clean-shaven, as was his face. She could also see beautiful blue dragon scale tattoos protruding from his shirt collar. He was buff, and his eyes were intense. This guy knew what he wanted, and, based on his build and hard stare, he probably knew how to get it.

"I'm looking for someone, a patient from the Dancing Buddha fire."

Ehani's hands went to her keyboard, ready to type in the patient's information. They had quite a few people from that fire laid up here, and she told the hulking visitor as much.

"What's the patient's name? We have several people from the Dancing Buddha here."

The visitor leaned in. "His name is Jhony."

"Are you friend or family?" she asked.

"Neither," he replied. Ehani looked up from her computer. "I'm just here for information." His eyes bore holes into her. Ehani swallowed back her rising fear. "And I think it would be in everyone's best interest to keep my being here off the books."

Ehani blinked. "Wh—why do you say that?"

"Because my friend doesn't appreciate uninvited guests, especially police."

A much smaller man stepped around him. Ehani hadn't been able to see him behind the guy with the dragon scale tattoos. The other visitor wasn't as immaculately dressed or kempt and wore a coat, even though the hospital was a little warm. One of the air conditioning units for this part of the building had been down for over a week.

She half-expected the second man to open his coat to reveal a vest strapped with C4. But he didn't, thank God. Instead, he hefted a duffel bag onto the counter, setting it down with a clunk. Next, he unzipped it far enough to see inside. Anyone with half a brain knew a bomb when they saw one.

Ehani's breath caught.

"If," he said, his voice low, "anyone disturbs our visit, the entire floor burns. Do you understand?"

Ehani nodded her head emphatically. Her eyes darted back and forth between both men, settling on the one in charge. "Won't you die too?"

He had the gall to smile. "Many have tried and failed. Now," he leaned in closer, "where's Jhony?"

9

"Wait, hold on, they killed your wife?"

May was equally as shocked as she posed the question to Thapa. She had floated many possible reasons through her head as to why Thapa may have left Shangri-La, the Valley of Petals, but this one hadn't been on the list. The murder of a loved one in an otherwise eternal environment hadn't even been in the same atmosphere of reasons.

"Yes," Thapa replied, "but she wasn't my wife. I did love her, though." He sighed. "My real wife was here, in the world of ordinary men."

May did her best to clue Jack into everything she and Thapa talked about. It wasn't easy. Nepali was one of four languages she spoke besides Chinese and English, the other being Korean. She had also wanted to add Japanese to her portfolio of dialects but had never found the time to do so.

"Who was she?" Jack asked.

"Celia," May translated, "was a Swiss climber that had gotten lost in a storm. She was brought to the valley by the Snow Lions and me."

"The Snow Lions?" Jack asked.

May shook her head. She had no idea what it meant, and she didn't get to ask. Thapa continued in rapid-fire succession. His eyes were glazed over, lost in a memory, or in this case, a nightmare.

"They denied her what she needed to survive." Thapa patted his chest. "It's an excruciatingly painful way to die, and I was forced to watch Celia suffer through it until the end." The Sherpa gritted his teeth, enraged. He locked eyes with Jack and spat his next words. "I left that godforsaken place because I wanted to make them pay for what they did to Celia. I wanted to come here and bring back an army of miscreants and burn the valley to the ground."

Thapa broke out into another coughing fit. May couldn't move. She was too stunned. Jack did, however. He reached out and steadied the ill man until he caught his breath. Thapa placed a gentle hand on Jack's and squeezed it, thanking him.

"Water," Jack said, pointing to the table next to May. She glanced down and saw a cup, blinked out of her stupor, and handed it to Jack.

Thapa accepted the cup and drank, relaxing when he was done. He sat back against his pillows. "The hierarchy is filled with treacherous snakes." He gazed up at his faux great-great-granddaughter. "They must be dealt with. The people—the families—of the Valley must be freed of their tyranny."

It hurt May to lie to this man. Everything he had gone through was so incredible, and yes, May believed it all. His conviction was as solid as stone. There was no deception in his words. That was enough for her, and based on Jack's reaction, he was thinking the same thing.

Thapa raised a shaky hand. In it was a remote connected to the rear wall. He depressed a small red button and sent a soft chime ringing throughout the room. Moments later, a short, petite woman entered. She was one of the nurses May had seen wandering around.

"Ah, Binsa," Thapa said, smiling wide. "My dear, this is Mayleen and her fiancé, Robert."

Binsa clutched May's hand. "It's a pleasure to meet you. Dhonu has told me so much about you."

May blushed, mostly because everything she had told Thapa was a lie.

"Binsa," Thapa said, "if you could be so kind as to retrieve the item I arrived with."

Binsa's eyes widened, and she nodded and quickly left.

"An item?" Jack asked. "That's awfully cryptic."

May could only shrug. "That's what he said."

Binsa returned a few minutes later, clutching something inside her scrub top. May knew the woman was trying her best to be inconspicuous but had utterly failed in her attempt. It was obvious that she had something of significance on her person, something she wasn't supposed to have.

The nurse removed a leathery wad of what could only be animal skins. It contained an object roughly the size of a drink coaster. May couldn't think of anything else to compare it to than that. Instead of unwrapping it herself and revealing its contents, she handed the package to its owner.

Then, she was gone. Binsa slipped out of the room with little more than a nod.

Once again, May and Jack were alone with the Sherpa.

"This is all I have left from the Valley of Petals," Thapa announced, carefully unfolding the skins. May and Jack stepped closer and leaned in. "But," he added, looking up at both of them, "it is all you need."

"Holy crap," Jack said, taking the words right out of May's mouth.

The object was a medallion of some kind, and it was beautiful. It appeared to be made of solid gold and was a quarter of an inch thick and four inches in diameter. *Bigger than a drink coaster.* It gleamed, perfectly polished. Thapa held it up, showing off the intricately engraved artwork on each side.

Side one contained an ornately conceived tree, though May didn't know what kind. Whatever it was, it was obviously important to the people responsible. Tiny characters were etched into the outer edges. May thought she recognized the language, but she couldn't translate it. Thapa flipped it over to reveal the other side.

The deep mountain valley was plain to see. Like the tree, it was super important to the person who had designed the medallion. At its center, floating in the air just off the surface, was a star.

Thapa convulsed and coughed, dropping the priceless artifact. Blood ran down his lip and chin. The Sherpa had held it together marvelously but was quickly coming undone. His illness—whatever it was—was killing him before their eyes.

"What's wrong with him?" Jack asked.

May asked.

"I've been without the nectar for too long. It's how my Celia died."

"Nectar?" Jack asked. "What nectar?"

He heard the door handle turn but didn't open his eyes to see who had entered his room. Jhony's skull was splitting. The smoke inhalation and concussion had both done their job on his head and throat. It hurt to speak, along with the burns up and down his arms. Jhony was in rough shape. At least he was comfortable. The ointments and drugs were keeping him relaxed as his body attempted to heal itself.

"Can I have some water?" Jhony asked.

The nurse didn't reply. Shockingly, she threw the cup at him instead.

He opened his eyes in shock and agony. The cool water fiercely stung Jhony's skin, making him wail. A thick hand covered his mouth. It didn't belong to his nurse. It belonged to a man with maniacal, penetrating eyes. They were the only outward emotion he showed. Everything he was doing was in control.

But who was he?

"If you speak, you die."

Jhony nodded.

The stranger released his mouth.

"Help!" Jhony shouted.

The hand covered his mouth again. Then, he was punched in the biceps of his terribly burned left arm. Jhony whined. The pain was agonizing.

"Shall we try that again?"

Tears streaked down Jhony's face. He nodded, getting himself under control. This time he'd stay quiet to see what his visitor wanted.

"What did you tell the police?"

He released Jhony's mouth. "N—nothing. As far as they know, I'm just a victim of an attack."

"Good."

"Who—who are you?"

The tattooed man stood tall and crossed his arms. "I am Shenlong, and I represent two interested parties."

Jhony had a feeling he knew who one of them was.

"Minister Zhao?"

His interrogator didn't need to reply, but his eyes confirmed it. Now, Jhony was curious as to who the other "interested party" was. But he was too scared to ask.

"So," Jhony said, choosing his words carefully, "is that it?"

"For you, yes." He turned away. "But my task is far from complete." The stranger moved so fast that Jhony had no way of getting his hands up in time. His injuries slowed down his movements, as did the drugs. Everything he did felt sluggish.

The man called Shenlong placed one hand over Jhony's mouth and squeezed. Then, to Jhony's terror, his other hand pinched his nose. All supply of air had been cut off.

"Sorry, but all loose threads must be cut."

Jhony thrashed against the attempted suffocation, but he couldn't remove the man's hands. Jhony was in no shape to fight back. But he had to, or he'd die. He swiped at Shenlong's face and slapped at his hands, trying desperately to free himself.

For Jhony's efforts, Shenlong leaned into him, pushing him deeper into his bed. The pressure in Jhony's chest built, and it burned. He needed to take a breath. His vision was already beginning to fade.

His muscles tensed and convulsed. Then, they released.

Jhony was dead.

The larger of the two men—the one with the blue dragon scale tattoos—had left to see the patient in Room 417. Unfortunately, his friend had stayed to keep watch. Ehani was "asked" to stay put until the other man returned. She had also done as she was told and had not revealed their intentions. As far as she knew, they were only here to talk to the patient in question.

She glanced away from her computer screen, eyeing the duffel bag. It sat, nonchalantly, in the other man's lap. The bomber's expression was cold and unemotive, just like his friend's. Whoever these people were, they must've done stuff like this often enough for it to seem so routine.

The phone next to her rang. Ehani answered it as if nothing was the matter. She needed to act natural. Her life and the lives of the surrounding people depended on it. She did her best to focus on the caller. The woman on the other line was inquiring about her son. He had just gotten out of hernia surgery and was resting comfortably in Room 411. Ehani told her as much. The mother was thrilled to hear the news and said she'd be in to see him later that evening.

"Yes, very good," Ehani replied. "We look forward to seeing you then."

She took a deep breath and hung up the phone's receiver. She didn't want to, but she did.

She glanced again at the duffel bag, and *only* the duffel bag.

Its owner was gone.

She frantically looked around for the one with the tattoos but didn't see him anywhere. The bag man had vanished, as well.

A scream erupted from somewhere down the hall. Ehani spun to see what the commotion was all about and spotted one of her coworkers backpedaling out of 417. Oddly, a light as bright as the sun winked to life behind her.

Everyone within thirty feet of the *sun* was incinerated, including Ehani.

10

"Nectar?" Jack asked. "What nectar?"

"It is what sustains us," May translated.

"So, you really were born in 1865?"

But Thapa didn't get to reply. A sound of thunder rumbled through the hospital before the entire eastern wall of the room was annihilated. Shrapnel of all types and sizes exploded into the room. Jack and May were equally thrown, catapulted into the wall behind the Sherpa's bed. They landed, entangled with one another, and IV tubing, unable to move for some time. Sirens blared, muffling the sound of screams and running water. Had a pipe burst? Jack's eyes opened.

It wasn't water.

It was blood.

May was the first to get up. "No!"

Jack shook his head, feeling warm wetness beneath his hand. He stopped what he was doing and saw that his fingers were resting in a growing crimson pool. He traced its origin back up to Thapa's bed.

He leaped to his feet and surveyed the damage. Unfortunately, the damage had been done, intentional or not. A three-foot-long piece of construction rebar had impaled the Sherpa in the gut. It had traveled at such a high velocity that it had penetrated a foot through the backside of the bed.

Thapa was in shock, staring down at it.

May said something to him, getting his attention off the mortal wound and onto her. He looked up at her and grazed her cheek as only a loving family member could. May's relationship might have been a lie, but Thapa believed it, and that's all that mattered. He'd die thinking that he had a badass great-great-granddaughter.

He muttered softly to May. Jack gave them some space, checking on the area immediately outside his room through what he would constitute as drink goggles. There was nothing left. The nurses' station was a blackened husk of itself. Jack could barely make out the pieces of whoever was manning it during the blast.

Was it a terrorist attack? Jack asked himself, holding his head as he moved.

The neighboring rooms were in similar disarray. People moved within a few of them. Others contained only the dead. Thapa's room had been spared a direct blast, though the Sherpa hadn't been so lucky.

Jack turned and watched as Thapa held his medallion in his shaking hands. With the last ounces of strength, he shoved it into May's chest, further slathering her in his blood. As soon as the artifact touched her breast, his hands fell away, and his head rocked back.

Thapa's eyes closed forever.

Jack coughed against the billowing smoke. They needed to move before the fires spread to them, or worse, the hospital fell apart. He stepped over next to May and coaxed her away, noticing the tears running down her face. She felt something for the old man. Jack did too. He respected him and everything he'd been through over the years.

A hundred years.

He still couldn't believe it. And what of the nectar? There were too many questions, like, how the hell were they going to get out of here? Fires raged down the hall. Most of the ceiling had fallen in too. The only way through was directly into the central blast radius of the nurses' station.

May clutched the medallion to her chest, unable to do much else. Her eyes were glued to Thapa.

"Hey," Jack said, trying to get her attention. When she didn't reply, he gently took her chin in his hand and forcibly turned it toward him. "Hey."

She didn't say anything. His ears rang. Maybe hers did too?

"Hey!" he shouted.

She flinched. "I heard you the first two times!"

"We need to get out of here," the building shook, "fast."

Oh, crap, not again. He looked around. *Two buildings in less than twenty-four hours?*

Jack found a half-burned towel and held out his hand. May reluctantly handed him the medallion. He quickly wrapped it up and shoved it inside his jacket pocket. The pair ducked through the charred, smoldering husk-of-a-doorframe. The walls were an unnavigable tangle of blackened drywall and rebar. When Jack's foot landed in the hallway, it bowed. He looked down in time to see his left boot disappear through the floor.

"Shit!" he yelped, expecting the rest of his body to follow it.

May grabbed him under his right armpit and pulled. With their combined effort, they successfully plucked Jack's foot out from between the third and fourth floors. They stumbled to the right and fell. Jack landed hard, right in front of an unrecognizable body. The only thing discernible was the person's melted nametag. It read, "Unnat."

Sorry, buddy.

"Come on," May said.

Jack was already moving. They got back up, avoiding a jumble of sparking wires hanging from the ceiling.

"What the hell happened here?" May asked.

Jack knew. He had heard similar explosions during his time with Delta, specifically during his time in Iraq. Someone had detonated a "small" bomb, but why? He knew they needed to leave, but Jack also needed answers. He spotted a mostly closed door across the hall from the nurses' station. It hung from one of three hinges and was missing what Jack guessed was a piece of square fogged glass. The blast had originated here. The outward stretching black circle on the floor indicated as much.

The sign was missing, but Jack guessed it was an office. He headed towards it, ripping the door from its last hinge. He disposed of the kindling and stepped through. A pair of moans greeted him.

"Help them!" Jack shouted, pointing to the rear of the rectangular room.

May rushed in while Jack searched for what he was looking for. He found it a short while later. Thankfully, it had been open and lying on the desk to his left. It was a logbook…and of course, it was in Nepali.

"May!"

She came over. "What is it?"

"See if you can find anything helpful in here."

She nodded, and Jack took her place in the room's rear. He unbuckled a man's belt to use on his female coworker's leg. The injury didn't look bad, but Jack had no idea how long it would take for emergency services to get here, let alone get up to the fourth floor. The belt's owner was dazed and filthy but otherwise fine. Jack motioned for them both to stay put, and he rejoined May.

"Here!" she shouted, coughing against the noxious air. "I found something."

"Whatcha got?"

She stabbed at a name in the middle of the left-hand page. "Jhony."

"What?" Jack picked up the book. "That can't be a coincidence, right?"

May shook her head.

"What room was he in?"

"417." She held up the ruined logbook. "That's further down the hall, I think."

He looked at her. "Think we have time?"

She shrugged. "As long as the building doesn't come down around us, sure."

"Yeah," Jack laughed, "don't count your chickens."

They slipped out of the office and edged around a hole in the floor. A hallway started twenty feet to their right. Jack kicked a bent piece of metal as he walked. It was a directional guide for the rooms.

May saw it too, and she pointed north.

"Back in the room," Jack said, "what did Thapa tell you before he gave you the medallion?"

"He told me to find the others—to find our—his—family. He said they'd guide us. He said that his bloodline has known about the Valley of Petals for generations, though none of them have ever seen it besides himself. It's how he originally found it all those years ago."

"Thapa's family? The Sherpas?"

"Yes, in the Langtang Valley, specifically. He also said to find the Valley of Petals and avenge Celia."

Jack placed a reassuring hand on her upper back. "One thing at a time."

"Okay." May pointed forward. "417 is just up here."

This section of the fourth floor had been mostly untouched by the blast. Mostly. Ceiling tiles had fallen, and glass had broken, but other than that, it was fine.

Jhony, on the other hand, was not fine.

"He's dead," Jack said, stating the obvious.

And he hadn't gone peacefully. His arms were stretched out to his side, and his back was slightly arched. There were no bullet wounds or cut marks, and Jack didn't see any visible sign of blunt force trauma.

"Was he suffocated?" Jack's question wasn't directed at May. He was just thinking out loud.

"Doesn't matter," May said. She turned away but stopped. "They're tying up loose ends."

Jack nodded, hands on hips. "Makes sense. But who's doing it?"

The room shook. May stepped towards the door. "Perhaps a question for another time?"

Jack agreed. And he had a few of them. Another thing that bugged him was that they got to Thapa so quickly. Wouldn't a bio company want the man's DNA? This was nothing more than a straightforward hit.

He and May left and headed back the way they had come. They nearly got back to the decimated nurses' station but paused just inside the hallway. Just in time, too. A squad of gun-toting men came hurrying forward. They each wore different getups ranging from ordinary citizen to steroid-injected surgeon. Jack figured they were coming for Jhony, but that didn't make sense. He was already dead.

Two men turned and entered the remains of Room 405, Dhonu Thapa's room.

Jack held an arm out in front of May. The killer look on her face was plain to see. She wanted to exact revenge on behalf of the late Sherpa. If she did, they'd both be killed.

"No," Jack whispered. "They're here for his DNA, I guarantee it."

"Then why not get it while he was alive?"

It was a valid question. Jack's best guess was that BIOfinity Genetics didn't have any local contacts at the hospitals here. The only way a Chinese biotech conglomerate could get their hands on it was with a dramatic stunt like this. Plus, how on earth were you covertly moving a bedridden patient? Jack looked around and refrained from calculating the dead. He couldn't. It would just piss him off more.

He sneered in disgust and was mere seconds from drawing his pistol and gunning these guys down himself. But he didn't.

"Let them get what they came for."

"What, why?" May asked, shocked he'd say such a thing.

"If we stop them here, they'll be on to us. At this point, they have no idea how much we know or where we are." May didn't look so sure or happy. "Believe me, I'd love nothing more than to jump out and kick the shit out of them myself. But think, what are the chances these guys came alone?"

Her face soured. "Zero. They'll have more people down on the streets."

"Exactly," Jack said, slinking back with May in tow. "We'll wait for them to go and then slip out with the other survivors."

"Hang on," May said, edging back toward the hall juncture. She dug into her pocket and produced her phone. Jack watched from behind as she opened her camera app and then swiped over to the video function.

After thirty seconds of filming the unknown team, she locked the phone and waved it at Jack.

She grinned. "The online conspiracy theorists are going to love this."

Clever girl.

11

The wait was excruciating. Jack and May hid until the foursome disappeared. Moments later, an emergency team rushed into the fold. That was their cue to emerge from hiding. They staggered into view, mostly on accident. Jack's legs really were jellified, and it was hard to breathe.

They clutched one another and cried out for help. One of the medics aided them, slapping an oxygen mask over May's face, then transferring it to Jack fifteen seconds later. The short supply of fresh air was enough to clear Jack's head and allow him to make it to the nearest stairwell.

Between Jack and May's combined strength and willpower, they pushed through the door. Jack spilled down the first half of the flight when it came free from its hinges. It was a slow and arduous descent. Jack landed on his back and slithered head-first down the entire length of the tiled steps, coming to a rest with only the top half of his body on the landing between floors.

May had tried to hurry after him, but she couldn't keep up. Jack stayed on his back, unmoving, barely showing any reaction at all. He had fallen so slowly that none of the bumps hurt. It had only been an inconvenient and slightly embarrassing occurrence and nothing more.

Jack folded his hands on top of his stomach and waited for his partner to appear. She did, standing over him with her hands on her hips. Neither of them said a word. Jack sighed and silently held up his hand.

May took it and helped him to his feet.

"Thanks."

She dusted his shoulder off, but to no avail. "You're welcome."

Jack stretched his lower back.

"Are you okay?" she asked.

"Yeah, fine." He shifted his hips to the right and popped his lower vertebrae. "Coulda done without that, though."

They took the next flight slowly, walking side by side.

"I have to say," May said, "I've never seen someone so at peace with falling down stairs."

Jack shrugged. "It's nothing new to me."

"Do you fall down stairs often?"

He glanced at her and cleared his throat. "Weirdly, yeah. It's as if I'm a character in some jerk's book who gets his rocks off by making the hero hurt himself."

"Aw, poor baby," May said, mocking him.

"It's not all bad." They parted and allowed two more paramedics through. "I've been able to see some really cool stuff along the way."

May tapped away at her phone.

"What are you doing?"

"Uploading the video and any additional information I have to the web."

Jack understood. "Time to make the roaches scurry?"

She nodded, tapping furiously. She grunted in Chinese. Her tone made it sound like a curse, and Jack had to know.

"What was that?" he asked.

"What was what?"

"What did you call your phone?"

It took May a second to recall what she had said. "Oh, I called its mother a wart-covered salamander. I'm having trouble getting a signal in the stairwell."

Jack nodded his approval. His phone had also been a wart-covered salamander at times. Once they emerged onto the first floor, May whooped into the air and pocketed her phone.

"It's only a matter of time now. At the very least, it'll slow them down."

Once the video caught fire, there'd be no stopping it. Jack had to trust May's ability to cover her tracks. Her phone was now a major liability. And she shared the same sentiment. She smashed it against the floor, picked up its remains, and dumped half of them in a nearby garbage can. The other half went into a separate can. There would be no tracing her now. Jack needed to remember that this was May's life. She was the professional when it came to living off the grid while avoiding murderous dictatorial regimes.

"And if it doesn't?" Jack asked.

"'And if it does't, what?'"

"What if the video doesn't slow them down?"

May thought for a moment. They hurried for the front doors, beckoned along by a line of medics, police officers, and firefighters. The cavalry had officially arrived on the scene.

"I still have a phone call I can make."

Jack didn't know what that meant, but he hoped it was like having an ace up her sleeve.

Kathmandu, Nepal

Four of his men had just finished collecting whatever blood and tissue they could from the old man. Two of them weren't actually on Shenlong's team. They worked directly for David Cho's biotech company. The other pair belonged to Shenlong alone. Two additional members of his outfit were out roaming the streets in plain clothes. The mercenary leader sat in a van down the street from the hospital, watching from afar. He was currently coordinating comms within his team, having fulfilled his part of the plan.

Shenlong had interrogated and executed the bartender.

His professional callsign, Shenlong, had been borrowed from a spiritual dragon originating deep within ancient Chinese mythology. The immense, blue-scaled, serpentine beast was said to be the "bringer of rain and master of storms" and had been a very important being to his people's culture. He had even used the name while devoutly serving in the military as a Falcon Commando.

Until his methods had become too severe.

Cowards.

The mercenary was in the process of contacting Cho with an update. He had just dialed the CEO's private line and was waiting for him to pick up. Cho didn't always answer right away. It was both understandable—considering the man's position—and infuriating. Shenlong and his team operated as a well-oiled machine, and any stoppage, no matter the cause, was a nuisance.

The line picked up. "Hang on."

Shenlong didn't like to do anything of the sort. Still, he waited for his employer to make himself available. Shenlong could hear the man excusing himself from what sounded like a meeting. Cho didn't mind. Shenlong had been told to contact him whenever he needed, twenty-four hours a day, seven days a week. It was only a two-hour time difference between Kathmandu and Shanghai, so that would never be an issue.

"Okay, I'm here," Cho said. "What do you have?"

Shenlong cleared his throat. "The contact has been neutralized, and our men are currently collecting the samples." He shifted in his seat. "I'm not sure why we didn't take the Sherpa alive."

"Because it would've drawn too much attention," Cho said.

"And bombing a hospital won't?"

"Yes, well, no matter. It's still early enough post-mortem for me to get what I need."

"Hopefully," Shenlong added. "You mentioned that this may not work."

Cho sighed. "Yes, that's true. Let's hope I'm wrong."

Yes, let's hope.

The quicker he got this job over with, the better. Working for a multi-billion-dollar tech company was much more of a high-profile job than he typically took. Add in that they were partnering with China's MSS, and Shenlong was feeling something he hadn't experienced in years.

Nerves.

There were too many moving pieces. This job was not as cut and dry as he'd been led to believe.

"What of the Minister's daughter?" Cho asked.

"No sign of her. She went underground shortly before I arrived."

"She is the only person that can ruin everything. She must be taken care of."

Shenlong leaned forward, squeezing his phone hard. "Remember who you are talking to, Mr. Cho. I know exactly what I'm doing, unlike some. If Zhao's people had done their job in the first place, you and I wouldn't be having this conversation."

Cho let out a long breath. "Too true. And—"

"Cho?"

"Hang on."

Shenlong growled. "I will not hang—"

"We have a problem."

The mercenary's anger subsided, and he waited for Cho to explain.

"A video was just uploaded online."

"And?" Shenlong would love nothing more than for Cho to get to the point.

"It stars our men dissecting the bloodied corpse of a media-darling Sherpa."

Now, Shenlong was experiencing something else he hadn't felt in years. Surprise. He climbed out of his van and walked into the middle of the road, uncaring if any cars were coming. The wider angle gave him a better view of the smoldering fourth floor of Kantipur Hospital. He pictured the cameraman—or in this case, camerawoman —sneaking up behind his recovery team only to film them.

Why not kill them?

Cho spoke up to reveal the reason.

"The video is titled *BIOfinity Genetics Dissects Famous Sherpa.* There's also a jumbled list entailing Minister Zhao's involvement and a vivid description of what happened inside the Dancing Buddha. We're being labeled as terrorists!"

Shenlong sat back. His people had not been mentioned, and that's all that mattered. It was obvious to him who had filmed his recovery team. Mayleen Wu was playing a very impressive card. The global media was surely going to eat this story up. Pressure would be put on them. Maybe enough for Cho to pull back his people—Shenlong and his team. All in all, Wu might just get away with it and disappear.

"You need to stop her!" Cho cried.

"Me? This is a BIOfinity problem."

"It is all of our problem." Cho got very serious. "I'll tell everyone you were involved. I'm sure some agencies around the world would love to meet you. CIA, Interpol, the Mossad…"

"You do that, and you're a dead man."

Cho chuckled, enraging Shenlong further. "You forget, my friend, I'm already dead—and so will you be unless you get rid of Wu and bring me my samples!"

In a matter of minutes, Shenlong had been pummeled by a series of emotions he had long thought been dead. First, was *nervousness.* Then came *surprise.* Now, the ruthless mercenary leader felt *concern.*

Cho had him. Shenlong couldn't threaten a man that was already destined for death.

"She must still be in the area," Shenlong said, thinking aloud. "We'll find her, and I'll personally put a bullet in her head."

"And my samples?"

"You'll get them soon enough."

Shenlong ended the call. A car horn blared behind him, but Shenlong was too absorbed in what was in front of him to turn his attention to the driver. The car horn had also gotten the attention of someone else. There, just outside the hospital's front doors, was a stunned Mayleen Wu. She jabbed a finger out at Shenlong, getting the attention of a man he had never seen before.

The Caucasian's outfit and haircut screamed, "America!"

He also needed to die.

May was too skilled to be afraid of her father's repercussions. He'd have to catch her first. The one thing May excelled at more than anything was disappearing without a trace. Her covers had covers. She owned several alternate identities with backstories, each a mile long. She had never been found out, and she had no intention of ending her streak today.

She and Jack held one another, looking the part of a scared couple. As if on cue, the pair took in a large lungful of air upon reaching the sidewalk. They stopped and did nothing else besides breathe. Jack gripped her shirt atop her left shoulder, refusing to let go. May didn't know if his protection over her was purposed or if he'd just forgotten he was holding onto her.

May didn't voice any condemnation. Jack was an honorable man. That much was for sure. He was charming in an innocent, boyish way. Some would've called it juvenile. May would describe it as youthful. Jack didn't act his age, and May didn't disapprove. She'd met way too many uptight bureaucrats in her life who had forgotten how to enjoy themselves.

Jack was a pleasant change of pace.

A combination of patients and visitors followed May and Jack out of the ruined Kantipur Hospital, forcing them forward and into the middle of the street. The roadway had been shut down and was now overflowing with those involved in the attack. Victims outnumbered the relief by more than four to one. May and Jack were in better shape than most, and they continued across the street to keep out of the way.

A car horn blared off to their right. May's attention shifted from the encompassing mayhem to the irate motorist. She assumed she'd see someone standing outside their car shaking a fist at the dozens of people laid out in the street like some internet shrew. Instead, she spied someone she recognized, staring down the angry driver.

Hmmm, it can't be.

He turned, stopping cold. He had seen her too.

May pulled Jack in the other direction. "Move!"

"Wait, what?"

"We need to get out of here!"

Jack was understandably confused. In the chaos of everything, it was easy for May to *acquire* a vehicle. She simply opened the nearest car's driver's side door, a compact, economy class four-door Hyundai, and ripped its owner out. The petrified woman didn't fight back. Jack didn't voice his opinion on the matter. It was easy to see that May had been spooked. He rushed around to the passenger side, looking back where May was currently staring. A single man was in the middle of the road walking towards them. He had his hand to his left ear, and he was shouting into his phone.

All hell broke loose as soon as May sat down behind the wheel. Bullets flew, impacting man and automobile alike. The shooters didn't seem to care which got in the way. Jack flung himself into the busted rear passenger window, screaming for May to "punch it!"

"Go, go, go!" he shouted, tucking his feet in before they got shredded.

More automatic gunfire erupted behind them.

May cranked on the steering wheel and slid them through the next intersection and around the corner. She checked her rearview mirror and saw nothing except Jack's feet. He righted himself and braced against the sideways g-forces, gripping the front seats' headrests as May took another corner.

"Who the hell was that guy?"

"Shenlong." She eyed Jack in her mirror. "He's very bad news."

12

Wu and her new friend got away, but not before Shenlong's men turned their vehicle into Swiss cheese. They wouldn't be getting very far, regardless of the Hyundai's condition. It wasn't exactly the best choice for a getaway car. It was built for economy, not speed.

Shenlong still held his phone to his ear. He calmly gave his men their orders as a group of police officers rushed his way. If they had been smart, they would've initiated a shoot-first strategy with Shenlong.

Oh, well.

"Red Team, pursue targets. Yellow Team, standby for orders." The police surrounded him. There were six in all. "Blue Team, regroup on my position."

"Don't move!" one of them yelled.

Predictable.

"Oh, and Blue Team? You know what to do."

Shenlong ended the call and lowered his phone.

"I said, don't—"

A barrage of gunfire took down all six police officers. Shenlong did as he was told and stood as still as a statue and allowed his men to do what they did best. None of the policemen got off a single shot. Every person within a hundred feet of Shenlong dove to the ground. He stepped forward and brushed a speck of dirt from his shirt as four people with scoped rifles emerged from the crowd like a band of specters. Onlookers shrunk back as they pushed through.

Two vans blared their horns, removing the gathering bystanders from the street. Shenlong and the rest of Blue Team climbed in, and they took off with a squeal of rubber.

And they weren't alone. There was an extra passenger inside the van carrying Shenlong and two other members of Blue Team.

"Who's this?" he asked, motioning to the understandably distraught woman. She was a nurse, and she was filthy. Twin streaks of mascara-laced tears ran down her dusty face. She'd been crying.

Shenlong leaned in and read her nametag. "Binsa, is it?"

His guest could not speak due to the duct tape covering her mouth. So, she just nodded.

"So, Ms. Binsa, what do we owe the pleasure?"

One of Shenlong's men spoke up. "She was the Sherpa's nurse. She came to check on him while we were upstairs." That didn't give Blue Team a good reason for abducting her, though. "We questioned her, and she blabbed on about some medallion the old man had brought in with him."

That piqued Shenlong's interest. He reached out and peeled back a corner of the tape.

"This may sting." He pulled.

To her credit, the nurse didn't cry out in pain. She let out little more than a wounded whimper.

He drew his pistol and sat it on the seat next to him. "Tell me about this medallion."

Kathmandu, Nepal

The Hyundai was missing most of its windows, but the engine was still running, and that's all that counted. Jack had since moved into the front passenger seat and strapped in next to his white-knuckling wheelwoman. May had done a fabulous job evading the initial assault. However, Jack wasn't stupid. He knew another bout was coming. So, he'd keep his head on a swivel and do his best to spot trouble before it was too late.

Jack shifted and yelped. "Ow, dammit!" He lifted his right butt cheek.

"What is it?" May asked.

He plopped back down and held up what he had plucked free. The object was an inch long and razor sharp.

"Glass."

He tossed it into the backseat and winced. He now had another hole in his ass. It wasn't anything to write home about, but it did sting. His jacket had shielded his arms from the glass when he had crashed into the rear of the car head-first. The only other injury he had sustained from the quick exit was a microscopic shard in his left palm.

He looked down at his ruined t-shirt. "So much for the new clothes, huh?"

May glanced down at her own destroyed outfit. "Yeah, I really liked these jeans."

They headed north, zipping past a Sampurna Pharmacy and an NMB Bank. There was even a McDonald's Café here. Jack would've given his pinky toe for a coffee right about now.

"Man, this place has everything."

May shot him a glare. "Including psychopathic mass murderers."

"Now that you mention it... Who is Shenlong?"

May looked uneasy. That told Jack all he needed to know. He really was bad news.

"He's a ghost. I didn't think he existed until I started hearing different stories, but all about the same guy."

"That bad?"

She nodded. "Former Falcon Commando, if you can believe it."

"Woah, really?"

"Yeah."

Jack's heart raced. "Damn, they're no joke."

She laughed. "You're telling me! I heard he was discharged from service because he continually crossed the line during interrogations."

"It's hard to make the dead talk," Jack said, shivering.

Five sport bikes came screaming up behind the Hyundai, closely tailed by an imposing, black SUV.

Jack spotted them first. "They're here."

"I see them," May said, eyeing her overhead mirror. "What next?"

Jack watched the crotch rockets maneuver towards them in the reflection of his side mirror. The bikes were fast, but they were lightweight. Their Hyundai wasn't all that heavy compared to the SUV at the rear of the pack, but it was a rhinoceros compared to the smaller two-wheelers.

"Separate the chicks from their mother."

May looked at him like he was crazy before putting it together. She sat up and adjusted the mirrors to see better. Jack drew his pistol, not sure what he could do besides call out their pursuers' movements. God forbid he took a shot and hit an innocent passerby.

He slid the weapon under his left leg. "Okay, who first?"

One of the bikers pulled forward, edging over to Jack's side.

Gotcha.

"Give it some gas, but be ready," he said, turning away from May.

"Ready for what?" May asked.

The biker sped up to match the Hyundai's speed, then attempted to overtake them. The bike was only a couple of feet from the rear right quarter panel, and when he swung back left just a hair, Jack signaled May.

"Brake!"

She did, and Jack threw open his door. The biker didn't stop in time and slammed into it. Jack snagged his pistol and snapped off a pair of point-blank shots. Each round hit the biker in the chest, and the two-wheeler bucked and went tumbling behind them. It nearly took out another of the motorcycles.

May spun the wheel right and took a turn at high speed. The force of the turn slammed the door on Jack, knocking his gun out of his hand and into the footwell. He knew he was lucky it hadn't fallen outside instead.

"Ow!" he yelled, shaking his hand.

"You'll live," May said, ducking as bullets tore into their headrests.

Jack slunk down low. "You sure about that?"

An unaware motorist pulled out too far into the road and was t-boned by one of the motorcycles. It impacted the sedan near its front tires, launching the rider into the air like a flesh missile. He hit and tumbled. His body acted as a biodegradable speed bump for the weighty SUV. It cleared the biker with little trouble.

"That's two!" Jack shouted, holding on tight.

May was putting the four-banger through the gauntlet, taking turns without slowing down a lick. It was seriously impressive to watch, not that Jack had his eyes open. They had just missed a school bus, clipping a smaller coupe instead. May had to decide, and she chose wisely and sideswiped the smaller of the two options.

During all the commotion, neither Jack nor May saw the SUV pull up beside them. It slammed into the driver's side of the much smaller Hyundai, pinning it against a row of slow-moving cars. The shriek of grinding metal and fiberglass drowned out all other sounds. Sparks flew, and Jack's door was sheared off. Now, the embers of the metal-on-metal contact threatened to cook him alive.

"Ah!" he shouted, leaning as far left as he could. He would've leaped into the backseat if he hadn't been buckled in.

May dug into the front of her jeans and drew her pistol. She leveled it at the SUV and pulled the trigger as many times as it took. After six rounds, the larger vehicle veered away. Jack looked up in time to see a person slumped in the front passenger seat. He couldn't see if the driver had been hit, but he prayed he had.

May pulled away, the Hyundai billowing smoke from several places. Jack's doorframe was red-hot and scorched. Traffic thinned up ahead, giving Jack a clear view of the road.

"Is that a bridge?"

"Yep, Tinkune Bridge. The Bagmati River runs directly beneath it." They snaked through a line of slower-moving cars. "Plenty of places to lose them on the other side."

"Why's that?" he asked, reaching into the footwell to retrieve his felled pistol.

"It's mostly residential over there. Roads are a lot tighter." They arrived, zooming onto the concrete river crossing. May looked over her shoulder. "But we can't do anything with these damn bikers on our butts!" Jack looked at her and was about to say something. "I know, I know," she said first, "one thing at a time, right?"

He grinned, then went wide-eyed as May stomped on the gas. The "oh shit!" handle tore free with the slightest pressure. He shrugged and casually tossed it out his window.

The plastic handle glanced off one of the biker's face masks. Jack had no idea who was startled more, himself or the crotch rocketeer. The simple, non-threatening vehicle accessory caused the biker to swerve and clip the rear fender of a pickup truck. The motorcycle went flipping into the right-hand guardrail, sending its rider over the side and into the river below.

They were halfway across the bridge when they realized they weren't being pursued anymore. May slowed a touch to give herself the ability to look around with Jack. Together, they confirmed that they were alone, going with the flow of regular traffic.

"Um…" Jack didn't know what to think. He looked out his window in time to see a demon rise from the depths of hell. "Holy shit."

May saw it too. "Are you kidding me?"

It was an attack helicopter, and it hovered right along with them, matching their speed with little effort.

It backed away and increased its altitude.

"Is it going to do what I think it's going to do?" May asked, speeding them back up.

Jack looked at their car and then down at the road passing beneath them.

He gazed at the aircraft. "Oh, God, I hope not."

It fired.

Four rockets streamed toward the bridge directly in front of their Hyundai. May did what she could to stop. The brakes locked, and they skidded forward and were rearended by another motorist.

A second burst of rockets was enough to destroy the bridge.

It broke apart beneath them, swallowing Jack and May whole. They didn't have time to unbuckle and climb out. All they could do was hold tight and ride it out. The splintering concrete reminded Jack of a string of howitzers going off. Saying that it was deafening would've been an understatement.

Then, they fell forty feet and plunged into the cold mountain water.

13

The chilling temperature of the Bagmati River punched the air from Jack's lungs. But it also got him moving. He quickly found his seatbelt buckle and disengaged it. Jack's exit from the Hyundai was easy since the passenger side door had been torn off. The entire car slipped under as he made his exit.

Now, all they needed to do was swim to shore.

"May?" he asked, spinning around. He waded in place for a moment, then called out her name even louder. "May!"

Jack swam in a circle and could just barely see the roof of the Hyundai under the surface of the water, but it was sinking fast. The water was too gray to see any deeper than that. He dove beneath the murky surface and kicked for the descending four-door. As he neared, Jack could see the outline of a person still sitting behind the wheel.

May!

Jack kicked like mad and reached out and grabbed hold of the bent and twisted passenger side doorframe. He cut his hand on something but paid it no attention. He pulled himself closer and ducked back into the Hyundai.

May floated lifelessly, still buckled into her seat. A trace amount of blood drifted away from her forehead. Jack guessed that the steering wheel was to blame for the injury and loss of consciousness. He launched at May's seatbelt assembly and depressed the red button, freeing her. As she was released, she rose to the ceiling while the vehicle continued to sink further.

He pulled May through the empty doorframe, then repositioned his arm underneath her left armpit before heading for the surface. He looked up and was just able to see sunlight. They had traveled much deeper than he had thought.

Not good.

Jack kicked and clawed at the water. He was a fine swimmer, but that was in a bathing suit. And he rarely had to carry another clothed, immobile adult with him. His lungs ached. Jack focused on the sun. It grew brighter with each stroke. But each stroke was slower than the one before.

Come on!

They broke the surface. Jack took in a lungful of precious air and kicked until he reached one of the nearby concrete supports. It sported a small platform and a ladder that reached down to the water. A second ladder began there and then continued up to the road itself. They were east of the smoldering breakage, somewhere between it and the shore. May didn't have time for that. In fact, she might already be dead.

Jack mentally burned the thought, refusing to believe she was gone. He slipped his shoulder under her body, using his slight buoyancy to his advantage. Then, he climbed, using only his feet and one hand. When they were high enough, he flopped May onto the small platform. Jack finished the ascent and knelt next to her, immediately starting CPR. He went through the steps in a haze and found himself pumping her chest with both hands clasped together. Jack leaned in, tilted her chin up, locked his lips with hers, and gave her mouth to mouth.

He blew.

"Come on, May."

After the second deep breath, May convulsed and coughed, and for a fraction of a second, her lips tightened around his, causing them to share a passionate kiss.

Or not.

May gagged, opened her eyes, and vomited the Bagmati River all over Jack's face and neck. He froze. The spewed water dribbled down his face and smattered the concrete between his knees, one disgusting drip at a time. May had no idea what had happened. She was too busy regaining her air to notice.

But Jack did.

She reached a hand up and stroked his cheek. "Th—thank you."

"Yeah," he replied, "no problem."

She leaned up on her elbows, confused by his demeanor.

"What's wrong?"

Jack pointed at his face. "See this?"

May sneered in disgust when a long string of viscous fluid connected his nose to the ground. "What is it?"

His eyes found hers. "You threw up on me."

"Oh, sorry," she said, grimacing.

"Yeah, no, it's fine." He sighed. "Everything is fine."

"Sir, it's confirmed. The target is in the river."

The remaining members of Blue and Red Team were gathered around their leader atop a hill overlooking the river. The middle of the bridge was a smoking, fiery husk.

Yellow Team's work had always been something to marvel at. The aircraft had disappeared as quickly as it had shown up. Red Team had suffered fatalities, though. Four of his men were dead. Three bikers and one of his men inside the SUV had been killed by Wu and her American friend. Casualties were nothing new to Shenlong, though it had been some time since his group had suffered any losses. Years, in fact.

It was just another reason that they needed to be killed. He looked over his shoulder at no one in particular.

"Bring me their heads."

Lalitpur, Nepal

Jack and May climbed down from the truck bed and thanked the good Samaritan for his help. They had decided to re-enter the frigid water and swim for the shore to the south of the river rather than climb straight up into the chaos. Once topside, they tried to hail a taxi, only no one was willing to give two sodding individuals a ride.

After three such rejections, a local with a rusted-out pickup rolled up to them. He stopped and looked the pair over before tipping his head back toward the bed. Jack and May glanced at one another and then climbed in.

"Our boat sank," Jack explained.

He had no idea if the local understood English. If he did, he didn't let on, nor did he say a single word to them the entire trip back to May's safehouse in Lalitpur. It was the only place they could think of heading until they figured out their next move.

May keyed open the apartment door, shivering as much as Jack. They were both cold and soaked. As soon as Jack crossed the threshold, he immediately ripped off his jacket and shirt. Then he did his best to wring them out in the sink. The safehouse had no power and no running water. The only reason it was here was for a day like this. He and May needed to lie low after a heated altercation.

"I need to—" he started, turning, and finding May hurriedly taking off her clothes.

She stood in front of him in only her jeans and sports bra. She had even ditched her shoes and socks. Her eyes lingered on Jack's muscular upper body the same way he had locked onto her rock-hard six-pack and innie belly button. May also showed off a circular scar on the front of her right shoulder. Jack recognized it for what it was.

She had been shot.

May noticed the change in Jack's eye level. "Four years ago. Bangkok."

"How'd it happen?"

"Another agent and I were attempting to smuggle out information against a morphine manufacturer. The plan was to blackmail the company into giving us priority access." She glanced down at the scar. "I guess they didn't like us being there after hours. Killed my partner."

Jack lifted his hand and placed it on her shoulder. He rubbed his thumb over the ragged scar. His eyes lingered before shifting to meet May's intense stare. Neither operative spoke. They were too lost in the moment. He playfully squeezed her shoulder tighter. Jack really wanted to kiss her again, without the vomit this time.

But he didn't.

"So, the medallion…" He released May's shoulder and stepped back, feeling his heart beating in his ears.

"Yes, the medallion," May said, trying to find something more important to look at. She was about to turn away from him but stopped. "What about your friends back home? Think they can help?"

Jack hadn't thought of that.

He removed his phone from his pocket, thrilled that he'd upgraded the case recently. Jack moved back into the kitchen, dug into his jacket, removed the wrapped artifact, and dialed the number for Raegor again. As always, it was answered on the second ring.

"Go ahead, Jack."

Jack stepped up to the same wall he and May had sat against the night before and leaned back against it, sliding himself down into a seated position.

"Sir, I actually need Eddy this time."

"Copy that," Raegor replied. Jack was thrilled to work for someone without ego. If Jack needed Eddy more, Raegor was happy to take the backseat.

"I'm here, Jack," Eddy said. The Georgia Peach's drawl was thick.

"Switching to video," Jack said, pulling the device away from his ear. He tapped the camera icon and waited for Eddy to accept it. Eddy and her short blonde hair came to life a second later. Unlike Raegor, she didn't take calls veiled in shadow. Eddy was out in the public, like Jack. Raegor was supposed to be dead and hid his identity at all costs.

Her eyes dipped. "Where's your shirt?"

Jack smiled. "Yeah, about that…"

He gave Eddy the short version of what had happened since the last time they had spoken. It had been less than a day, and still, so much had occurred.

"Wow, yeah, okay." Eddy looked concerned. "Well, it's good to see you're still in one piece."

A smirk formed on Jack's face. "Is that worry I see on your face?"

She shook her head. "No, gas. Too much queso last night." Eddy never skipped a beat. "So, what do you have for me?"

"This."

Jack held up the medallion, showing off both sides. "It belonged to our Sherpa friend." He sat up taller. "Can you do some digging for me? I don't exactly have the means right now."

Eddy nodded. "No problem. Already captured images of both sides."

May slid in next to Jack, unintentionally showing off the straps to her sports bra. Eddy's eyes locked on her.

"Ms. Wu, I see you are also missing your shirt."

May looked down, then looked at Jack.

"Calm down, *Mom*," he said. "The river, remember? We're just trying to dry out our clothes." He held up his right hand, tucking in just his thumb and pinky. His ring, middle, and forefinger stood up straight. "Scout's honor."

Eddy rubbed her temples. "At least tell me you're wearing pants."

Jack nudged May. "For now."

Thankfully, May got the hint. Both burst out laughing at Eddy's expense.

The peach's face reddened.

"Jack." It was Raegor. He was just off camera.

"Sir?"

"This Shenlong character, what do you know about him?"

May repeated everything she had told Jack, which wasn't much.

"He sounds like a ghost," Raegor said.

"That's what May called him," Jack added. "Guys like that are tough to pinpoint."

"They don't give up easily, either," Eddy added.

"No," Raegor said, "they don't." He let out a long breath. "We'll do some digging on him and your medallion and call you back ASAP. Raegor out."

Eddy leaned in close to the screen. "Jack, I really am happy you're okay, you know that, right?"

That made Jack feel good. "I know, thanks."

"And Jack?"

"Yeah?"

Eddy grinned. "Put on a shirt." She winked. "Eddy out."

They hung up with Eddy and Raegor and worked on trying to dry their clothes. Jack laid their shirts and jackets on the floor and opened a window to get some much-needed airflow into the stagnant apartment. It was the best he could do under the circumstances. Unfortunately, his actions caused the safehouse's internal temperature to drop significantly.

He and May decided to turn in early, knowing that Eddy could call them back at any time. Once again, they lay down. It was different this time, though. At least, it was for Jack. He had done his best to ignore his rising feelings for the former MSS agent. There was something about May that he was gaga over. She was the perfect woman in his eyes.

Get ahold of yourself!

Jack was flat on his back, flexing and releasing the muscles in his lower back. He felt a slight tremble but paid it no attention.

Until he realized what it was.

May was facing away from him, shivering. He turned and watched her. Every few seconds, her body trembled and broke out in goosebumps. Jack felt bad for her. He wanted to do something for her, but what? There were no furnishments here. Jack racked his brain to come up with a solution. When he did, he knew it would take some convincing for May to partake.

"Hey," he said.

May looked over her shoulder. "What?"

Jack lifted his right arm. "Come here."

She scoffed at the idea. "I'm fine."

"Yeah, right." He laughed. "I can see you shaking from here."

"Jack, I—"

"May." She flipped onto her back and leaned up on her elbows. "Shut up and get over here."

Jack could see she was trying her damnedest not to smile. He locked eyes with her and willed himself not to break contact. He almost did, but she gave up and huffed in annoyance at her defeat. She slid into Jack's awaiting embrace. He wrapped his arm around her, instantly feeling her ice-cold body against his warm skin. Jack was the kind of guy that slept with his AC cranked as low as it could run.

His heat caused May to melt into him, and just when he thought they were going to have a "moment," she was sound asleep, snoring like a chainsaw.

14

BIOfinity Genetics Group
Shanghai, China

It was late, and David Cho fidgeted in his chair. Most of the staff had gone home hours ago. Only he, Li, and a few other lab rats remained. David had told his assistant several times to leave and get some rest, but the young man had denied his boss each time. David admired Li's work ethic and drive to succeed. He reminded David of himself when he was fresh out of college.

Where did that person go?

His cell phone buzzed, and the screen lit up. The name on the screen made his armpits dampen.

It said, ZHAO.

David swallowed back his fear and picked up the device. He would have to break the news of Shenlong's failure lightly. Wu and the American had evaded Shenlong and his men at the hospital, though not all was lost. The Sherpa's blood and tissue samples were currently being analyzed.

David answered the call. He couldn't ghost Zhao, not yet.

"Hello, Minister."

"The gaps within your updates are bothersome."

David nervously tapped the desktop with his fingertip. "I…I figured you'd be asleep and didn't want to wake you."

"Did your man come through?"

David let out a shaky breath. "He was unable to apprehend your—Agent Wu." He was lucky he had caught himself. If David had called Wu Zhao's daughter, he would've been a dead man. "But," he said quickly, "we did recover samples from the Sherpa. Tests are being done as we speak. We will know if the samples are viable or not soon."

"So, you failed."

David was confused. "Quite the contrary, sir, we—"

"Wu is still at large. Just because you succeeded in one facet of the mission doesn't mean I should just overlook your failure in apprehending Wu."

"With all due respect, Minister, the mission has always been the Sherpa's tissue samples."

Zhao growled. "I will tell you what your mission is." He paused. "One more blunder and I will be forced to send in my own men."

"My people can handle it."

"The results say otherwise. I have a team standing by as we speak."

No! David thought. *If his people get involved, I'll lose everything!*

David needed to keep the Minister in the dark about his health concerns. It would be seen as a weakness, and men like Zhao only dealt with weaknesses in one way.

He got rid of them.

Lalitpur, Nepal

An obnoxiously loud buzzing noise stirred Jack. He tried to ignore it, but it persisted. With a heavy heart, he opened his equally heavy eyelids and attempted to roll onto his left side. But he couldn't. It was pinned down by another human being.

After May had fallen asleep in his arms, Jack had, likewise, passed out. Neither, it seemed, had moved the entire night. Jack tipped right, positioning himself better to remove his appendage from beneath his partner. He gently gripped May's left shoulder and coaxed her to roll forward. May subconsciously complied and rotated away from him, much to his displeasure. Jack frowned, eyeing her for a moment longer before reaching down onto the floor and finding his phone beside the thin mattress.

Jack checked his watch. It was 5:05 a.m. local time.

Ugh.

He answered the call. His voice was low and gravelly. "Hello?"

"Jack, that you?"

It was Eddy. Jack flopped his head back onto the mattress and closed his eyes.

"I'm sorry, but I can't come to the phone right now—"

"Jack?"

"If you could leave your name, number, and time you called—"

"Jack, this isn't funny."

"I promise to call you back in, say, three hours, and—"

"Jack!"

He sighed and opened his eyes. May did too. She faced Jack, showing off a matted head of black hair. She parted it around her face and smiled at Jack when she found him staring at her.

Jack put the call on speaker.

"Oh, hey, Eddy. That you?"

The senior TAC operative muttered incoherently under her breath. It was early in the morning here, but it was dinner time on the previous day back home.

"Agent Wu there with you?" May propped herself up on her left elbow and stared at the phone.

"Yeah, we're still in bed."

May's chin fell to her chest, and she shook her head, mortified.

"Jesus, Jack? TMI. Look, I found something."

That instantly woke up both of the fatigued field operatives. Jack struggled into a seated position and stretched his arms high into the air. May stayed put, looking very comfortable, but she was also laser focused.

"Okay, Eddy, whattaya got?"

"Do you have the medallion handy?"

May slinked out of bed and disappeared into the living area. She quickly returned with the artifact in hand. Instead of returning to her earlier posture, she sat on both knees next to Jack.

"The first side," Eddy said, "the one with the tree…"

May held it up.

"What about it?" Jack asked.

"There wasn't much to go on from ancient history."

"So, we got nothing?"

Eddy laughed softly. "I didn't say that. I found something from a recent discovery that I think you should look at. Here, I'm sending you a photo."

Jack glanced at May. She had no clue what Eddy was talking about.

Eddy's text came through, showing off a replica of the medallion's front face, or at least what they were calling the front face. The tree was plain as day and had been carved into stone.

"Where is this?" Jack asked.

"On the outskirts of a village called Langtang."

"Langtang?" It was the same place they had planned to go to find Thapa's Sherpa family.

May flashed her eyes to Jack. She was thinking the same thing. "Yeah. I know it. We actually have a lead there. Our Sherpa's family is from Langtang. We're supposed to locate them for help."

"Hmmm," Eddy said, "that can't be a coincidence."

"No, it can't," Jack agreed.

"But," May added, "Langtang Village doesn't exist anymore."

That Jack didn't know.

"No, it doesn't," Eddy agreed. "Erased during the earthquake of 2015, right?"

"Yes," May replied. "It was a total loss. The entire village was destroyed."

"Hang on, 2015?" Jack asked, recalling something from the deep recesses of his memory. "Wasn't that the one that ransacked most of Nepal?"

May nodded. "Nearly nine thousand people died. Over four hundred of them were in Langtang, wiped out by an avalanche. But," May continued, perking up Jack's hopes, "Langtang is slowly being rebuilt. Thapa wouldn't have known any of this, though. A man in his situation would've naturally assumed the village was still intact."

"Hey, Eddy?" Jack asked, moving them along. "I don't mean to be a bastard here, but what does this have to do with our medallion?"

"Right… Well, the carving you see was photographed a year ago during an excavation of what's believed to be the entrance to a newly discovered tomb beneath a monastery's foundation."

"A tomb?" Jack and May asked simultaneously.

"That's what the article said. And there was no reference to the writing engraved into the edges."

"And you said 'believed,' as in they aren't sure?"

"Correct."

Jack smiled. "That means they haven't opened it yet."

That was very good news.

"What about the other side?" May asked, flipping the medallion over.

"What do you think?" Eddy asked. "It's a mountain valley. There are thousands of similar carvings floating around the net."

"Nothing revolving around Shangri-La?" Jack asked.

Eddy snorted a laugh. "Of course, there is, but most of the other information to go along with them is utter garbage based on what we know." That deflated

Jack. May's shoulders dipped. She felt the same way. "Until we can find someone to translate the text, I'm afraid this is all I can help you with. I'm sorry, Jack, but you're on your own."

"Yeah, no problem, Eddy. Thanks for the info."

"So," Eddy said, "Langtang?"

Jack looked at May. She nodded.

"Yeah, Eddy, Langtang."

It was a four-hour drive to Langtang, give or take. Jack and May dressed, cringing as they each slipped into their cool, marginally damp shirts and jackets. As they had done, not even a day prior, they picked up a change of outfits from the same retailer before embarking on their journey north. Jack also insisted on grabbing another round of beverages from Ju Yang's favorite coffee shop.

Jack and May were set up with an exact duplicate of the wears they had purchased the day before, and the coffee was even better than the one he had ordered yesterday. Now, the only thing they needed to figure out was a car.

"Ju has already taken care of it," May said, flashing Jack a smirk.

Drinks in hand, they continued their trek through the northern end of Lalitpur and hung a right a quarter of a mile further up. The area opened into a parking lot. May led Jack through the quaint maze of vehicles, stopping in front of a boxy, white SUV. The rental was a four-wheel-drive Mahindra Scorpio, sporting a robust diesel engine. It reminded Jack of a budget-friendly Land Rover.

May offered to drive the first leg, which was music to Jack's ears, and knees...and back. Plus, he really wanted to savor the rest of his coffee. Jack didn't know the area either, so having May drive was the obvious choice.

For his part, Jack plugged "Langtang" into his phone's map app but muted the robotic woman's voice. He was happy to see a charging cable ready to go. Jack plugged in his phone and vanished into his beverage. May had already polished hers off and looked somewhat coherent.

Jack was still pretty far off from that.

"Turn left," Jack said, imitating his phone's female, Australian-accented voice.

The traffic light changed, and May cranked the wheel. "Cute."

Jack smiled. "How 'bout some music?" She shrugged, indifferent. "Do you like Bob Seger?"

Bidur, Nepal

They stopped once for breakfast and a bathroom break at the Namaste Café. Jack was tickled to the death that the name rhymed. To his amazement and enjoyment, a traditional Nepali breakfast consisted mostly of tea and fried dough—donuts. Jack substituted the tea for more coffee and then dunked his cinnamon-sugar donuts into the hot beverage, much to the dismay of the nearby locals. The first bite transported Jack to heaven.

"Enjoying yourself?" May asked.

Jack nodded. He closed his eyes, and he breathed in deep. When he opened them, he discovered that May was also dunking her donut. Her eyes glazed over when she took a bite. Her lips were caked in cinnamon and sugar deliciousness.

She was also clearly enjoying herself.

They took a bag of fried dough to go and climbed back into the car. Jack drove this time. He was wide awake and well-fed, even though it had all been just a bunch of caffeine and sugar.

Jack connected his phone to the Scorpio's Bluetooth but the device got ripped from his hand.

"Hey, what gives?"

May scrolled. "My turn to choose the music."

She must've found what she wanted because her eyes lit up when she tapped the screen. A chord progression unlike anything Jack had ever heard started up. The drums were killer too. Their style was like a blend of hard rock and modern jazz with a touch of metal. He couldn't wait to hear the vocals.

Only, there weren't any.

"Instrumental?" he asked, glancing at the screen. "Plini?"

May nodded. "Yeah, they don't have a singer."

These guys were a progressive rock band. How May had found them was beyond Jack. They were good too. His left knee found the rhythm, and it bounced along until the band switched to a tempo that Jack had no chance of counting. So, instead, he focused on the road, zoned out, and enjoyed the groove and beautiful view.

May spoke for the first time in over an hour. She'd been doing some research on her own, trying to dig up as much information as possible on this tomb.

"Huh."

"Find something good?" Jack asked, spying a sign for the city of Dhunche. He was happy that the larger communities had included English translations to their signage.

He couldn't see anything on her screen without leaning over. Seeing as that could cause a wreck, Jack decided to wait for May to reveal her discovery.

"Supposedly, our tomb belongs to the first chief of Langtang."

"Really—beneath a monastery?"

She showed Jack the screen, not that he could read much of anything. "That's what it says."

"I'll have to take your word for it."

"The archaeologist in charge of the dig says he's certain of it based on the site's timeline and the symbology."

"What symbols?"

"Mostly carvings—along with some fairly legible script, all things considered."

"What about the illegible script surrounding our tree?"

May shook her head. "Doesn't say. I don't think they've been able to decipher it either, from the looks of it." She smiled. "And here's our medallion."

May clicked on the image and showed it to Jack. It was exactly the same photo that Eddy had sent them. But something was off—different—something neither of them had noticed before.

Jack couldn't help himself. He leaned over a little to give himself a better view of the phone while also attempting to navigate the winding mountain road. Thankfully, the trek was slow. If they had been traveling any faster, the move would have been all but impossible. Not that it was safe to do now, especially with a river riding right alongside you.

The Pasang Lhamu Highway had followed the Trishuli River for nearly the entire trip. The road weaved back and forth along the waterway's eastern shore, giving travelers something else to marvel at. The water was peaceful in some areas, reminding Jack of the Little River in the Great Smoky Mountains National Park in Tennessee.

It was tranquil—beautiful.

"What's that at the bottom of the petroglyph?" Jack asked, motioning to the bottom of the screen.

May zoomed in. "I'm not sure, pots?"

Jack nodded. "Maybe clay jars?"

"Whatever they are," May said, squinting, "they were important enough to add."

15

Syapru Besi, Nepal

"Turn here," May said, pointing at a road sign. "Take it slow."

"Yes, ma'am," Jack replied, doing as he was told.

He edged the Scorpio off the main road and down a soft decline. The road changed from paved to stone. Luckily, the densely packed crushed stone path seemed firm enough to drive on. The four-wheel-drive SUV performed beautifully as the narrow two-lane switchback hairpinned sharply back to the right. Forty feet later and twenty feet deeper, it leveled out. Jack guided them around to the east, depositing them at the foot of a modern-ish concrete bridge.

"The Trishuli River," May announced.

Jack kept liking this place more and more. The peace it projected was comparable to Yellowstone and the Smokies. Jack could see tiny communities dotting the waterway from their slightly elevated position. The Trishuli flowed faster here. It was also wider and looked deeper.

Jack pushed the Scorpio across the bridge. He silently prayed that there wasn't a murderous mercenary behind them planning to blow it up. For good measure, Jack sped up a hair and finished the short trek in no time flat. May gave him a look when the SUV shot forward at the last minute. They segued back onto the compacted, rocky road with a gritty crunch.

"This it?" Jack asked.

"Almost," May replied. "We're about seven miles from the western edge of Langtang Valley. Follow the road until you can't."

"Until we can't?"

May nodded. "There's a hike coming up."

Jack sighed and readjusted in his seat. "Can't wait."

Usually, he was always game for some exploration, but given his body's condition and their lack of proper supplies, Jack wasn't thrilled with the prospect of roughing it through the wilds of Nepal.

I guess it could be worse, he thought, appreciating the view.

Nepal really was breathtaking. The drastic elevation changes meshed seamlessly with the powerful, fast-moving Trishuli River. But there were also rolling hills featuring slow, trickling streams. The beauty was consistent.

"What's that for?" May asked.

Jack blinked. "Huh? What are you talking about?"

May reached over and softly tapped his lips. "This."

Jack was smiling.

"It's because of that," he said, pointing out his window. "All of it."

May smiled. "I agree."

Jack got caught staring at her, and he didn't care. May blushed and pulled a loose strand of hair behind her ear. Her eyes went wide.

"Jack!"

He turned his attention off her and saw only the tree line to the road. Jack yanked on the wheel and righted their course. Now, it was his turn to be embarrassed.

"Sorry," he said.

"It's…fine," May said, blowing out a long breath.

Jack, once more, shifted in his seat. "To be fair, I was distracted by something beautiful."

"Jack, I—"

He grinned. "Oh, you think I'm talking about you?" May's face hardened. "I mean, come on, perfect skin, stunning eyes, excellent trigger finger… Why would I be attracted to that?"

She blushed again.

Jack never had the intention of planting *that* seed even a minute ago, but he couldn't help himself. May was flawless in every single way. She'd been at the forefront of his mind ever since she kicked the crap out of him on the third floor of the Dancing Buddha. And she had, literally, *kicked* that crap out of him.

The Scorpio's interior fell into an awkward silence. Jack prayed that he hadn't overstepped an invisible boundary. Not only could his actions have ruined things between him and his partner, but they might've also harmed the mission.

May turned slightly. "What were your grandparents like?"

Jack nearly ran them off the road again. He course corrected and swallowed hard. It wasn't exactly the comeback he'd been expecting. He didn't know what to say. So, he told her the truth.

"Grandma and Grandpa raised me from when I was six. She was a historian. He was a British army vet."

May smiled wide.

"What?"

"I can see where you get it from now."

"Yep," Jack said, "and you aren't the only one to notice."

"You should be proud of it."

Jack glanced at her before returning his attention to the road. "Oh, I am. I loved them a lot. They were my mom and dad longer than my actual parents were."

Is this an interview? Jack thought. *It kinda feels like an interview.*

May was looking into Jack's background, attempting to gauge the kind of man he was. He didn't blame her, either. Jack had already done the same thing with May. Both of her folks had heavily influenced her. The biggest difference between them was that her father had dragged her into his business—a business of espionage, distrust, and murder. At least Jack had been given the opportunity to build his life in his own way. He had joined the military on his own accord.

His grandfather—the veteran—had wholeheartedly approved the move but, had in no way forced Jack to do it. Jack couldn't imagine May willingly signing up to work for the MSS. She seemed too grounded and normal to be a radical, nationalist spy.

May's hand was still on his shoulder. Jack was close to acknowledging it but caught himself. Instead, they just drove, jamming to another of May's prog-rock bands.

Jack couldn't hide his delight.

"There's that smile again," she said, forming her own.

Jack shrugged. "What can I say… Despite everything that's happened," he gazed out the windshield, "I'm really enjoying myself."

Kathmandu, Nepal

It had only taken one night for the quaint hotel room to be transformed into a working laboratory. Shenlong didn't recognize most of the equipment, and he didn't understand half of what the two men said. This wasn't his world. His was more straightforward and to the point. He existed for action, not sitting around and waiting.

The two scientists were optimistic about getting results, though unsure if they would be the ones David Cho sought. If the samples weren't viable, the next phase in Shenlong's mission in Nepal would commence. He kind of hoped it would happen too. Cho's survival meant very little to him, personally. Yes, if the wealthy CEO died, Shenlong would lose a valuable client.

There are always more clients, Shenlong thought, cleaning his pistol. The weapon wasn't dirty, but the work kept his mind busy.

He sat in a folding chair, working atop a cheap card table. He faced the door, as he always did when sitting idly. It was a quirk of his, one that had come in handy several times.

A buzzer caught his attention. He turned in his chair and watched as a spinning machine, a centrifuge, slowed. The two science types dove at the connected laptop and spoke in hushed tones. From here, Shenlong could see the screen come to life with data, none of which made sense to him.

So, he waited.

They took too long.

"And?" Shenlong asked.

Both men faced him. The one on the right, a man whose name was never mentioned, spoke. "Results are negative. We have nothing viable."

Shenlong didn't respond to him. He removed his phone from his pocket and called his employer.

"What do you have?" Cho asked.

"Nothing of use."

"No…" Cho said. "That can't—no!" Shenlong allowed the dying man to vent and, once more, waited. "You must continue the mission."

"My fee?"

"Double it," Cho replied. "I don't care the cost. Find Wu and find Shangri-La!"

Shenlong eyed the door. He couldn't wait to get moving again. His men were scattered throughout the building, all in different rooms. A simple text would get them moving in minutes.

"Oh, and Shenlong?"

"Yes?"

Cho's voice grew quiet. "No witnesses. I trust you know what to do."

"I do." Shenlong hung up and set down the device.

"What did he say?"

Shenlong stood and looked over his shoulder. "Pack up. We're done here."

They quickly began to get their gear together. Shenlong quietly slid a magazine into his empty semi-automatic pistol as they did. Once it was loaded, he racked the slide, chambered a round, and shot both scientists in the back.

Forty-five seconds later, the hotel room was ablaze.

Padmaarga, Nepal

May was enjoying herself too. She couldn't remember the last time she had felt joy of any kind. A person in her line of work typically felt more stress and loss than joy. There was a sense of purpose being alongside Jack.

He appreciated May as a person and not just a professional. They had relied heavily on one another, which was okay. It was a change of heart for May. She usually hated to work with someone else. She had only trusted herself. It was an easier existence for a spy. Relationships didn't happen often for her, and when they did, they ended in sorrow.

"End of the line," Jack said, braking. He pulled off into a makeshift parking lot and threw the SUV into park, and then yanked on the emergency brake.

From what May could see, he was right. The road seemed to end at the start of the village of Padmaarga. From her estimation, Langtang was still three miles due east along a path only accessible by foot or hoofed beast. May didn't see any horses or donkeys around, so she guessed they'd be going by foot. She didn't mind either. The car ride had tightened her legs, and they were in major need of exercise.

Jack didn't look as eager to get out and venture. Still, he popped his door and climbed out. He was an impressive man. The temperature outside was significantly cooler than it had been down south. May's breath was visible— barely—but it was there. By nightfall, it would be freezing. They hadn't packed for that.

They hadn't packed for anything.

She watched him take in the village. He was one hundred percent enthralled with the landscape. This wasn't just a job for him. He was thoroughly relishing in everything around him. She admired that.

Padmaarga comprised a collection of random structures. Most had been constructed of rocks meticulously pieced together by hand. A few of them had been built of more modern design, using concrete and stucco siding. All of them sported the same blue, metallic rooftops. May wasn't sure about the significance of it, nor was she concerned as to why.

The first thing they needed to do was ask about Thapa's family. Then, they'd need a guide to Langtang. If they were lucky, Thapa's relative would also be that guide. If not, May was confident she and Jack could figure it out independently, but not confident enough to attempt it recklessly.

Jack agreed.

"Let's find us a Sherpa," he said, heading off.

They were currently in the north-central part of town. To their left was a handful of small tea houses and cafes. Jack stopped and studied each one before turning and heading south. May didn't follow. The sign for a small "hotel" was in a language that wasn't Nepali.

"Um, Jack?"

He stopped. "Yeah?"

"We might have a problem."

Jack rejoined her and waited for her to explain. She pointed at the sign that had caught her attention. "That's Tibetan, not Nepali." She faced him. "I don't speak Tibetan."

Jack broke into a full-body shiver.

"Geez," May said, "I didn't think that would bother you so much."

"Oh, it didn't. I'm freezing. I don't have enough layers."

She turned and saw a sign for a corner store. In places like this, that's where they'd find something to wear.

Let's hope they take credit cards.

They did.

Most places like this were built on tourism dollars, and it was impossible to rely on out-of-towners to carry cash with them. They entered the small store. Jack was forced to duck through the low opening. May spotted a wall of coats to the right and headed that way. Jack followed closely. His demeanor had instantly changed now that he was out of the cold.

He inhaled deeply.

May smelled it too. It wasn't a rank stench but one of mustiness. Central air was a luxury that some places didn't have. A small, wrinkled woman happily greeted them.

"Hello," May said, praying she understood Nepali.

The local didn't respond as if she did.

"Hi there," Jack said.

The shopkeeper smiled. "Hello, sir."

May tripped over her own feet and faced the woman. "You speak English?"

She held up her hand, putting the slightest of spaces between her thumb and forefinger. "Little."

Okay, May thought, *keep the conversation simple.*

"We need coats," she said, holding herself and shaking.

The local nodded. "Yes, coats. Yes, please." She held out a hand, showing off her wares.

Jack plucked one of the larger sizes off the wall and checked it. Whatever size it was, he must've been satisfied. He slid out of his thinner jacket as he was about to sport a heavier one.

"Hang on," May said, stopping him. "You need a better shirt too."

Jack looked down at his shirt and then went shopping for one. He eventually found a heavier, long-sleeved shirt on a rack behind them.

"Is there a changing room?"

"I don't think so," May replied.

Never one to feel ashamed, Jack shrugged and pulled off his t-shirt, much to the delight of the aged shopkeeper.

She glanced at May and flexed her arms. May smiled.

"Husband?" she asked.

May nearly choked on her own air. She coughed and shook her head, trying to regain her composure. Jack froze, looking hurt by her reaction.

He answered in a very Jack way. "Someday, maybe." He gave the local a playful wink.

The older woman enthusiastically applauded the statement. "You take." She pointed at the long sleeve. "You have. A gift."

Jack shook his head. "No. I'll pay."

The local bowed. "Thank you." She looked at May, clutched the operative's hands together, and then pointed at Jack. "You keep, yes?"

She found Jack's eyes but didn't say anything. How could she?

May decided to pick out her own coat. Jack had chosen a black one with a thick layer of gray insulation. May's coat was nut brown and it contained a cream-colored inner layer.

She held up her credit card. "Please tell me you take credit."

The shopkeeper snagged the card out of May's hand and looked it over. "Yes, Ms. Yang. Not Stone Age."

Thank God.

"May, hang on a sec. I want to grab a few more things." He stepped away in search of more gear but stopped. "Oh, and ma'am?"

"Yes?" the shopkeeper asked.

He stepped up next to May. "Do you know anyone here by the name of Thapa?"

"Kalsang?" she asked, looking up from her old school manual card swiper. She paused what she was doing and stood erect. Her friendly demeanor vanished. "What you want with him?"

16

After Jack explained that they were here to deliver Kalsang the news of his relative's unfortunate passing, the shopkeeper, Ditya, bid them farewell and offered them a ten percent discount if they should ever need anything else.

Ever the saleswoman.

They headed outside, and Jack barely felt it. His new coat blocked all the wind the Himalayas could throw at him. He tucked his hands inside the front pockets and found them equally effective against the elements.

"Here."

He turned and found May holding out a flap of black. As Jack realized what it was, he took the stocking cap and slid it on his head. He looked at her with a raised eyebrow.

"It was a gift." She smiled. "I tipped her well."

The temperature was dipping fast. They needed to find Kalsang Thapa before it got dark. Jack had no idea what awaited them here after sunset. Places like this were often too dangerous to navigate at night. The terrain was harsh and ever-changing. Even the most experienced mountaineer needed to proceed with caution.

Ditya had confirmed Kalsang was a Sherpa guide like his ancestor before him. But in between clients, Kalsang worked at the Monastery Hotel. It sat at the southern edge of Padmaarga. Based on that, it would offer guests an unmatchable view of the surrounding landscape. Not that there was a bad view anywhere around here.

The sky was unbelievably clear with a great sun. A picture-perfect paradise.

"I think I'm gonna move here," he joked, "just as long as there's decent pizza."

May rolled her eyes. "That might be a problem."

Jack shrugged. "Oh, well. You see our hotel anywhere?"

"Not yet." She pointed ahead where the main road split into two. "Let's try that way first."

They marched forward. Jack was thrilled to see English at some of the establishments. Like Ditya, a handful of other locals spoke enough of it to get by. He also recognized a smattering of Nepali, but most of the readable signage was in Tibetan. They continued south, quietly walking with one another. The sound of their crunching footsteps was second to the whipping wind and bray of livestock.

Sheep roamed the streets freely, though they stuck closely to a specific property. Jack guessed it was their owner's residence. One of them was the same color as his coat's lining.

Possibly the source of the wool? He cringed and held up his arm and stared at his sleeve. *What about the skin?*

"Something the matter?" May asked.

Jack shook his head. "No, I'm fine." He spotted something at the end of the road and pointed at it. "Is that a church?"

"It is," May replied, "well, a monastery anyway."

"Monastery Hotel?"

May shrugged. "Only one way to find out."

They beelined for the structure, buffeted by the cold mountain air. The center of Padmaarga featured a symbol the Himalayas were well known for: Prayer flags. They stretched across from building to building and in all sorts of colors. The flags were a Tibetan tradition meant to bless the surrounding lands and the people traversing them. Some had been dulled by time. Others looked new and vibrant.

Jack needed to do something.

He removed his phone and flagged down a younger boy. "Excuse me."

The Padmaargan looked at him oddly. It was easy to see he didn't speak English. Jack turned his phone sideways and mimicked the use of a camera. The youth caught on quickly and nodded.

"Come on," he said, holding out his hand to May.

"Jack, we—"

"Have time. Humor me…please?"

She gave in. "Fine. You win." May took his hand and stepped up next to him. Jack eased his arm onto her shoulder and drew her in close. She gave in again. May leaned into his embrace and smiled wide for the camera, and for herself.

The teen said something, but Jack and May didn't understand him.

"What?" Jack asked.

The youth repeated it and then made an exaggerated kissing noise and face. He repeated the action when neither Jack nor May responded. Jack swallowed down his fear and gazed down at his companion. She similarly looked up at him. Both parties didn't budge, not until the local made the kissing noise again.

Oh, to hell with it.

Jack went in.

As did May.

Less than an inch away from his personal utopian wonderland, Jack got hit from behind and knocked forward. He stumbled away from May and spun around, about to draw his gun. But he stopped. His attacker wasn't a viable threat…because it was a sheep. The teen laughed, and so did May, though she did everything in her power to hide it.

The moment, like Jack's self-esteem, had been shattered.

By livestock.

The same damn sheep he had seen before, the one with the same color wool as the lining of his coat, had butted him in the ass while on his way to his wonderland. Now, Jack felt like a circus clown. He spun and pounded away, not giving a damn that he didn't retrieve his phone first. Luckily, May didn't seem to believe the same about him. She hurried after Jack.

"Hey," she called, "wait up."

Jack didn't acknowledge her. He just kept moving.

"Jack."

He slowed and stopped, closing his eyes and taking a deep breath.

"Hey," May repeated, "you forgot this."

When he opened them, he found May holding out his phone. Jack held out his hand, unable to look at her.

"Hey." May's hand found his shoulder which persuaded him to make eye contact with her. She smiled broadly at him. "You still with me?"

He sighed. "A sheep headbutted me in the ass."

May grinned. "I was there." She motioned at the phone. "Great picture, by the way."

May headed off without Jack. He lifted the device, unlocked it, and gazed at the screen. The picture really was amazing. They were posed under dozens of waving prayer flags with a background that no graphic artist could properly replicate. Even the sheep was visible behind him. He guided his pinched fingers away from one another and zoomed in on him and May.

They both looked so happy.

He turned and found the "ruiner of dreams" right where they had left him. It bleated at Jack, almost mocking him.

"You coming?" May called out.

Jack looked over his shoulder and found her further ahead.

He gave the sheep one more stare. "Bastard."

He turned and caught up with May.

"What was that all about?"

Jack shrugged. "Nothing. I was just thinking about what sheep tastes like."

Monastery Hotel
Padmaarga, Nepal

The monastery Jack had seen from a distance was, indeed, their hotel. So, technically he was correct on both counts. From what he could tell, the former house of worship had been retrofitted into a place of rest for weary travelers. There were plenty of places to stay in Padmaarga, actually, though most only offered a handful of rooms. In reality, they were closer to small bed and breakfasts than a hotel or a motel.

The Langtang Valley Trek was a renowned hiking excursion that drew the attention of thousands annually. During his time as the Scorpio's passenger, Jack had looked ahead and researched the area a bit. The trek, initially, seemed like a cool thing to do, but it took nearly eleven days to complete! If it had been a day or two—maybe three—Jack would've been game. But eleven? No way. His feet ached thinking about it.

May made it to the front steps first and began her ascent. The incline, like the monastery itself, was made of fit stone. The architecture was something to admire. And given its remote location, Jack gave the builders a couple of extra brownie points and an unspoken "attaboy!" This monastery wasn't as elaborate as the others Jack had read about, but it was still a sight to behold.

She entered through a rickety louvered wood door. Jack's closet back home had a similar one. The slatted construction was designed to allow airflow in and out of the separated rooms, i.e., Jack's stuffy closet and his bedroom. The windows were a matching set. All of them were. The monastery sported two floors that Jack could see, though he wasn't sure if basements were a thing in the Himalayas.

Is the ground too hard to dig? It would make sense if they existed. Basements would easily be the warmest rooms during the harsh Nepali winters.

He, once again, had to duck his head to enter. Apparently, no one in Padmaarga stood taller than five-ten—minus the hulking monster at the center of the lobby, if this was the lobby? To Jack, it still looked like a functioning house of worship. In fact, he was pretty damn sure it was.

Behind the Yeti-sized man was a trio of seated figures. Each of them was bowed in reverence to their deity. The enormous individual was currently performing some sort of ceremony. He stood at least six feet seven inches, and he must've weighed north of 275 pounds.

Jack leaned in close to May and spoke softly. "Our Sherpa?"

May shrugged.

The two waited for the ritual to conclude. It didn't take long. Jack and May must've come when it was near its completion. The threesome of parishioners stood and exited through a backdoor, leaving Jack and May alone with the burly fellow.

Jack nudged May forward. She looked at him as if he were crazy. Jack didn't know what to say. He wasn't even sure the guy would understand him. Jack coaxed May forward again and received a slap to the hand for his effort. He shook the sting away and waited for her to do something.

"Go," he silently mouthed, shooing her away.

May gave Jack the finger before speaking. She greeted the man in Nepali first. Jack now recognized the language after listening to her converse with others. The local didn't react. He just kept mumbling along to himself. Was he deaf?

May switched gears and greeted him in Chinese, just in case.

Still, nothing.

Jack could see that she was about to give up. She looked at him and then got an idea.

"Hello," she said. Ditya couldn't be the only person here to understand English. The behemoth turned and eyed the newcomers. "We are looking for…" he stepped toward them. May's voice caught. She coughed and cleared it and tried again. "I'm May, and he's Jack, and we're looking for Kalsang Thapa. Ditya said we could find him here."

He stopped in the middle of the space, directly beneath the glow of a skylight. It illuminated the giant fully, and Jack couldn't fathom how this guy fit through such a small front door.

"Do you understand me?" May asked, leaning closer to Jack as she spoke.

"Yes," bellowed the beast. His voice was thick and deep.

Michael Clark Duncan, eat your heart out.

"Will you help us?"

He didn't reply or move. The man's lightly bearded face was as unemotional as stone.

May opened her mouth to ask the question again but was cut off.

"No." He turned and headed toward the same back door as the others.

Jack was sick of the games. If this guy was who Jack thought he was, then he'd stick around if he told him the truth. Jack dug into his coat pocket and removed the medallion.

"Dhonu Thapa." The name paused the mammoth man's departure. "We just had a little chat with him."

"Impossible," the local said. He didn't turn. "Dhonu Thapa died a century ago."

Jack took three steps forward. Now, he was in the same overhead light as the big guy had been earlier. He held up the medallion. "Then, how did we get this, I wonder?"

The show was too much for the other man. He turned. When he did, his eyes went from Jack to the artifact. His expression changed from annoyance to shock.

"Where did you get that?"

"From your great-great-grandfather," May said, stepping up next to Jack.

"Im—"

"Impossible?" Jack interrupted. "Funny thing about impossibilities... They sometimes get proven otherwise. Dhonu said he had been in the Valley of Petals for the last one hundred years."

"How do you know that name? Most just call it—"

"Shangri-La?" May asked.

Kalsang nodded.

"Look, buddy," Jack said, "there's an awful lot to unpack here. Is there anywhere else we can talk? Maybe somewhere a little more private."

Kalsang glanced behind him and tilted his head toward the backdoor. "Come. I... I will make us some tea."

17

Kalsang led Jack and May to a modest dwelling at the rear of the Monastery Hotel property. An older man spotted them walking toward him and paused his duties. He had been tending to a small herd of yak. Kalsang spouted off something to the elder, and the shepherd quickly dropped what he was doing and headed up toward the hotel.

"Friend of yours?" Jack asked, hurrying along after the Sherpa. Kalsang's strides were long and swift.

The bigger man nodded. "Taral helps me at the hotel."

"Your English is very impressive," May said.

Kalsang paused in front of the second structure's door and faced them. "Believe it or not, I spent a few years in the States."

"Really?" Jack asked, genuinely surprised. "Doing what?"

"Wrestling scholarship at Penn State."

Jack looked at May with his mouth hanging open. She seemed just as stunned as he was.

"Don't believe me?" Kalsang asked.

"Oh, no, I do," Jack said. "I mean, look at you! Did it not work out?"

Kalsang gripped his right shoulder. "Torn rotator ended my career, and I came home to help here."

"I'm sorry to hear that," May said.

Kalsang shrugged, then swept his hand across the landscape. "I'm not. Now, I own the business. My mother and father passed a few years ago. The Monastery Hotel is now mine and mine alone."

They headed inside.

"Do you still do guided tours?" May asked.

He waggled his hand back and forth. "Only when it's worth it for me."

Jack patted the giant on the shoulder as he passed by him. "Oh, believe me, this'll be worth it."

The dwelling turned out to be Kalsang's residence. It was simple and sparsely decorated. The Sherpa lived simply. His home wasn't meant to entertain guests. It had been designed for very specific reasons, such as eating and sleeping. A tiny stove was situated in the corner of the main living area. Next to it was an equally small kitchenette, including the equivalent of a mini fridge from back home.

"Sit," Kalsang said, "I'll start on the tea."

Jack and May sat. Jack placed the medallion in the center of the square table.

"What do you know about the medallion?" Jack asked, getting down to business.

"I was about to ask the same thing," Kalsang countered.

"Not much," May replied. "Only what Dhonu told us."

Kalsang looked over his shoulder. "And you know that was actually my great-great-grandfather?"

"We have no reason to refute anything he told us, except for maybe the part of him being 157 years old. His eyes told the story."

Kalsang mumbled something and bobbed his head.

"What about you two?" the Sherpa asked.

"Us?" Jack asked. "Well, I was in the military before leaving and becoming a park ranger for a few years."

"Which park?" Kalsang asked.

"Yellowstone."

"Beautiful place," he said.

Jack looked out the window. "Yeah, but it has nothing on Nepal."

"Quite true." He clinked away. "I guess it's safe to assume you aren't a park ranger anymore."

"No, I'm not."

"What do you do now?"

Jack shifted in his seat. "Let's just say I work for some people who value history more than others."

"Treasure hunter?"

Jack laughed. "Why does everyone ask me that? No, we aim to protect history, not profit off it. Like now, there's currently a nasty biotech company out of China that would love to find the Valley of Petals and violate it to the tenth degree."

Kalsang actually snorted a laugh. "They'll have to find it first."

"They will," May said confidently.

Kalsang paused what he was doing to give her his full attention. "How?"

"The biotech company is working with the Ministry of State Security."

"And you know this, how?"

May leaned forward and clasped both hands atop the table. "The Ministry… I'm one of their best agents."

Kalsang clenched his fists and stepped forward.

"Former agent!" Jack added, essentially shouting the words. "May is why I'm here. Our goal is to stop it from happening. She threw her life away because she didn't agree with the move."

"Why should I believe you?" Kalsang asked. "Either of you."

"Because," Jack said, picking up the artifact, "this medallion means something significant to you." Kalsang's eyes shifted to the artifact. He longed for it. Jack put two and two together quickly. Kalsang's odd reaction said it all. "You've seen it before, haven't you?"

"But how?" May asked. "Dhonu would've had it with him the entire time he was in the Valley of Petals."

She and Jack waited for the Sherpa to divulge.

"First, tea," Kalsang said, turning around, "then, I will tell you what you want to know."

Tea wasn't exactly Jack's thing, but this brew was better than decent. It contained a mixture of herbs and spices with subtle fruit tones buried in it. Jack enjoyed the temperature of the drink more than the drink itself. He was presently cradling the still warm cup in both hands, cherishing the sensation.

"So," May said, setting her teacup down, "how do you know about the medallion?"

Kalsang stood and began to clear the table. "First off, it is *not* a medallion." Jack and May stared at one another. "It's a travel passport, of sorts. A permit, if you will. I've also heard it called a key."

"A permit?" Jack asked.

"How do you know that?" May added.

Kalsang set the dishes in the sink and faced them. He leaned back against the counter, looking back and forth between Jack and May.

"Her first," Jack said, pointing at May.

Kalsang nodded and returned to his seat. "I come from a long line of Sherpas whose purpose was to deter the unworthy from discovering the Valley of Petals, a trail called the Sacred Path. The Thapas, and Thapas alone, knew the way."

"Your family guarded its location?" Jack asked.

"Once... But everything changed the day my great-great-grandfather disappeared. My grandfather passed down a few of the stories to me when I was young. Until now, I only thought of them as just that, stories."

Kalsang stood and went back to his kitchen. He stood on his tiptoes and reached his bear-sized hand up and over the top of the cabinet positioned above the sink. Whatever he was looking for, he found it. Jack couldn't quite make out what the Sherpa had retrieved. It was bound in animal skins, much like the medallion—the travel permit—had been.

He returned to his seat between Jack and May and carefully folded back the wrapping. Inside was a simple, leather-bound book. He paused before laying a finger on it. You could tell that Kalsang was deeply spooked by whatever was inside. As he said, everything about his family's past had been a mishmash of truth and lore until now. Kalsang had grown up unsure of what to believe.

"This," he said, "was my grandfather's journal. In it, he recounted what his grandfather, Dhonu Thapa, had told him."

Jack's eyes lit up. May reacted the same way.

"Unfortunately," Kalsang continued, "it doesn't divulge much about the Sacred Path. But it does describe your artifact vividly." He carefully opened the cover and flipped to a seemingly random page. Jack could tell Kalsang had read the thing cover to cover several times by the way he navigated the pages. "Here..."

He turned the book upside down so Jack and May could see. The book had been penned in a language he had never seen before.

"Is that Tibetan?" Jack asked.

May shook her head. "No, it's something else."

"You are both correct."

They turned their attention from the journal to its owner. "The Thapas developed their own language to keep their secrets their own. This," he tapped the page, "is a combination of both Nepali and Tibetan." He sighed. "I'm the only person alive that can read it."

That hit home.

"You're it?" Jack asked.

The big guy nodded. "I'm the last of the Thapa bloodline. I have no heirs, and my father had no other siblings."

That seemed strange to Jack. When Kalsang ultimately passed on, so would an entire language. Kalsang's home fell into a deep silence. The revelation was difficult for everyone to process.

"These," May said, pointing at the words engraved into the glided permit, "they're the same language, aren't they?"

Kalsang nodded.

"What do they say?" Jack asked.

Kalsang took a second before handling the item. This thing had been in his family for generations, yet it was the first time he'd laid eyes, or hands, on it. With the care of a trained archaeologist, Kalsang plucked the ancient relic off the table and examined it.

"It's exactly as my grandfather had said. This says, 'the way to paradise is paved in blood.'"

"It's a warning?" May asked.

"Yes," Kalsang replied. "I believe it implies that the Sacred Path is a difficult journey, not that it is literally paved in blood."

Jack tapped the side with the tree. "Did you know there's a petroglyph in Langtang with this on it?"

To his surprise, Kalsang nodded. "Yes, I do. I prayed it was nothing more than a coincidence."

"Why's that?" Jack asked.

"Because my family was torn apart because of this thing." He set the artifact down. "If you're looking for my help, you can forget about it. I want nothing to do with the Valley of Petals."

He pushed his chair away from the table, stood, and headed for the front door. May stood too, but Jack didn't.

"And the families that call the valley home, what about them?" Kalsang reached for the doorknob but stopped. "When they are discovered and slaughtered—and they will be—what will you say then?" Jack stood. "I don't know about you, but I don't think I could sleep knowing that I could've done something to help them and chose not to."

"You're a soldier. I am not."

Jack shrugged. "I'd like to think I'd do the same thing regardless. My time in the military gave me the ability to do something about it, not the want to do it." He headed out, but not before stopping in front of the Sherpa. "You know, your great-great-grandfather gave us this thing with the hopes of his family saving lives, not hiding in the shadows."

May followed Jack but paused in front of the Sherpa. "My father is the Chinese Minister of State. He's trying to kill me." Kalsang's eyes rose from the floor to her. "He will stop at nothing to find your family's valley. He has unlimited resources, and now that he knows Shangri-La exists, in whatever form it is, he won't rest until it's his. If he gets what he wants, everyone there will die, or worse, be corralled into labor camps and studied like lab rats."

"And how do you suppose we stop such a man?"

"We get there first," Jack replied.

"It's not enough."

Jack shrugged. "Then, at least we tried." He placed a hand on May's back and guided her outside. "Come on. We'll find someone else."

Jack and May made it as far as ground level.

"Wait."

They turned. Kalsang stood just inside the door. He stooped low and stepped out. "What is your plan for the valley once you've found it? When this is all done, what do you want from it?"

"Nothing," Jack said. He motioned between him and May. "We just want peace."

"There's nothing of gain here for either of you?"

Jack grinned. "Well, yeah, a good night's sleep, for one. It's been a while."

May looked equally exhausted.

Kalsang took a long breath and looked out over Padmaarga. "Fine."

"Fine?" May asked.

The Sherpa eyed them both. "I'll help you." He held open his door. "Come. We have much to discuss before we make the trek to Langtang Village."

"Like what?" Jack asked.

"My grandfather's journal. There's much I haven't told you."

Kathmandu, Nepal

"The nurse said Thapa had a medallion with him," Junfeng relayed. He had recently seen to the nurse's interrogation. No one on Shenlong's team was better at *interviews* than his second in command.

Shenlong was confused. "We found nothing of the sort."

"I know, which means—"

"That Wu now has it," Shenlong finished.

Junfeng smiled. "Exactly."

Four men, including Shenlong and Junfeng, stood beneath the bright moonlight. The other six team members remained in the SUVs and awaited orders. The nurse's body had been dumped down a roadside hill. If they were fortunate, her bloodied corpse wouldn't be discovered until morning. By then, they'd be long gone.

"What did the medallion look like?" Shenlong asked.

Junfeng stood with his hands clutched behind his back and continued the debrief. "On one side was a tree with a script she couldn't read."

"An ancient language?"

Junfeng shrugged. "Perhaps. The other side contained a deep mountain valley."

"Gang," Shenlong said.

One of the four men stepped forward. "Get online. Find me anything you can."

Gang nodded and headed off. He popped the rear hatch of the second vehicle and dug through their bags for a laptop. The description was vague, but Shenlong was confident Gang could still find something given the information provided.

"Sir," a fifth man said, stepping out of the lead SUV, "what should I tell Yellow Team?"

He was talking about the helicopter.

"Tell them to stand down," Shenlong replied. "We've drawn too much attention to ourselves already. From now on, we're on our own."

18

Padmaarga, Nepal

The Sherpa suggested that they wait until night to make the hike to the tomb. The excavation was a high-profile story in the area and would surely be watched. Plus, Kalsang needed to protect himself. His livelihood depended on him not being implicated in an off-the-books probe such as this.

So, they sat and ate, preparing for the journey ahead. Kalsang concocted a supper of freshly made lentil soup, steamed rice, and yak meat. Jack had never eaten yak before. The meal was uncomplicated and delectable.

"There's one thing that still bothers me," Jack said.

"Just one?" May added.

Jack didn't respond to her interjection. He simply held up the permit and asked, "Why would the family assigned to protect the Sacred Path need a license to do so?"

Kalsang leaned back in his chair. "That's just one of the mysteries, isn't it? Once Dhonu disappeared, my great-great-grandmother forbade anyone to speak of the old ways. Eventually, as the elder Thapas passed on, all was forgotten. Now, the only thing left is what my grandfather wrote down, though it's only a fraction of it. Many of the pages are illegible due to time."

Jack belched. "Dinner was awful, by the way."

May grinned, as did the cook.

"Happy you enjoyed it," Kalsang said, clearing the table. He leaned toward the window above the sink, peering through it. "It's time."

Jack gazed out a different window and saw that the sun had fully set. He met May's nervous stare. Traveling through the Himalayas at night was never a wise move, even with someone as versed in its terrain as Kalsang.

They checked their weapons under the watchful eye of the Sherpa. Kalsang stepped over to a drawer and removed a keyring from his pocket. Jack now saw that the drawer had been locked. The local quickly singled out a brass key and inserted it into the cylinder. Once unlocked, he drew it open and removed a large caliber handgun.

"USP?" Jack asked, recognizing the legendary Heckler & Koch pistol. "Chambered in .45 ACP. That's a big bullet."

Kalsang nodded. "There are lots of big things out there."

He didn't elaborate. Jack was pleased to see that the guy was armed. He slid it into a leather holster and lifted his jacket, tucking both of them into his waistband. There, the firearm would be kept warm and away from the harsh elements. Kalsang had taken the liberty to pack bags for Jack and May. They contained everything a person would need during a cold-weather hike.

"Alright." Kalsang slipped on his pack. "Let's go."

Langtang, Nepal

The moonlight was so bright that it made Jack a little nervous about being seen. However, he calmed, aware that the person spotting them would have to be right up on them even to have a chance. None of them were sure what to expect regarding site security. They were in such a remote area that Jack couldn't fathom someone coming out here to do a little tomb raiding.

Unless you're us. He shook his head and pushed aside the thought and moved on.

Kalsang led them east with May between him and Jack. Jack kept his ear to the ground, listening for anything coming up behind them. Not that there was anything to hear besides the wind. It whipped about, stinging Jack's face. The rest of him was covered enough to survive the four-mile trek. His locally made wool coat was a godsend, keeping out everything the Langtang Valley could throw at him. His legs were cold, but he could handle that.

The Sherpa slowed up ahead, scaling a subtle incline. He motioned for Jack and May to stay low as they approached. Kalsang knelt behind a manmade wall, showing just the top half of his head to whatever was on the other side. Jack slowed and lightened up his footfalls, keeping the sound of crunching earth to a minimum. May moved as silent as a spirit, arriving at the wall ten seconds before Jack. She knelt to Kalsang's right, and Jack took up position to his left.

Jack gazed over the low wall and expected to see trouble but found harmony instead. A small group of locals were gathered around a fire up ahead. The wall had blocked out the red aura upon approach. The wall's construction was similar to a few buildings back in Padmaarga. Stones had been cut and laid atop one another with little to no mortar. Jack noticed that the handful of homes here surrounded their properties with similar walls, much like people did with picket or chain-link fences. There were also wide walkways cut in between the properties acting as rudimentary roads. It was a unique way to build a community.

Rebuild, actually.

Langtang Village wasn't yet prospering, but it was on its way.

"This way," Kalsang whispered, heading south along the wall.

Jack and May followed closely behind him. They only made it thirty feet. A low growl suddenly emanated from somewhere on the other side of the wall. All three explorers glued themselves to the wall, using it as cover. Galloping feet approached, stopping on the opposite side of Jack. He glanced behind him at May. She could only shrug.

Deep inhalations followed. Jack knew a dog when he heard one. Whatever this one was, it had heard them moving close to its territory. It growled, then barked, standing tall and looking over the wall. Jack looked up but couldn't see the animal from his vantage point. Two voices quickly called after the dog. Jack didn't understand a word of it.

Go home, Rover.

Two sets of feet crunched their way over to the dog, continuing their calls. A bright light blinked to life and swept back and forth across the valley beyond. It cut deep across the land. The flashlight, and the person's hand, appeared directly above Jack, protruding across the wall. The local swept the beam back and forth, causing Jack's heart to race. So far, they had done nothing wrong except for acting shady.

The voices discussed something before extinguishing the light. The dog didn't sound happy, but it dropped down and followed its owners, presumably back toward the communal fire. He, once more, glanced back at May. The look in her eyes told Jack that her heart was racing too.

Wherever the monastery was, Kalsang must've known its location intimately. It made sense, too, since his family was originally from here. Jack and May hadn't asked Kalsang, but Jack guessed the surviving Thapas had moved to Padmaarga following the devastating earthquake of 2015. It's why he and May had found Kalsang living there. The Langtang Village monastery was likely a place the Thapas had frequented many times, Kalsang included.

Until now, Jack didn't think about how hard this might be for the Sherpa. This had been his home, and it had been ravaged by Mother Nature in mere minutes. Jack wondered if this was the first time Kalsang had been back since then.

Kalsang pushed away from the wall and headed due south. The firelight vanished, transporting them back into the land of the moon. It took a second for Jack's eyes to readjust to the lower level of light. They moved down a slight grade. He couldn't see it yet, but Jack could hear that they were slowly approaching rushing water. A raging river—hopefully just a fast-moving, narrow stream—was up ahead. Jack willed a crossing point into existence. He really didn't want to get wet again.

"Thank God," Jack mumbled, seeing a narrow footbridge emerge from the darkness.

The current state of the bridge didn't seem to faze Kalsang in the least. The beefy man scaled it without stopping, pausing at its humped peak when Jack and May didn't immediately follow.

"It's safe," Kalsang ensured.

"And how would you know?" Jack asked, starting his crossing.

Kalsang turned and continued down the other side. "I helped build it."

That wasn't exactly a reassuring reason, but the bridge held, and it didn't creak once.

"How much further is it?" May asked, now walking beside Jack.

"Not too much more," Kalsang replied.

The next leg of their journey only took three minutes. Kalsang slowed but didn't kneel into cover like he'd done back at the village wall. Jack watched him dig into his coat pocket and remove a small flashlight from it. He clicked it on. The beam landed on a wide military tent. The heavy-duty structure came complete with an operable door and had been tied down in several places to keep it in place throughout its stay. It seemed as if the entire site was beneath it, or at least, the key pieces. Jack understood its presence too. The weather wasn't such that it would behave regularly. The beefy covering was a way to keep the elements out while the crew worked and while they were away.

Like now.

Jack was astonished to see that no one was keeping guard. He wasn't going to complain about it, however. Kalsang didn't move. He showed his light over the tent and waited a nauseating length of time before he moved again. Jack respected the Sherpa's display of caution. Jack procured his own light, as did May. Once Kalsang stepped toward the excavation, Jack turned his on. May quickly added hers to theirs.

"It's not big enough," Kalsang said under his breath.

The village was far enough away now, and uphill, so Jack felt some reassurance that the residents wouldn't see their beams. Still, they needed to be careful in what direction they shined them.

"Give me your light," Kalsang said, flicking his off and removing his backpack.

Jack and May surrounded him, using their bodies to mask the light from behind. The Sherpa removed a pair of collapsible bolt cutters. Jack turned his attention to the door and saw that there was, indeed, a padlock.

With a flick of his wrists, Kalsang removed the padlock. He quickly disassembled the bolt cutters and stuffed them and the lock into his bag. Kalsang slipped back into its shoulder straps and gripped the doorknob. He paused before opening the door and did so when a dog's bark echoed down the hill. The three wrongdoers rushed inside and shut the door. In May's light, Jack jammed a random chair beneath the knob.

"That won't hold them for long," Jack said, backing away.

"Who?" May asked.

Jack shrugged. "Them."

"Them who?" Kalsang asked.

"You know, *them*!"

"Just go with it," May said, looking at the Sherpa.

Kalsang did as instructed and ended the line of questioning. All three of them turned toward the innards of the structure. Kalsang added his light back to Jack and May's and was taken aback by what they saw.

"Woah," Jack said. He now understood what Kalsang had meant when he said that the tent wasn't big enough.

Just a section of the floor had been excavated, but what it held was a thing of beauty. They stood five feet above a great seal featuring the same tree as their passport. The intricacy of the artwork was phenomenal. It was easily ten feet in diameter and had been carved directly into the rock bed beneath their perch.

"I thought it was carved into the wall," May said.

Jack shook his head. "Apparently not.

"There," Jack said, aiming his beam at the tree's center. "What's that?"

May and Kalsang added their light. Jack spied a circular depression at the heart of the tree. He needed a closer look and placed his hand on the low, hip-high perimeter fencing built around the site. Kalsang stopped him with a firm hand.

Jack paused with his foot in the air and gazed up at the taller Sherpa. "We have to."

Kalsang let out a long breath and nodded, releasing Jack's shoulder. May followed him over the side, but Kalsang didn't. He stood by and watched from afar, refusing to desecrate his people's legacy. Jack and May stepped lightly, doing their best not to damage anything.

Jack got into a catcher's squat and dug into his coat pocket. May knelt before him, keeping her light trained on the odd recession. Jack unwrapped the medallion—the travel permit—and examined it before lowering it into the circular cut depression. Once in place, he pushed, and a low *clunk* answered him. Then, a section twice the size of a manhole separated and dropped away from the rest of the seal. It was irregularly shaped, following along the cutout of the tree trunk.

It happened to be the section Jack and May were squatting on.

Jack and May grabbed one another and steadied themselves as a surge of air buffeted them as it entered the newly created passage. They only fell a few inches, but it was enough to startle them both. They gazed between their feet, hearing the third member of their team approach. The events had been too much for the Sherpa. He needed to know what was going on for himself.

Jack plucked the artifact free and held it up. "I guess this thing really is a key, huh?"

"All of this was beneath the monastery?" Kalsang asked, speaking to no one in particular.

Jack stood, helping May up as he did. "Looks like it, my friend."

"What do you think is down there?" May asked.

"Well," Jack replied, "I know one way to find out."

19

Jack and Kalsang dug in and pushed. The stone slab wasn't all that thick and was stuck into place after years of inactivity. With the Thapas out of the picture, no one had been maintaining the entry point. Luckily, the engineering on display was top-notch, especially considering how long ago it had been constructed.

Centuries ago, Jack thought, feeling the golden key's weight shift in his pocket.

The entrance moved a few inches before grinding to a halt. May had joined in at the last second, and the combined strength of the trio had been sufficient. They shoved the slab open far enough for a grown man to slip inside. Jack stuck his head in, along with his light. A set of stairs greeted him. They were carved directly from the rock, the same as the great seal. The way through was pretty tight.

"Well," he said, popping back out, "I hope you guys aren't claustrophobic." May and Kalsang looked a bit uneasy. "Oookay, let's see what we have."

Jack handed his flashlight to May, turned, and entered feet first. She aimed it down the stairwell so he could see what he was doing. He stopped at his shoulders and held out his hand. May handed him back his light, and he disappeared beneath the ancient seal. The ceiling was low. Jack was forced to stay in a squatted position as he moved lower. When Jack thought he was far enough in, he stopped and waited for the others to join him.

May went next. She and Jack climbed down lower to give Kalsang the room he needed to make the trip. He barely fit through the opening they had created. Jack took an extra step lower, turned, and aimed his light toward the bottom of the stairs.

He saw an opening that looked tall enough to walk upright through.

Besides the impressive engineering, there wasn't anything else remarkable to drool over. The way forward was dull and unfinished. The roof was marginally rounded off, but inconsistently so. This didn't look like the path of some great king, not to Jack anyway. This place had been created and used, and that was it. No extra effort had been made to perfect it.

"Does this feel like a tomb to you guys?" Jack asked.

He wasn't an expert in worldly crypts, but this one just felt off.

"No," May said. "Eddy said the article implied that this was a tomb and that it housed the first chief of Langtang."

"They were wrong," Jack said, standing up. He rubbed his lower back and stepped further back to allow his cohorts to do the same. Unfortunately, Kalsang was too tall. He couldn't fully unfold his large frame. "You're awfully silent."

Kalsang gazed down the dark passage and then faced Jack. "There was nothing about this in my grandfather's journal. Your guess is as good as mine, but no, this does not feel like a tomb."

"Any thoughts as to what it is?"

Kalsang shook his head.

"Okay then," Jack said. He pointed his light straight ahead. "Forward, march."

The simplicity of the construction kind of disappointed Jack. The seal above his head had been so intricately produced that he figured the rest would be the same. He guessed the architect that had designed the first level was not the same one that designed the level they were on now. Whether by choice or, more than likely, by death, the principal builder had been replaced during the production timeline.

"Dhonu would've known about this place, right?" Jack asked.

"Yes, he would've known about all the locations along the Sacred Path."

"'All' of them?" May asked. "How many are there?"

"Three," Kalsang replied. "That's what my grandfather's journal says, anyway."

Three? Jack thought. He had a feeling this expedition was going to take much longer than he, Raegor, or Eddy had thought. *Days? Weeks, maybe?*

"I've got something up here," Jack said, seeing the corridor open up into a high-ceilinged room.

As he entered, the first thing he noticed was a heavy-looking rectangular table positioned lengthwise in the middle of the room. It was definitely *not* a tomb. Then, he showed his light against the left-hand wall and found three ledges. They had been cut directly from the earth like everything else around him. Situated atop those ledges...were bodies.

Okay, so it is a tomb.

The floor was littered with clay jars. Some were broken, but most were still intact.

"More bodies," May said, inspecting the right-hand wall. It, similarly, held three corpses.

"So, is it a tomb or a storehouse?" Jack asked.

May shrugged. "Both?"

Kalsang was off in la-la land somewhere. He was too absorbed in the room to hear anything Jack and May were saying. The Sherpa stood at the right side of the room, reading a faint line of text beneath the body on the middle ledge. Jack saw that all of the bodies had the same thing. They looked like nameplates.

"What's it say?" Jack asked.

Kalsang didn't answer. So, Jack left him alone and took in the rest of the square space. The jars were piled up big time along the back wall. He glanced at May, and together, they headed over to them.

"What do you think they're for?" he asked.

"I'm not sure, holding things?"

Jack snorted. "No, shit, really?" He squatted down and tried to lift one of the sealed jars. "Woah, that's heavy!"

He rotated it around a few times but didn't find anything discernable. Jack set it down on the table for a closer inspection but got distracted by their third group member.

Kalsang finished reading the inscriptions on all six bodies and then joined them at the back end of the table. He placed his fists on top of it and leaned forward, causing the table to creak. Jack practiced patience and waited for Kalsang to clue him and May in.

"You alright?" May asked, voice soft.

Kalsang nodded. "Yes, it's just, I..." He couldn't gather his words.

"Take your time, bud."

He nodded again and blinked hard. "The dead..."

"What about them?" Jack asked.

Kalsang picked his head up and looked at Jack. "They're all Thapas."

"They are?"

"Yes," he replied, "all of them. They're my ancestors."

"Do you know any of the names?" May asked.

"No, which means they are very old—hundreds of years old." His eyes found the jar. "What's this?"

"No idea," Jack replied. "I was kinda hoping you could tell us."

"It's a jar. It holds things."

Jack rolled his eyes. "You two, I swear..."

Kalsang picked it up. "Heavy." He shook it. "Solid too." Like Jack, Kalsang tried to open it, but it was sealed tight.

"Give it here," Jack said. Kalsang obliged and was shocked when Jack lifted it high overhead.

"What are you doing?" he said, reaching for the artifact.

"We need to open it."

"Not like that!"

Jack stepped back. "Look, I get it. This is an important piece of your people's history, but we need answers, and if this thing can clue us in..."

Kalsang knew Jack was right. He lowered his hands and stepped back. "Fine."

Sorry.

Jack slammed the jar down onto the floor, cracking it in several places. The three explorers gathered around the desecrated relic and were stunned to see that its contents were rock solid and a dark, yellowy color. Whatever it was, it had hardened years ago.

"Looks like wax," May said. She rubbed her finger across its surface. "Feels odd, too."

Just for a moment, Jack's eyes flicked up and away from the broken jar. What he saw nearly gave him whiplash after he jerked his head back up to look again.

"Holy crap."

May and Kalsang looked at Jack and followed his line of sight above the doorway. A seventh body was present, but this one's remains were positioned differently. Like the person's present company, this one was also on a ledge cut from the rock. But unlike the others, this was someone important.

"Is that a sarcophagus?" Jack asked, already knowing the answer to his question.

It was, and it was adorned with beautiful artwork, and most of it depicted people walking from right to left. *Pilgrims?* It was also covered in petroglyphs and the Thapian script.

"How'd they get it up there?" May asked, looking to Jack for answers.

"Isn't it obvious?" Jack looked long and hard at her. "Aliens."

Once again, Kalsang was too absorbed by the discovery to listen. He rushed over to the doorway and stood on his tiptoes to get a better look. Unfortunately, he still wasn't tall enough. The ledge was over ten feet off the ground, and the angle and lighting weren't making it any easier.

"Hang on," Jack said, getting an idea. "Here. Help me."

The three of them leaned into the heavy table and slid it across the room with a loud, persistent shriek. The shape of the tomb and the solid walls amplified the sound to a horrific crescendo. Jack closed his eyes and gritted his teeth until they banged into the front wall and doorway.

Jack and May stood back and allowed Kalsang to mount the table alone, but not before Jack had dug the key out of his pocket.

He handed it over to the Sherpa. "Just in case."

This was Kalsang's family. Plus, he'd be able to tell Jack and May more about it than they ever could have gotten otherwise. After a minute of silence, Jack spoke up.

"Anything exciting?"

Kalsang nodded and slowly turned around. He didn't climb down, though. He was too lost in thought. His eyes were now glued to the back wall, staring through it.

"It's him."

Jack and May met glances.

"Who?" May asked.

Jack rubbed his forehead, needing the pace to pick back up.

Oh, 'Who' better not be on first!

Kalsang finally broke eye contact with the back wall and found his colleagues. "It's the first chief of Langtang."

"Oh, damn," Jack commented, "I guess he really is here." He glanced at May. "Eddy was right."

"How long ago was Langtang founded?" May asked.

"Um," Kalsang said, still kind of lost, "about six hundred years ago. He supposedly came from Tibet."

"Woah, hang on! Six hundred years?" Jack asked, nearly shouting the question.

"Yes, and…"

"There's more?"

Kalsang nodded. "He was also a Thapa. My family owes this man everything."

Jack and May took it all in while Kalsang returned his attention to the stone coffin.

"Hmmm," he murmured. "Interesting…"

"What is it?" May asked.

"I…" Kalsang started, once again on his tiptoes. "I think there's a place to insert the key on the lid, but I can't see." He looked over his shoulder and down at Jack and May. "I need a boost."

Jack and May looked at one another, then at the table. Jack bonked it with the base of his fist. "I'm not sure this thing can handle the extra poundage."

"Speak for yourself," May countered, climbing onto the table with little regard for its age.

Jack lifted his hands and then allowed them to flop back down to his sides. "Fine, but don't say I didn't warn you."

He joined them and got into position against the wall beneath the sarcophagus. May slid in beside him, and they both cupped their hands together. Kalsang used each as a stirrup and stepped into them, giving him a couple of extra feet of elevation.

"Okay, perfect. Hold me there."

"Pfft," Jack said, straining, "I can do this all, *ugh*, day."

May wasn't faring any better. She wasn't as strong as Jack. Thankfully, Kalsang was leaning a little to Jack's side. He must've been thinking the same thing, not that Jack was thrilled with it.

"Okay. Inserting the key… Oh!"

Jack heard a *shink* as something shifted up above. "What was that?"

"Two doors slid open to reveal a carved map. It's an area of the Himalayas, and—oh, I know this place!" He shifted his weight to access his front pocket and removed his phone, snapping a picture. "It's Lam—"

The table groaned.

"That can't be g—" The ancient furniture buckled and collapsed. "Woah!"

Jack and May fell four feet and landed hard on their backs and asses. Kalsang was a few feet higher, and his prodigious frame crashed on top of his comrades. The only positive result from the incident was that Jack and May broke Kalsang's fall instead of him breaking his skull.

"Ouch…" Jack moaned, crumpled between the wall and Kalsang's hip.

May had fared better, falling backward into the open doorway.

"I told you s—"

"Jack?" May asked, on her back.

"Yeah?"

"Please, shut up."

Jack was immediately released from the unpleasant cuddle as Kalsang rolled away from him. Jack took a second to regain his breath before climbing to his feet. May got up first and helped Jack with the last half of his ascent. They dusted each other off, getting a look out of Kalsang. His right eyebrow was raised skyward.

Jack cleared his throat, and he stepped away from May. His eyes darted up to the ledge, then back down to the Sherpa. "Please tell me you got the key?"

Kalsang held it up and smiled, but the joyous reaction faltered and cracked.

"What's wrong?" May asked.

"There's one more thing about our friend up there."

Of course, there is, Jack thought amid a bout of pain and information overload.

"Everyone here died according to the average age of time for a human," Kalsang pointed at the chief's resting place, "except for him."

Uh, oh.

"How old was he?" Jack asked.

Kalsang sighed. "He was 138. It seems that our chief may have spent some time in the Valley of Petals too."

Jack inhaled deeply, then let it out slowly. He did it once more before asking the next obvious question.

"So, where to from here?"

Kalsang handed the key back to Jack. "Our next stop is Lamabagar."

"Our?" Jack asked. "So, you're coming with us?"

He nodded. "I must see this through. I still have so many questions."

Kathmandu, Nepal

"I found something!" Gang shouted. He had set up shop on a picnic table and was currently waving for Shenlong to join him.

The mercenary leader and Junfeng climbed out of the lead car and hurried over.

"What did you find?" Shenlong asked, leaning over his man's shoulder.

"This," he replied, pointing at the screen.

There had been a discovery in the Langtang Valley. A tomb with similar artwork to what the nurse had described had been located a few weeks earlier. It was the only thing of note that Gang had found within Nepal's borders.

"Do you think that's our spot?" Junfeng asked.

"It's not close," Gang added, pulling up directions to the valley entrance. "It will take us four hours to reach, at best."

Shenlong didn't like to waste time, but what choice did they have? This was all they had to go on.

"We leave in five minutes."

20

Syapru Besi, Nepal

The biggest problem so far was that they couldn't cover their tracks. Their presence would be found at sunrise. They tried to relock the seal but couldn't push it back together. The broken padlock would've been enough alone. Jack knew that news would get out, and if Shenlong was as resourceful as he seemed, he'd eventually make his way to Langtang.

"And kill everyone on site," Jack said, explaining his worry to Raegor. "I think we have a serious problem, sir."

He stared out of the front passenger side window of May's Scorpio, though she wasn't driving. Kalsang was currently behind the wheel. May was taking a break, lying across the backseat. They had decided to rotate driving duties while one person navigated. The third person would get some much-needed rest.

"Langtang has seen enough heartache for one lifetime," Jack continued, "they don't need more."

"Yes, I understand," Raegor said.

"But…" Jack added, knowing it was coming.

"But I'm not sure what we can do. We aren't an army, Jack. We don't have the manpower to plant in such a remote area." Jack knew he was right. "Even if we could get enough people to deter this Shenlong character long enough, it'll take days to roundup that kind of force."

"They don't have days."

Raegor sighed, breathing heavily into the phone. "I know."

"I may know someone that can help." May sat up. "But it'll cost you."

"Ms. Wu," Raegor said, "you seem to forget that money really isn't an issue for us. Who do you have in mind?"

"Well, see, that's the thing. She's wanted by Interpol at the moment, and—"

"No way!" Eddy shouted, butting in. "We aren't getting dragged into an international incident with Interpol!"

"Agent Marker." Raegor's words were stern and final.

Jack turned and nodded for May to continue. "To her enemies, she's known as the Blood Dragon. But those closest to her know her as Yana."

"Yana?" Jack asked. "Russian?"

"Yes. She's former Russian Intelligence. Yana specialized in, what you'd say, *erasing* people. We have worked together over the years."

"Former?" Raegor asked.

"Yes," May replied. "Like me, she was…*let go*…by her superiors. Now, she's freelance, like Shenlong, though she prefers to work alone."

"Alone?" Raegor asked.

"Yes, and I've seen her in action." May eyed Jack. "Yana doesn't need a team."

Yikes, Jack thought. To him, it sounded like Yana was a badass, for sure.

"Give us a second," Raegor said. His side of the call muted.

He was no doubt arguing with Eddy over the prospects of hiring a former Russian assassin turned mercenary. But Jack had to give it to May. It was a good idea. Yana's involvement wouldn't be traced back to TAC, the organization wholly responsible for putting the people of Langtang in harm's way. *That* was Jack's biggest worry, not anything relating to international relations. It was TAC's fault, which meant it was Jack's fault.

"Okay, Ms. Wu, contact your friend. Tell her what's going on and get her moving ASAP. We'll give her whatever her going rate is. Jack will handle the rest. Raegor out."

Jack ended the call and handed his phone back to May. She did as Raegor asked and got to work contacting the Blood Dragon. He returned his attention to the landscapes of Nepal as they motored back down the Pasang Lhamu Highway. The mountains dictated travel around here, and they told humanity there wasn't a direct route to anywhere. Instead of making the short fifty-mile jaunt straight to Lamabagar, they were being forced to retrace their steps south to Kathmandu, then journey east before heading back to the north.

The 170-mile trip still didn't seem so bad to Jack until Kalsang and May gave him the elapsed timeframe for the whole trip.

"If we can keep stops to a minimum," Kalsang said, mentally calculating the drive, "we'll get there by dinner time."

The sun had only come up two hours ago. Kalsang needed to prepare the Monastery Hotel for his absence. His impending absence was coming at extremely short notice, and the Sherpa required a brief sit-down with his friend, Taral. The old-timer lived deeper into the valley and owned no phone. Hiking to his place at night would be a death sentence from what Kalsang had said. So, they waited until after first light to leave Padmaarga for Lamabagar.

Jack kept forgetting how the roads worked here. They wound back and forth and rose and fell with the earth. Speeds were slow everywhere in the Himalayas. Luckily, it meant they'd be slow for anyone following them.

Except they have a friggin' helicopter!

May finished her call. "Okay, Yana will contact us after payment is transferred."

"That's bold of her," Jack said. "Expect payment without work."

May laughed. "You haven't worked with her kind before, have you?"

Jack turned and faced her. "I've worked alongside people in her line of work several times before, but I've never been on the hiring side of things."

"Fair enough," May said, giving Jack the benefit of the doubt.

Jack accessed a special bank app on his phone and then handed the device back to May. "Here you go. Just don't bankrupt us, will ya?"

She accepted it and got to work. "Somehow, I doubt I could do that even if I tried."

Jack had no idea what his company was worth. It wasn't his job to keep track of it, either. Finances weren't exactly his strong suit. Jack was a man of action and someone who paid others to keep his money straight.

"It's done," May announced. "You are now—"

"Don't tell me," Jack said. "I really don't want to know how much."

"I would like to know."

Jack eyed Kalsang.

May shrugged and showed the Sherpa the screen. The large man gagged on his own air.

"That much?" Jack asked. Kalsang nodded. Jack bit his lip, thinking what it could be. "No," he said. "Don't care."

May handed him his phone, and he quickly closed the app, erasing the data from the device. Just another security protocol set into place by Eddy's IT guys.

Jack looked out his window, then realized something. He turned back to May. "Did I just order a hit on someone?"

Kathmandu passed by in a blur. They purposefully stopped just before entering the city limits to switch drivers. Jack was now near the end of his shift, with May up next and sitting beside him. Kalsang was snoring loudly in the backseat, catching up on the sleep he had lost last night. Jack was used to going a long time without sleep. A few hours a day was all he'd need to perform his duties, though he preferred to get more. It just wasn't all that common for him to stay in one spot long enough for that to happen.

He doubted he'd be able to nap in the cramped backseat of the Scorpio, but he'd sure as hell try. He'd dream about two nights ago—when he and May had snuggled atop the uncomfortably thin mattress inside her safehouse.

"What are you thinking about?"

The question caught him off guard. So, he told her.

"You and me after we took that swim in the river."

May's eyes opened wide. "Oh."

"Hey, you asked, and that's what was on my mind."

"Sure. That was nice, wasn't it?" She grinned. "Except for everything else that happened that day."

Jack laughed but cut it off when Kalsang's snore transformed into a snorting diesel engine. "Yeah, that day mostly sucked."

"At least this one hasn't been too bad."

Jack agreed. "True, but the day is young."

May turned and faced him. "How do you do it?"

Jack was confused. "Do what?"

"Stay so calm and in control all the time."

"I honestly don't think about it. I'm just me, and this," he motioned to his body, "is what you get."

May gazed past him. "I wish I had that kind of confidence. I could've rid the world of my father years ago."

"Don't say that," Jack implored. "You were young and doing what you were told. You were a soldier like I was."

"Was it hard, you know, being a soldier?"

Jack nodded. "Every day was a nightmare, but I learned a lot too."

"Like what?"

Jack thought about it for a second. "It was nice to have so many people have your back. It's been a little lonely for me since."

"What about your friends back home?"

Jack shrugged. "They're still there, but that doesn't do much for me out here," he looked at her, "does it?"

She nodded. "I know the feeling."

Jack glanced down at her hand. It was just sitting there resting on top of her thigh. May had returned her attention to the world outside. Jack removed his hand from the shifter knob and hovered it three inches over her hand. He lowered it just as an alarm in the backseat went off. Kalsang snapped awake, and Jack put his hand back on the shifter. May had seen none of it.

"My turn," the Sherpa said, yawning and leaning forward.

"Yeah," Jack said, signaling and pulling off, "okay, sure."

Lamabagar, Nepal

The bumpy road woke Jack. He had no idea how long he'd been out. In fact, he didn't remember falling asleep at all. By his estimation, he had napped for a couple of hours. It felt like it too. He was groggy, and his head hurt. Jack's time clock had reset, and he'd need caffeine. But he'd most likely have to wait to get it.

Charikot-Lamabagar Road had forked up ahead. The paved portion kept going straight and true. Kalsang had slowed and went left toward the dirt, unpaved portion. It's what had jostled Jack awake. He tried to sit up, but his lower back balked. Jack was flat on his back with his legs tucked against the bench seat's backrest.

Seatbelts be damned.

"Here."

Jack peered through heavy eyelids to see May holding out both hands. One held a bottle of water. The other contained four pills. Jack didn't ask what they were, assuming they were ibuprofen or something similar. He didn't think May would drug him with something nasty.

Jack nodded his thanks and drained the entire bottle. He hadn't realized how thirsty he was. His lack of sweating was confusing his body. He was exhausted, but not in the same parched, lack of hydration kind of way. Come to think of it, the only consistent beverage he'd drunk since landing in Nepal was coffee. Now, add the pills to his empty stomach, and…

That can't be healthy.

"So," Jack said, "that's our next monastery, huh?"

"Yes," Kalsang replied, "the Emerald Lotus."

"But it's not green?"

The monastery was a small, plain white tiered structure with silver and gold accents. There was literally zero emerald coloration anywhere. Unlike the Langtang Monastery, which natural causes had torn down, the Emerald Lotus Monastery still stood, and only by sheer will and bird shit, by the looks of it. It was in seriously rough shape. Jack spotted a bit of concrete lying off to the side. The building was crumbling to the ground right in front of them.

"Yikes," Jack said under his breath. He leaned between May and Kalsang.

May glanced at him. "My thoughts exactly."

"Wait until you see the inside," Kalsang said. Without further explanation, he pulled them into the large dirt expanse that acted as a parking lot.

Buddhist monks meandered about, conversing with one another quietly. They paid the trio of newcomers no attention. Their nonreaction told Jack that they saw people like them regularly. Tourism was a big industry in these parts, so it made sense.

Jack winced against the setting sun. He had followed the terrain west, up the vertical cliff, and got blinded by the remaining sun. Soon it would slip over the precipice and disappear until morning.

"The language here is Tibetan, just so you know," Kalsang said, "though some speak Nepali." He looked at Jack. "A little English too."

"How little?" Jack asked.

Kalsang didn't reply.

Jack waved at the nearest monk. "How y'all doin'?"

He didn't answer.

Not much, apparently.

21

Emerald Lotus Monastery
Lamabagar, Nepal

The Emerald Lotus Monastery was in major need of a facelift. But Jack had to hand it to the monks living here. They were doing well with what they had been given. Kalsang said this place was a popular tourist destination but by accident. Evidently, there were other, more remarkable places to see in the surrounding area, but the Emerald Lotus was the first one you saw when reaching town.

Jack looked north and spotted a marvel of modern engineering. Where the Tamakoshi River narrowed, the Upper Tamakoshi Hydroelectric Plant spanned its breadth. It's what supplied power to everything here. Jack also had to hand it to them. They, too, were making something out of nothing.

Kalsang greeted two men in Tibetan before opening the door and stepping aside for Jack and May to enter first. The roof hung low, and the single room smelled of incense. The air was thick with it.

"Can we open a window?" Jack muttered, feeling his nose tingle.

He swung his head right and spied a large emerald-colored lotus encased along the back of the room.

Oh, well, there you have it.

The emerald lotus was an artifact within the monastery, not a name describing the monastery itself.

"Beautiful," May said.

They followed Kalsang over to the display case and edged up to the single rope used to keep intruders away. Jack was honestly shocked that it was all they used unless...

"It's a fake," he said.

"How do you know?" May asked.

Jack motioned to the monastery and then flicked the rope. "Would you willingly plop a gemstone the size of your head in a place like this?" He kept his voice down for fear of upsetting the monks. They didn't deserve any ridicule.

"I think he's right," Kalsang said. "Initially, the lack of security had been disturbing. Now, it made sense. Why go to all the trouble of guarding something with no monetary value?"

"So, is this place our second marker?" May asked.

"It still could be," Jack said. "I doubt any of this makes a difference." He looked around and spotted a hole in the floor. A monk appeared from within it holding a basket of random, touristy stuff. "We need to have a closer look."

They split up and combed the interior, taking in everything. Nothing stood out to Jack. He prayed this place hadn't been renovated in the past. Their lock may have been erased in the process decades ago. The only other place left to look was inside the hole the monk had climbed out of.

"Come on," Jack said, casually making his way over. In reality, he was making a bigger show of not being up to something.

"What are you doing?" May whispered.

"Um, sneaking?"

May shook her head. "Well, you're terrible at it."

Five feet from the entry point, Jack spotted narrow, wooden steps. Then, a head, Jack startled the poor guy half to death. He shouted his surprise in Tibetan and dropped the basket back down into the hole.

Jack cringed. "Sorry."

More Tibetan was slung his way, and from the look on Kalsang's face, the monk had a potty mouth. The local reemerged. Jack gave him plenty of room to climb out, even offering him his help. The monk refused the aid and huffed his displeasure, standing tall in front of Jack as if he were a competitor. But he wasn't. Jack was six to seven inches taller than the monk and had at least fifty pounds on him.

Kalsang said something to him and bowed slightly. Jack took it as an apology, then got down to business.

"What's down there?" he asked.

"None of your business," Kalsang quickly interpreted.

Jack was again taken aback by the monk's brashness. This guy walked his own path, for sure.

"Can we see?"

The monk shook his head and said something.

"He says, 'no,'" Kalsang translated.

Jack rolled his eyes. "Thanks, I kinda got that."

He glanced at the Sherpa. "We need to see what's down there."

Kalsang shrugged. He didn't know what to do.

Jack grinned. He did because there was a language that everyone spoke.

"Tell him I'll donate one thousand U.S. dollars to the monastery if we can go down there."

The monk held out his hand. "Make it two thousand, and you have deal."

"You speak English?" Jack asked, confused.

"When it counts."

Jack couldn't help but be impressed by the size of this guy's balls.

May pulled Jack away. "Are you bribing a Buddhist monk?"

"What choice do we have?"

She didn't like it, and neither did Jack, but they were desperate. Jack rejoined the monk and Sherpa and shook the offered hand.

"I hope you have Venmo."

The monk smiled wide. "Of course."

Jack transferred the man his money and started his descent. "Don't steal anything!" Jack paused and looked up at the monk. He was still on his phone, tapping away and swiping, doing God-knows-what.

Jack didn't reply, ducking beneath the floorboards of the main level. The wooden steps creaked beneath his weight but held. A single overhead bulb lit the basement. It was too dark to see much of anything, but Jack noticed that the lower level was larger than the one above his head.

That's a start.

He reached into his pocket and removed his flashlight. The high-powered beam instantly landed on the far wall. Jack looked up and reoriented himself. He was facing north. Shelves lined the wall, filled with supplies and cheap trinkets to sell to visitors.

Jack inspected the physical wall the best he could and didn't see anything of note. May joined him, sweeping her own light east. If she saw something, she didn't voice it. Jack assumed she didn't and kept looking. At first glance, there was nothing here. Jack closed his eyes, deep in thought.

What did we miss? he asked himself.

A light bloomed in his face, interrupting his thoughts. "Can I help you?" He opened his eyes and blocked May's light with his free hand. But she wasn't looking at him.

She was looking past him.

Jack turned around and gazed at the western wall just as Kalsang cautiously descended the steps. He paused at the base and was about to speak but stopped himself. Jack and May stood as still as statues, staring at a wall filled with random supplies.

"Find something?" Kalsang asked, breaking the silence.

Jack rushed forward. "I think we did."

He pocketed his flashlight and went about clearing the shelf. May kept her light on, focusing it on where Jack was working. Three baskets later, Jack stepped back, smiling wide. There, carved into the wall, was a circular depression depicting their tree.

"We found it."

Jack and May emptied the remaining baskets off the three remaining shelves while Kalsang gave them light. Jack was about to drag the storage unit away but was stopped by May.

"Hang on," she said, grabbing his arm. "What about him?" She pointed straight up.

Jack understood what she meant. She was talking about the monk with the mile-long hustle. If they were discovered messing around with his property, then he'd have every right to kick them out.

He turned to Kalsang. "Can you keep an eye on our friend upstairs?"

The Sherpa nodded and began his climb but stopped. "What do I do if he insists on coming down here?"

Jack patted him on the shoulder. "No clue, but I'm sure you'll think of something."

Kalsang didn't look so confident. Nevertheless, he climbed back up to the main level and disappeared from view.

Jack faced May. "Ready?"

"As ready as I'll ever be."

They each gripped an end and pulled. The metal feet cried in agony against the stone floor, making them pause.

"Up," Jack whispered.

He and May lifted it high enough in the air and carried it the rest of the way. They set the shelving in the middle of the room and showed both of their lights on the wall for a second time. The lock was still in decent enough shape, but the rest of the wall had been worn away over the years. Jack could just make out a few other petroglyphs but couldn't tell what they used to be.

He removed the key from his coat pocket. "Here goes nothing."

Jack slotted it into place and pushed. The wall exhaled dust all over the place, covering Jack and May in the stuff. The duo wheezed against it but refrained from making too much noise. Through the cloud of grime, Jack saw that a seven-foot squared section of wall had sunk inward.

Jack stepped over to the obstacle and pressed on it with his palms. He got nothing.

"Give me a hand, will ya?"

May joined him, and they each planted their shoulders into the wall.

Jack counted. "One, two, three!"

They drove their weight into the wall. It didn't budge.

Then, it did.

"Keep…going," Jack said between grunts.

May growled too, and thankfully, the barrier kept sliding back. Once it was two feet from where it had been, Jack saw space around the edges. They weren't through yet, but at least they'd made enough progress to see that their hard work wasn't for nothing. Jack wanted to stop and rest but dug in and kept going. May did too. Her growls transformed into feral snarls. Jack just got quieter. If he'd been as animated as his partner, his vocalizations would've come out as whimpers, not primal snarls.

Finally, a gap large enough to fit Jack appeared, and he stopped and collapsed. Jack fell against the wall and slid down onto his butt, panting hard. May landed next to him. Both were filthy, caked in what must've been years of dust. They were soaked in sweat too. The stuffy air and warmer internal temperatures made Jack's coat feel a bit much.

He laughed and closed his eyes. When he opened them, he turned just his head toward May and was stunned when she leaned in and planted her dirty lips on his. Jack froze. He felt like a middle school boy all over again. He had wanted to do this exact thing several times before but couldn't. Too many things had gotten in the way, including a sheep. He pressed into May and thought about wrapping his arms around her and bringing her in even closer.

A voice from just outside the basement entrance forced them to part. May leaned around him to check on what was happening. Jack, on the other hand, didn't move an inch. He was still sitting against the western wall, lost in what had happened. His eyes were on the east wall, but they saw nothing. All he could do was replay the last ten seconds of life over and over in his head.

"You okay?"

Jack blinked out of his lover boy stupor and focused on the voice's owner.

"Um… Yeah, I think so. A little hungry. Could use a beer. You?"

May smiled. "I could also use a beer."

She stood and reached a hand down to Jack. He gladly took it and gritted his teeth as he stood. He was about to say something about what had just happened, but May was already back into business mode. She clicked her light back on and slipped through the opening they had created.

Jack sighed, looked around the basement, and tossed his hands up in a combination of frustration and confusion. He also ignited his flashlight and squeezed through the narrow opening, humming the chorus to Bob Seger's "You'll Accomp'ny Me" as he did.

22

Jack and May continued west, deeper into the mountain. The air was still and reeked of mildew. The tunnel entrance was tall enough for Jack to walk upright and wide enough for him and May to comfortably walk side by side. The skill to build such a place rivaled the more known worlds, like Egypt and Mesoamerica. All of it, even the prospect of being crushed by a mountain, had taken a backseat in Jack's mind.

And what mattered was the next leg of the adventure.

But he was also still thinking of the kiss. It had become precisely what he had feared, a distraction. He both rejoiced in it and wanted nothing more than to cast it aside—the distracting part of it, not the kiss itself. The spontaneity and passion filled Jack with joy, but also confusion.

Get your head in the game, Reilly!

It's what his coach used to say when he had been in high school. Like many athletically gifted kids, he had dabbled in several sports, but Jack didn't necessarily excel in any of them. He was good at a lot of things but not great at one thing. His versatility paid off in the end, though, and he always seemed to be on the field or court. But the memory had popped up for a good reason. He *did* need to get his head back in the game. It was a cliché thing to think, but it was true.

"So," he started, "that was some kiss."

Instantly, Jack had catapulted himself further out of *the game.*

"Yes, it was," May agreed.

"You do that often in the spy world?" Jack didn't know why he was asking the question. He just needed to know if there was a motive behind it.

She narrowed her eyes at him with an obvious, "No."

"Then—"

May stopped but didn't look at him. "Are we talking about this—now?"

"Well, I—"

"Jack." She faced him, cutting him off. "Look, I like you, okay? But if we don't finish what we started, then it might not matter. We could both die before we can see where *we* end up."

We?

With that, May turned and marched off. Jack, on the other hand, could only stand still and reflect as any boy did when finding out the hot girl in class liked him. He did a mental fist pump and happy dance.

"Jack?"

He pulled himself out of the cerebral celebration. "Yeah?"

"You need to see this."

He hurried to catch up with May. The tone in her voice said she had found something amazing. Jack skidded to a halt six feet past the tunnel exit. The space beyond was a yawning void. A slow drip of water somewhere in the darkness validated the sheer size of the cavern. It softly echoed around them.

Jack could just pick out the left-hand wall and followed it up to a domed ceiling. He voiced his hypothesis as he uncovered new details.

"Natural cave," he said. "Builders probably removed stalagmites and stalactites to give the place a more polished look."

"But how?" May asked. "There's no way a man, or even dozens of them, could pull this off."

Jack shrugged. "Don't let it bother you. A good chunk of the crap I see makes zero sense. I just appreciate it and go along with it."

"But don't you care to find out?"

Jack faced May. "Of course, I do, but I rarely have time to dawdle."

She glanced back at the tunnel. "Oh, right."

"Hey." She met his eyes. Jack reached out and took her hand. "Would you do me the honor…" his voice was serious, "of exploring this creepy cave with me?"

May smiled and rolled her eyes.

They released their hands, holding them for a second longer than needed.

"The shape of this place reminds me of a *stupa*," May said.

"A stupa?" Jack knew the word. "A Buddhist burial complex?"

May nodded. "Yes. Traditionally, they contain important relics, and also the remains of men and women of faith—monks and nuns."

Jack stopped. "What about giant stone lions?"

May turned toward him only to find Jack looking up, not at her. She followed his light, adding hers to it. Near the rear of the domed room, there were not one but two mammoth stone lions.

May stepped away from Jack, examining the fifty-foot-tall beasts. "They're guardian lions."

Jack knew about the Chinese variations of the lions. They were common in the artwork of the region. They were huge and muscular with long curled manes and generously proportioned teeth.

"Though, these are different," she added.

"How so?" Jack asked, out of his element.

They started off again. "Lions, such as these, are customarily seen standing guard outside a family's home," her light dropped between them, "not keeping watch over a house of worship."

"Wow," Jack said.

They were halfway to the lions when Jack passed the first stone bench. It reminded him of the prayer temple he had discovered in Poland while searching for Hitler's gold train. Like everything else here, including the lions, the benches had been chiseled out of the stone.

"Plus," May added, "look at their coats. They're all wrong. These aren't the guardians I'm used to seeing back in China."

"Aren't lions symbolized in different ways all over Asia?" Jack asked, piecing together what he knew about them.

"Yes, that's true, though I'm not overly familiar with the Nepali or Tibetan variants." She sighed and looked over her shoulder. "We need Kalsang."

"I got this," Jack said, producing his phone. He snapped a dozen pictures and even took a circling video of everything his light touched. Then, he tucked the device back into his pocket.

They picked up their pace as the floor sloped forward. They drew nearer to their destination and the dripping sound increased. Jack lifted his light from the floor to the cave's back wall, but he didn't find it. The expanse continued far beyond the looming guardians.

"What the hell?"

They left the rows of benches behind and entered the lions' realm. Between it was a raised, stepped platform. Again, it was like the one in Poland. The slanted floor gave the seats in the rear a higher elevation and a better line of sight. Modern sporting stadiums and concert halls were set up in the same manner.

But it wasn't the benches or platform or even the fifty-foot-tall lions that currently held Jack's attention. It was the lake of ultra-clear water that stretched into the blackness beyond his and May's lights.

Jack could barely see a smudge of land in the middle. To the right was the slow leak from the ceiling overhead. Jack figured that it must be from mountain runoff, making it some of the cleanest water on earth. He edged around the platform rather than scaling it. Jack swiped his hand across the left-hand lion's pedestal, marveling at its engineering and detail. Jack could make out every imperfection of the big cat's mane and coat. Its bushy tail too. The tail made Jack think of a cheerleader's pom-pom, but with fur and not synthetic fibers.

Hmmm, definitely 'not' a traditional design. These were something else.

Kalsang would know what they were.

May headed around to the right. Jack spotted her talking to herself. He knew she was trying to work it out in her head. Sometimes, vocalizing your thoughts was easier than keeping it all inside.

"Incredible, isn't it?" he asked.

May met him at the rear of the platform. "It really is. But…"

"But what?"

"I don't see anywhere to insert the key."

Damn!

Jack had been so enthralled with their discovery that he hadn't even begun to look for a keyhole. They did their due diligence and searched the platform and the surrounding area, including the lions, but found nothing.

They returned to the water's edge and sat on the lowermost steps of the platform. Jack hung his head and felt a hand gently massage his back. May was attempting to relax his peaking anxiety. Everything they had uncovered was amazing, but it wasn't enough. They needed to find the Valley of Petals before Shenlong did. They needed to confirm its existence and then defend it against the incoming threat because it wouldn't stop. Ever.

So, Jack wouldn't either.

He stood and, once more, looked out over the tranquil waters, finding the small island of stone.

He pointed at it. "What about that?"

May looked up from the floor and followed his outstretched hand. She leaped to her feet and joined Jack.

"That would be elaborate of them."

He snorted, laughed, turned, and presented the five-story tall lion to his left.

May shrugged. "I guess it can't hurt to check. But how?"

Jack looked down at his body and sighed. "Dang."

"No," May said, "I'll go." He opened his mouth to argue. "Please, let me do this."

Jack didn't like being sidelined, but he also really, *really* didn't want to get wet again.

"Okay, you go, but here," he handed her his phone, "you're gonna need this."

She didn't accept it right away. First, she stripped.

The awkward moments Jack had felt earlier were nothing compared to what he was experiencing now. Their dusty kiss had unlocked long-dormant feelings. May removed her coat, then her shirt. Her pants, socks, and shoes were next. He couldn't get himself to blink or look away. May noticed but didn't seem to care. If anything, Jack's boyish response amused her.

She stepped toward the water with nothing but her underwear on and Jack's waterproof phone, and the key stuffed deeply into her sports bra. Her movement away spurred Jack into motion, and he reached out and grabbed her shoulder. Her skin was already cold to the touch. He knew the water would be freezing, even lower than the temperature of the Bagmati River back in Kathmandu. May peered over her shoulder and met his gaze.

"Be careful," he said, unable to hide his worry.

She winked. "It'll be a piece of cake."

Then, she dove in.

23

This was nothing like cake. Cake was sweet and comforting. The icy Himalayan water was not sweet and comforting. The sting May's skin experienced was relentless, forcibly purging the air from her lungs. She gasped but kept moving. She couldn't slow. If she did, it would only make it harder to speed back up. Plus, she didn't want Jack to worry more than he already was.

Seeing a man like him proudly display emotion was a Godsend. She didn't have that growing up, or with anyone else in her adult life, for that matter. Jack was always himself, and May liked that about him. It's why she didn't react negatively to him ogling her body. Jack's feelings and intentions were sincere, and he wasn't a threat to her in any way, even in her most vulnerable state.

Like, mostly naked and alone in an underground temple with an armed man.

The cold snapped her back onto her task. She kicked and pulled at the water like an Olympian. She focused on her strokes, counting them, desperately trying to keep her mind off the piercing temperature.

She made it halfway there before losing her ability to take a deep breath. Still, May pushed on. Her body was in peak condition, and she knew she'd make it there with something left. The trip back was going to be brutal. Luckily, she wasn't alone. She didn't want Jack to have to come to her rescue but was satisfied knowing that he would at any sign of a struggle.

The last leg of the swim went by in a numbing blur. She reached the stone island and grasped it with unresponsive fingers. They moved fine. She just couldn't feel anything beneath them. May kicked a leg up and rolled atop the landmass. She didn't stay down. She dug deep, got to her feet, and broke into a series of jumping jacks. May needed to warm up her body any way she could.

She couldn't see what Jack was doing, but he was undoubtedly watching her like she was a crazy woman. He wouldn't be far off, either. But it worked. May's internal temperature rose steadily, as did that of her skin. She could even feel the worn stone beneath her feet.

She slowed, then stopped, puffing hard. Her hands found her knees, and she took a few seconds to catch her breath.

"You good?" Jack shouted, his voice resonating around her.

May didn't verbally reply. She waved him off and got to work, breathing on her fingers as she did. They had yet to return to full function, though she hardly noticed. A circular cutout featuring their tree had been carved into the center of the ten-by-ten stone island.

"I have something!" she shouted.

"What is it?"

"I'm not sure! Give me a second!"

May struggled to remove the key from her sodden sports bra. She nearly dropped the wrapped artifact, bobbing and catching it before it could go overboard. It was still wrapped up in the burned towel from the elder Thapa's hospital room. The memory of watching the man die rushed back. May swallowed hard and squeezed the key tight. She knelt, setting the irreplaceable relic on the ground. Then, she dug Jack's phone out and set it down on her other side.

With great care, May unwrapped the key. Her fingers still weren't all the way back, forcing her to concentrate heavily on what they were doing. The gold was cold, that much she could feel. Holding it by its edges, May lowered the key into place, hearing a satisfying click as it unlocked something.

She pushed.

But nothing happened.

"Hmmm."

She removed the key and placed it above the lock, taking a closer look. Like the other two locks, this one was supposed to do something once it was in place and depressed. Unsurprisingly, something had malfunctioned after what must've been hundreds of years of existence.

May leaned in closer and dug her fingertips into the narrow crevasse between but could barely get a grip. Plus, she still couldn't feel her hands. She brought them up to her mouth, breathed on them several times, and tried again. This time, she slipped her fingertips into the gap and pulled. She cringed when she felt her nails being pried up and away from her nail beds. But it worked. The lock opened slightly.

She removed her hands and breathed on them again.

"Anything yet?" Jack asked, his voice echoing.

"Almost got it!" she shouted back.

With more room to work, May reached into the lock, getting her fingertips into the first knuckle, and pulled. With one final grunt, it slid open to reveal an image she had never seen before. May knew a decent amount about the Buddhist culture, but not everything. This engraving fell into the latter category.

But that's not why she was here. May was only supposed to gain access to the marker. She picked up Jack's phone and snapped four pictures of it, changing distance and angle with every tap of the screen. Satisfied that she had completed her task, she re-wrapped the key and jammed it and the phone back into her bra. The fit was even more uncomfortable than before.

She stood, turned, and waved to shore. "Got it!"

"Awesome!" Jack replied, fist-pumping the air.

This was the part May was dreading. The swim back to Jack was going to be extraordinarily difficult. She had only now regained the feeling in her fingertips. The rest of her was fine—cold—but fine.

"I…I'm coming back to you!"

"You sure you're okay to do that?" Jack asked. Worry laced in his voice.

May eyed the perfectly flat water and mumbled, "I don't really have a choice, do I?"

She took a deep breath and dove.

May was a strong swimmer. She looked very comfortable in the water. But this wasn't your average swim. Jack knew how quickly cold water could sap your strength. Even without his and May's unexpected dip in the Bagmati River, Jack had some experiences dating back to his first years with Delta.

He knew May could make the swim, but she was tired and beat up, like him.

He understood what a weakened body and mind could do to your ability to function at a high level. Even now, Jack saw May's pace was slower than before.

"Dammit," he said, slipping out of his coat. He tossed it aside, never once looking away from May. If she went under, he needed to know exactly where.

Her speed was steady but not all that rapid. To May's credit, she didn't stop.

Jack's shirt was next to hit the floor, as were his socks and shoes.

The air within the cave was chilling. Uncomfortable, at worst.

He edged forward when she slowed and dipped under the surface. All the pressure was on the balls of his feet. May popped back up and immediately shook the water free from her hair. Somehow, her pace increased following the quick submersion. The woman's resilience was inspiring. Jack wondered if the dive had somehow refocused her, like when he would splash cold water on his own face.

Whatever works, I guess.

May was twenty feet from him when she went under again. Jack's legs flexed, ready to go in. He launched up and forward but stopped himself with waving arms as May's head broke the surface. He teetered over the edge, then got down on a knee and reached out for his partner.

May's hand found his, and he dragged her out of the water. They fell back onto the platform's rear steps. May curled into Jack's chest, dousing him in the freezing lake water. He didn't care. Jack's survival training kicked in, and he blocked it out. He knew his own body temperature would help slowly bring May's back to normal, but he needed more help.

He reached for his and May's clothes, specifically their wool jackets. Jack laid his on her first, uncaring if it absorbed the icy water. Her welfare was above all else. Then, he added her jacket to his, and leaned back against the steps. There, he held May tight and waited for her body's convulsions to reduce in frequency.

"You okay?" he asked, tipping his chin down to see her.

May lifted her head but kept it against Jack's chest. "P-piece of c-cake."

Their eyes locked, and this time, Jack initiated the kiss. He leaned in and locked his lips with hers. They were cold to the touch. She relaxed, and so did Jack.

May twitched, pulling them out of the moment.

Jack also shivered.

"Goosebumps," May said, lightly running her hand over his right arm.

"I'm cold," Jack said.

May smiled. "Sure. We'll go with that."

"I am!" Jack chirped, laughing.

"Says the guy that stayed on shore."

Jack gazed up at the lions and shrugged. "True." His eyes returned to May. "You know I was seconds away from coming in after you."

Her hand slid off his arm and found his bare chest. She affectionately caressed it with her fingertips. "I can see that." Jack guided his hand up her arm, finding the same hand on his chest. He gently squeezed it. May leaned into him. "Thank you."

"No problem."

"No, Jack," May said, pulling her face away from him and looking him deep in the eyes. "Thank you."

The corner of his mouth rose. She was offering more than just politeness in her thank you. His presence was what she was thanking him for. May had been lost for a very long time. Jack could say the same thing about himself. He knew what was going through her head.

He simply said, "You're welcome."

They sat there until May's internal temperature righted itself. When it did, Jack eased May to her feet and helped her get back into her dry clothes, which helped her immensely. Once she was fully clothed and moving around on her own, Jack dressed. He relaxed when he was back inside his wool-lined coat.

"So, what did you find?"

May handed him back his phone. Jack selected the photos app and cycled through them, spotting the one from Padmaarga. He and May posed beneath the lines of prayer flags. Jack liked that one. May saw him stop and leaned in to see what he was staring at.

"That's a good one," she said.

"It is."

Jack swiped up to the end of the folder and found four nearly identical pictures. He picked out the one with the best resolution and looked it over, unsure what he was looking at. Three orbs aligned in a pyramidal shape were all that the Emerald Lotus lock had revealed. It was too cryptic for Jack to decipher.

"We need Kalsang."

"Yeah," May agreed, "come on."

She and Jack navigated around the platform and left it and the two remarkable stone lions behind. The benches were next, and then the expanse of nothing between them and their entrance. May stepped through, but Jack stopped and gave the cave one last look before following her. He wanted to stay and have a better look at things but knew he couldn't.

The tunnel ended back at the musty basement storage room. Jack sighed at the uninspiring sight but was still shocked by what lay beyond.

"How the hell do we close this thing?" Jack asked, inspecting the doorway for anything useful. He raised his arms, and then they flopped down to his sides. "First Langtang, and now this. This is becoming the easiest game of 'follow the leader' ever."

May shook her head. She didn't have an answer for him.

"Help me with this," Jack said, gripping onto the shelving unit.

The pair dragged it back into place and replaced the baskets, covering the temple entry the best they could. It was bound to be found sooner or later and by Shenlong, no doubt.

Unless May's friend is successful.

Jack hoped the Yana could, at the very least, delay the man's arrival here. At best, she'd kill him.

Jack was fine with that too.

They climbed back up to the first level and were immediately assailed by the monk. Verbally, not physically. Something had sent the guy off and Jack had a feeling that they were being held responsible. Kalsang was nowhere to be found.

Had he been arrested? No, Jack didn't think so. He doubted the Sherpa would ever do anything to get himself locked up.

"Your friend is a monster!" the monk shouted.

Oh, Jack thought, *maybe he did do something terrible.*

"What's the problem?" May asked.

"The problem?" The monk was irate. "He tell everyone the lotus is fake!"

Jack shrugged, beginning to see what Kalsang may have done. He had created a diversion to give him and May more time below. A man of Kalsang's upbringing would've been incredibly off-put by the monk's operation here.

"Well, it is!" Jack said, raising his voice. "It's a big phony!" The monk flinched as if Jack had gut-punched him. Patrons stopped what they were doing and took in the confrontation. "I'm enraged that a man who represents Buddha would lie like this." Jack faced the dozen or so onlookers. "And for what— profit? Sorry, everyone, but you've been duped!"

The monk shrank away from his understandably upset clientele. Kalsang had sniffed the bogus emerald lotus out as soon as he stepped foot inside the monastery.

Jack leaned in close to the monk. "When you recover from his speed bump, and I'm sure you will, how about you start putting some of the money you swindle out of people back into this place instead of your pockets."

May stepped up next to Jack. They didn't come here to intimidate a Tibetan monk, but here they were. It comforted Jack to know that this guy was far outside what people of his faith should've been doing. Maybe this little hiccup would serve as a reminder of who he serves.

They left the astray holy man to fend for himself and swiftly exited the monastery. Jack didn't care that he had paid the man two thousand dollars. It was well worth it, considering what they had found downstairs. Jack was also filled with slight regret. The monk would surely use it as a way to make even more money.

He and May found Kalsang leaning against their rental with his arms crossed. He pushed away from it and met the two halfway. Between Jack and May's physical state and the fresh hullabaloo emanating from back inside the monastery, the Sherpa's eyes were filled with concern.

"What happened to you two?" he asked.

A gust hit them, causing May to shiver noticeably.

"Car first," Jack said. He stuck his hand out. "Keys."

Kalsang didn't look so sure. He pointed at their clothing. "But you—"

"I'm fine," Jack said, waving him off. "Plus, you have a lot of research to do in the backseat."

His eyes opened wider, and he nodded, handing Jack the keys. In exchange, Jack gave the man his phone and guided May over to the front passenger side door. He opened it and helped her in. Jack shut it and hurried around to the driver's side. Kalsang was already inside by the time Jack made his way in.

The Sherpa's next word uttered was, "Wow."

Jack started the engine and cranked up the heat. "Yes, much wow."

24

Langtang, Nepal

She watched them from afar. Sheep, all of them. Her power was undeniable. In the blink of an eye, she could remove one of the villager's existences from the face of the earth. *That* was true power. She wasn't here for the locals, however. Yana Fedorov was here for someone infinitely more dangerous.

Like herself, Shenlong had made a name for himself over the last decade. Yana worked alone, operating with practiced stealth and patience. Shenlong walked an entirely different path. He preferred to use brute force and large, imposing numbers. Yana's tactics let her live a normal life in Norway. No one there knew who she really was. Her blonde hair and tall, lean, muscular figure allowed her to blend in perfectly, as did her honed use of the Norwegian language and perfected accent. She also spoke a bit of Chinese.

The former Russian Intelligence Officer even had friends back home in Bjerke. If she were able to complete her contract here and purge the world of a man like Shenlong, Yana would be able to go home and brag to...no one. She regretted living a lie at times. But her cover of living out her life as an early Bitcoin investor was easy enough to believe. No one questioned the retired thirty-something's jet-setting lifestyle.

Except, Yana wasn't retired, even if she was well-off financially. She didn't have to accept contracts any longer. She didn't need the money. The Blood Dragon just enjoyed the thrill of the hunt too much to give up, though she was much pickier about the jobs she accepted nowadays.

Taking out a target like the infamous Shenlong was too much for her to refuse.

"Where are you?" she said, staring through her rifle's scope.

The white and gray weapon matched Yana's clothing. She was currently perched on an outcrop of rock three hundred feet behind the excavation site and two hundred feet above it. The distance wouldn't be a factor for someone of her capabilities. No, Yana's real challenge was going to be the weather. A low fog hung over the valley, and the wind was steadily blowing and swirling. Precision was even more important in conditions like these.

I've seen worse.

And she had. Countless missions in hellholes such as Siberia and Greenland had sharpened her skills even more. Once, in Norilsk, Russia, Yana had been tasked with eliminating a traitorous target while he did a cash drop outside the Valok Airport. The weather had been very similar to what she was dealing with now. The man receiving the payment had also been dealt with.

She swung the rifle up and to the right, away from the dig site's tent and its handful of occupants. She did so using the weapon's bipod as designed. The village outskirts came into view. A couple tended to their boisterous dog, a Nepali sheepdog. It had barked at Yana earlier, much to the shock of the assassin. The animal's ears and nose must've been exceptionally keen to have detected her. Its owners had been completely unaware, reacting as they did now.

This time, however, *was* different. Yana zoomed out just enough to catch the locals and the dog but also a line of men marching up to the village boundaries. Although no weapons were visible, the newcomers screamed military, or in this case, mercenary. If she took the shot now, Yana was sure she could hit one of them. Still, she waited.

She zoomed in on each of the men as they neared but couldn't see their faces. She had no idea which one was Shenlong.

"Dammit!"

So, Yana waited and kept watch on both the line of men heading her way and the locals. Part of her mission was to keep the residents of Langtang alive at all costs. Her own life, however, would not be one of those costs. The man that hired her—May's friend—was different from anyone Yana had ever worked for. It was the first time she had been paid to preserve lives. Nowhere in May's texts had it said to kill anyone, though it had been implied.

Yana had been paid. She could do as she pleased, but she had pride. She would do the job as intended and play overwatch for the people of Langtang because that's what the contract demanded. Yes, the Blood Dragon was a killer, but she also believed in honor.

At over one thousand yards, Yana lined up her initial shot. The first to die would be the man left behind to keep track of the villagers. Then, she'd track the lead mercenary and move down the row from there. Eventually, her position would be discovered. Yana planned to be long gone by then. But there was always the scenario of these guys not having any way to engage the enemy at a distance. If that were the case, Yana could dig in and take her time.

She counted ten men.

Yana had brought plenty of American-made .308 AP rounds with her. AP, of course, stood for *armor piercing*, but they were also known as *black tips*. They had been her go-to caliber since she had been forcibly retired from active duty. The second man she had killed back in Norilsk, the one receiving the briefcase full of money, he'd been a monster to young women inside Russia's Federal Security Service (FSB). Yana had heard horror stories about him and decided, in the moment, to do humanity a favor. Alas, the act had cost Yana her career and nearly her life.

But it had been worth it.

The fifteen-ounce, ten-inch-long Advanced Armament Mk13-SD suppressor and the rifle, a Remington Semi-Automatic Sniper System (RSASS) made the weapon feel like a vaulter's pole. However, her dedication to the craft had made the perceived clumsiness fade long ago. It had become a part of her.

Now, the primary chunk of Shenlong's men was in a type of no man's land. There was no cover between the village wall and the dig site's tent.

And the wind had died down.

She shifted her aim back to the merc left behind, lined his chest up, and quickly pulled the trigger. The shot was heard as a slight cough by anyone within earshot. Yana knew they'd hear it, but Langtang's surrounding mountains would undoubtedly confuse all parties. She didn't wait for the puff of red to confirm that the target was down. Yana knew he was. She turned her attention to the lead man and gunned him down as soon as her scope's crosshairs floated over his sternum.

Black tips could tear straight through most body armor. The AP round didn't slow when there was nothing to combat its velocity other than human flesh, bone, and organ. The black tip entered the base of the man's neck, directly below his Adam's apple, and continued straight through his spine, killing him on his feet.

The line of mercenaries panicked. Guns swung up from beneath winter coats. Yana smiled ear to ear when she spotted only stubby submachine guns. While great in close-quarters battle (CQB), the ultracompact firearm was a major liability in the open such as in environments similar to Langtang Valley. It's why Yana preferred to use the in-between design of a Designated Marksman Rifle (DMR). The weapon wasn't as cumbersome as a traditional sniper rifle and possessed much better range than an infantry rifle, such as an M4.

This was Yana's perfect storm. She breathed easy and snapped off another shot. This AP round nearly took a man's arm off at the shoulder. Yana moved on. There was no reason to verify the man's demise. She knew he'd bleed out in no time.

"Three," she said, calling out the kills. When she reached ten, she'd stop.

The third man fired wildly into the mountain, missing Yana by over a hundred feet. For good measure, she took aim at the new rearmost man, watching him turn and flee to the village perimeter. Before jumping the nearby wall, Yana splattered his brains all over it. Some of the gore made it into the sheepdog's yard.

"Four."

Yana opted to box them in. She'd flip back and forth and take out the man at either end of the line until no one was left. Next up was the frontmost gunman. This one was thin and fast. Yana had to hurry to catch up to him, but her distance and elevated position helped her compensate for his foot speed. She was only forced to move her RSASS' twenty-inch-long barrel down and to the left a few inches. Yana led him and then put him down.

"Five."

She lined up her next shot and squeezed the trigger. Nothing happened. Her DMR malfunctioned. The trained professional quickly ejected the magazine and yanked back on the charging handle, clearing the jammed round from the upper receiver. She reached underneath her chest and snagged a fully loaded magazine from her chest rig. There were still two more twenty-round mags waiting for her there. She had sixty more rounds of black tips and only five targets remaining.

She allowed a grin to form on her face. The Blood Dragon understood how good she was.

Yana's self-assurance nearly got her head taken off. A stray bullet pinged off the stone next to her head. The deflection caused her to flinch and kick a puff of snow down the mountainside. More rounds immediately ricocheted around her, forcing her to roll away and onto her back. Her perch was such that she was now completely hidden from view. Yana had dug out a small ditch as soon as she had gotten into position three hours prior.

The sniper thumbed the bolt release and rolled back onto her belly. She leaned into her scope and eyed her next target. He was in the middle of the remaining pack, making Yana's heart sink.

He shouldered an RPG-32 Barkas. The reusable Rocket Propelled Grenade launcher maintained an effective range of well over a thousand feet. Yana pulled her RSASS's trigger just as the mercenary released his payload. The black tip struck him in the chest and knocked him back. But the damage was done. Through her scope, Yana watched the deadly explosive steak across the sky in her direction.

This was it.

Yana Fedorov, the infamous Blood Dragon, was finally getting hers.

Miraculously, a sharp gust forced the projectile off course, sinking it below its intended target at the last moment. The explosive warhead slammed into the mountain some thirty feet beneath Yana's position. The impact rattled her teeth. But for now, she was still alive.

Not if they get off another shot. If they do, I'm—

The sound of splitting rock filled the air. Yana looked left, then right, but saw nothing. Then, she rolled onto her back and gazed straight up, and saw something that dismantled her earlier confidence.

A wall of snow rushed down the aggressively slanted slope. It wasn't a full-fledged avalanche, but that didn't mean it couldn't rip her from her perch. The only thing she could do besides leap from the side of the mountain was to move closer to it. Yana rolled right, tucked the RSASS into her chest, and shut its dust cover. Then, she took a deep breath and closed her eyes.

Like so many before, Yana was buried alive, wrapped in the Himalayas' chilling, wintery embrace.

Silence returned to Langtang Valley. There were no pain-filled screams. There was no gunfire or explosions. Shenlong lifted his head and slowly surveyed the damage his team had sustained. He knew of at least four deaths but suspected there had been more. After the man in front of him had been killed by sniper fire, Shenlong did the only thing he could do—the smart thing to do. He threw himself to the ground and played dead.

He had landed, aiming toward the village, and witnessed one of his people shoulder the RPG-32. Shenlong also witnessed him depress the weapon's trigger while simultaneously having his life ended. The veiled threat had instantly made Shenlong reassess his plans. The survivors would regroup back in Padmaarga and rearm themselves for a long-distance engagement. Until now, he had no reason to believe Wu would have a skilled sniper at her disposal.

Shenlong wondered who would though. The precision the shooter displayed was second to none. He knew of a select few in this hemisphere that had the ability to pull off such shots. None of them were friends of his. He stood and counted the dead.

Six, he thought. To his recollection, there had only been six shots fired.

He glanced back and forth between his people's position and the roundabout location of the now incapacitated, hopefully deceased, shooter. The fact that six of his men had been taken out with just six pulls of a trigger was hard to imagine. The conditions weren't ideal either.

Such a shame.

Shenlong would've loved to have employed such a talent.

"Haitao."

Shenlong spun and raised his select-fire QCW-05 bullpup submachine gun (SMG). The bullpup's unique configuration allowed the magazine to be loaded *behind* the handgrip and trigger assembly rather than in front of it like most traditional firearms. It was also in current circulation within the Chinese army. It was how Shenlong had obtained it. He still had friends in high places within the PLA.

"H—Haitao."

He found the voice's owner. He was Shenlong's second in command and the only man in his outfit that knew Shenlong's given name. They had served together a lifetime ago and were friends, not just comrades in arms. Junfeng had sustained a gruesome injury to his left shoulder. Blood poured from the wound. Even behind his friend's partially masked face, Shenlong could see his skin had paled. He also owned a faraway look.

Junfeng would die soon.

Shenlong didn't have time for emotions. He shouldered his weapon and shot his long-time companion in the head. Junfeng had served Shenlong admirably, and his sacrifice wouldn't be forgotten. It had been Junfeng's response to the sniper that had given Shenlong the inkling to move and, ultimately, survive.

Ten was now four.

The three other survivors rushed to their leader's side and awaited orders. Shenlong pounded across the snow-dusted plain, making his way to the abandoned excavation. His team's arrival and subsequent gunfight had caused the workers to scamper away like rats.

The others fanned out and took up sentry positions around Shenlong. One man looked east. Another gazed out to the west. The third man guarded the north, their backs.

"Stay here," Shenlong ordered, entering the tent. The stock of his submachine gun was already planted in his shoulder.

He stepped through and quickly cleared the interior. When he was sure it was empty, he lowered his weapon and slung it around his back. The seal carved into the floor was impressive, but the opening was even more notable. In one fluid move, Shenlong planted his hand on the guardrail and vaulted over it. He landed with a heavy thud and moved off.

Shenlong knelt before the dark opening but spotted a subtle glow emanating from within. The excavation team had no doubt discovered the entrance earlier this morning and had been in the middle of documenting it when he and his team arrived. They'd also left a light source behind.

He slid into the opening feet first and descended through a narrow, low-roofed staircase. When it ended, Shenlong came to a stop and listened. There was no way of knowing whether a crewmember was hiding down here. For their sake, Shenlong hoped they hadn't been that stupid. Hearing nothing, he stood and moved off, unsheathing a razor-sharp combat knife as he stepped lightly. There would be no guns fired down here. The report in the tomb's tight confines would easily destroy his hearing.

The corridor ended at a broken table and a lifeless room that resembled more storehouse than crypt. Six bodies adorned the walls, three on each side. Their burial was simple. The dead had been wrapped in clothes and laid atop stone ledges. Shenlong also found six jars separated from the others and lined up on the floor. These were wholly intact and would fare a nice price on the black market, but that's not why he was here.

The nurse had described the seal before she had been dealt with. Shenlong's men dug deep into the web to find this place, as did a few of Cho's people back in Shanghai. The article's author wrote about a little-known legend of a "path to heaven." Few knew of it, and even fewer cared to investigate it further. But this place affirmed the tale.

"And a path requires markers to follow." *This* was one of those markers. "But how?"

Shenlong didn't know what he was looking for. He turned back toward the doorway and paused, noticing something he had missed on his first pass. A modern ladder had been set against the wall to the left of the opening. It led up to a much more elaborate burial. The stone sarcophagus was beautiful.

He mounted the ladder and scaled it, stopping when he was face to face with the coffin. It was covered in a script he couldn't read. There was also a duplicate tree carved into the lid. The tree itself had been split in two to reveal a map beneath it.

Shenlong smiled. He removed his phone from his pocket and snapped three pictures. He'd need them too. Shenlong had no idea where to go next. Regardless, he and the survivors needed to get moving. The action here had surely been brought to the attention of the authorities.

25

Lamabagar, Nepal

They made it a hundred yards north before Jack was forced to pull over. Kalsang's initial reactions were of the "ooh and aah" variety, but it wasn't until he saw what lay beneath the lock that he had anything to say that was noteworthy.

"I've seen this exact carving in the side of a monastery further to the north."

"You have?" Jack and May said together.

"Yes, but only once. The Triratna Monastery."

"Triratna?" May asked.

Kalsang nodded. "Yes, it's a symbol representing the Three Jewels of Buddhism. They don't matter much. Only the symbol as it relates to the monastery does." He sat back. "But there's a problem with that."

Jack turned around as much as he could. "What problem?"

Kalsang nodded. "The monastery was abandoned over a century ago due to issues with the locals."

"A century ago?" May asked. "That also fits the timeline of Dhonu Thapa's disappearance. Could it be related?"

No one had an answer.

"Tell me about these problem locals?" Jack asked, moving the conversation along.

The Sherpa was visibly uncomfortable with what he was about to say.

"Spit it out," Jack said as politely as possible.

Kalsang gave him an irritated stare but spoke. "Stories from the devout populace of that particular mountain valley say that the Lions of Buddha roam the land in search of the unworthy."

Jack would've laughed a couple of days ago. But not now.

"Hang on, lions?" May asked. "Like the two from the pictures on Jack's phone?"

Kalsang pulled them up. "Yes, exactly like these."

"What are they?" Jack asked.

"These," Kalsang said, turning the phone so Jack and May could see it, "are, like I said, the Lions of Buddha, but they're also called Snow Lions. They are the legendary protectors of Buddha, and they are fearsome."

May fidgeted in her seat. "Are you telling us that a pride of mythological creatures terrorized the monks at the monastery so badly that they drove them out?"

"That's what the local populace thinks, yes," Kalsang replied. "There isn't much in the way of written history in their community. Nearly everything that has been passed down, stretching over several generations, has been passed down by word of mouth."

"So, there could be a lot of accidental misinformation, right?" Jack asked.

"Naturally." Kalsang took a moment to collect his thoughts. "Do I believe that actual Snow Lions forced the abandonment to occur? No."

"Doesn't matter why it happened," May said. "We still have to go up there."

"Yeah," Jack said, "it's not like we have much choice in the matter."

"Hang on, Jack," May said, "didn't Dhonu say something about Snow Lions?"

His eyes opened wider. "He did. That's gotta count for something, right?"

Kalsang silently nodded. He didn't look thrilled about the prospect of revisiting Triratna Monastery. He let out a long breath and pointed to the road ahead.

"Take us north until the road ends. There's a supply store along the way." He eyed Jack. "We have quite the hike ahead of us."

May glanced at Jack. "Where are we going?"

Kalsang sighed. "Tibet. To the foot of Bardo Ri."

"Bardo Ri?" May asked. "I've never heard of it."

"Few have. No one goes there for a good reason."

"Bardo Ri, what does it mean?" Jack asked.

Kalsang rubbed his neck and explained. "In Buddhism, *Bardo* is the state of existence between life and death. And *Ri* means mountain."

Jack frowned. "Sounds an awful lot like Purgatory."

"Wait, so we're going to Purgatory Mountain?" May asked, looking extremely unhappy about it.

"No, it doesn't represent Purgatory," Kalsang replied, "and no, we are not going to Bardo Ri. We're staying beneath it…in the Forbidden Valley."

"Now's there's a forbidden valley?" Jack turned and sat back and groaned. "Sure, why not?"

Langtang, Nepal

A hand burst through the snow, reaching toward the heavens. It shook, its owner filled with rage. She was also incredibly cold. Little by little, Yana Fedorov dug herself out of her impromptu tomb. She refused to become a victim of the Himalayas.

Luckily, Yana had felt around and could tell she still had all her gear, minus the magazine that had failed to feed earlier. But she had also sustained a head injury. Blood freely flowed from a wound on the back of her head. She guessed it had come from a rock within the miniature avalanche. The compacted snow had frozen a good deal of the plasma to her skin, creating a nasty, crimson layer. She imagined her hair was matted down to her skull too. Yana must've been a sight to see.

She wiggled free and got to her knees, breathing hard. She was already feeling warmer. The layers she wore beneath her snow camo jacket had stayed mostly dry. Now, free of the mountain's embrace, Yana returned her attention to the mission. She had survived and was now solely focused on the task she had been contracted to do.

Yana took a deep breath and stood, feeling woozy. She took a moment to regain her balance, then went about checking over her RSASS. Everything seemed to be in working order. She'd need to fire it to be sure, but she wasn't about to try now. Yana needed to, first, confirm that the enemy was no longer in the area. Even from here, she could see the bodies littering the once unblemished landscape of the valley floor. Now, it looked like a warzone. She counted five black lumps. The sixth, the first target, was up near the wall and out of sight.

The path back down to ground level was arduous. Before the avalanche, it had been a chore to make the climb. Now, the trail had been completely wiped out and her only way down the mountain was by sliding on her backside.

Once she reached the bottom, she lay prone and readied her RSASS. Yana owned a mostly unobstructed view of the battlegrounds through her scope. But nothing moved. She aimed higher and tried to spot the villagers. More nothing. Either they had been smart and taken refuge during the shooting, or Shenlong's remaining men had cleaned house before leaving. If that had happened, Yana wouldn't know what to do with herself. The mission would be a failure.

Slowly, she got to a knee, shouldering the large DMR as if it were a standard battle rifle. Though it was more than capable of being fired while standing, the RSASS fared much better down on its attached bipod.

Speaking of which…

Yana reached beneath the barrel and folded the feet forward. Then, she moved out.

She stepped inside the tent and confirmed her earlier supposition. The archaeological team had fled before they could be boxed in and killed. Yana aimed at the open door and checked for enemies. Confirming she was alone, Yana stepped out and headed for the first body. Shenlong sported blue dragon scale tattoos. Besides being a former Falcon Commando, that's all Yana knew about him.

The lead gunman was not Shenlong. She angled slightly left. The next of the dead wasn't the mercenary boss either. The third one, the one she had hit in the shoulder, had bled out a significant amount of blood, but that's not what had ended his life. He'd been shot in the head by a small caliber round.

She ignored the fact that someone had ended this man's life before he could bleed to death and checked for tattoos. She removed his mask and then pulled down the killer's shirt collar. It was tattooed, but not with blue scales. He was not Shenlong.

Yana gritted her teeth and moved on.

None of the men, including the one wielding the RPG-32, was Shenlong. Success came in many forms. Had Yana killed six well-trained targets? Yes. Were the villagers safe? Possibly. Was Shenlong still alive? From the looks of it, yes.

The mission wasn't yet a success for the Russian Blood Dragon. Her standards were much too high. She'd continue the hunt. But first, she needed to know where they had gone. Once Yana was back at her car, she'd call May for additional details.

BIOfinity Genetics Group
Shanghai, China

David's office phone buzzed. Only one person called him on the intercom.

"Sir," Li said, "you have a call from Minister Zhao...again."

David growled. "Tell him I'm in another meeting."

"Um," Li said, sounding tense, "he said that if you used that excuse, he'd be on the first plane to Shanghai to speak to you in person."

No! David thought, lifting his hand and hovering it over his desk phone.

"He sounds furious, sir."

David flopped back in his chair, defeated. "Fine. Transfer it in."

His phone beeped.

He picked it up and put on a little of his trademark, fake charm. He hated schmoozing people, especially people like Minister Zhao. The government was overflowing with bureaucrats, overpriced file clerks, and wannabe dictators. It's why David preferred the private sector. But the government contracts were just too lucrative to pass up. If he didn't do it, some other biotech company would.

"Minister Zhao, hel—"

"You've been dodging my calls, David."

"No, sir, I—"

"I don't react well to such disrespect."

David's blood went cold. The last person he should be pissing off was the head of the MSS. Even someone of David's status could be "disappeared" overnight. He repressed his fright and folded his hands atop his desk to keep them from shaking.

"Now," Zhao continued, "to neglect my calls, you must either have found something noteworthy or you have nothing at all. Which is it?"

David needed to be very careful what he was about to tell Zhao.

He decided to be honest.

"The tests failed, Minister. The samples were not viable."

Zhao sighed, no doubt boiling over with rage. "That is unfortunate to hear. I—"

"I'll make you a deal," David interrupted, throwing all his cards on the table.

Zhao laughed. "You have nothing to offer me that I can't take for myself."

He meant David's company. That had always been a possibility ever since he began dealing with the government. David knew that any failure on his part could lead to a company takeover. He never thought it could happen so soon. Not that it mattered. If they turned up nothing in Nepal, he was dead, either way.

So, David decided to use his potential fate as an ace up his sleeve.

"If you send reinforcements, I'll give you *Project: Eternity*—not the Ministry, but *you*."

Zhao knew all about the long-term experimental project. And he had the nerve to scoff at it. "Is that what you're *really* after in Nepal?"

"To stretch my lifespan far beyond their limits? Absolutely. If I get what I want, I'll easily be able to add another century to my life." He grinned. This was his ace. "If you had the opportunity, wouldn't you do the same, Minister? What if you could outlive your superiors? *You* could lead China into a new era."

The lack of response told David that he had won.

"Fine. You can have your team."

"Thank you, but they will answer to my men."

Zhao grumbled. "Where do I send them? And David?"

"Yes, Minister?"

Zhao's voice deepened. "If you fail, it'll be your head."

"Yes, Minister," David replied, uncaring what Zhao could do to him. "So be it."

26

Lamabagar, Nepal

Jack opted to stay in the car while May and Kalsang picked out their gear. He needed to touch base with Raegor and Eddy back home. He also needed time to think. A lot had happened in a very short amount of time.

He opted to text Eddy instead of calling them, stating it was safer at the moment. In reality, Jack just wanted some peace and quiet, not that he didn't enjoy May and Kalsang's company. He had sent Eddy all the pictures they had gathered. A short description and explanation accompanied each one.

"This is incredible, Jack!" Eddy replied.

"Yeah, it's been a wild ride."

Jack tried to picture what awaited them in the Forbidden Valley, but he couldn't come up with anything. There wasn't much online either. The Triratna Monastery was a Google ghost. No one had mentioned the place in decades, it seemed. Even the claims of there being mythological lions roaming the area hadn't made it to any of the cryptid websites.

"What's next?" Eddy asked.

He tapped out what Kalsang had told him.

"Really? That's pretty far out there, even for a Jack mission. LOL."

Jack rolled his eyes, but knew she was right. His tasks had been something else since joining TAC.

He ended the text thread with a simple, *"Gotta run. Talk again soon."*

"Good luck, Jack. Eddy out."

Jack specifically neglected to mention anything about the budding connection between him and May, if that's what it truly was. It wasn't any of TAC's business anyway. Honestly, Jack had no idea what to make of him and May.

He laid his head back against his headrest and shut his eyes. "What are you doing, Jack?"

What he was doing with May was stupid, but she stirred something in him that he had thought long dead. The prospects of forming a close-knit bond with a person of the opposite sex had died over twenty years ago. Until a few days ago, Jack had been dedicated to his work—his life. The busyness of it all helped fill the natural void in his heart. It had gone unnoticed for a long time.

Until now, he thought, chuckling at the absurd timing.

Jack had hidden his emptiness well, but he had become increasingly lonely over the years. His friends also helped fill the space, though they were in short supply, and back in Wyoming. Being on the road helped keep the demons in his mind at bay, but only perpetuated his feeling of isolation. It was a fair trade in the end. Jack's mind could destroy him. The little ache in his soul was navigable.

He'd been close to adopting a dog before joining TAC. He had always wanted a Belgium Malinois named Duke, and not from John Wayne, mind you. The name came from his favorite computer game growing up, *Duke Nukem*.

He grinned. "Come get some." It had been one of Duke's catchphrases.

The crunch of footfalls caused him to open his eyes. He sat upright and discovered that May and Kalsang were marching toward him with three overflowing packs, and God knows what else. He exited the vehicle and helped them load everything in the back. They still had another mile to go before beginning their hike, and there was no reason to carry this stuff any farther than needed.

"So," Jack started, "what did you—"

His pocket vibrated, cutting him off. He needed to take the call because there were only two people that would be reaching out to him right now: Raegor or Eddy. The number came up as a bunch of random garbage, by design. Just another method of inscription.

Jack swiftly answered it. "This is Jack."

"Well, hello, Jack. It's nice to finally meet you."

The voice possessed a heavy Russian accent. Jack looked at May. "Hi, I'm guessing this is Yana?"

Jack removed the phone and activated its speaker mode. The mercenary either didn't notice the change in acoustics or didn't care.

"Yes, this is Yana."

Jack didn't know what to say. He had been caught wholly off guard. "So, how are things?"

Yana softly laughed. "You're a funny man, Jack. By things, I believe you are inquiring about the status of my mission."

"Yeah, that," Jack replied.

"First off, no villagers were harmed. I know that was an important part of our agreement. Secondly, Shenlong's team suffered substantial losses." Jack perked up. "But unfortunately, he was not among the dead."

"Oh, I'm sorry to hear that."

"Me too. And I intend to rectify that. It is why I am calling. Is May there?"

May leaned closer. "I'm here."

"Good. I just wanted to be sure. I also need to know where Shenlong is headed next?"

Jack wasn't overly fond of giving a Russian assassin that information, but he didn't have another choice. If Yana were willing to continue with her contract, then it would be foolish not to use her abilities to the fullest.

"If Shenlong solves the next clue, which he undoubtedly will, he'll be headed for the Emerald Lotus Monastery in Lamabagar."

"Lamabagar?"

"Yep," Jack replied. He even spelled it out for her. "L-A-M-A-B-A-G-A-R."

"Copy that. Goodbye."

"Same to you. Happy hunting."

Yana hung up. Jack handed his phone to May, and she plugged it in.

Kalsang leaned forward. "She sounds intense."

May nodded, lost in a memory. "You have no idea."

Jack wanted to know what May was thinking. He was curious about what May had seen the last time she had paired with the Blood Dragon. It wasn't a priority, though. They needed to get moving.

He put the Scorpio into gear. They traveled north along the western shore of the Tamakoshi River, crossing it at the hydroelectric plant. A compacted dirt road continued on the other side, guiding them deeper into the wilderness beyond Lamabagar. The path snaked for another mile before dead-ending at a circular cutout of land designed as a turnaround for vehicles like theirs.

"This it?" Jack asked, already knowing the answer.

"Yes," Kalsang replied, opening his door, "we walk from here."

Jack and May exited the Scorpio, helped unload the gear from the trunk, and set everything off to the side.

Kalsang tossed Jack a pair of black waterproof Gore-Tex pants. "Put those on over your jeans. It's cold and wet where we're going."

"What about the car?" May asked, slipping into a similar pair. "Even if Shenlong doesn't figure out where the next marker is, he'll eventually find the car and know we came this way."

Kalsang shrugged.

Jack zipped the fly of his outerwear and looked around. The tree line wasn't an option. It wasn't dense enough around here to hide an automobile. He heard something that might work and faced it.

"I vote for the river," he said.

"The river?" Kalsang asked.

"Yeah. The water is dark enough to hide the car. Looks deep enough too."

May bit her lip but nodded. "I agree."

Jack climbed back in and angled the car at the river, pointing it west. The descending terrain was made of flat stone and was steep, ending at the sweeping waterway. He lowered the windows, killed the engine, and got out, leaving it in neutral. Kalsang went around back, and Jack and May picked a door.

They pushed.

It took a second to get the Scorpio moving, but when it did, gravity took control. Ju Yang's rental bounced down the grade and crashed into the water. May's hand found Jack's, and she laced her fingers into his and rested her head on his shoulder as she watched. The car resisted going under for just a moment, but once the river realized the vehicle's windows were down, it was all she wrote. The trapped air within the Scorpio kept it afloat for a little longer, but even it couldn't prevail.

Then, it was gone.

Jack released May's hand, wrapped his arm around her shoulder, and hugged her. May took it a step further, leaned in, and wrapped her arms around his back. She laid her head on his chest. They embraced, never taking their eyes off the sinking Scorpio. Neither spoke. It was just the two of them confirming the car's demise too. Kalsang had moved on and went about double-checking their gear.

The Sherpa cleared his throat. "We're ready."

Jack and May parted and turned. Jack gave May a reassuring wink. "We'll be fine. I have a lot of experience in the wilderness, and Kalsang has spent a lifetime out here."

"I'm not worried about that," May said, heading over to Kalsang.

"Then, what's wrong?" Jack asked, walking next to her.

She stopped and glanced back at the river. "I'm just trying to think of what to tell the rental company about their car."

Jack grinned. "Yeah, Ju Yang is kinda screwed, isn't she?"

"It'll be dealt with when it's dealt with."

It was another way of saying, "It is what it is," and Jack couldn't agree more. Right now, the fate of the Scorpio didn't matter. Getting to the next lock was at the top of their list.

"How far is it to the Triratna Monastery from here?" Jack asked, hoping he wouldn't regret asking the question.

Kalsang hefted on his pack and looked north. He was obviously calculating the distance in his head. "It lies at the end of the Forbidden Valley, roughly thirty-two kilometers."

Jack's shoulders fell, as he did the conversion. *Twenty-ish miles… Ho-ly shit.* May looked sick to her stomach.

"Right," Jack said, sounding as chipper as possible, "shall we?"

"What about the sun?" May asked, looking up. It was currently behind a cloud. "I thought hiking through the Himalayas at night was bad practice?"

Kalsang nodded. "Usually, it is. I will take us as far as possible." He checked his watch. "Sunset isn't for another three hours. If the land allows it, we will continue after nightfall."

"And if it doesn't?" she asked. Her nervousness was showing.

"We'll be fine." Jack placed a hand on her shoulder. "Also, do you like camping?"

The terrain was precipitous but traversable. Kalsang kept them close to the river, following its winding path. It was their map. There was no manmade route through the trees and brush. They were forced to create their own. Kalsang had opted not to use a machete to clear any obstacles away. He understood their need for stealth. They'd be easily tracked if they made too much of a mess. So, if they came across a dense area, they tried to squeeze through it without causing too much damage, or they'd avoid it altogether.

Jack loved the excursion. It reminded him of home. He used to do stuff like this all the time with Bull. In a way, Kalsang was his Bull right now.

And that makes May, what, Hawk? He looked at her. *No friggin' way.*

They made it four miles before losing the light completely. Kalsang paused and ignited his flashlight and swept it around. He must've been okay with what the land gave them because he started off again.

Three miles after that, they came upon a clearing on the bank of the Tamakoshi. It was fifty feet in diameter and entirely devoid of growth. The empty space was a natural occurrence due to the rocky ground. Jack found evidence of a landslide. It had cut straight through the forest eons ago.

Kalsang stopped and held his light against the tree line ahead of them. He dropped his bag and turned to Jack and May. "We'll camp here for tonight."

Jack didn't argue, and neither did May. They both shrugged out of their bags. Jack knelt and dug into his.

"Oh, and…" Jack looked up at the Sherpa, "welcome to Tibet."

27

Tibet

They had crossed the border into Tibet a mile previously. Jack had never been to Tibet, or Nepal, for that matter. The temperature was borderline unbearable now. The clearing they had found was a perfect spot to put up a tent, but it was also inviting in the wind. They used loose rocks to anchor the shelter down before climbing in. The trio's bodyweight and gear would do the rest.

Jack was perplexed why Kalsang would pick out a tent with a removable Velcro divider running up the middle. Typically, you'd want everyone's body heat to work together to help warm the tent's interior. The *wall* made that much less efficient.

Then, it dawned on Jack when May climbed into his side of the tent. Kalsang had figured that the two of them were a couple and didn't need to worry about keeping the interior warm.

"We made that shopkeeper very happy," May said, tossing in her sleeping bag. The battery-powered light illuminated the room well. It shined like a soft bedside lamp.

"Yeah, I'm sure, and you're welcome."

May stopped. "Who said it was your card?"

Jack stopped prepping his own sleeping bag. "Ju Yang?"

"It was the least I could do."

"Besides sinking your rental, of course." Jack slid inside and laid on his back.

She shrugged. "Hazard of the job. I've done much worse."

"Oh, yeah?" Jack rubbed his hands together. They were cold. "Please, do tell."

May unlaced her boots and set them aside. She unfurled her heavy sleeping bag, set it next to Jack's, and slipped in. She laid on her left side and propped her head up with her hand, facing him.

"Once, I set a very nice truck on fire."

Jack's eyes widened, and he leaned up and looked at her. "Why?"

"I was being hunted by someone with Night Vision and knew the light would mask my escape. Took me two days to get back to town with no transportation."

He laid back down. "Where were you?"

"Middle East."

Jack rolled onto his right side and propped his head up. "Really?" He was suspicious. "And who was hunting you?"

May looked away from him.

"May!"

She laughed. "How was I supposed to know American forces were in the area?"

Jack rolled his eyes. "Yeah, I'm sure you had no idea where they were."

She smiled sheepishly. "Well, maybe one or two of them."

Jack let it slide. He wasn't a soldier anymore. The light on Kalsang's side went out. The Sherpa was going to sleep. But Jack was too awake to follow suit.

Plus, he enjoyed talking to May like this. Just two people with a lot in common talking shop.

"So," he started, keeping his voice down, "what's next for Mayleen Wu?"

"If we survive," she added.

"Pfft," Jack said, waving away the comment, "I don't know about you, but I think we're doing great." He smiled. "Come on. Tell me. What's next?"

All the delight faded from her face. "Honestly, I'm not sure."

"What about Ju Yang? Couldn't you live out that persona?"

"Yes, but..." Her eyes welled with tears. "I'm so tired, Jack. I..." the tears fell, "I just want to live in peace."

Jack reached out and grabbed May's free hand and held it. "I promise you'll get there one day. I know what you're going through—I really do. I wasn't just blowing smoke up your butt." He affectionately caressed the top of her hand. "After I retired from service, I had no direction, and don't get me started about the nightmares."

"That bad?"

"Yeah, they were. Let's just say I'm happy they're finally gone."

"What did you do when you were in the military?"

Jack had never told anyone besides Bull and Hawk what he had done. Trust was in short supply but May had earned it.

"I was with Delta. Team leader, if you can believe it." May didn't seem surprised. Jack forgot. She was very smart and had figured out that he had been in the Special Forces. "For over a decade, I exterminated bad guys with extreme prejudice."

"Iraq?"

"Mostly, yeah. I was really good at what I did until I wasn't." He told her about his last mission with Delta—about the kid's face that had been burned into his memory forever.

"That's awful."

He nodded. "It was."

"And the nightmares? How did you get them to go away?"

Jack released May's hand and motioned to the air around them. "This. My job with TAC. Once I got back into the world, they slowly faded away to nothing. It originally started with becoming a park ranger, though. That's what sped up the healing the most."

May held up their clasped hands. "And what about this? Is this a part of that process too?"

Jack felt painfully awkward, but he calmed himself and looked over their hands. The sight made him beam. "I don't know, but I kinda like it." His eyes found hers. "A lot."

"You're an odd man, you know that, right?" She smiled, amused.

Jack softly chuckled. "Would you have me any other way?"

May's tone got serious. "I'll let you know after I've had you."

Jack blushed and he didn't care how visible his rosy cheeks were. It was much too late to hide the feelings he had for May.

He leaned in to kiss her and was, once more, startled by Kalsang. The Sherpa mumbled in his sleep, and Jack looked over his shoulder and held his breath to hear if he was awake. When the mumbling subsided and the snoring resumed, Jack mentally wiped his brow. They were in the clear.

But he didn't get his kiss.

He turned and was elated to see that May was still waiting for it. Jack leaned in and gently applied his lips to hers. They passionately carried on for a moment and then separated and grinned at one another. Jack was confident it would've progressed even further if they had been alone. But with an important mission still on the line, and a roommate snoring loudly less than three feet away, they smartly decided to be patient and wait for whatever else might come later.

May shifted her posture and rolled into Jack. They were still in their individual sleeping bags but were now in the classic *spooning* position. Jack hadn't felt this happy in years. He found May's hand again, and he pulled her in closer. Both yawned, and they laid down. May gladly, almost eagerly, used Jack's right biceps as her pillow. Jack was relegated to using his wadded-up backpack.

"For what it's worth," May whispered, "I like it a lot too."

Jack and May woke up to a shuffling sound outside the tent. They were also in the same position they had fallen asleep in. May's body was curled into his, helping to create a comforting layer of heat between them. Jack lifted his head, feeling a slight kink in his neck. Through blurry eyes, he spotted the culprit. His backpack had failed as a viable replacement for a pillow. His arm seemed to have worked for May, though. She yawned, stretched, and began to sit up.

But Jack had other plans.

He wrapped his arm around May's waist and pulled her back down. She yelped in surprise, then laughed. Heavy footfalls approached upon her outburst, and their side of the tent was ripped open with a rush of cool air. A thick man greeted the entangled pair. He was backlit by a touch of sunshine.

"We need to get moving." With that, Kalsang let them be.

May's hair was half-draped over Jack's face. He reluctantly released the squirming woman and allowed her to get up. The Sherpa was right. They needed to get going. They still had a long hike ahead of them.

Another thirteen miles.

May rolled onto her feet and gave Jack a death glare. But she couldn't hold it. The corner of her mouth twitched, revealing the pleasure she was feeling.

She picked up her bag and shoved a hand inside. "You don't deserve it."

"Deserve what?" Jack asked, leaning up on one arm.

"This."

May tossed a small, vacuum-sealed package of instant coffee at him and stood.

Jack quickly got to one knee and held it up as if it were a wedding ring. "Marry me."

She didn't respond. She just collected her boots and tossed open the flap. Chilling air burst into the tent, earning a shout and shiver from Jack. May enjoyed the hell out of it and stepped out. Her laugh was loud and boisterous. For his part, Jack slipped out of his sleeping bag and collected his gear. He put on his shoes, picked up the instant coffee, and headed outside. The sun had just begun to rise. His campouts in Yellowstone had been similar. You used whatever light you were given.

All of it.

May was waiting for him with three collapsible plastic cups. She had thought of everything. That, or it had been Kalsang's idea. Jack decided it was May who had thought of it since she knew he loved the drink. The trio of cups were already filled with water. The coffee wouldn't be hot, but it would undoubtedly do the job.

He took a sip after stirring it in with his filthy finger. The brew was average at best, though it was still roasty and chockful of caffeine. That's all Jack could ask for when camping...in Nepal. He sipped it and stepped over to the river. A family of eight deer was gathered on the other side, grazing on the grass, and drinking from the crisp river.

May joined Jack, and they watched them in silence.

"Tibetan red deer," Kalsang announced, startling one of the creatures. That one alerted the others, and they all took off into the trees.

"Thanks," Jack said, annoyed.

Kalsang didn't notice his irritation. "Makes a good stew." The Sherpa headed back to the tent without another word.

Jack watched him leave. May didn't follow him. She stayed with Jack.

"I'd try it."

Jack agreed. "Same. I'm starving."

"Here."

Kalsang tossed each of Jack and May a sandwich baggy. They were packed with dry, brown tree bark. Upon closer inspection, Jack realized that it wasn't bark. It was jerky.

"What is it?" he asked, intrigued.

"Yak," Kalsang replied, packing his stuff. "Dried it myself."

Jack had never eaten yak jerky before. He separated the Ziploc seal and dove in while walking back to the tent. He sniffed it. The jerky didn't smell overly spiced. It just smelled like a bag of beef. Yaks were nothing but cattle.

May didn't look as intrigued. But, like Jack, she required sustenance. They each tore off a hunk and looked at one another.

"*Salud*," Jack said, stuffing the jerky into his mouth.

May forced a smile but didn't say anything.

It was juicier than it had looked, and it was somewhat bland. Still, it was edible and satiated Jack's hunger. Once he ate half the ration, he resealed and pocketed the rest. It would be a snack in a couple of hours. He drank half a bottle of water, then switched back to his coffee. He was now semi-hydrated, and his stomach was full enough to function.

May struggled through her ration, but she ate. She knew how important it was to get her calorie intake. Jack wasn't the only one aware of the journey that lay ahead.

The tent collapsed quite easily and went into a bag strapped to the top of Kalsang's pack and his own sleeping bag. The Sherpa was plenty strong enough to carry an excess load. Jack and May were also ready. They looked over the campsite and noticed something.

"The rocks we used," Jack said, pointing at the pile.

"What about them?" May asked.

He walked over to them and picked one up. "Put them back. We need to keep our presence here to a minimum."

The trio scattered the various stones. Satisfied that the grounds looked back to normal, Kalsang led them northeast, around a thicket of pine trees. It must've been the cluster that had made him decide to stop the night before. They were now moving away from their map—the river. Jack respected the decision even more now. The Sherpa had made the right call to pitch camp.

Jack brought up the rear and mumbled, "Thirteen miles…"

28

Kathmandu, Nepal

After losing six men in Langtang, Shenlong moved his remaining force back to their safehouse in Kathmandu until further notice. They needed to re-up on supplies and figure out where Wu and the American went. Shenlong wasn't an expert in Nepali or Tibetan history. He was a soldier, and he excelled in its many facets. Cho had been no help, either. The man had sounded flustered and offered Shenlong no usable information.

Instead of utilizing unreliable, historical references, Shenlong used high-def topographical maps. He was comparing every Himalayan valley to the one he had taken a photo of. A few years ago, Shenlong had obtained access to specific servers within the Chinese army. The officer he had paid off had eventually been found out and tried with treason and killed, but the secret access point still lived on.

The main reason Shenlong typically operated in Asia and the Middle East was because of this access. His information for those regions ran deep. European jobs were doable but with a lower success rate than he was comfortable with.

The ratcheting sound of a charging handle got his attention. He turned and watched two of his men checking over their own DMR precision rifles. The identical Type 95 bullpups were in perfect working order, thanks partly to Shenlong's meticulous maintenance habits. He personally kept up with all his people's firearms. It was a great way for him to relax and zone out.

Suddenly, his laptop dinged. Shenlong spun to find that his program had found a match of eighty-nine percent. He quickly looked it over as his men closed in around him. Lamabagar was eighty miles northwest of Kathmandu, and it would take some time to get there.

He stood and closed the machine. "We leave in ten minutes."

Lamabagar, Nepal

Jack's tip landed Yana in Lamabagar well before Shenlong, or that's what she assumed. She had seen no evidence of his arrival. Yana decided to scout the area before heading to her selected post in the western mountains. There were fewer people in Langtang than in Lamabagar, which meant there was a higher chance of collateral damage. Yana needed to be smart in how she proceeded.

She followed a group of tourists who had just exited a dust-covered tour bus. Yana no longer wore her white and gray kit. She currently donned fake eyeglasses, a messy bun, jeans, and a white designer winter coat. Beneath her coat was a holstered pistol, a Walther PPQ.

To the untrained eye, the Blood Dragon's outward appearance looked anything but dangerous. She had made a life of blending into her surroundings. Sometimes, the best place to hide was in plain sight. She looked down at her watch and then up at the sun, calculating when it would disappear behind the mountain, making visibility poorer.

She'd give Shenlong a few more hours to arrive, then…she didn't know what she'd do. The mission needed completion, but she couldn't just go hunting for Shenlong and get into an open conflict with him and the remainder of his team. Plus, she had no idea if he had picked up more men.

"Patience," she told herself. "He will come."

Forbidden Valley, Tibet

Three hours into their hike, Jack, May, and Kalsang saw their first signs of life, or death. The shredded remains of a Tibetan red deer, the same species they had seen back at camp earlier, greeted them. The kill was somewhat fresh—less than a day old—and sat as a dark omen at the entrance to the Forbidden Valley. The predator, probably more than one, had picked the deer clean.

"What do you think it was that did this?" May asked.

Kalsang stopped to look over the carcass. "I'd say either a pack of Himalayan wolves or, possibly, a snow leopard."

"Any bears around here?" Jack asked.

"Yes," Kalsang replied, moving again, "but they are rare."

"What kind?" he asked.

The Sherpa looked over his shoulder. "Tibetan blue bear. They are a type of brown bear. Very big and extremely territorial."

"Yeah, I know brown bears well," Jack said, earning a look from May. "I've had a few run-ins with them back in Yell0wstone."

May got the conversation off bears and onto something more important to the mission. "Kalsang, what do you think drove out the Triratna monks? I can't imagine you believe it was really Snow Lions."

"Hard to say, and no, I don't think it was Snow Lions. Man does not have many threats out here besides himself and the mountain."

"Take a stab at it," Jack said. "We won't hold you to it."

Kalsang didn't answer right away. Jack figured the guy was working out his theory before spilling the beans. "I'd say it was either a pack of unusually aggressive wolves, possibly rabid, or a family of blue bears. That makes the most sense."

"Is it common for animals out here to contract rabies?" May asked.

"No, though it can happen." Kalsang pushed aside a thick limb and allowed Jack and May to pass. "Plus, our wolves aren't all that big. The average male only weighs in around, oh…" he silently counted out the weight conversion on his fingers, "seventy-five pounds, or so. I've seen them bigger, but not all that often."

They snaked north, further away from the western flow of the Tamakoshi River.

"Why again do they call it the 'Forbidden Valley?'" Jack asked, keeping his head on a swivel.

"There have been an unprecedented number of deaths here. Expeditions into the valley are scarce because of it. Local superstitions are truth around here, and getting a guide is nearly impossible."

"Money talks," May muttered.

Kalsang looked at her. "Not always. I wouldn't be caught dead here except for my family's involvement."

"That bad?" May asked.

Kalsang slowed and looked over his shoulder at her. "You'll see…"

Lamabagar, Nepal

The next village was much larger than Langtang or Padmaarga but still quite small compared to Kathmandu. Shenlong preferred the larger cities for one reason only: variety. Back in the Nepali capital, he'd have plenty of options regarding hideouts, transportation, and contacts. Here, in the heart of the Himalayas, he had nothing besides himself and what was left of his team.

The Langtang sniper still had him shaken.

He cautiously climbed out of his SUV and surveyed the immediate area. For being such a quaint village, Lamabagar was much busier than he would've expected. He'd have to be careful of witnesses. Bigger metropolises, like Kathmandu, offered someone like him a surprising amount of anonymity. The hustle and bustle helped conceal his doings in a way. But places like Lamabagar did nothing else except focus the attention on the loudest individual, which was bound to be him.

His three remaining men converged on his position from their individual vehicles. They had decided to play it safe and travel separately. Shenlong could picture a single transport being compromised and all four of them killed, especially without a confirmation of the sniper's demise. If the shooter was still alive, they were still a target.

"Fan out," Shenlong said, keeping his voice low. Tourists moved about close to their position at the rear of a shared parking lot. "Contact me as soon as you find something."

He adjusted the short black wig taped to his bald head. He wasn't taking any chances on being identified. He also wore simple sunglasses and a turtleneck beneath his coat to hide his tattoos.

"What are we looking for exactly?"

Shenlong faced the speaker. "Anything of note." He looked at his watch. "We'll meet in fifteen minutes." He looked around for a central location and found a rundown monastery. "There." He pointed at the place of worship. It was the tallest building in the vicinity.

A monastery, hmmm, he thought. *It can't be that easy, can it?*

The men dispersed. Shenlong's gut told him to check out the monastery first. His gut was usually a reliable source of intuition. People like him and Wu had learned to live on their instincts. It's what had kept them alive for so long. But they worked in an industry of depreciation. Their occupations, while not exactly the same, shared one absolute. The longer they stayed active and the more enemies they made, the better chance they'd eventually find themselves on the other end of a bullet.

The roadside stop contained trinket shops and a corner store. Further up the road was a sign for an outdoor supplier. Shenlong couldn't see the business but assumed it was around the next bend, north of the monastery.

He was less than a hundred yards from the monastery. A family of four pushed past him, excitedly chatting with one another. Shenlong shuffled to a stop when he heard them mention something about a commotion at the monastery the day before.

"Excuse me," he said, speaking Nepali.

The father stopped, shooing his wife and sons away. "Yes?"

"I apologize, but did I overhear you say something happened at the monastery?"

The dad looked back at his family, obviously wanting to rejoin them. "I did. Why?"

"Is it still open? I have traveled very far to visit it and would be devastated to hear if it weren't."

The father relaxed and smiled. "It is, but I'm sorry to have to say this…"

Shenlong tensed to hear grave news.

"But the Emerald Lotus is a fake." He shrugged. "It's still worth seeing. Sorry if that ruined it for you."

He went to turn away but was stopped.

"How was the forgery discovered?" Shenlong asked, painfully upbeat.

"An American and his girlfriend caused a big scene yesterday." Shenlong hid his enthusiasm. "I'm sorry, but I have to go."

Shenlong blinked out of his thoughts. "Uh, yes, and thank you."

He spun on a dime and strode to the monastery. He didn't care if it was a hallowed house of Buddhism or not. Shenlong was prepared to burn it to the ground and sift through the ashes to find what he needed.

29

Emerald Lotus Monastery
Lamabagar, Nepal

The inside of the monastery was musty and not lit well. Shenlong could see the Emerald Lotus at the rear of the room. A few people hung around to have a look, but the space was mostly deserted. A monk hurried over to Shenlong, his hands nervously fidgeting.

"Something the matter?" Shenlong asked, speaking Tibetan.

The monk stopped and sized him up. "Yes—no!"

Shenlong's right eyebrow rose. "Well, which is it?"

"I've been better, but we will survive." The monk's attitude was un-monk-like. He was worried about himself and whatever Wu and the American had done to upset him, rather than focusing on his duties.

Shenlong took in more of the room, specifically the people inside. There was an older couple huddled in front of the lotus and a taller, spectacled blonde jotting down notes in a journal. Shenlong guessed she was a student, maybe even a journalist, and she'd come to study the fabled Emerald Lotus. She casually spoke to another woman.

"Is there anything else?"

Shenlong returned his attention to the rude monk. "Do you have somewhere to be?"

"Well, no, but—"

He stepped within an arm's reach of the monk and held his gaze. "How about I make you a deal?"

The monk swallowed back his fear. "What kind of deal?"

"Show me what you showed the American yesterday."

The monk's brow furrowed, but then he calmed. "Yes, of course. I offered him a good deal, and you'll get an even a better one. Three thousand U.S. dollars and you can go anywhere you please."

"Just like that?" Shenlong asked, disgusted. "You'd sell your soul, just like that?"

The monk looked genuinely offended but didn't get a chance to rebuke him.

Shenlong moved to within inches of him. "How about I pay you nothing and let you live instead?" he hissed. "Like your lotus, you are counterfeit—a liar! I don't care much for liars."

The monk's lower jaw hung loose, and he nodded his head, eyes wide. "C-come," he blinked hard, "I will show you where they went."

He was led to the back corner of the main level. A narrow staircase greeted him, descending into what looked like a storage basement. Interestingly, a soft breeze passed alongside Shenlong. He focused on the current of air and found that it was being pulled *into* the basement.

Hmmm.

He touched the earbud in his left ear. "To the monastery, now."

Less than a minute later, his team arrived.

"Guard the entrance. Gang, with me." He looked at the monk. "You're coming too."

Shenlong descended first. The monk was forced to follow him along with one of his men, Gang, who brought up the rear. The two remaining men headed back outside to observe and report.

The stairs ended at a dark storage room with no exits. But Shenlong could still feel a gentle pull of fresh air. The monk didn't seem to notice it, though. Shenlong was getting the feeling that the monk didn't know what the American had found down here, if anything at all.

"What was the American searching for?"

The monk shrugged. "I didn't ask."

Shenlong wheeled on him. "And yet, you let him do as he pleased?"

"I don't answer to you."

"True, but your life is one hundred percent in *my* hands. If I were you, I would show some respect." The monk staggered back and bumped into the thickly built Gang. "Also," he pointed at the western wall, "do you know you have a draft?"

Shenlong waited until the monk felt it. When he did, his reaction was one of confusion.

"Gang!"

The mercenary went straight to the shelving and pulled it to the ground, scattering the monk's possessions everywhere. The monk was surprised, but not because his belongings had been treated so roughly. His reaction came from the recession in the wall behind the shelving. It was wide enough to fit a grown man through.

Shenlong clicked on his flashlight. "Shall we?"

The passage ended at a large, naturally formed cavern. Although it had been built by nature, the space had later seen assistance from mankind. It appeared to be a secret temple of some kind. Shenlong would be lying if he said he was an expert in the subject. It wasn't his job. He was here for Wu and Shangri-La. Everything else along the way was a mere speed bump and an afterthought.

The monk had trouble keeping up and had to be reminded to keep his feet moving by Gang. His attention, as Shenlong figured it would be, was divided. The discovery of the ancient temple quietly resting directly beneath his feet was a lot for him to grasp. And knowing the monk, he'd use it for profit. It sickened Shenlong, but that was his choice and meant very little to him in the end. After he figured out where Wu and the American were headed, he'd never step foot in Lamabagar again.

Gang shoved the monk between the first pair of stone-cut benches, and he fell. Shenlong was too busy to notice whether he'd been hurt. The two enormous lion guardians awed even a man of his ilk. They guarded a platform and stood before a long, flat subterranean lake. That was good and all, but Shenlong had yet to see anything in the way of a map or directions.

He mounted the platform, much to the displeasure of the monk, and continued down to the other side. He slowed his descent. The floor and rear steps were wet. Shenlong knelt beside the disturbed area and examined it. The path of water connected to the lake.

Someone went for a swim. But why?

There was only one way to find out.

He stood and looked out over the glassy body of water, hearing the slightest water droplets reverberate past him. He spotted a small island of stone only inches above the surface.

Shenlong put it together. Whatever Wu and her partner had found, it was on that sliver of stone. It meant that Shenlong was also going for a swim.

"Gang," Shenlong said, beginning to undress.

The mercenary ushered the monk around the right-hand side of the platform. The local immediately noticed what Shenlong was about to do.

"You must not enter!"

"And why is that?" Shenlong asked, pausing.

The monk motioned to the cavern. "Based on all of this. This water is obviously sacred. We must pay respect and not defile it."

Shenlong chuckled and eyed Gang. "How about that, he really is a monk!" He continued to undress. "Step aside, or you're coming in with me."

She did her best to stay calm. Yana was nearly caught watching Shenlong's exchange with the monk. At first, she didn't know it was him. His disguise, like hers, was designed to do precisely what it had done. It had thrown Yana off. But his demeanor and intimidating walk, combined with his laser focus, had given him away.

Yana had been doodling incoherent nonsense in her notebook, acting as if she was sketching the lotus, when she turned and found her target coming up behind her. She spun back around and said hello to the woman to her right, hoping the innocent exchange would be seen as exactly that.

Yana tucked a loose section of hair behind her left ear. She then angled herself to see the two men's reflections in the lotus' glass case while also giving the impression that she was still sketching. The pair moved to a hole in the floor and were met by three more men. This was all that was left of Shenlong's original force. If Yana acted now, she could wipe the slate clean.

But others would die.

Jack wanted no additional casualties. As menacing as the Blood Dragon could be, Yana drew a line with drawing a pistol and getting into a gunfight inside a Buddhist monastery. The trio conversed with their boss, and two of them returned outside. Guards, more than likely. Shenlong and the larger of his men descended the stairs with the monk.

She casually strolled over to gain a closer look. The larger merc was halfway in when he quickly snapped his eyes up at her approach. Luckily, Yana had looked away in time, only having to shift her eyes back to her sketchbook. She could feel him staring at her. So, Yana kept her head down and her strides slow and easy, all while doodling away. Her cover would be blown if she met his eyes at this distance.

She took a deep breath and hummed a random song. Then, she stopped and faced the wall and gazed at it curiously. Yana flipped the page and started a new "drawing."

Come on, she thought, *go!*

The merc did as she had willed, and he ducked his head inside and disappeared. She could've followed and gunned them down, but not without putting the monk in danger. Yana closed her sketchbook and headed for the exit. If she moved fast enough, she could get up into the hills and set up her RSASS.

She paid the guards no attention, even when one of them called after her. There was no way they could've known she understood Chinese. The fact they would be so openly obscene spoke to their character. Then again, they were killers for hire, who, as most people in their profession, owned no moral compass.

But Yana did.

A sound like approaching thunder slowed her departure. She stopped in the middle of the large, shared parking area and watched three blacked-out SUVs appear from around the bend to the south.

Yana cursed under her breath in Russian.

The disguised assassin picked up her feet and fled the scene as fast as she could without running. Yana tucked the sketchpad against her chest and rolled her shoulders forward. She'd resemble nothing more than a frightened onlooker to the untrained eye.

She had no idea who the newcomers were, but they weren't here to help her. That was certain. She guessed that Shenlong was receiving a team of much-needed reinforcements. Yana's chance to close her contract may have just been delayed indefinitely.

She hurried along and found her car, and climbed in. Gone was her terrified persona. Yana pulled her phone free and videoed the incoming convoy. They parked in a line, cutting the open center of the parking lot in half. These people weren't disguising their arrival. Whoever they were, they were dreadful news.

Several doors opened, and twelve men spilled free. Yana identified them all as Chinese. These were military types. Yana recalled what little information she had on Shenlong.

He'd been a Falcon Commando.

If that's who these men were, everyone from here to Everest was in grave danger.

Yana couldn't keep this to herself. She dialed Jack's number again and tossed the device aside when the call refused to connect. He and May were too deep into the mountains to have a signal.

She gripped the steering wheel hard and pondered what to do. But Yana already knew what her course of action was. Once Shenlong emerged with the location of his next stop, Yana would follow them and, with any luck, find May, Jack, and their Sherpa friend before it was too late.

This was the worst-case scenario.

Gang helped his boss ashore, clothes in hand. Shenlong didn't accept them quite yet. First, he allowed the freezing water to naturally run off his muscular, scarred body. He was also lost in thought and not paying attention to his subordinate.

Like the sarcophagus back in Langtang, the lock built into the stone island had been opened to reveal their next destination. Shenlong recognized the Three Jewels but was unsure of its significance in connection to his mission. So far, the two dots on his map had been monasteries. That's where he'd start.

Gang didn't bother to ask him what he had found. His job wasn't to ask him any questions. It was to take orders and get paid. His loyalty was unquestionable. If the information were pertinent to his job, he knew Shenlong would relay it to him.

The monk, however, asked.

"What did you find?"

"Nothing that concerns you."

The monk stepped in front of him. "What? All of this concerns me."

Shenlong accepted his long-sleeve thermal first and slipped into it. "Why, so you can profit from it?"

"I don't answer—"

"To me?" Shenlong leaned in, nearly touching noses. "If you're curious, go look for yourself."

"But…I can't make that swim."

Shenlong shrugged and received his pants. "Not my problem."

Next were his socks and shoes and his sidearm. The latter dangled in his hand as he mounted the steps up to the platform, unaware whether the monk was following or not. But he did care. If the monk revealed any of this before Shenlong could finish his task, it would surely complicate the matter.

Shenlong sighed, lifted his pistol, turned, and pulled the trigger.

The gun's report echoed violently around them. The monk stumbled backward. He flopped onto his back and into the sacred waters of the Emerald Lotus Monastery's subterranean lake. The gone astray, holy man's robes billowed out around him like a beta fish's fins would. Arms out wide, he gracefully floated toward deeper water where he'd ultimately sink.

Shenlong and Gang returned to the basement and re-hid the temple entrance. They replaced the shelving unit and restocked it. They needed to delay its discovery for as long as they could. Eventually, it would be found, as would the monk's body.

They exited the basement and went straight for the exit. Shenlong stepped outside and stopped atop the first stair. A rigid line of twelve plain-clothed men were waiting for him. Shenlong waited for an attack. But it didn't come. In addition, he noticed that his men hadn't even been detained. Then one of the twelve stepped forward.

Shenlong recognized him.

"Hello, Haitao."

Shenlong sneered at hearing his birth name being uttered in public.

"Fan. It's been a long time." He looked over the other men. "I can see you're still one of the Empire's dogs."

"Says the stray."

Fan had been Shenlong's team leader when he had served as a Falcon Commando. Shenlong believed in only what he could control. He had lost faith in his birth country's leadership long ago.

Shenlong snarled. "Why are you here?"

"We are a gift from Minister Zhao. We are to report to you…for now."

"For now?" Shenlong asked, hesitant to accept such a *gift*.

Fan stepped closer. No weapons were in sight, but Shenlong knew the Falcon Commandos didn't go anywhere unarmed.

"Yes, for now," Fan replied. "If I deem it necessary to the mission's success, I will take command."

Shenlong took that as a threat. "What does David Cho have to say about this?"

Fan smiled slyly. "This was Cho's idea. He cut a deal with Zhao."

Shenlong hated being out of the loop, but there was nothing he could do. He was currently outnumbered four-to-one, and if he was being truthful, he needed the support.

"Fine. Let me bring you up to speed."

30

Forbidden Valley, Tibet

The terrain became fully snow covered five miles ago, and they were an untold amount of feet higher in elevation. The transition had slowed the intrepid adventurers down significantly. By Jack's calculation, they had lost an hour, bringing their total hike time to seven and a half hours. Each step was as important as the last. Kalsang moved steadily forward but at a leisurely pace.

"We are here."

Jack and May joined Kalsang at a wide shelf of rock. So far, they had maneuvered over tight, death-defying footpaths. This was the first piece of land, in hours, that the three of them could stand on side by side.

Jack's hands found his knees. He took the time to catch his breath. A stone path was barely visible, but it continued into the trees. But neither the Sherpa nor the former MSS agent was paying the pathway any attention. Jack picked up his head and craned his neck back.

"Are you shitting me?"

Five hundred feet above his head was the Triratna Monastery. It had, somehow, been built directly into the side of the mountain—Purgatory Mountain. But Jack didn't know where the line of recognition between valley and mountain started or ended, so he let it go. The monastery resembled more of a fortress than a place of worship. As Jack stared at the wondrous marvel of architecture, he realized something. The four-story-tall outside wall had been constructed as a cap of sorts. If Jack had to wager, gun to his head, he would've put his money on it being a retrofitted cave.

How the hell did they get the stones up there?

And there, carved into the bottom, left-hand wall face, was the same three-ringed symbol May had photographed in Lamabagar.

"The Monastery of the Three Jewels," Kalsang announced. "Constructed over a thousand years ago."

Looks like it too, Jack thought, remembering this place had been deserted over a century ago.

Jack's hands found his hips, and he stared. The construction method reminded him of another monastery he had read about on Instagram. "Reminds me of the Sumela Monastery in Turkey. That one is twice as old."

May and Kalsang waited for additional information. But he offered none.

"How do we get in?" Jack asked. "I don't see a path up to it."

Kalsang turned away from them. "Yes, there's a problem with that."

"What problem?" May asked.

"The bottom half of the stairs were broken apart a half a century ago. No one has been able to gain access since without a little free climbing first."

"But people have made it, right?" Jack asked.

Kalsang nodded. "A few."

That was not what Jack wanted to hear. Not only did they have to survive the climb up to the monastery, but they also still needed to find the third marker. Honestly, Jack was surprised they had gotten this far. But this, the final test, as it were, was a doozy.

"Right," Jack said, stretching his lower back, "so, where did the stairs start?"

"Over here." Kalsang led them over to the left-hand side of the cliff.

When they got closer, Jack saw it. A path had once existed, cut directly into the rock itself. That passage was currently filled with man-sized boulders and other debris. Since the mess included rotted trees, he guessed it had been an avalanche that had taken out the entrance.

"Is this area seismically active?" Jack asked, curious.

"I'm not sure, but it's usually safe to assume that all the Himalayas are."

May removed a rugged-looking monocular from her pack, put it to her eye, and followed the path up. "Got it." She dropped the device away from her face and pointed to a section of the rockface halfway between them and the base of the monastery.

"Let me see," Jack said, accepting the device. It was one he knew well.

He peered through the Vortex 10x25 Solo Monocular and found what she had seen after a couple of tries. It was tough to spot, but he could just make out a snaking depression in the side of the cliff face. The stairs cut back and forth across it, once again, showing off the builders' skill.

"Yeah, getting there is going to be rough."

A sniffing and snorting sound spurred them into action. Jack and May quickly went for their pistols. They drew their weapons and aimed them toward the grounds behind them. Kalsang didn't move for his weapon. He froze and waited.

The wind whipped up and rubbed through the trees. With it, the feral noise returned. Jack glanced at May. Together, they relaxed and returned the sidearms to their places beneath their coats. They were, understandably, on edge and jumpy.

"Just the trees," May concluded.

"Yeah," Jack said, "but damn if that didn't sound alive." May agreed with a nod.

"I'm curious," May said, "did we ever come up with what animal drove these people out?"

Jack and Kalsang shook their heads in unison.

"Wonderful," May said.

"Yeah, just peachy," Jack added, facing the blocked staircase.

Each of them had a red ice axe attached to the side of their packs. Jack wasn't all that familiar with their applications but had played enough *Tomb Raider* to get the gist of it. But since Kalsang didn't go for his, neither did Jack. May didn't either.

You know what? Screw it!

Jack removed his pack, unbuckled the ice axe, and looked it over. He had no idea what made a good one good. This particular one had a single word printed on the side, SWITCH. After putting his pack back on, he clipped the toothy tool to his belt via a carabiner clip for easier access. It dangled and bumped his leg, but he didn't mind.

Kalsang looked at him like he was an idiot.

May shrugged and followed Jack's lead.

"Hey," Jack said, "you're the expert out here, not us. And I'm not taking any chances becoming another climber's landmark."

Kalsang commenced the climb without a word. He quickly found solid footholds and scaled the sealed entry, pausing when he reached the top.

"Step where I step," he instructed. "Always keep three points of contact with the mountain."

Jack let go and backed away from the rocks. "Okay, just because I said we weren't experts didn't mean we were newbies either." He reached out and started his ascent. "I'll have you know that I climbed Devils Tower once before."

"How was that?" May asked from behind and below.

Jack looked over his shoulder. "Not as cold."

May smiled and shook her head. Jack was nearly to the top when the breeze picked up again. When it did, so did the animal calls. Neither of them paid the sounds any attention…until they carried on even after the wind died down.

"Um, Jack?"

Jack rolled onto the top and stayed on his stomach. He beckoned her forward. "May, climb!"

May leaped onto the rockface and got her legs beneath her. There was definitely something out here with them. It didn't sound like a wolf or a bear. Jack had no idea what it was. He couldn't do anything expect wave for May to climb faster.

A howling gust came out of nowhere, nearly ripping May away. If she fell, it would only be a ten-foot drop. Not enough to kill her. Jack wasn't worried about the fall. He was more worried about what was hunting them.

They were blinded by a gale. Snow pounded the mountainside and the climbers. Jack closed his eyes, fighting the stinging, icy blast. He opened them just in time to grab May's outstretched hand and pull. Kalsang found her other hand and aided him. They got her halfway up just as something large shot out of the tree line, hiding within the storm. It bolted straight for May and swiped at her, missing her feet by inches. Its claws scraped against stone like nails on a chalkboard. Whatever it was, it didn't stop, continuing into the trees on the other side of the natural ledge. Its rage-fueled roars faded and then cut out altogether.

Jack panicked and yanked May farther than needed. She stumbled back, bringing him with her. They spilled back onto a less-than-uniform section of boulders. One of them jabbed Jack in the back, forcing the air from his lungs. He wheezed for breath.

"What was that?" May asked.

Jack couldn't speak. He only shook his head and coughed.

Kalsang's face was whiter than the snow. "It is them."

"Them?" Jack croaked.

"Yes, them. It is the Lions of Buddha."

May stood and helped Jack to his feet.

"I thought you said they were nothing but a myth," May argued. "You said you didn't believe they were real."

Jack took in a pair of deep inhalations and then settled in. "What did you see, exactly?"

"You didn't see it?" May asked.

"Not really. I was a little preoccupied, you know, making sure you didn't die."

"I didn't see much, but it moved like lightning and was bigger than me. The snow and wind made it hard to get a better look."

"Which means it could've been anything," Jack added. "Tibetan blue bears, right? They live out here?"

Kalsang nodded. "Yes, though rare."

"I don't care about rare. I care about fact." He slid in front of Kalsang's line of sight. "Do you believe that Snow Lions are real and are terrorizing this monastery?"

The way Jack had said it made it sound ridiculous. The Sherpa had proven himself to be a rational person. From what Jack could gather, Kalsang's belief in his people's superstitions was minimal.

Kalsang blew out a long breath. "No, I do not."

"What do you think it was?" May asked.

Jack shook his head. "Let's get to the monastery first."

Kalsang nodded and hopped over a few rough looking areas. Jack and May mimicked him as he instructed. May's heel clipped a small pile of loose rocks, and they took off tumbling like a handful of Skittles on a sidewalk.

They mostly followed the original stairway but had to deviate away from it every so often.

"Ouch," Jack said, spotting the remains of a femur beneath a foursome of boulders, each the size of a car.

May sneered in disgust. It was impossible to tell when the person had been killed, though Jack assumed it had happened during the original landslide. If that was true, then the body would have been from the sixties, and was still here.

They were forty feet beneath the still intact section of staircase. The biggest issue was that there was no way to get it except straight up. At one time, they could tell that the path had turned right before acting as a switchback and darting back left. That section was now impassable.

"Up?" Jack asked.

"Yes, the path is too loose to traverse. Too much risk."

"More risk than scaling a rock wall in this crap?" Jack asked, as he was hit with a chilling gust.

"Much more," Kalsang said.

Jack and May watched the big guy go.

The Sherpa reached as high as he could and found a pocket-sized ledge with his right hand. He gripped it with his fingertips and snagged a second small outcrop. Then he found one with his foot and began his vertical free climb. Typically, people as big as him battled with climbing. Kalsang was beefy and heavy. Even Jack struggled at times. But May was built perfectly for it.

Jack waited for Kalsang to get halfway up before beginning his ascent. Having a guide ahead of him made his climb easier. He took his time and searched for the same hand and footholds Kalsang had used just moments earlier.

Kalsang finished.

Jack was halfway.

May began.

The Sherpa swung his leg up and over a ledge and disappeared from view. But Jack was too busy, sore, and tired to pay attention to where he had gone. Only once did he stop, and when he did, he looked down. May was adhered to the wall and looked comfortable. Jack also spied the area directly behind them.

Nothing was following them.

Something grabbed Jack's wrist and locked on like a vise. He was startled and lost his footing. Jack's left boot slipped and sent a few small pebbles bouncing down the rockface, and right into May. She shouted and looked up, blinking away the dirt and snow that had just found itself in her eyes.

Jack looked down at her. "Sorry!"

He gazed up at the thing that had grabbed him.

Kalsang.

He had gripped his wrist to help, not scare.

"Thanks," Jack said. "I nearly soiled myself."

Kalsang didn't find anything Jack did or said to be funny and quietly went about pulling him over the edge. Jack landed feet first on heavily slanted earth of compacted rock, snow, and tree limbs. More evidence of an avalanche. Both men waited for May. When she was within reach, the two men easily plucked her from the side of the mountain and set her down next to them.

"You okay?" Jack asked, feeling awful.

May wiped the debris-induced tear from her right eye. "Yeah, I'm fine."

Kalsang was already moving again, heading left and up. The staircase wasn't very stairy. Decades of inactivity and a lack of maintenance had ruined the once impressive passageway. There was no way to tell how far down the stairs were buried beneath their feet. Jack just wished there was a guardrail of some kind. His anxiety surged. He really didn't want to be ripped off the mountain and thrown back to Lamabagar.

Lamabagar, Nepal

Four SUVs holding sixteen armed men headed up the road. Yana watched them from her car. She shifted into gear and quickly followed them but stayed far enough back not to be noticed. Wherever they were going, it was deeper to the north, further away from civilization. She spotted them a half mile later speeding across the bridge spanning the Tamakoshi River.

Once they disappeared into the tree line, she traversed the bridge. Yana tried Jack's phone again, but to no avail.

"Shit," she muttered, tossing her phone aside. Soon it would be no use to her as well. The low valleys and high mountains caused a natural dead zone. "The same for Shenlong too." That calmed Yana a little. No one would be calling for help.

She kept her speed moderate, wanting to sneak up on them without being seen or heard. The crunch of her car's tires on the packed dirt road would be easy to hear in the silent forested areas. The only noise out here was from the rushing river and the gusting winds.

The road ended up ahead. Yana didn't push it any further. She pulled off and waited and watched but saw no movement. She had only been a couple of minutes behind them.

After another sixty seconds of nothing, she lifted her foot and rolled forward until she was within shouting distance of the four parked SUVs. No one jumped out to challenge her being there.

They were already gone.

She threw her car into park, grabbed her phone, and leaped out, drawing her pistol. Even without service, the device's camera could still be of use. The rest of her gear was in her trunk. Yana stayed low and edged up to the closest SUV, careful not to touch it. She listened and heard nothing except the nearby waterway. That's what concerned her the most. The river would conceal her footsteps, but it would also conceal that of Shenlong and the newly arrived Falcon Commandos.

One by one, Yana cleared the SUVs. When she was certain there was no one around, she rushed back to her car and popped the trunk. Yana changed, not wasting any more time. There was enough snow on the ground up ahead for her to wear her white and gray winter gear again.

Outfitted exactly as she had been in Langtang, the Blood Dragon entered the trees and didn't look back.

31

Triratna Monastery
Forbidden Valley, Tibet

Matching the height of a fifty-story high-rise, Jack, May, and Kalsang finally made it to the Triratna Monastery. Oddly enough, they found the entrance on the second floor. The wooden doors were simple and looked incredibly heavy. They'd be perfect to keep the oncoming chill out, as well as any unwelcome visitors.

And they were ajar.

"That's convenient," May said, hurrying toward them.

"And creepy," Jack added. "We're about to break every rule in the horror movie survival handbook."

He didn't elaborate, and without stopping, followed May inside. Kalsang was right behind them. They all wanted to get out of the storm, even at the cost of running headlong into a Freddy or Jason-type.

"Give me a hand, will ya?" Jack asked, grabbing the open door.

Kalsang obliged and helped him pull it shut. The wind cut off some but was still being funneled in by the busted-out southern windows. Jack discovered a thick wooden post on the back of one of the doors and slid it sideways and into place, much like the stalls in a public bathroom. The lock was old, but serviceable. It should hold.

For now.

Jack removed his gloves and breathed on his fingers. Now out of the bitter cold, he could already feel the warmth returning. He fumbled with his flashlight before clicking it on and showing it around the room, not that it was all that dark inside. They were in a great hall, and it had been beautiful once. A hundred years, and zero upkeep had ruined the place. That, and Jack could see that the place had been ransacked and robbed of anything valuable.

The last of the monks, perhaps?

It could've also been someone else altogether. Kalsang did say that a few people had been here in the not-too-distant past. Not all of them lived to tell about it, however. Jack was willing to bet that they'd find more than a few bodies in their search for the third, and final, marker.

"We have a problem," May said, stepping away. "This place is a lot bigger than the others."

"Yeah, I was thinking the same thing," Jack said, scratching his head. "I say we start from the bottom and work our way up. The last two locks were in the basement, why would this one be any different?"

No one argued.

The inner walls were covered with worn frescoes of Buddhas and strange beasts. It was an odd mix of artwork to Jack. The creatures didn't look at all like the Snow Lions from beneath the Emerald Lotus. They did possess fur, but they more closely resembled bears than large cats. The paintings had faded long ago and weren't as vibrant as they would've been during the monastery's heyday, making identifying the animals that much harder.

"Are these typical of a Buddhist monastery?" May asked, holding her light over one of the beasts.

Kalsang silently shook his head.

Jack didn't think so, either.

The largest of the Buddhas had been vandalized, smeared with a grimy, brown liquid that had dried many years prior. Unfortunately, Jack was pretty sure he knew what the substance was.

Blood. Something awful had happened here.

This was more than just Dhonu Thapa neglecting his duties as Keeper of the Sacred Path to Shangri-La. And it was impossible to put a timeline together. Had he been here before, during, or after this place had been abandoned? Plus, for all Jack knew, the smear could be nothing more than animal blood.

No, Jack thought, *vandalism denotes intelligence. A bear or wolf wouldn't purposely deface a painting of a Buddha.*

Jack needed to consider all options. He pictured a blood-soaked bear, fresh off a kill, rubbing its fur against the wall as it passed by. The open front door would've invited anything in that was attempting to avoid the elements, wild animals included. That could've absolutely happened. If it were the case, Jack figured they'd be seeing more of the same style of defacement during their search.

The elephant in the room was Grandpa Thapa's Snow Lions, the ones from his journal. The story that had been told was that the lions terrorized the monks that lived here and drove them out. There were too many things wrong with that. First off, the Lions of Buddha were supposed to be protectors, not menaces. Also, in order for them to be responsible, they needed to exist.

Jack wasn't ready to admit that.

"This is the last stop, right?" May asked, reconfirming what they already knew.

"Based on my grandfather's journal, yes," Kalsang replied. "There should only be three markers."

May stopped to look at a mural. "Which means it'll more than likely be the hardest one to find."

Jack had also considered that. This place was a mountain stronghold for a reason.

Hmmm.

"What if this place was built around the third marker with the purpose of hiding it?" Jack asked, thinking aloud. "What if the builders of this place found something in the mountain and decided to hide it away from prying eyes? I mean, look around you, does this look like any Tibetan monastery you've ever seen?"

Neither May nor Kalsang said a word. They were just as awed and confused by this place as Jack was.

They turned left and headed down the first hallway they found, essentially moving deeper into the mountain itself. Every twenty feet, there was a vertical cutout, a doorway. But no doors were present. It appeared as if they hadn't survived the abandonment like their stronger brothers out front. Jack played his light inside and found what appeared to be somebody's bedroom.

A flat, rotted mattress sat on the floor up against the rear wall. The walls were also decorated with paintings, but Jack didn't pay them too much attention. He verified that the space was empty.

May copied Jack, but on the right side of the hall. Kalsang stayed in the center and kept the group moving forward.

Jack stopped, hearing something.

He turned and aimed his light back the way they had come. The wind outside had picked up again, recreating the thunderous roaring from before. Jack couldn't tell if it was the wind this time or if their attacker had returned. He held his ground and slid his right hand into his coat, resting his palm atop his pistol.

Jack counted to ten.

Nothing came at them.

Satisfied they were still alone, he retreated his hand and let out the air he had been holding. The monastery was creeping the hell out of him, making him jumpy. His skin crawled. Haunted houses had done the same thing to him as a kid.

"Ugh," May said, standing in a doorway up ahead.

Jack arrived and was allowed access to the room as his partners stepped aside.

"Oh, damn."

The center of the room was packed with the dead. Jack counted at least ten bodies. All of them were of the very dead variety. They'd been here for some time based on the stage of decomposition. His light swept the room and he found something interesting, considering the massacre that had taken place.

"No blood."

"What do you call that?" May asked, illuminating the floor.

"I meant that there isn't any on the walls or ceiling. These men weren't killed here. They were placed here afterward."

"By what?" May asked.

"Or whom," Kalsang added from outside the doorway.

Jack shrugged. "Our friend outside, perhaps?"

"What is that?" Kalsang asked, concentrating his light on one of the corpse's heads.

He wore a hat. The emblem was caked in dirt and dried blood, making it difficult to identify. Jack crept forward to get a better look. When he was within four feet of the burial mound, he stopped and knelt. The cap was sideways and pinned between two other corpses. Jack turned his head to match its direction. He squinted and recognized the insignia, pulling the information from the deepest parts of his knowledge of the Second World War.

The hat's logo featured a star with a dot at its center. There were also a pair of eagle wings present.

"The United States Army Air Forces."

"The 'Army Air Forces?'" May asked.

Jack nodded. "They routinely flew back and forth over the Himalayas between China and India during World War II. The AAF operated out of China to help resupply their efforts against Imperial Japan." He chuckled. "Anyone else find it kinda funny that the U.S., China, and Russia—well, the Soviet Union—were buddies back then?"

Nobody laughed.

"And their presence here?" May asked.

"Quite a few planes went down over the Himalayas during the war. Can you imagine flying a plane from that era around here? No thanks. My guess is that they went down, and they discovered this place and hunkered down—"

"Until they were slaughtered," May finished.

"Yup."

"What's that?" Kalsang asked, directing his light at another body's shoulders.

It was a patch and a ranking. "And there you go," Jack said. "Chinese Air Force." He stood. "These guys have been here for eighty years."

Jack spotted something that he had to have. "Anyone have a knife?"

Kalsang snapped one open and handed it to Jack, grip first. Jack carefully used the blade to obtain a pair of dog tags from one of the Americans. When it was exposed enough to grab, Jack handed the knife back to Kalsang and snapped the chain off with a quick flick of his wrist.

Jack stood and smiled wide, much to the horror of both May and the Sherpa.

"What?" Jack said. "This is history." May opened her mouth to argue, but Jack cut her off. "I'm going to call Eddy and give her the soldier's ID number so she can notify the next of kin. These men's families will finally have closure."

"And the tags?" Kalsang asked, holding his knife as if it were covered in acid.

"Oh, I'm keeping these for myself."

He pocketed them and exited the room before they could say another word.

May wasn't having any of it. "Jack, you can't—"

"Shhh!" Jack hissed, holding up his hand. He tapped his left ear and looked left, back towards the front doors.

They weren't alone. The heavy inhalations of a scenting animal could be heard around the corner, just out of sight. None of them bothered to check if there was another way in, nor did they check to see if they had locked something inside with them.

"Bear," Jack whispered. He knew them well.

Footfalls followed, as did grunts. A second set of garbled growls responded to the first.

Check that, 'bears.' Plural.

A third one joined the party.

Jack motioned for them to follow him. He placed his extended forefinger to his lips, not caring that it was the one that had just touched a corpse's necklace. There were more pressing issues to deal with. May drew her gun but earned a shake of the head from Jack. Shooting a bear, the size of a Grizzly, with a nine-millimeter bullet was going to do nothing except piss it off more.

We're in their territory.

They had waltzed into a four-story bear den, uninvited. And the owners were home.

Jack backpedaled further down the hall, beckoning May and Kalsang to follow. They did, moving like molasses. Jack doubted they'd get away undetected. At this rate, they just needed to get further away before making a break for it. The stone floors should prove difficult for the bears to keep up. Jack could've really used a "You Are Here" map in the worst way.

The storm outside paused long enough to allow a stream of sunlight in. The angle of the rays was such that it partially backlit the hunter. The bear was already on its hind paws, which confused Jack. Bears hunted on all fours. They only stood to intimidate their foe or to reach for something that was high up.

Then, the grunts and growls started up again.

"What the hell?" Jack mouthed.

May heard it too and was equally as perplexed. She silently asked, "Are they talking?"

Jack couldn't make out the words if that's what they were. Either way, the beasts seemed to be conversing with one another in a way that Jack had never heard of before. This wasn't Yogi and Booboo. Bears were smart, but they didn't hold conversations with one another.

Unless they 'aren't' bears.

The sniffing rose to a fever pitch. Jack pointed at the room across the hall, and they practically dove into it just as an enormous figure crossed in front of the light. Jack was last to enter and was the only one who saw *it*. He leaned out and tried to spot it again, but it was gone.

Jack backed away from the doorway, desperately trying to make heads and tails about what he had just witnessed. Whatever called this place home, they weren't bears, that was for damn sure! Jack was happy to see that the room was like the first one, and completely devoid of anything, including the dead.

His shaking hands found his knees and he breathed hard. Kalsang crept back over to the doorway, knelt, and kept watch. May decided to wear a path in the floor in front of Jack, pacing back and forth. The search for the third marker had just become more interesting.

"One more time," Jack said, getting the Sherpa's attention, "tell me about the Lions of Buddha."

32

"Why?" Kalsang stood and joined Jack. "What did you see?"

Jack knelt in the center of the room. "You won't believe me."

"Try us," May snorted, stepping up next to him.

"It walked like a man but looked like a bear—what I could see, anyway. Fur covered its thickly built body." Jack looked up at May. "You heard the grunts, right?" She nodded. "That was speech."

"We don't know that," May said. She sounded like she was trying to convince herself that was the case.

Kalsang sighed. "What do you want to know?"

"Everything," Jack said, burning holes into the man.

The Sherpa nodded. "The Snow Lions symbolize strength, so if they were real, I'd imagine they'd be big and powerful."

"Check," Jack said.

"They also represent protection, that of the physical Buddha. And they are thought to only exist in the high mountains as they are seen as the 'king of beasts' and would tower over other animals of the lower realms."

"Anything else?" Jack asked.

"Yes," Kalsang replied, "when you grow up in the very same mountains, you learn a thing or two, though I still don't believe they are Snow Lions."

"What do you think they are, if they aren't bears or wolves? Give me something crazy."

"Well, when I was a boy, I once heard an elder at my village describe them as being similar to a *migoi*."

"Migoi?" Jack asked. "I know that word."

"You do?" May asked.

Jack eyed her. "Yeah, but I'm not sure from where." He returned his attention to the Sherpa. "What does it mean?"

Kalsang looked uncomfortable with what he was about to say.

"What's wrong?" Jack asked. He removed his ski cap and tossed his hair with his free hand.

"You won't believe me."

Jack grinned. He used May's line from earlier. "Try us."

"Okay, well..." Kalsang blew out a long, calming breath, "in Tibetan, migoi means 'wild man.'"

Jack's eyes opened wide, and he stood and stepped away from his companions. His hands found his head and he gripped his hair. Everything came rushing in all at once. If he wasn't where he was and had seen what he had seen, he'd have thought the idea of a 'wild man' being in their midst was crazy.

"What's wrong, Jack?" May asked, worry creeping into her voice. "What are you two talking about?"

Jack faced her with a serious gaze. "Well, you see, in some Himalayan cultures—and I can't believe I'm saying this—but a 'wild man' is also commonly referred to as a Yeti." He sighed. "I think we're being hunted by

Yetis."

May smiled, but Jack and Kalsang didn't join in on the joke. "Wait, you're both being serious?" She exhaled out a short laugh. "I don't believe it."

"Me either," Jack said, "yet, here we are. You don't have to believe me, but I know what I saw."

"You didn't see much of anything," she countered. "It was dark, and you're tired. They could be anything."

He closed his eyes and turned his head up to the ceiling. "I am, and boy, I hope you're right."

May's hand found his shoulder. He opened his eyes and met hers. "Yes, let's hope I am."

"We need to find the third marker, either way," Kalsang said.

"Yeah, I know." Jack removed the key from his coat pocket and looked it over.

"Can I see it?" May asked.

Jack handed it to her and inched toward the door. Kalsang was right. It didn't matter what was in here with them. They needed to get moving again. He peeked down the hall exposing only the left half of his face. The large common area of the second floor was empty, and the weather outside was calm. Jack leaned away from the hall and turned to his friends.

"Okay, coast is clear. Let's go."

Jack stepped out, keeping his steps slow and deliberate. He turned left and aimed for the rear of the long hallway, where the outside light was. He ignited his flashlight and could just barely see their destination. The hall dead-ended at a staircase. One side descended, and the other ascended.

Jack didn't dare speak. The plan had been to start at the bottom and work their way up. He trusted that May and Kalsang remembered. They passed by more rooms until the area opened up into a second common area. It was circular and featured an open ceiling, much like the Dancing Buddha had. Jack edged beneath the opening and saw that it reached to the fourth-floor ceiling. If there had been railings before, they were gone now. The third and fourth floors looked like precipitous ledges to him from down here.

Thin, mattress-like pads sat in a circle below the open ceiling. Like the bed back in the first room, these were also ruined and rotted. Jack guessed this was where monks could sit as a group and talk about their monkly duties.

Talk about bringing your work home with you! Jack thought, failing to cheer himself up.

They were halfway across the central common area when Jack heard growling. He spun and aimed his light behind them but saw nothing. May and Kalsang had turned along with him, but they weren't looking where all their lights had flocked. Their necks were craned back, peering straight up. Jack swallowed his fear, lifted his head and his light, and found the source of the noise.

And as soon as the flashlight's beam touched the creature, it roared and leaped from the fourth-story balcony. If it were a man, the thirty-plus-foot drop would've broken his legs. But this was no man!

Jack grabbed May and Kalsang and pulled them toward the staircases, screaming, "Run!"

He peeked behind him and watched the beast land like Iron Man. Its superhero pose was both extraordinary and terrifying. Its white and gray fur was perfectly suited for the mountainous landscape, and it was thick and matted down, making it difficult to figure out what the hell it was, Yeti or not. That, and Jack couldn't hold his light steady because of fear and the running.

May and Kalsang pulled ahead of Jack and disappeared into the stairwell. The clambering of their steps pushed him onward. He bolted down the set on the left, moving as fast as he could without falling.

Jack quickly realized something.

He was alone.

May and Kalsang had gone up to the third floor instead of following the plan. Then again, they might have been the smarter ones. They'd have twice as many places to hide and twice as many opportunities to find an exit. Jack only had the one floor to navigate, and typically, basements didn't have outside access.

He was alone and, quite possibly, trapped.

Jack kept going, hitting the landing at full speed. He rounded it to the left and made it halfway down the second set of stairs before leaping to the floor and rolling upon impact. He got back to his feet and discovered that the first level—the basement level—wasn't at all like the second floor.

It's a tomb!

He hurried forward. The ceiling wasn't as finished here. Halfway across the expansive room, it turned rough and craggy. In his light's candela, he saw that large chunks of rock had come free at some point in the past and had smashed the tomb's belongings to bits.

Similar sarcophaguses to the Langtang chief dotted the floor, as did something infinitely eerier. Jack power-walked down the central pathway, unable to meet the stare of the fully exposed, seated mummies on either side of him. He had heard of such practices of Buddhist self-mummification, Sokushinbutsu. One of the more notable displays of the practice was in Taiwan. That particular corpse was later given sunglasses by his caretakers to hide his decomposed eye sockets.

These guys had no such sunglasses. If Jack was creeped out before, now he was at an all-new level. Heavy footsteps signified that the creature had decided to pursue him instead of May and Kalsang. From what he could tell, there had been only one.

May!

Jack checked his pockets. She still had the key. Even if Jack could find the third marker, he wouldn't be able to unlock it without her. He looked back and then scurried behind a beautifully ornate sarcophagus.

"Okay," he whispered, "hide and seek it is."

Luckily for Jack, the tomb was so dank that he couldn't take a breath without smelling the dead and dust. His scent should be easily masked as he moved about.

The basement level was a giant circle roughly two hundred feet across. If Jack could sneak around the beast, he could make it back to the stairs and meet up with May and Kalsang on the floors above. But he also needed to search for the third marker. Somewhere around here was a lock that required their key.

This wasn't the recon Jack had expected to do. He was normally fine with doing two things at once, but not when one of them was trying not to die at the hands of a myth. But Jack wasn't some rookie. At the end of the day, his life was more important than the mission, mostly because if he went too far and died, the mission was toast. He peeked around the corner of the sarcophagus.

His pursuer was in the same place, unmoving. The beast had all the time in the world.

Shit.

Jack rolled back into cover and gritted his teeth. Time was of the essence. Shenlong's force was bound to show up, and they needed to be long gone by then.

Tibet

Yana had kept the rearmost man in sight for most of the hike. They'd been at it for a few hours already. Only once had she thought she had been spotted. But when the commando turned, a deer jumped out and sprinted away.

The Russian's camo was doing its job. She kept to the snow-covered areas along the route and only moved when the soldiers were out of sight. Once she caught up with them, she'd hide and wait for them to vanish again. The cat-and-mouse game was tiresome, but necessary.

The terrain was such that Yana could've shouldered her RSASS and taken out three or four of the commandos. That wasn't enough, though. They were China's best, and if she left even one of them standing while also being within shouting distance, she'd die.

The trees thickened to the left, further up the mountain. She grinned and slid away, changing tactics. Yana would follow them, but she'd do so from a higher elevation.

She planted her left foot down and froze when a twig broke beneath it. The stick had been concealed under the topmost layer of snow. As a result, the line of men stopped. Yana dropped to the ground like a marionette with its strings cut, landing with her shoulder buried in the snow and her ass in the air. She didn't dare adjust herself. One of the soldiers called out in Chinese, but luckily, none of them ordered the other to go have a look.

She had dodged a bullet.

Yana knew she'd be forced to dodge actual bullets next time if she did something like that again. Not that it was her fault. There was no way of knowing a twig was buried there.

"All clear!" a voice shouted. "Move out!"

Yana took the unplanned respite to catch her breath. She turned her head to the left and eyed the landscape, plotting her course up the mountain.

33

Triratna Monastery
Forbidden Valley, Tibet

Jack inched right, away from the central walkway lined with the mummified monks. The rest of the room was crammed with stone sarcophaguses. Some must've dated back hundreds of years, maybe even back to the monastery's construction a millennium ago. He would've given anything to stop and observe the tomb, but he was too busy playing the most frightening game of hide and seek ever. He had also overrated the beast's patience. After only a few minutes, it shifted into hunt mode.

Each time Jack slid behind new cover, he'd stop and listen. The beast's footsteps were light in respect to its prodigious size. But in an environment as noiseless as the basement tomb, they gave away its position as much as a white light under NODs. Jack kept his movements silent by staying on all fours and going sloth slow. He planned to "foot hand crawl" in a long arc back toward the stairs.

He slid in behind another sarcophagus and scuttled to the other side. He leaned out to check on the creature, but it wasn't there. It had disappeared into thin air.

Or, better yet, it's wise to my game and joined in on the fun.

Jack bit his lower lip and thought about his next move. He was almost halfway back to the stairs and could pop up, gun drawn, and try to shoot his way out. There was even a possibility of his shots pinning the beast down long enough for him to get away.

Maybe. He sighed and got real. *Probably not.*

Jack leaned out and deliberately searched for the beast. It had gone up and disappeared on him. A low, guttural growl made Jack freeze. It wasn't the sound that had spooked him. It was the sound's proximity to him.

"You're above me, aren't you?" Jack asked, slowly looking up.

A massive shadow loomed directly over him. The migoi was squatted down, resembling a Yeti-sized gargoyle perched atop Notre-Dame. Jack's hand shook as he brought up his light. If he was going to die, he was at least going to look into the eyes of his killer.

It somehow understood what Jack was attempting. It snarled, stopping his hand.

"Okay, fine, no light."

Why hasn't it killed me yet?

Jack didn't argue the fact that his heart was still pumping. He kept the light on, tried his luck, and backed away from his would-be killer. He slowly stood as he moved.

"You're big, aren'tcha?" Jack nervously laughed. "Don't suppose you know Harry Henderson, do ya?"

The *Harry and the Hendersons*-inspired joke did nothing to ease the tension of the situation. Jack was known to use humor at inappropriate times to deal with stress. This was no different.

He glanced over his shoulder and steered around a coffin while also angling himself back toward the stairs. The creature dismounted and followed him. Jack kept talking too.

"I would advise against eating me. I had a slight sniffle four days ago, and I think I'm still contagious." He faked a cough. "I don't think there's a hospital around here, so don't get sick!"

It growled again.

"Or, you know, you do you, and YOLO…or whatever the kids are saying these days. But seriously, I'm overripe, covered in bruises." He motioned to his body. "You don't want any of this. Also, I smell like a past-its-prime gas station egg salad sandwich—definitely not on the menu at Downtown Flavortown."

It sneered.

"Oh, so you don't know Guy Fieri. Well, let me tell you—"

The beast roared, sending Jack running for his life. He zigged around sarcophaguses, even vaulting over the lower ones. The migoi was in hot pursuit and would've sliced Jack to ribbons if it hadn't been for his chaotic directional changes. If he looked as strange as he felt, Jack Reilly must've been the spitting image of Jack Sparrow right about now. Johnny Depp's *pirate run* had become iconic.

For good measure, Jack shouted, "Where's the rum!"

Jack's attacker landed with a boom to his left, swiping at his head. Jack ducked and darted right, now moving further away from the exit. He tried to correct his course but was unable to when the beast roared and gave chase. It landed to the right of him and raked its claws across his right shoulder. The cuts were shallow and stung like hell. Jack's cozy, wool-lined coat now sported an air vent.

He tried to zag left but couldn't. The creature had successfully corralled him against the south wall. He spun and reached into his coat but was stopped by a head-rattling bellow. Jack's hands went to his ears instead of his pistol.

He felt the floor beneath him shift slightly. He looked down and found himself standing atop a slotted grate. When he realized what it was, it was too late. His added weight caused the ancient drain cover to crumble and fall apart, taking Jack and a nearby sarcophagus for a ride. Jack fell and tumbled, leaving behind the enraged migoi, if that's really what it was. Eventually, he settled onto his belly and slid face first like a penguin. He moved in tandem with that of a decrepit mummy, though the deceased monk slid alongside him on its back, arms crossed, stiff as a board. The steeply descending conduit was angled south from what he could tell. He pictured their entry point.

It had been to the west.

"Oh, shit!" he screamed, grabbing at his waist.

Just as he was regurgitated from Purgatory Mountain and into the open air, Jack slammed the tip of his ice axe into the rocks on the edge of the drain's exit. He had somehow hooked the climbing tool's aggressively serrated head on a jagged rock formation. The sudden stoppage nearly ripped the pick from his hand. His body went horizontal before getting slung back into the cliff face.

When he hit, he snagged the same section of stone with his free hand. He squeezed with all his might and immediately kicked for purchase with his booted toes.

He caught a finite ledge with his right foot and another with his left and stood in place five hundred feet above the valley below. Jack did his best opossum joey impression and hung on for dear life. He shook with nervous energy and the cold and looked over his shoulder. He couldn't help but laugh, hooting into the air as if he'd won an award for being the luckiest man alive.

The monk wasn't so fortunate. The Mummy Missile sailed out into the Himalayan sky like an ancient biological weapon, disappearing into the low-lying fog beneath Jack's feet.

May followed Kalsang up the stairs as fast as her tired legs could carry her. They hit the landing between floors and hooked left, immediately climbing the next half up to the third floor. May stumbled but didn't lose her footing. It caused her to look down at what she had tripped over, and instead of identifying the object, she noticed something else far more important.

Jack wasn't with them.

She was about to reverse course and take up the search for him but was pulled along by Kalsang. May fought against his grip but lost in the end. The Sherpa led her right, and they continued down a corridor. He darted left and changed course one more time before ducking into a random room. The two explorers sucked in heavy breaths with their hands on their knees.

"What about Jack?" May asked, keeping her voice low.

"Couldn't risk it," Kalsang replied. "We will reconnect later."

"But—"

Kalsang held up his hand and stopped her rebuttal. "The creatures."

May understood. If they had turned around on the steps, they would've more than likely been slaughtered. Running was the only option and the only way for them to stay alive long enough to find Jack. They would need to trust that the former soldier could keep himself on this side of the soil for a little bit longer.

"Where—" May started, but she stopped once again.

Kalsang's raised hand didn't upset her. The look on his face did. He closed his hand until only his forefinger was left. It went to his mouth. It went to his right ear next.

May followed his instructions and stopped to listen.

She heard it.

More sniffing. One of the beasts was near, and it was searching for them.

"We need to keep moving," May whispered.

Kalsang nodded and leaned out into the hallway. He looked both ways twice and then edged out. May was right behind him. She was slightly lost but was pretty sure she could find her way back to the staircase if forced to.

Like now.

If they could circle around and keep the creature behind them, they would be able to do just that. She hoped Kalsang was thinking the same thing. But after a few direction changes, May got lost. Still, they kept moving. Staying put would only get them killed. The beast was tracking them by scent. Everything here smelled musty, dank, and filthy.

Everything except the three humans.

They heard a guttural sound emanate from directly behind them, and Kalsang yanked May into a large circular chamber. They backed into it without taking in its contents first.

May spun and wished she hadn't done so.

The room was full of bones. At its center was a mound similar to the one they had seen downstairs but ten times larger. This seemed to be the creatures' primary feeding station, and they had waltzed right into it. But unlike the mound downstairs, this one seemed to be mostly made of animal remains.

Mostly.

May did see a handful of human skulls intermixed with the other species. The multitude of antlers present suggested the remains mostly belonged to deer. The hunter neared, sending its prey scurrying around to the other side of the bone pile.

May got an idea. She snagged Kalsang's coat sleeve and pulled him in close. Together, they sidestepped and kept whatever was stalking them on the other side of the pile. She hoped that its stench would mask their scent. They edged right, stepping light. Luckily, there was a walkway encircling the bone pile. If the path had been filled with debris, there would've been no way for them to do this.

She looked down and spotted evidence of the floor having been swept clean. The walkway was purposely being kept clear. The things were intelligent, not geniuses, but smart enough.

But they still have animalistic hunting traits.

They were nearly back to the front entrance. Their plan had worked so far. May peeked over her shoulder and saw that the doorway was only ten feet behind them. She elbowed Kalsang. He nodded, noticing the doorway too. They quickly, but quietly, turned and hurried out of the room.

They headed back the way they had come, but this time, they followed a worn pattern on the floor. They had missed it earlier. It looked like the creatures habitually traveled along the same path every time they came here. All they had to do was follow it in reverse. They spotted the same staircase they had used earlier in no time, but it was currently occupied.

One of the massive beasts was standing atop the steps but was happily facing the opposite direction. May and Kalsang entered one of the rooms off the main corridor and caught their breath. There was nothing they could do but wait. Guns were also an option, but the report would give away their position and also destroy their hearing.

So, they'd wait.

May hoped Jack was doing better than them.

34

The first thing Jack did before he moved out was secure his ice axe's wrist lanyard. In the event he dropped the lifesaving climbing tool, he wouldn't lose it down the rockface. Jack ascended high enough to see that the drainage tunnel was no longer passable. It, like the tomb's floor, had collapsed in on itself.

The mummy's ornate sarcophagus had become a giant cog in the Tibetan blockage. Jack felt bad about the destruction, but the weakened foundation had saved his life. He needed to somehow make it back up to the monastery and find May and Kalsang before the migoi did. Jack was too busy keeping himself from joining his mummy friend below to analyze what he had seen regarding the beast.

First, climb.

Jack couldn't go straight up because of the drainage exit. The cliff formed an overhang further up too. So, he shimmied left toward the gated entrance—a gate that was bound to still be locked.

Because of me. He shook his head. *One thing at a time.*

He reached left and found a solid handhold, following along with his other appendages. Jack drove the pick into the cliff, feeling it dig in and catch. He hugged the mountain, relaxed, and breathed. Jack moved sideways for another fifty feet before starting his ascension. Now, there was a clear climb straight up.

"Yeah, no problem."

Jack was a skilled mountaineer but had never navigated an ascent quite like this. Uneven cutouts merged with flat surfaces. Fortunately, the cliff wasn't all that icy. He decided to play it safe and treat it as if it was. Double and triple-checking his footing and hand placements were paramount. The methodical slowness wore him down immensely. But it was worth it. Jack was making great progress.

There was no tempo. This wasn't long-distance running. Jack didn't get lost in the trail's rhythmic steps and scenic landscape. He was breathing hard, grunting, and groaning while scraping his frozen face as he made his way up the rockface.

Mother Nature tried her damnedest to peel him off her back several times. But Jack fought and stayed put like an annoying tick.

His left hand slipped, but his axe hand held. Jack pulled himself back into the wall and cringed when he inadvertently thrust his nether regions into a spike of stone.

"Oof!" he wheezed. "Coulda done without that."

The next leg of his climb went without incident. He aimed for the solid outcrop to his right and was thrilled to see that it jutted over a foot from the rockface. He stepped onto it gently, testing its strength. It held him. Jack released his death grip on the mountain and leaned into it with his arms dangling down by his sides.

The break was a Godsend. Jack craned his neck back and saw that he was nearly there. He only had twenty-five feet to go.

Well, no time like the present.

Jack kept the ledge beneath him and climbed, much to the angst of his body. His muscles ached, as did his lungs. The deep inhalations of cold air stung. He would've been in a heap of trouble if the air had been thinner. Thankfully, he'd spent the last few years of his life working in Yellowstone National Park, where the average elevation was roughly 8,000 feet above sea level.

The end was in sight, but just out of reach. He removed the pick from the rock and pushed himself higher, driving it into the ledge above. The added pressure of him forcing his weight up caused the stone beneath his feet to crumble. In a last-ditch effort, he pulled himself up with his axe and found something to grab onto with his left hand.

He dangled for a moment, unsure of what the next move was. Jack was too tired to simply pull himself up. He tried to dig his toes into something—anything—but couldn't find a suitable crevasse. So, he squeezed tightly with his left hand, did the crazy thing, and popped his axe free. The motion swung him to the left a little. He held on and waited for his body to return to the right. When it did, he used that little bit of momentum to his advantage and pulled himself skyward, popping himself up a couple more inches. At his swing's peak, he drove his ice axe back into the earth.

Now, he was high enough to crawl just using his arms. The rocky surface gave him plenty of choices, though not all of them were sturdy enough to use.

But he did make it.

Jack got a knee up and rolled himself up and onto his back. Exhausted, he lay there, uncaring if there was anything nearby about to eat him. If there was, he was too spent to fight back.

"Get...up...Jack," he said between breaths.

May and Kalsang needed him.

Begrudgingly, Jack rolled onto his belly and undertook the arduous task of standing. He pushed himself up on his knees, then stood, stumbling away on rubbery legs. Jack headed straight for the gate, and as he had suspected, it was still locked from the inside. His decision to bolt the door was coming back to haunt him.

"Ease up, Jack. You didn't know."

He didn't either. How could he? The decision to cover their asses had been a good one. There was no way of knowing that the monastery would be occupied. Regardless, Jack needed to find a way in.

The trees behind him shook.

Jack was exposed here. He looked left, then up. There was no access from the outside except through the doors.

His shoulders fell. *That's not true.*

Jack turned toward the open air. He thought back to the busted windows lining the exposed southern face of the monastery.

Maybe I can get in that way?

The trees rustled again. This time they were accompanied by a growl.

He hurried over to the edge. "Window it is."

Jack couldn't control the urge, and he looked down. He could just see the ground through a gap in the fog. He swallowed down his anxiety and turned his attention to the outside wall of the monastery. It jutted out farther than where he stood, making it difficult to formulate a proper plan of attack. The monastery's western side, the one staring blankly back at Jack, sported a series of horizontal running ledges, each three feet apart from the other.

He hurried forward and estimated that they were six inches wide, max.

Yikes.

The wind swirled. The monastery's location in the back of the valley was causing all kinds of mayhem with the weather. The cold air swooping down from above was duking it out with the warmer air rising from the valley floor.

But Jack didn't have a choice.

He grumbled incoherently and followed the west wall out as far as it could take him. Jack assessed his footing and edged out over nothing. For good measure, he reached his ice axe up over his head and hooked in on one of the ledges. Technically, he was using three points of contact. He gripped the ledge in front of his face with his free hand and said a quick prayer.

Jack shuffled sideways, sliding his body along the stone-cut wall like a slug. He rotated his attention up and down, from his ice axe to his feet. Each time he moved one, he made damn sure they were secure before moving the other. His left hand wasn't doing much of anything except giving Jack a little peace of mind.

He had made it to the southwest corner but now he had a problem. Jack wasn't exactly sure how to go about slinking around to the south face. He released his pick's hold on the above ledge and wrapped his arm around the corner, scraping the wall vigorously with the sharp head. On his fourth attempt, he caught something solid.

"Okay, so, right foot next?" Jack was guessing here.

He slid his foot forward, grinding it along. His toes were first to leave the ledge. Once his heel was about to follow, he stopped and pivoted it ninety degrees to the left. In doing so, he leaned far enough right to clear his knee. The wind pushed and pulled at his clothes and nipped his face. He closed his right eye against the onslaught but kept moving.

So far, so good.

Jack slid the ice axe further right to give himself more room to maneuver. He was halfway there, split down the middle on the southwest corner. Jack could just make out the first window twenty feet away. He was confident that he would make it as long as Mother Nature didn't have a tick up her butt.

He put more weight on the pick and quickly slipped his left foot closer. Next was his left hand. He followed with his right foot and then with his right hand. He was three-quarters of the way around to the southern façade. This was going to be the hardest part so far.

Hmmm. Foot or hand?

The mountain decided for him.

A gust of wind pulled him away from the wall. Jack panicked and released his left hand. He snagged the ledge again, but this time, on the south face. The wind changed directions and forcibly shoved him back into the monastery wall with a clunk of his forehead.

"Ouch," he said, wincing against the knock.

Cliffhanger, eat your heart out.

The wind died down, and Jack wriggled his left foot around too.

Jack's entire body was where he needed it to be. But Jack was also nowhere he wanted to be. The wind shoving him back against the monastery gave Jack an idea though. He moved when it died down, then hung on when it reversed course and attempted to yank him off. When it blew back in, Jack moved again.

His strategy allowed him to speed up a little. Jack only had to time the weather a few more times before his ice axe hovered over nothing. He released the handle and left it to fall, allowing the wrist lanyard to do its job. The climbing tool fell away, but not forever. Jack reached inside the window and gripped the inside wall with his fingertips. He let the wind do its thing one more time before scrambling right and throwing himself into the window.

But he didn't make it.

"Oh, shit!"

His poor footing hampered his best efforts, and he fell into the window frame and not over it. He landed on his armpits, crashing down atop the bottom edge of the window. He kicked at nothing, finding no purchase. Jack's toes scraped across the wall, doing little else than scuffing his already destroyed footwear.

He rolled his shoulder forward and inched his right arm further into the opening. Jack did the same thing with his left shoulder and arm. He was effectively rocking back and forth, army crawling into the window. Once he made it to chest level, the going got quicker. Jack snaked forward a few more inches, falling head-first back into the Triratna Monastery.

He landed hard on his right shoulder and flipped ass over teakettle onto his back.

Jack stared wide-eyed at the ceiling, gasping for air, waiting for the adrenaline high to subside.

"Never again." He huffed a breath. "Never, ever again."

35

A commotion picked up in the hallway featuring the room with the bodies from World War II. Jack climbed to his feet and slipped his hand free of the wrist lanyard. He reattached the ice axe to his belt as he shuffled forward, feeling his ribs and shoulder protest the action. The climb through the window had done a number on him.

Jack reached into his coat and drew his pistol. He knew it wouldn't do much against whatever was hunting them. Still, he needed to try. Maybe the firearm's report and the sting of the nine-millimeter rounds would, at the very least, spook it.

Jack hurried forward until he came to within six feet of the hall. He kept to the left of it, staying out of sight of whatever was about to greet him. Jack raised the gun and softened his steps, rolling them from heel to toe. He didn't stop. He launched himself out into the hall and was bulldozed by a mammoth being.

The sudden collision tossed the weapon from Jack's hand. He and his attacker landed hard, with Jack taking most of the impact. He gasped for air but wasn't swiftly killed.

"Jack, oh God!"

May slid into view and held his face in her hands while he desperately tried to refill his lungs. Kalsang climbed to his feet, looking mortified by what he'd done. Jack wrapped his hand around May's and squeezed, then he released it and patted the top of it. He raised himself onto his elbows and looked up at the Sherpa.

"Wrestling scholarship, huh?" Kalsang shrugged and reached out a hand. Jack took it and was hauled to his feet. "Probably shoulda gone with football instead." He looked at May. "Find anything?"

She shook her head. "You?"

Jack shrugged. "Oh, you know, the usual. Lots of bodies."

May and Kalsang stared at him. He gave them a quick rundown of everything that had happened after they had gotten separated. May then gave Jack the play-by-play of the jaunt that she and Kalsang had just had on the third floor.

"Everything about this place is off," Kalsang said, looking around.

Jack nodded. "Yeah, tell me about it."

A pair of roars reverberated from somewhere in the hallway.

May moved for the front door, but Jack stopped her.

"No!" He grabbed her arm. "Not that way!"

"But—"

"Trust me."

Kalsang glanced over his shoulder. "It's not much better in here, either."

The grumbled discourse neared.

"There." Jack pointed east and steered May and Kalsang past the hallway. "Hurry."

Jack fell behind but kept moving at a steady pace. A dead sprint was out of the question. Hopefully, they could sneak down another hallway before they were detected.

More odd frescoes lined these walls. The ceiling was dotted with them too. Like before, they featured monks and the creatures that happened to be chasing them now. Jack knew the paintings were, at the youngest, a hundred years old. He'd love to know when the first frescoes featuring the beasts had been created. And how long had the monks lived among these beings and when did they discover their existence?

There was something important being hidden from them.

"In here!" May whispered, darting into a doorway on their left. She stayed just inside the opening and kept an eye on the way they had come.

The room was high-ceilinged and domed. The paintings here were more "traditional" than the ones in the common area. Four thick, hand-cut columns supported the weight of the crushing stone above their heads. A platform, similar to the one beneath the Emerald Lotus Monastery, was built up against the rear wall, though this one wasn't stepped.

A prayer temple. Jack didn't know what else to call it.

"Hide!" May sprinted deeper into the room.

Jack wanted to ask, "Where?" but never got the chance. Her actions gave him the answer that he needed. She picked the rear-right pillar and disappeared behind it. Kalsang chose the rear-left pillar, having to turn his larger frame sideways to do so. Jack hurried over to the front-left pillar and slid behind it just as a set of heavy footsteps settled outside the doorway. Jack hoped the unforgiving stone walls was veiling their movements.

I guess we're about to find out.

The footsteps' owner entered the room. Jack listened intently, picturing the migoi's movements in his mind's eye. Animalistic inhalations followed. It was checking for scents. A strong gust poured into the prayer temple, hopefully concealing the aroma of the terrified, unclean humans. Then again, the creature's own scent must've been ripe enough to choke a great white.

"Go away," Jack mouthed, willing it to happen.

He looked diagonally across the space and spotted May pressed up against her pillar, back first. Jack found himself breathing through his mouth to get him through the ordeal. The cold air had been playing with his sinuses since he had left civilization behind.

The beast waited an excruciatingly long time before moving again, and when it did, it left.

Jack heard it turn and walk away. Then, he caught its footfalls fade as it continued its search elsewhere.

May carefully leaned around her pillar and gave Jack a thumbs up. Kalsang must've seen her signal as well. He stepped out of cover in time with Jack. They met at the center of the temple but didn't utter a word.

Jack's heart rate slowed, and he tipped his head toward the doorway. May and Kalsang nodded, and they headed towards it. Jack leaned out and checked both ways. He didn't see the beast anywhere. That unnerved him. A thing that big shouldn't have been able to move that quickly and silently.

Jack put a finger to his lips and stepped out without a sound. May followed his example perfectly. Kalsang did his best, moving quietly enough for a big guy in big boots. Jack turned left. He didn't take off at a mad dash. He kept his pace even and steady. Their predicament required silence over speed.

Jack spotted an anomaly in the eastern wall. It was still a way off, but if he had to guess, the oddity resembled another door. So far, the only intact door he'd seen had been at the western entrance. Could this be another way outside?

They made it twenty more feet before Jack felt that something was off. The hairs on his neck stood, and a shiver snaked its way up his spine. He felt like he was being watched.

He stopped and peered over his shoulder. May and Kalsang made it a little farther east before realizing he wasn't with them. But when they did, they were in just as much a state of shock as he was.

Three of the massive creatures stood hunched, watching them from the other side of the second level. For the moment, the two trios were at a stalemate. Neither provoked the other to move. Jack took the pause in the action to take them all in and study them, the low light made identifying them difficult. Now the distance and snapping breeze was making it hard for him to concentrate, but he tried.

Their fur was thick and covered every square inch of their humanoid frames. Jack was pretty sure he spotted nasty-looking claws protruding from their hands or paws, depending on what they truly were. Their faces were the grandest enigma. There was nothing to see. Only more heavy fur.

"Jack," May whispered.

"Yeah?"

"We need to keep moving."

Tell that to them.

"Okay. Back away slowly. Do not run."

Jack took a deep breath and took the first step away. It had been the only move, and of course, it had also been the wrong move. The three migois took off after them. Jack spun and was happy to see May and Kalsang were already moving too.

"Head for the door!" Jack shouted.

"Where do you think we're going?" May retorted, glancing behind her as she ran.

Kalsang didn't look back. He was solely focused on the exit, it seemed. In spectacular fashion, Kalsang pulled ahead of them and lined himself up with the exit. Jack couldn't believe it. Kalsang was planning on ramming it. Jack banked left a hair to see around him and saw what he must've seen. This door also had a sliding lock, and it was currently disengaged. But that didn't mean it would open so easily.

Eh, to hell with it.

Stopping and opening it would take too much time. Jack put on more speed, much to the dismay of his body. His quads burned. But Jack was an expert in dealing with pain. It was an unfortunate, yet valuable trait that he possessed.

Jack made it to the door in time with Kalsang, rolled his right shoulder forward, and leaned his head away. The two well-built men blasted straight through the barrier, turning it to kindling. The unexpected success threw Jack off, and he didn't spot his landing well enough. Just outside the door was an iced-over landing of stone. He and Kalsang hit it, slipped, and went down in a tangle of limbs.

The steps came next.

They shouted and slid down them. The slide turned into a tumble halfway down, and they instinctively grabbed one another. Jack had no idea what had become of May. He spotted solid ground. Then, they hit it. He and Kalsang spun through the slight snow cover, stopping ten yards later.

The two men climbed to their feet and took in the grounds. They had entered an empty, snow-dusted courtyard. A stone wall sat between them and the cliff to the south. The northern section was lined with iron benches and dense trees. Straight to the east was a passage that led deeper into the forest.

"Jack!" May called out nearly at the bottom of the steps.

He rushed to her and stumbled when something landed behind him with a concussive boom. May slowed and stared straight past Jack and Kalsang in shock. Jack instantly knew what had shaken her. One of the beasts had leaped the distance of the steps between the monastery and the courtyard, boxing them in.

The two other creatures emerged from the monastery but chose to use the stairs. And why not? It's not like their prey was going anywhere.

May joined Jack and Kalsang.

Another of the things emerged from the northern tree line. And another clambered over the low wall to the south. The humans were outnumbered and about to become lunch.

"We came so close," May said, turning and backing into Jack. Kalsang also turned. The three of them stood together and waited. "The third marker is lost forever."

"As is the Valley of Petals," Kalsang added.

But Jack was too deep in thought to hear the Sherpa.

The third marker. He had hoped to discover the lock in the tomb, which may very well still be down there.

The lock. Jack rubbed the outside of his coat pocket, feeling the outline of the golden key inside.

Keys unlocked things, but this key, in particular, had also been called a travel permit or a passport. Permits and passports allowed people access to places, same as a key, though typically on a grander scale, like when you traveled across borders.

Is that what it is? His eyes lit up, and he dug into his pocket.

"I get it now."

"Get what?" May asked.

He glanced over at her. "There is no lock here."

"How do you know that?"

"What are you two talking about?" Kalsang asked, pressing deeper into them as the beasts closed in. All five of them had formed a ring of death.

"The key. It's all about the key."

Jack drew it from his pocket, but before he could reveal it, one of the creatures shouted a warning, and he was torn away from his party and hurled into the air like the Mummy Missile. Jack landed twenty feet to the north and slid to a stop.

The world went black.

Jack didn't feel his skull hit the iron bench.

Tibet

Her vantage point of the men was much better now. Yana was two hundred feet above them, moving within the snowy trees of the western elevation. Shenlong and the Falcon Commandos had stuck closely to the river so far. Once they were further out, another mile or two, Yana would begin her assault.

Or, she thought, *I could leave them and go warn May and Jack.*

She slid behind a large pine tree and waited a moment before moving again. Warning May and Jack of the incoming attack would be a great service, but so would bettering the odds. Maybe if she was lucky, she would take out Shenlong. But if she killed him, then what? Was she really going to leave and let the Chinese military march onward?

She placed her hand on her chest, fingering the three reloaded magazines in her rig.

No, she decided.

Yana had enough ammunition to send all of these bastards to hell.

36

Triratna Monastery
Forbidden Valley, Tibet

"No!" May shouted, rushing to Jack's side.

Kalsang was surprised when the beasts closest to her allowed her through without conflict. Why?

He stayed put, realizing something. None of their attackers were paying them any attention now. Their odd behavior was how May had evaded capture, and death, so easily. Kalsang could probably run as well, but his curiosity got the best of him. He wanted to understand what caused the hunt to end so suddenly.

The Sherpa slowly turned in a circle and then looked down at his feet. The gold key was buried halfway in the snow.

And the creatures' attention was glued to it.

Kalsang replayed the last words Jack had said. *It's all about the key.*

"It's a travel permit," Kalsang mumbled, recalling what his grandfather had called it.

Kalsang's eyes darted up to the largest of the monsters. Slowly, he bent down and picked up the key. He held it in front of him and turned, showing it to each of the five hunters.

"Where did you get that?"

Kalsang took a step back. The creature had spoken, and did so in a language only known to the Thapas.

"You speak my family's language?" Kalsang asked.

"You're a Thapa?"

Kalsang nodded. "My great-great-grandfather was Dhonu Thapa, Keeper of the Sacred Path."

The largest one raised its arms. As it did, Kalsang noticed something. Though massive and thick, its paws weren't paws. They were hands. Its claws weren't natural, either. They were connected to a wooden pole held within the mammoth individual's clenched hands, resembling a set of taloned brass knuckles.

It took some effort, but eventually, the hunter pulled the fur on its head. Kalsang discovered that it wasn't naturally grown. It was nothing more than a thick hood.

The creature beneath it…was a man.

Sort of.

The individual resembled a Neanderthal more than anything else. His forehead was wide and flat, and his lower jaw jutted out at extreme angles. He also had longer canines than your average human being. He was carnal and evolved. His hair was black and flowed beneath his garb. Whether on purpose or by sheer coincidence, he looked exactly like a migoi—a Yeti. Kalsang deduced that the hunters had inspired the stories surrounding the Yetis. They might have even been the inspiration behind the mythos of the Lions of Buddha.

Kalsang was stunned by the revelation. An ancient tribe of brutish mountain people could clarify so many of the region's legends.

Kalsang blinked out of his shock. "How do you know my family's language?"

The furred hunter stepped closer. "Because it was never yours."

"What?"

"It belongs to many others, not just the Keepers of the Sacred Path." He put his huge hand on his chest. "Including us, the Protectors of the Sacred Path."

"You?"

Kalsang spun as each of the tribesmen removed their hoods.

Two of them were women.

"Yes, us. For generations, we have been tasked with guarding the path against the unworthy. That," he pointed at the key, "is the only thing keeping you alive."

"So, if we had shown this to you earlier—"

The hunter looked at Jack and May. "We wouldn't have hurt your friend." He bowed slightly. "For that, we are sorry."

The four other tribesmen also bowed in apology.

As far as the language was concerned, Kalsang understood why these people would've spoken it. They had dealt directly with the Keepers, so sharing a common language would have benefitted both parties. Kalsang doubted it was the tribe's natural tongue, though. He had heard the tribesmen communicate earlier through grunts and growls.

"Where did the language originate?" Kalsang asked.

The large man crossed his arms. "Where do you think?"

Kalsang held up the key. "The Valley of Petals."

The other man nodded.

"Are there others like you—other tribes?"

"Yes."

"And the Thapas?"

"They bridged the gap between worlds. Being a Keeper was great honor. When Dhonu Thapa disappeared—"

"So too did the Sacred Path."

"Correct."

Kalsang leaned around one of the women and saw May tending to Jack. She wasn't screaming desperately for help, so Jack must be okay.

"So, no one has entered the valley in the last century?"

"He's awake!" May shouted.

The tribesman tilted his head. "Come, let us help your friend. You will have your answers soon enough."

He recalled being carried back inside the monastery by something huge and furry, and he didn't think it had been Kalsang without his shirt on.

He had drifted in and out of consciousness. When he finally came to, he felt that he'd been propped up on something firm but comfortable, and he was lying on his back in front of a small fire and was wrapped in furs. The covering stunk, but it was warm and inviting.

Jack covertly checked his surroundings. He listened closely and smelled the air. Sensing nothing usual, he slowly peeked open his eyes. His head was killing him. The fire had been built next to one of the open windows for ventilation. But the breeze was also helping spread the warmth created by the flames.

"Hey."

He turned his head slightly to the right and found May sitting next to him with a similar fur over her shoulders. She was unharmed. In fact, she looked at peace.

"I guess I missed something."

May smiled. "You could say that. Kalsang!" she called. "He's awake."

But it wasn't the Sherpa who appeared above Jack. His head tilted straight up, and his eyes opened wide. A massive, fanged man with a thick skull leaned in over Jack and gazed into his very soul. Jack's eyes snapped over to May.

"Yeah," she said, gazing up at the newcomer, "you definitely missed something."

Kalsang came into view from around the giant's back and took a seat on Jack's left. The *guy* joined them and knelt on the opposite side of the fire.

Jack sat up a little to stare into the eyes of all three of his compatriots.

"Is someone going to fill me in?"

Kalsang nodded. "Yes, I'm just trying to decide where I should begin."

"How about right after I blacked out?"

Kalsang told Jack everything.

"So," Jack pointed at the gargantuan, "he's the chief of an ancient tribe of Neanderthal-Human hybrids who are tasked with protecting the Sacred Path."

"Yes," Kalsang said, "although Anthropology isn't a strength of mine."

May cleared her throat. "And don't forget the part of them being the inspiration behind both the local Yeti lore and the Snow Lions from Buddhist mythology."

"How could I forget that?" Jack asked, trying to be jovial about the amazing discovery. But he couldn't. He was in pretty piss-poor shape.

Other disclosures shocked him too. The reason the monastery was here was a result of a covert deal that had been struck by a sect of monks and the tribe. The monks ensured the tribe that the Sacred Path would be maintained and that they'd regularly donate resources to the tribe that called the mountain home. When Dhonu Thapa gave up his duty as Keeper, the tribe revolted and drove out the monks.

Also, chief's name was Dorje.

"Dorje means 'indestructible,'" Kalsang explained.

"I bet," Jack said, eyeing the beast.

"Drilha!" Dorje said, calling out behind him.

Another member of the tribe joined them. Given this one's slighter build and more feminine features, Jack guessed that this one was a woman.

"This is Dorje's wife, Drilha."

May took over. "Her name means, 'Goddess of Scent.' She's their best hunter."

Kalsang said something and pointed at Jack and said his name twice.

"Jack. Jack."

Dorje tried it out, pronouncing it like "Jahk." Then, his wife said it.

Drilha handed her husband a bowl and nodded. Dorje passed it around to

Kalsang.

"He says to drink this. It will assist you with your recovery."

Jack accepted the bowl. Inside was a steaming, semi-milky substance. He looked up at the woman. She cupped her hands and lifted them to her face, motioning for him to drink.

He did as he was instructed and sipped the liquid. It had a touch of sweetness but also had an underlying funkiness that Jack couldn't quite place. It tasted a little spoiled.

"What is this stuff?"

Kalsang relayed the question to Dorje.

The wife, Drilha, rambled off something, getting an odd reaction from the Sherpa. Kalsang repeated a single word, getting a nod of confirmation from both Protectors.

"What's wrong?" Jack asked.

May looked just as curious. She leaned in closer.

Kalsang shifted. "Nothing is wrong, but…"

"But what?" May asked.

"Yes, but what?" Jack added.

Kalsang couldn't hide his discomfort. "The, uh, drink, it, you see… In Tibetan lore, it is said that two of their most important heroes were raised by Snow Lions."

"Okay, but—"

Kalsang cut off Jack. "Please, Jack. I'm getting there."

Drilha repeated something and once more mimicked a sipping motion. Jack looked down at the drink and then at the smiling wife. She'd probably break him in half like a twig if he hurt her feelings.

He lifted the bowl. *Happy wife, happy life.*

Jack backed off on his questions and drank. The liquid was less pungent now.

"Like all mammals," Kalsang said, "the hero children were raised on—"

"Oh, no," May said, covering her mouth and shaking her head.

"What?" Jack asked.

He took another sip. The drink was clearing his mind like only the best cups of coffee could do. He gazed into the bowl, impressed.

"The milk of a Snow Lioness is believed to contain special nutrients to heal the body and mind and calm the soul."

Jack held up the bowl. "Snow Lioness milk? But—" His eyes went from the bowl to Kalsang to May.

May bit her lip, closed her eyes, and nodded.

Drilha smiled, looking very proud.

Jack sniffed the bowl's contents. "Breast milk…" He looked at Drilha. "This is your breast milk?"

Kalsang translated.

The wife emphatically nodded.

Jack stuck a fingertip in the bowl and lifted it out. The liquid slowly ran off it. He glanced at May. She was visibly disgusted. Drilha grunted and, once more, made the drinking motion with her cupped hands.

Her husband quietly sat across the low fire. His eyes had never left Jack.

Oh, what the hell! When in Rome…

Jack tipped the bowl back and polished off the boob juice much to the disbelief of his friends. A little ran down his chin, but he didn't notice. The euphoria he was feeling was like a high he had never experienced. He was on a cloud. He felt no pain in his back or limbs, and his headache vanished.

He lowered the bowl and opened his eyes. May and Kalsang were staring at him. Dorje and Drilha were too, but not in the same way. They were proud. May and Kalsang were appalled.

Jack held up the bowl, feeling great. "Got any more?"

37

The pelt that Jack had been using as a blanket belonged to Dorje, the tribal chief. And it wasn't actually a blanket. It was his Yeti cloak. Dorje morphed right back into the same beast Jack had seen earlier when he put the cloak back on and his hood raised up. May had been wearing Drilha's.

There were three other tribesmen present. Jack had not been properly introduced to them. Honestly, it didn't matter. They were more standoffish anyway, keeping watch on the immediate area.

Bodyguards for the chief and his bride?

Jack, May, and Kalsang were now being led back outside through the door that they had destroyed. Their owners didn't seem to be bothered by it, thank goodness. But they did have ill-feelings towards the monks.

Jack glanced at Kalsang. All of this was because of Dhonu Thapa's dishonor. He had left his sacred duties and caused a rift between the two worlds. Jack was beginning to think that the old man's decision to leave hadn't been so virtuous. But there was still a lot they didn't know.

This time, Jack took the steps the way they were intended to be used. He descended them carefully and returned to the courtyard. He looked around and saw a skid mark in the snow that had been left by his body. Thinking back, Jack still couldn't believe that he was up and moving about so well after taking such a nasty hit.

The "Snow Lioness Milk" had done as advertised.

It was jampacked with nutrients, and God knew what else. Jack knew that BIOfinity Genetics would love to get their hands all over this. He pictured these tribeswomen being captured and then handled like barnyard animals. He wouldn't put it past Cho or Zhao to do such a thing.

"Where are they taking us?" May asked.

"Huh?" Jack asked.

"You okay?"

He nodded. "Yeah, I'm good. Just have a lot on my mind, you know?"

"Yep."

Kalsang stepped up next to Jack to answer May's question. "They are taking us to the gateway between our worlds."

"Now there's a gateway?" Jack asked, tired of all the stops.

"Not literally. I think it's more of a metaphor than a physical gateway."

"Oh, right. Just like the Maya, though their pathways, the sacred cenotes, were entrances to the underworld, *Xibalba*, the 'place of fear.'"

"The 'place of fear?'" Kalsang asked.

Jack nodded. "Yeah. I read up on it a while back. Always intrigued me."

May nudged him with his elbow. "Thinking of looking for it next?"

Jack laughed. "Hell no! I actively try to avoid spots with names like 'place of fear.'"

"You mean like Forbidden Valley?" Kalsang asked.

"And Purgatory Mountain?" May added.

Jack looked back at the both of them. "Oh, you two can go straight to *Xibalba*!"

It felt good to laugh. "Seriously, though, where are we going?" Kalsang asked.

"Into the trees," he said. The Sherpa shrugged.

The lack of explanation was as good as a period at the end of a sentence. They were going to be shown the destination, not told where it was. So, they walked.

Dorje led them beneath a canopy of mostly dried leaves and gnarled branches. The natural cover would conceal them from above. Not that anyone was watching them.

The chief and his wife walked in front of Jack. Both were nearly a foot taller than him. Dorje was thickly built. His wife was somewhat leaner, but still outweighed Jack by a good sixty-plus pounds. Even Kalsang looked small compared to them.

They stayed on this path for over half an hour.

It hooked left, turning into a V-shaped, open-air passage of stone. Dorje didn't stop. He entered the rocky pathway and kept the line moving. No one spoke. They just marched on like good little soldiers. What could they have done different? They were at the mercy of an ancient Himalayan tribe. They felt like a "my way or the highway" kind of bunch.

Jack thought back to the room full of corpses. He tapped Kalsang on the shoulder. "What?"

"Ask them about the bodies we found, the ones from World War Two."

"What, why?"

Jack rolled his eyes. "Humor me." What harm could a question bring?

Kalsang spoke up. The answer he got was short and to the point.

"He says that they arrived without a key and were hunted and killed."

"But they were only trying to get in from the cold."

Kalsang said something.

Dorje grumbled a response.

"They didn't belong, and we have a duty to uphold." Dorje stopped. His wife stepped aside and allowed him through. "We protect the Sacred Path...from everyone so that we can prevent it from being discovered by the masses."

He stared Jack down before returning to the front of the line. Jack rarely responded to threats well, but this one he'd happily let go. As long as they didn't piss the tribe off, they'd be seen as an ally and not a foe.

Still...

"For what it's worth," Jack said, through Kalsang, "I have no intention of revealing any of this to the masses. We're here to protect it."

Dorje stopped again and looked over his shoulder. As he met Jack's stare, Jack knew Dorje understood his sincerity about protecting everything about the Valley of Petals and the Sacred Path. The chief nodded and started off again.

The falling snow thickened as they traveled further away from the Triratna Monastery. The trek would've been so much worse had there been a breeze. It was cold, but not intolerably cold.

That changed in a matter of seconds.

The protective rock walls disappeared to reveal a flat expanse of nothing. The wind howled, battering the inhospitable landscape.

"Oh, my God," Jack said. "Where are we?"

"It is called Desolation," Kalsang replied.

"Desolation?" Jack stared at the expanse. "Of course, it is."

Kalsang conversed with the chief for a moment while Jack and May huddled together and leaned away from the direction of the wind.

"Dorje says that this is the final test to gain entry into the Valley of Petals. This place symbolizes the boundary between worlds." The tribal leader stepped up to the three travelers. "Everyone who has entered this void without permission has perished."

"By whose hand?" Jack asked.

Dorje held his up. "Either by ours or the mountain's wrath."

They descended an embankment. The wind was beyond abusive and must've been blowing at near tropical storm forces. Jack didn't know much about hurricanes, but if he was a betting man, he'd bet that these winds were close to the strength of a category one storm.

The plain itself wasn't as flat as Jack had originally thought. It rose and fell, much like the barren Sahara Desert. In reality, this was also a barren desert. Jack doubted it had ever received liquid water. One of Jack's favorite factoids was that Antarctica was the driest place on Planet Earth.

The wind died down slightly.

Jack was surprised to find out why.

The five tribesmen walked in a line on the left of May, Kalsang, and himself. They were using their bodies and furs as shields against the onslaught. The effort made the hike much more bearable. Jack was amazed with the efforts of Dorje and his people. They really did take their life's duty seriously. Even after a century of inaction, they performed as they had been taught.

How old are they?

If they weren't fully human, then all bets were off. If a female's body could naturally produce a substance like the milk that had healed Jack, then who knew what else their DNA possessed? They lived long lives, grew to massive sizes, and had the instincts of a primal apex predator. But they could also communicate at a high level.

This tribe was special—more special than modern man in many ways.

Jack, May, and Kalsang were exhausted from the trek even though they had help with the hostile winds. Jack had never done anything like this before. He imagined that he was experiencing something very similar to what the early explorers had felt as they traversed across the earth's poles.

A large, rectangular boulder took shape. It would act as a barricade against the raging storm. The nearer they drew, the more Jack recognized that it wasn't a boulder at all. At one time, it had been a building. His shoulders sagged. Possibly even someone's home.

"They used to live out here?" Jack asked.

Kalsang shrugged and asked Dorje.

"He says, long ago the mountain shook, and fell, burying those living here. It used to be a livable plain with many homes."

"It fell?" May asked, keeping close to Jack.

"That's what he said," Kalsang replied. "Sounds like this region had a major geological event that changed the ecosystem overnight."

Jack shrugged. "Whatever had been keeping the elements at bay came down with an earthquake, opening the door to this?" Jack held his hand up.

"Possibly. This was probably a valley, at one time. If a section was compromised, then sure, it could have altered the conditions."

"And kill dozens—hundreds?" May asked.

Jack nudged her. "Langtang."

"He's right," Kalsang agreed. "Out here, anything can happen, and the results can be catastrophic."

Dorje held up his hand and signaled for everyone to rest.

They arrived at the other side of Desolation relatively unscathed. Besides losing feeling in random parts of his body, Jack had faired fine. May looked a little worse for wear. Annoyingly, Kalsang looked as if he had taken a walk in the park. Like the tribesmen, the Sherpa was built perfectly for this.

Now that they had reached their destination, Jack couldn't help but to compare it to the previous side. The entrance was a freezing expanse with another similar slope they'd have to scale. This slope, however, was scattered in a sea of bones. There were hundreds of bodies. It appeared as if people had perished here over several centuries. And the killers who were responsible happened to be shepherding them across the expanse now.

They climbed the ascension, unable to weave around the remains. In fact, Jack used their rock-hard bones as hand and footholds, making the climb faster and easier. When they reached the pinnacle, they found nothing but an ice-blasted stone facing, and a crudely cut hole in the mountainside. Based on the uneven shape and overall poorly constructed ceiling, Jack weathered a guess that it was a natural formation.

The ancient guardians backed away from the opening.

"They aren't coming with us?" Jack asked.

"No," Kalsang translated, "our place is here. Who will protect this path if we do not?"

Jack held out his hand to the tribal chief. It was engulfed by Dorje's. They shook once. Jack was thrilled that his hand hadn't been accidentally crushed.

"Thank you," Jack said, looking at both husband and wife.

Kalsang whispered, "Say, *Dhan che*, and bow."

Kalsang did just that. "*Dhan che.*" Then, he bowed.

"I'm bowing?" Jack asked.

Kalsang shrugged. "They're royalty, aren't they?" He lightly slapped Jack's shoulder. "Be respectful. He could've killed us, remember."

"Oh, I remember…" Jack stepped forward and bowed. "*Dhan che.*"

May followed their lead. "*Dhan che.*"

"One more thing," Jack said. "There might be people following us. They are very dangerous."

Kalsang relayed the warning, but Dorje didn't seem to be all that worried.

The chief pounded his chest.

"We are not afraid of anything," Kalsang translated. "We have endured many trials over the generations. And we have defeated many enemies."

"Not like this. These guys aren't simple bandits or thieves. What's coming is a wave of death."

Dorje grinned and snorted out a laugh.

"That may be, but we will give these intruders something to fear worse than death. We will give them the full might of the Protectors of the Sacred Path."

As soon as he uttered those words, eleven more tribesmen and women appeared from within the whiteout. Had they been trailing them the entire time? A few were as big as Chief Dorje. Jack had never seen a more intimidating show of brute force in all his life, and he hadn't even witnessed them in action.

That would be something to see.

Drilha bowed and then stepped forward and placed her hand on Jack's shoulder. The gesture was simple, but it spoke volumes. Even though she was built like a savage warrior, she had soft, caring eyes. She stepped back and mumbled something, meeting the gaze of all three of them.

"What did she say?" May asked.

Kalsang turned away from the storm, "She said, 'good luck.'"

They went to turn and leave.

"One more thing!" May said, looking to Kalsang for help.

The Sherpa translated.

"There may be another traveler—a woman—a mighty hunter. Please, grant her safe passage. She's an ally of ours."

No one answered. Dorje and Drilha gave Jack one last look, and then, all sixteen tribespeople turned and disappeared into Desolation.

38

Forbidden Valley, Tibet

The combined force had taken two breaks since entering the woods to the north of Lamabagar. Yana had not. She had used their stoppages to her advantage and had gotten ahead of them. And she'd done so while staying completely unseen.

Yana lay prone at the base of two trees. Their X pattern gave her perfect cover. The only thing visible belonging to her was the barrel of her RSASS as it protruded between the growth's "legs," though its white and gray paint job would conceal it from a distance. As she had done in Langtang, Yana had dug a small trench in the snow to use as additional cover. Only this time, she added in a few fallen branches and dried leaves to break up her shape.

Not that they'll see where the shot came from.

Her plan was to allow the column of men to pass. As they did, she'd attempt to identify Shenlong. When she did, she'd take the shot from behind and then hide for as long as it took. There were too many heavily armed, well-trained men for a frontal assault. The Falcon Commandos weren't a two-bit band of Congolese ruffians. They were the real deal and would surely have several marksmen within their ranks.

All sixteen of the men below wore civilian clothing. There was a variety of weaponry visible. Yana didn't recognize any of the weapons.

"Bastards. You upgraded."

Yana breathed in deep and slowed her pulse to a crawl just as the last man passed through her reticle. She lined the soldier's head up in her scope while also eyeing the man in front of him. If she were quick enough, she'd be able to take out both before the others could react.

The rearmost man leaned and gazed into the water.

She smiled. "Let's play."

When his attention returned to the trek, Yana squeezed the trigger. The RSASS coughed out a round, and Yana snapped the DMR up and a fraction of an inch to the left and squeezed the trigger again. She promptly rolled into her dugout. Yana had definitely killed the first one. The second one *should* have met the same fate, but Yana had moved too quickly to confirm it. She'd have to trust her skills.

Yana seriously doubted one of the two men she'd shot had been Shenlong. With a sniper on the loose, she knew he wouldn't be stupid enough to march at the end of the line. He wouldn't be at the front either. Not that it mattered. After this attack she had made on them they'd be sure to change their order.

And when it was time, Yana would take out two more.

Maybe three.

Fan and Shenlong's combined group had just entered what was dubbed the Forbidden Valley. Backpackers routinely went missing from the area, granting the valley earn such a foreboding title. Not all the missing persons had been found over the years. And those that had were found ravaged and discovered in pieces.

Shenlong was second in line, marching in front of the Falcon Commando squad leader, Fan. The group's point man was Fan's best set of eyes.

"He sees everything," Fan had said.

Seeing isn't everything, Shenlong had thought.

Shenlong had made the decision to not tell Fan that a majority of his team had been decimated in Langtang. If the Falcon Commandos all ended up dead, then they wouldn't be able to take over his mission.

When asked by Fan why Shenlong had such a small team of four, he had responded by telling him, "I believe a smaller force is all that is required out here. That, and patience."

Shenlong knew that his men would follow his lead and continue the ruse. They were paid killers, not soldiers, though, at one point, they had been soldiers, like himself. But like Shenlong, they also enjoyed operating with freedom and didn't want to be ordered around by a "Company Man."

Twin *thwaps* echoed around them, bouncing off the mountains. To the untrained ear, it sounded like a pair of two-by-fours being slapped together twice. Shenlong dove behind a pine tree and stayed put. Looking would result in his death. The mountainous terrain made it impossible to determine what direction the shots had originated without seeing the muzzle flash.

Fan shouted out orders.

"Stay down. Ears open. Eyes up."

Shenlong knew it wouldn't help. They were pinned down with two additional casualties. Since he, Fan, and the point man had been unharmed, Shenlong assumed it had been the last two men in line that had been killed.

Fan's men.

Shenlong grinned. The odds of him becoming a victim had dropped drastically with the Chinese military's arrival. With a little luck, he'd survive the latter portion of their hike through the Forbidden Valley, while also watching more of Fan's men fall.

Desolation

The three intrepid explorers stood just outside the fracture. No one was willing to make the first move. If this was, in fact, the end of their journey, then it meant their destination, the fabled Shangri-La, would be on the other side.

The Valley of Petals. Jack tried to picture it in his mind.

There had been so many interpretations since *Lost Horizon* had been published in 1933. James Hilton's inspiration for the mystical mountain utopia was said to be from several different Himalayan Beyuls. In Tibetan Buddhism, a *Beyul* was a hidden valley often encompassing hundreds of square miles, though Jack doubted *their* Beyul was that large. The valleys were said to be blessed by Padmasambhava, an important figure in the belief system.

Jack couldn't wait any longer. He stepped inside the passage, immediately relishing in the shelter it provided. He clicked on his flashlight and continued into the opening, keeping his steps steady. Just because this was the last leg of their trek, didn't mean there wouldn't be any dangers afoot.

"We are just like the *tertons*," Kalsang said, voice low.

"Tertons?" Jack asked, glancing behind him.

"Yes, they were kind of like ancient treasure hunters. Their discoveries were supposed to be purposefully shown to the tertons at very specific times by the gods. The treasure was said to be things like hidden scrolls concealed under rocks. No one found their prize on their own. They were gifted their treasure when they needed it most."

"Under rocks?" May asked. "Or how about within the rock?"

"The markers?" Jack asked.

May nodded. "Yeah."

Kalsang seemed to agree. He perked up. "It is also said that the treasure could be revealed in stupas and monasteries."

Bingo!

"What about the Sacred Path and the tribe of protectors?" Jack asked.

Kalsang shrugged. "Could all be a part of the reveal mechanism. In this case, the elaborate unveiling of the most sacred Beyul of them all, the Valley of Petals."

Jack didn't know what to make of the whole terton-blessed Beyul thing. This didn't feel like there had been any divine work involved. Was it elaborate? Hell yes. But had it been planned by a holy Buddhist master? No, Jack didn't think so. He wasn't even sure if he had understood half of what Kalsang had explained.

But the parallels were fascinating.

"Do you know what Shangri-La means?" Kalsang asked from the back. No one answered. "If you break down the name, like how we did with Bardo Ri, you see that *ri* is mountain and *la* is pass."

"What about Shang?" May asked.

"Shang means, well, Shang."

Jack glanced over his shoulder. "So, Shangri-La translates to Shang Mountain Pass? That's it?"

"Technically, yes."

Jack looked back at May. "Kinda figured it would be something cooler."

"Who was Shang?" May asked.

"Shang," Kalsang replied, "is in a district north of Tashi Lhunpo."

"Are we anywhere near there right now?" Jack asked.

Kalsang shook his head. "No, not at all."

The route ahead drastically changed. The worn path ended and turned into crudely cut, steep steps moving deeper into the earth. Jack was surprised by their poor condition. They had gotten a ton of foot traffic and were incredibly old. The steps dipped slightly in the center hinting at their age, supporting Jack's hypothesis.

Jack took the steps slow, keeping his light on the next one in front of him. "How many people do you think have used this path?"

"Impossible to say," Kalsang replied. "But I'd say the number is in the thousands. This has been here for a long, long time."

"How long?" May asked.

"My grandfather said the Valley of Petals was founded thousands of years ago by a band of weary travelers."

"More tertons, huh?" Jack asked, half-joking.

"Could be," Kalsang replied. "It's possible they were shown their treasure precisely when they needed it most."

The climb was interesting to say the least. It was apparent that several hands had been at work during its construction. The style and precision of the cuts were drastically different as they descended deeper into the mountain. It spiraled in some places and darted around wildly in others. Some lengths were more focused on the ceiling and walls than others. The only consistency was the condition of the steps themselves.

Periodically, artwork would show up, but it was unrefined and hard to make out.

"You're kidding me."

Jack and May stopped and turned and looked back at Kalsang. He was staring intently at the same petroglyph Jack had spotted. But it was plain to see that the Sherpa had found something profound within it that Jack had missed.

"What is it?" Jack asked from lower down the steps.

"It's a name."

"The artist?" May asked.

Kalsang nodded, eyes wide. "Possibly."

Jack stepped closer, now only inches from May. "Who is it?"

Kalsang faced them. "His name is 'Shang.'"

"Huh," May said, "so that's where the name came from?"

"Hang on, 'Shang?'" Jack asked. "As in the Shang Mountain Pass? You're telling me that this," he motioned to the surrounding stone, "is the real Shangri-La?"

"It's a distinct possibility, yes. This route may have been improperly associated with the lore, and then it took on a life of its own as the years passed by. People that spoke of Shangri-La meant this passage, but it could've easily been misconstrued as the kingdom we seek now."

"Man, that's so lame," Jack said, looking at the floor and shaking his head.

Kalsang shrugged. "Don't look at me. I'm just as confused as you."

The grade leveled off and the passage straightened out. Jack was so turned around. He had no idea which direction they had been traveling. In fact, he had lost his sense of it completely since they had left Desolation. They had originally been going north, so for now, Jack assumed they were still pushing on in that direction.

"Kill your lights for a sec, will ya?" Jack asked, turning his off. In the pitch darkness, he saw something encouraging. "There's light up ahead." But not enough to see by. He reignited his flashlight and started off again, this time, moving faster.

Speck by microscopic speck, the dot of light expanded. Eventually, it became strong enough that they could extinguish their flashlights and stow them. Jack's feet hurt, but the rest of him still felt okay. The hunter's milk's effects were permanent, it seemed. That was until he hurt something again. He doubted the stuff could do anything then.

Up ahead, the ceiling rose and disappeared, merging with the mountain. The walls remained, showing off a high cliff on either side. The path opened up wide enough for the trio to walk side by side. The weather warmed up quite a bit too.

What the hell? They were still in the Himalayas, right?

The mountain pass snaked around a bit, never giving Jack a hint as to what was at the end. His next clue was the sky he saw above his head. A persistent layer of cloud cover allowed in enough light to see by. It gave the pathway a calm morning dawn kind of feel.

The worn footpath narrowed again and rose, reducing the effect the cliffs had on them. A soft, cool breeze swirled around them, beckoning them forward. The overall temperature was significantly warmer, closer to what it had been in Kathmandu. Jack leaned into the incline and pushed himself harder. He raised a hand to shield his eyes from the ever-increasing sunshine. It wasn't overly intense. The slight discomfort he was feeling was from his eyes slowly adjusting. They had been underground for some time.

Then, the grade leveled off and opened. Jack, May, and Kalsang all stepped out onto a ledge that overlooked the most wondrous thing Jack had ever seen.

"The Valley of Petals..." he said, relieved. "We made it."

39

Valley of Petals

The Valley of Petals was the most magnificent thing Jack had ever seen. The entire valley, for as far as the eye could see, was a shade of soft pink, though it was more concentrated at the center. It was an odd sight, for sure.

Monasteries and homes—possibly even businesses—dotted the rising and falling valley floor. Jack could just make out specks of movement within the city, as well as out in the horseshoe of grassy fields surrounding the inner kingdom. Its overall shape was that of a turkey baster. The first half of the secluded sanctuary was a long stretch of intersecting streets. The roads ended at the same point, a large circular city center featuring a massive common area with deep green foliage mixed with soft pink.

A park?

A cool breeze whipped past them. Jack looked up at the cloud cover. It sat atop the entire valley and hid it from view. No spy satellite in orbit would know what was down here. His winter coat felt warm and like overkill here. The depth of the valley, as well as the high mountains, kept out the abusive Himalayan freeze.

"Holy crap!" Jack said, realizing something fantastic. He unzipped his coat, removing it. "This place has its own climate!"

May and Kalsang were too lost in the hidden civilization below to have noticed.

"Every major Asian culture is represented," May said, staring through her Vortex monocular. She lifted a finger and pointed at particular structures. "Chinese, Japanese, Nepali," she stepped forward, her hand darting left then right, "Tibetan, Cambodian, Mongolian… This place has been influenced by so many."

Jack joined her. "Or did this place influence them?"

She looked at him, thinking it through. "Depending on how old this place really is, I guess that's possible."

Jack grinned. "There's only one way to find out."

"Over here," Kalsang said, pointing left. "I found stairs."

May hurried over. Jack gave the lost city one last look from afar. He turned away but stopped when something floated past him. The small object gently landed on the overlooking ledge. He eyed it and then gave the Valley of Petals another glance before bending over and picking it up.

"What is it?" May asked.

Jack held up the pinkish-white flower petal. It was the same color as the city itself.

He held out his hand and faced the city. "Let me see that monocular again."

The sight tool landed in his hand seconds later. He brought it up to his right eye and scanned the streets, seeing so many amazing things that it was difficult to remember what he was looking for. But then, *it* came into view. At the deepest, pinkest point of the city...was a tree. It's what he had mistaken as a park. The tree was still too far away to identify what type of tree it was. Just then, Jack spotted another petal get plucked free by the swirling breeze. He watched it flutter and sail impossibly far away and land on the roof of a small hut.

It clicked. "The Valley of Petals, I get it."

"Get what?" May asked.

"The entire city is covered in these," he removed the monocular from his eye and held up the petal. "It's what's giving everything its color."

"What's the source?" Kalsang asked.

"There's a tree shedding them at the city's center, but I don't know what kind. It's big, though."

"How big?" May asked.

"Well, based on the surrounding structures and what goes for an average floor height in every major metropolitan city, I'd say the tree is at least fifty feet tall, give or take."

"Give or take?"

Jack nodded. "The average floor of a building in the U.S. is roughly eight to ten feet from floor to ceiling. But there's no guarantee these architects used the same base measurement. Plus, I can't see the bottom half of the tree from here. It's being blocked by buildings. Who knows how deep the valley is there? It could have another fifty or sixty feet to offer that I can't see."

Kalsang led them down a ten-foot-wide staircase. It had been meticulously carved right out of the rock in a long, switchbacking fashion. The walls beside them were adorned with intricately produced etched artwork. The entire thing was one massive piece of art depicting an infinite amount of people traveling together. And if Jack had to speculate, their destination had been the Valley of Petals.

"The original tertons," Jack said.

"That was my guess too," Kalsang said. "This is their story."

This portion of the staircase paused at a sizeable landing, then turned and cut back in the other direction. Kalsang and May continued down the next set of steps. Jack hung out on the landing for a moment longer to take another look at the paradisial city. The platform Jack stood on was speckled in petals as was the second half of the staircase.

Even though this place resembled what the Garden of Eden must've looked like, Jack noticed something that didn't belong. This heaven on earth sported a robust defensive wall similar to the Great Wall of China. Either the builders were incredibly paranoid of an attack way out here, or there had been one in the past and this was their way of preventing another from occurring. It made sense. Eventually, people would find this place, whether by accident or on purpose, like Jack, May, and Kalsang.

As they neared the bottom steps, May pointed toward the city. "Jack, look."

He slowed and saw what she had been looking at. A group of people had gathered atop the wall...and they were armed. Even from this distance, he could see the curvature of several recurve bows. More advanced weapons, like modern firearms, weren't present here. That made Shenlong's incoming force all the more dangerous.

These people are screwed if Dorje can't stop them.

May and Kalsang were a dozen steps ahead of Jack and finished the descent before him. She looked back at him in wonder. Kalsang didn't look up at all. He was too transfixed on the ground to do so.

"Look familiar?" May asked, stepping aside.

It did.

"It's the tree."

Artwork identical to the back of the key had been meticulously chiseled into the ground. Jack removed it from his pocket and confirmed as much. Whoever had made the travel permit had also been involved in creating the valley's welcome mat. Jack was confident now that he and Kalsang had been right by naming them the tertons.

Is that what we are?

Kalsang had made mention of it when they had been following Shang's mountain pass. He supposed that they were being shown their "treasure" when they needed it most. Jack wasn't so sure about that. Fate was a cruel mistress. Luck, on the other hand, was something Jack could get behind. They weren't just here to verify the Valley of Petals' existence. Now, they were here to prevent its destruction.

Jack flipped the key over, and the image of the tree took on a whole new meaning. It must be of immense importance to the people here. Jack didn't know why, but he figured they'd find out soon.

They crossed the seal and continued onto a gently arching stone bridge. Beneath it was a quick moving river that, intentional or not, acted as another defensive measure. Jack lost sight of it as it curved around the side of the Himalayan kingdom.

It has a moat! Jack thought, amazed. If the Valley of Petals were to be attacked, the bridge would force the assailants into a bottleneck.

A few smaller tributaries branched off the main waterway and snaked their way into the city, running beneath the wall.

Clean water, a self-sustaining climate, and natural defenses.

"This reminds me of the Meridian Gate," May said. "Wall and all."

"From the Forbidden City?" Jack asked.

"Yes."

Jack shifted his attention from the gate and wall to the structures sitting atop them. They weren't of the classical Chinese architecture, the traditional hip-and-gable design.

"The roofing is all wrong," he said. "This looks more like the spires in Angkor Wat."

May silently agreed with a nod. The Cambodian temple complex of Angkor Wat was famous for the corn-on-the-cob design of the Khmer Empire.

They descended the bridge and slowed their advance as more and more bow-wielding locals appeared overhead. There were forty in all by the time they were within one hundred feet of the tall gate. It was massive, stretching twenty-five feet across and thirty feet high.

Jack couldn't make out any of their faces due to their ornamental masks. They reminded him of the ones the samurai wore back in the days of feudal

Japan. These people's masks similarly covered only the lower half of the archers' faces. Some of them had long flowing hair too. Others sported shaved heads with tattooed skin, as well as everything else in between.

The standoff was surreal. Pink flower petals drifted to and fro, all while Jack, May, and Kalsang were getting a stare down from above. It felt as if they had been transported into a cowboy versus samurai movie mashup. A gentle breeze directed the petals left, then changed course and guided them back to the right.

"Now what?" May asked, keeping her voice barely above a whisper.

"We say hi," Jack said. "Kalsang, you're up."

The Sherpa looked at Jack. "Me?"

Jack nodded, smiling sheepishly. He waved at an armed guard. "Dorje said that your family's language didn't just belong to you, but to a great many, or something—blah, blah, blah. Try using it."

"Makes sense," May said. "The Keepers and Protectors spoke it. I'm pretty sure he said the people here would too."

Kalsang didn't look thrilled to be the one to make first contact, but he, nevertheless, did. The Sherpa cleared his throat and spoke.

"I am Kalsang, and we mean you no harm."

The Sherpa didn't know what else he could say to sway their opinion of them. He had decided to omit his last name. Dhonu had surely tarnished it.

No one replied. He eyed their weapons and decided on a different tactic. Instead of declaring their intentions, he'd tell them about the other inbound party.

"But we are not the only ones coming. There are more men on their way now. They are not friendly. They are quite the opposite." A few of the archers glanced at one another. Two others spoke amongst themselves. "We are here to warn you," he continued. "They are coming for your secrets."

"You led them here?" one man asked.

Kalsang decided to be honest. "It was unavoidable. They would've come regardless of our involvement." That much was true, though there was also a possibility that Shenlong might not have been able to decipher the way without their assistance.

"What's happening?" Jack asked.

Kalsang didn't reply. He stepped forward and raised his voice. "Please, if you want to protect the valley and the people who call this place home, you will allow us entry!"

All was quiet.

Jack looked on edge. Kalsang shrugged. He didn't know what else to say.

"To hell with this," Jack grumbled. He stepped in front of May and Kalsang and held up the key for all to see.

Kalsang quickly translated. "We have been proven worthy of entrance into the Valley of Petals! We followed the Sacred Path from Langtang to Lamabagar to the Forbidden Valley and were guided across Desolation by Dorje and the Protectors! Let us in, dammit!"

Kalsang replaced the last word with *please*.

The grounds outside the grand gate went silent.

Then, a clunk and a grinding noise filled the air. Jack didn't budge. Kalsang and May stepped up next to him. They were unified—a team. The gate split and opened at its center, and when the *doors* were ten feet apart, they stopped and out poured ten more men. They weren't outfitted with bows, however. The white-clad ground force dual-wielded a pair of gleaming, oversized *khukuri* machetes.

The forward curving weapon was a signature armament of the Gurkhas of Nepal and was usually used to clear brush. But they were also an acceptable means of self-defense. Kalsang owned several. His late father's service khukuri hung on the wall above his quaint fireplace in his home back in Padmaarga.

They spread out in a half-moon. The precision with which they moved was impressive. They faced the newcomers with a collective *hrah!* and rocked forward onto the balls of their feet into a left-handed fighting stance. They all held the forwardmost blade in a backhanded grip. The second khukuri was held closer to their body and in a traditional grip.

No one made a move to attack.

Their mempo masks featured decorative faces. Each face covering was unique too. The only similarity between them was their demonic theme.

An eleventh man marched forward. It was obvious that he was in charge. He held no weapon.

He was missing his left arm at the shoulder, and the iris of his left eye was white, which meant he must be blind in that eye. But whatever he lacked physically, he more than made up for it with his one intense eye. He stared daggers at Kalsang, Jack, and May and then removed his mempo mask. The first thing Kalsang took away from the man was that he was of Indian blood.

His harsh glare locked in on Jack. "Where did you get that?"

Kalsang was shocked.

The man spoke English.

40

Jack was more than a little confused. The militarized force that had greeted them was a lot to absorb. Now, add in the fact that their commander spoke English. In retrospect, it shouldn't have shocked Jack. English was the official language of India, after all. His accent was of the classic "Indian English" the country was often known for. As he spoke, Jack pictured the spectacled Prime Minister of Pankot from the *Temple of Doom*, even though this guy looked nothing like him.

The one-eyed, one-armed man stepped forward. "I will ask you one more time…" He pointed at the key in Jack's hand. "Where did you get that?"

Kalsang took a step away from Jack and May, calling the attention to himself. "From my great-great-grandfather, Dhonu Thapa, Keeper of the Sacred Path."

The baldheaded *local* faced the much larger Sherpa. "You mean *former* Keeper of the Sacred Path. He disgraced himself and his family when he turned his back on his responsibilities."

"And yet," Jack interjected, "he was allowed to live here for over a hundred years. Sounds like a major HR problem."

"And you are?" the commander asked, looking away from Kalsang.

"The name's, Jack, Jack Reilly," he replied, holding out his hand. "I'm with a special unit whose job is to protect places like this."

He sneered at Jack's hand and didn't move to shake it. "Yes, Thapa was given refuge here. However, if I had been in charge back then, I assure you, things would've turned out much differently."

"You would've turned him away?" May asked.

"Absolutely." His gaze never broke away from Jack. "You say you protect places like this, yes?"

Jack nodded. "We do."

"And who says we need your protection?"

Jack looked over his shoulder, up at the valley entrance. "Believe me. You're gonna need it."

The thinner man stepped toward Jack. "Is that a threat?"

Jack shook his head. "Not from me, no. But there are people on their way now who want to harm the people that call this beautiful place home."

The commander grinned. "Let them try."

Jack returned his gaze in spades. "Oh, they will, and a lot of your people will die because of your arrogance. Is that what you want?" The other man opened his mouth to counter Jack's insult. "Dorje and Drilha are going to try and cut them off, which is something I'd love to have floor seats for, but I fear even they won't be able to stop them."

The man snickered. "Nothing gets past the Protectors when they don't want it to. They are, what you say, effective."

"Yeah, so I've heard."

"These people will succeed," May said, her voice laced with worry. "They only care about the money and the mission. They do not care who stands in their way. Old, woman, child… It's all fair game to them."

The cycloptic leader turned away from them but didn't leave. He was thinking over what they had said.

"Please," Jack pleaded, "hear us out. If you don't like what we have to say, we'll leave and never return, and I'll make sure to omit this place's location from my report."

May glanced at Jack. He was being serious.

Jack was happy to see some swordsmen break their matching stares. They weren't as hardened as their boss. May's added warning had been the icing on the cake for a handful of them. Their commander must've seen the worry on their faces. His men must've had families within these walls.

"Fine," he sighed and faced Jack, "you have one night to convince us."

He snapped off two quick words that Jack guessed meant "stand down" because the swordsmen did just that. They stood at attention, spinning their blades over their shoulders and into the sheaths on their backs. It was an extraordinary display of blade control.

The bald man then rambled off something that got Kalsang's attention. The Sherpa looked at Jack and May. "You're not going to like this."

"What's wrong?" May asked.

"He just ordered a 'cleaning.'"

Jack didn't understand. "A cleaning?"

Kalsang nodded. "Yes, a cleaning."

Seconds later, six additional people came hustling out of the gates. They were all women, and they wore cloth masks over their noses and mouths. The sextet also sported steaming pales of water, towels, and short-handled mops. A seventh woman wheeled out a cart overflowing with neatly folded, white robes.

"Aw, crap," Jack said, now knowing what their intentions were. He looked down at his filthy, infectious body. "Dhonu Thapa had no immune system, right?" May nodded. "If you were these people, would you let three strangers in who could be carrying all kinds of nasties on them?"

May's eyes darted from Jack to the cleaning crew.

The one-armed man barked an order. The single word made Jack squirm.

"Strip!"

Jack wasn't the shyest person, but having May here changed everything. He'd been naked in front of plenty of people before, but never under these kind of circumstances. This was the most archaic sanitation room he'd ever seen.

May looked mortified.

So, Jack went first. He tossed his coat aside and removed his shirt. "Hey," he said, locking eyes with May, "look at me. Block them out."

Kalsang was facing away from them and was already working on his belt buckle.

May bit her lip and removed her shoes. Jack might see how someone could view this as wholly unnecessary. But he also saw it from the other side. These people were incredibly vulnerable to illness. If Jack, May, and Kalsang wanted to gain access to the real-life Shangri-La, they needed to play ball.

Jack removed his shoes and socks next. May's coat hit the ground, and she began to turn her head.

"Don't," Jack said, getting her attention back. "On me."

She nodded, untucked her long-sleeve thermal, and pulled it over her head. Jack undid his belt and dropped his pants. Luckily, the ambient temperature was comfortable. If he had been forced to do this a few hundred yards back in the other direction it would've been a bit more difficult.

Now came the hard part.

May was down to her bra and panties, and Jack only had on his boxer briefs.

"Ready?" Jack asked.

May sighed and laughed softly at the ridiculousness of the situation. "I've already gone this far."

Jack took a deep breath and yanked down his underwear as May removed the last of her defenses. Neither one examined the other. They respected one another's forced nudity. This wasn't them alone in a bedroom or on a beach in France. This act was necessary, not one of their own free will.

The cleaning crew came in fast and furious. A smirk formed on Jack's face. May caught it and tilted her head to the side in question.

"What's that for?"

Jack let out a subtle giggle as one of the women tickled his ribs with a towel. "Oh, I'm just visualizing us at the spa, not," he winced, "getting poked and prodded by six women who I don't know while standing butt naked in front of a girl I," May's eyes playfully narrowed, waiting for him to finish, "respect."

She rolled her eyes. "Respect?"

"Give me a break, will ya? I'm sore as hell, and these chicks are finding every last bruise."

May laughed, then cringed. "Ow. Same."

In no time, Jack was rinsed off by a fresh, warm pail of water, then wrapped in a soft white robe. May and Kalsang were too. Their clothes were collected, as were their weapons, and they were put on a separate cart and wheeled away.

"What are you—" Jack started.

"Your possessions will be cleaned and returned to you," the commander said.

Jack nodded. He hoped that meant their pistols too. "Thank you, Mister…"

"I am Veer Burman," he announced, standing tall, "and it is my duty to protect the Valley of Petals."

Veer turned on a heel and headed through the gates. Jack, May, and Kalsang quickly followed him inside. The two men standing in front of the gate's narrow opening stepped aside and allowed all four of them to enter. The other side of the barrier was as stunning as Jack had hoped. Pink petals floated around everywhere, giving a very Japanese cherry blossom kind of feel to the entire city.

Is that what they are?

The structures lining the main road were short and rectangular, reminding Jack of Cambodia, but not Angkor Wat this time. These were reminiscent of the famous jungle temple complex of Ta Prohm. The buildings there had been overtaken by nature decades earlier, giving the place a creepy horror movie vibe.

These roofs weren't that of Khmer architecture, however. They were closer to that of the flatter Chinese hip-and-gable design. The one constant addition to all the structures were the intricately carved Snow Lions. To Jack, they were acting as French gargoyles. In Gothic architecture, the creatures were meant to denote "guardianship" over the building, and it was believed that they protected against malevolent spirits.

It was plain to see that the Snow Lions served the same purpose.

"So," Jack said, clearing his throat, "I have to know, what exactly happened to you with, well, you know?"

Veer glanced at Jack, having to turn his head to do so. "Do you always point out someone's disability to begin a conversation?"

Jack shrugged. "I just got hosed down, and I'm going commando. I'm nervous. Sue me."

Veer rolled his eye. "I was found like this by the Dharmapala."

"The what?" Jack asked.

"The Dharmapala," Veer repeated. "It's what we call Dorje's tribe. It means 'Dharma Protectors' in Tibetan. Dharma can be loosely translated as *merit* or *righteousness*."

"How 'bout *worthiness*?" May asked.

Veer nodded. "Very good. They are the Protectors of the Worthy. Sound familiar? And in Buddhism, the Dharmapala are said to be fearsome beasts with protruding fangs. Terrifying creatures."

"That's them to a T," Jack said, chuckling. "You think that's where the description originated?"

"It wouldn't shock me."

They walked in silence for a moment. Besides the murmurs from onlookers, the only noise you could hear was the slapping of three sets of bare feet.

Veer greeted a group of skeptical residents with a slight bow of his head. "I had just retired and came here to celebrate. My expedition was caught in a storm, and I was severely injured by falling rocks. I was the only survivor out of ten."

"I'm sorry to hear that," May said, voice somber.

He waved away the concern. "That was nearly twenty years ago. There is nothing to be sorry about, not anymore."

"The Dharmapala brought you here?" Jack asked, trying out the name for the first time.

"Yes, Dorje himself picked me up out of the snow, and Drilha nursed me back to health with—"

"Her breast milk?" Veer slowed and then faced Jack. "Yeah, I know all about it."

"What did you think?"

A smirk formed on Jack's face. "Honestly, it wasn't that bad."

"Can we please move on?" May asked, looking ill.

"Yes, of course," Veer replied. "Dorje must have thought I was worthy and brought me here in the middle of the night. There have been others left to die over the years, but not me."

Was that the real reason they helped me? Jack thought. *Or was it simply because we possessed the key?*

Jack pushed the thought aside. "So, you were just another terton being shown his treasure, huh?"

Veer glanced at Jack again. "You know of the tertons?"

Jack waggled his hand. "Eh, sorta. Kalsang is the real expert."

Veer held up his hand, stopping the group. Even the ten swordsmen halted their march behind them. Jack had been so enthralled by Veer's story and the surrounding structures that he had completely forgotten about the armed escort.

"Kalsang Thapa," Veer announced, allowing the Sherpa's last name to hang in the air. "I can tell that you differ from your ancestor."

"What makes you say that?" the Sherpa asked.

Veer slowly paced back and forth while he explained. "Just you being here shows me that you seek knowledge and not recognition."

Jack playfully punched Kalsang in his meaty shoulder. "He's got you pegged perfectly, big guy."

Kalsang didn't respond to Jack in the least. "I could be here for something else."

Veer shook his head. "No, I don't believe that. You don't come across as a man looking to inflate his ego. You're curious—as you should be. The Thapas are incredibly important to this place."

"All I want is answers."

Veer nodded, thinking inwardly. "You'll get them soon enough. Come, we were just about to eat."

They were led into the fourth building on the right. There were already other people dining inside. The large single room reminded Jack of a quick-service eatery at an amusement park. The back wall was lined with people serving others.

"Everything we eat is grown locally," Veer said, leading them over to a table.

He sat on the floor instead of getting in line with the others.

"What about...?" Jack started, starving.

"Patience. Please, sit."

They did. May stayed close to Jack's side. She scooched nearer to him even after she sat down. The simple act earned Jack a smile from the army commander. May didn't see it. Jack made eye contact with Veer and smiled back. The message was clear, not that the local was attempting anything nefarious. It had been nothing more than a harmless observation.

A column of men and women poured out of a second room, one Jack had not seen when he came in. Each person carried a wooden tray with portioned food resting atop it. The meal wouldn't be overly filling, but it was loaded with proteins and would satiate his nagging hunger.

Jack eyed a delicious-looking peach on Veer's tray. His didn't have one. Nor did May or Kalsang's trays.

What gives?

He didn't get to ask.

"So," May said, looking over her food, "what was your treasure?"

Veer sat up. "Well, as I'm sure you can tell, I was in the military in my past life. This place desperately needed my leadership, and I was given the honor of rebuilding its fortifications."

"What branch did you serve in?" Jack asked, picking up a juicy leg of meat.

Pig? Lamb?

He bit into it and nearly passed out from delight.

"Indian Army. I was a colonel."

"So, they're your doing?" Jack asked, looking over his shoulder. He could see all ten swordsmen through the front windows, proudly standing at attention outside the cafeteria.

"No, but I did teach them how to better hone their skills."

"You know," Jack said in between bites, "you aren't as scary as you were outside the gate."

Veer grinned. "Yes, well, sometimes it pays to be able to switch gears from time to time."

Jack laughed. "I once knew a few drill sergeants that could do the same thing."

"Oh, so you also served?"

Jack nodded. "U.S. Special Forces. Retired a few years back. Now, I do this."

Veer leaned forward. "Back there. You said people were coming that wanted to do this place harm. Why? What do they want?"

Jack glanced at his friends. "I thought that was obvious. I mean, this is 'Shangri-La,' right? Once they found out how old Thapa was—"

"Who is *they*?"

Jack looked at May.

She folded her hands atop her lap. "The Chinese Ministry of State Security."

Veer's face fell. "The MSS? That is unfortunate to hear."

"Yeah, tell me about it," Jack said, closing his eyes and rubbing them. "They've been trying to kill us for a few days now. It's why we've been hurrying to get here first—to warn you."

"But you also may have very well led them here," Veer countered.

"True," Jack said, "but I think it's safe to say they would've found this place eventually, with or without our involvement."

"What makes you say that?"

May cleared her throat. "My father heads the MSS." Veer's eyes narrowed, though he didn't speak. "I know him well, and he was prepared to throw everything in the pot. And I mean everything. But I stopped him and offered to lead a covert investigation instead." She sighed. "I had intended to refute Thapa's claims but never got the chance. Then, Jack came to the rescue, and here we are."

Kalsang spoke up next. Jack was surprised to hear him ask the all-important question. "What gives you your long lifespan?"

"First, eat." Veer sat back. "Ponder the possible answers. You will be shown once we are finished."

Jack was shocked. "You're going to show us your big secret, just like that?"

Veer shrugged. "Should I not? It was once customary for us to reveal our 'big secret' to those who proved themselves worthy." He sat forward. "Are you not worthy?"

May held up her hands. "We aren't your enemy, Veer. We just want to help. There's a lot of lives at stake."

"Well, then we should finish quickly, yes?" Veer picked up his peach and a small knife. He cut off a hunk and took a bite, smiling at something Jack didn't know.

41

Forbidden Valley, Tibet

Yana held back and peered through her scope. The valley floor ended at a high cliff. She traced a line up the rockface and saw something amazing. A monastery had been built right into the mountainside. She'd seen similar ones before but never in person. She lowered her focus back to ground level and nearly squeezed the trigger. The reason she hesitated was because the number of men in the Chinese force had changed.

Two are missing.

She removed her face from the scope and panned around, listening intently while moving at a snail's pace. Yana tried her hardest to remain silent. Shenlong had no doubt ordered two men to hang back. Yana was now being hunted.

She grinned.

The Falcon Commandos were dangerous, for sure. But this was Yana's world. She was the assassin, not them. Plus, she was prepared for a fight like this. They weren't. It was her perfectly camouflaged garments versus their high-contrast civilian clothing.

She sneered when she looked back into her scope and saw a trail of men begin their ascent of the cliff to the monastery. These were easy pickings. But the missing commandos forced her to refrain. If she did, she'd give away her position.

I need to deal with these two first, she thought, adjusting her aim down to the valley floor. She scanned it, finding nothing as she figured. They wouldn't be dumb enough to travel out in the open, not again.

How about we dance and find out?

She lined up the topmost climber and pulled the trigger. The .308 black tip plucked the man from the mountain in an explosion of blood. A rustling sound to Yana's right caused her to spin out of position. This was where the RSASS' versatility shined.

Yana sat up and shouldered the DMR, same as you would a traditional battle rifle. A commando charged around a cluster of trees raising his own rifle as he moved. Yana wasn't given the time to properly line him up with her scope and she quickly squeezed off three rounds, hitting the soldier in the upper thigh and stomach. He dropped just as another disturbance picked up behind her.

There was no way for Yana to reposition in time. Instead, she laid flat on her back and drew her sidearm from its place on her hip. The Walther PPQ was chambered in .45 ACP and made a mess of whatever it touched. She lifted the gun over her head and lined up the other commando's chest, pressing the trigger.

She missed! The soldier dove behind cover at the last moment.

He blindly fired from behind a thick tree trunk. Yana rolled left just as the ground around her was peppered with bullets. Midway through the maneuver, she became tangled in her rifle's sling. Yana shrugged out of it, leaving it behind as she got to her feet and danced behind a low boulder. Yana was sufficient with a pistol, but she was much more comfortable with a rifle.

Now, her tactics needed to change. She stood and scrambled atop the large rock, purposely making a lot of noise. She kept her PPQ leveled at the clump of trees hiding her foe as she did. Yana didn't need to kill him here and now. She only needed to keep him pinned down as she made her move.

Yana squeezed the trigger. The round harmlessly impacted a trunk. When she surmounted the boulder, she sent another projectile into the same spot. Yana felt her perch dip and she followed it carefully, squeezing the trigger again. Yana slid down the front of the rock and landed, sending, yet another, round into the commando's cover.

She bolted straight for him, stomping loudly as she moved. Yana pulled the trigger and saw movement through a gap in the trees. She went into a baseball slide and tracked the man's trajectory. Just as she stopped, he spun out of cover, aiming much too high. Yana grinned and put two in his chest. It had taken eight rounds, but Yana had been successful.

Automatic gunfire tore up the ground around her. Yana got to her feet and bolted back to her rifle. She holstered her PPQ on her hip, scooped up her RSASS, and kept moving. She didn't attempt to return fire. Yana darted downhill, slipping back into the large weapon's sling all while spotting what would make an insane escape route. She dove headfirst and took the descent like a waterslide. Yana had no idea where it was taking her. At least the gunfire had stopped.

Yana shouted, seeing a drop off up ahead.

She spun onto her butt and got her feet in front of her. As she did, she unsheathed her knife and dug it into the earth beneath her, driving the heels of her boots in deep. She slowed but she didn't stop.

Yana was mere feet from the ledge when the blade finally caught. Her body was lifted off the ground by the sudden stop in momentum and then slammed back down. Her feet found nothing but air. Yana clawed back up the incline until she was wholly on solid ground, gasping for air as she did.

She fell face first into the snowy terrain and stayed there. The freezing ground stung her skin, but it also focused and reawakened her. She growled and pushed herself up, careful not to lose her footing. Yana took in her surroundings and saw a way up to her right. The wall looked climbable and wasn't all that tall. She used her knife, like one would use an ice axe, and dug it into the ground as she scuttled sideways. Once she was next to the wall, she sheathed her blade and began her climb.

"Five down, eleven to go."

Triratna Monastery

Four Falcon Commandos lay prone, watching over the vicinity of the gunfight. The lead man had already been stripped of his essential gear. The equipment had then been re-distributed to the rest of the men, accordingly. Shenlong and his three remaining men had been spared so far.

The sniper was quickly bringing Fan's headcount down. Soon, the commandos would lose the numbers advantage they had over Shenlong's team.

Shenlong looked down at his feet and dug his right toe into a crevasse. He drove his weight up and rolled atop a sizeable empty expanse of land. To his right was a pair of large, wooden doors. A footpath led into the trees off to his left. It disappeared around a bend, looking very ominous. Shenlong was curious as to who or what used it. If the passageway had been abandoned as long as the monastery had, it should've been overgrown and inaccessible.

As the two men before him had done, Shenlong spun and faced the cliff's edge. He aimed his rifle out over the void of the Forbidden Valley. Even though the assault weapon had a superior effective range over the submachine gun he had used previously, it was still just a light infantry rifle and mostly useless from where he laid now.

Shenlong waited for the rest of the men from his and Fan's teams to join them up top before they got moving again. Their idea was to look for muzzle flash and then return fire and hope to get lucky, though Fan hadn't put it like that. He had been told that Fan's men could take out their pursuer at this distance and in these conditions. The wind swirled like mad up here, and it wasn't much better further down the mountainside.

A bestial cry could be heard with the next gust of wind. Shenlong peered over his shoulder, focusing on the forested route. The noise seemed to have originated from there. Then, it echoed all around him. He shook off the ridiculous notion that there was something up here with them and did his part to keep watch over the valley below. Shenlong couldn't see much of the valley floor due to a low-hanging fog.

Gang, the fourth and final member of his original ten-man team, lay beside him just as the sound erupted. Gang silently inquired about what to do next. Shenlong was sure they could overtake Fan's force now, but he wasn't sure if it was smart to do it yet. There were only three commandos to their four mercenaries up top.

Shenlong shook his head. Fan's team was too valuable of an asset. *If* something was up here with them, then having the extra guns would be a godsend.

Fan was the next man up. There was one more man a dozen or so feet behind him, struggling against the elements. The wind slowed the last man down to the point that he stopped and hugged the cliff face until it subsided.

The guttural roar of the wind increased tenfold around them. Shenlong leaped to his feet, much to the disapproval of Fan. Shenlong's men followed their leader as he sprinted toward the monastery. They hit the doors and pushed but found them locked. The screams of both human and beast punched Shenlong in the back of the head. He refused to look, focusing on the doors instead. More animalistic howls exploded behind him, as did the frightened cries of Fan's hardened team. Shenlong peered between the doors and saw a thick horizontal post in place.

He stepped back and opened fire on the "lock." After emptying half his magazine, Shenlong threw himself at the doors hard enough to break the post the rest of the way. They swung open and spilled him onto the monastery floor. Shenlong felt himself being lifted off of the ground by two of his people as the third one opened fire at something outside. Then, the gunfire ceased, and he was dragged away.

Shenlong turned just in time to see an enormous, fur-covered creature take four rounds to the chest as if it were nothing. It impaled one of Fan's men in the stomach with its immense claws, then yanked them free and backhanded another of the commandos off the ledge. His screams died down as he disappeared below.

Shenlong's mouth hung open, and he stumbled backward. Gang and Ceba shut the doors but had no way to relock them. It didn't matter. They needed to get going before that thing noticed they had escaped indoors.

"Run," he said, choking on his words.

"What?" Gang asked, facing him.

Shenlong was terrified by what he had just witnessed. He took a deep breath, feeling his hands tremble. He lifted them and watched them shake. Then, he returned his attention to his understandably unsettled subordinate.

"Run."

They ran to the pulsating soundtrack of war, passing a long hallway on their left. No one could see what was happening outside, but Shenlong knew Fan's commandos were being overrun. Whatever the creatures were, gunfire did very little to harm them. He didn't think they sported some kind of high-tech, bulletproof clothing either. The animals were just *that* tough, maybe even invulnerable.

Shenlong spotted an exit on the far side of the room.

Ceba, the lone Tibetan in Shenlong's team, conversed with Gang as they ran. A figure passed by in front of their exit, stopping the threesome in their tracks.

"Back," Shenlong said, retreating. "The hallway. Go."

They retraced their steps and ducked into the hallway they had just passed. Shenlong waited, watching to see if they would be followed. But the figure had vanished. The battle outside was dying down too. Shenlong knew that whatever was killing Fan and his men would also come looking for them. He guessed this was the creatures' home. And they had waltzed right in and shut the doors.

"Shenlong," Gang hissed, getting him to turn.

Gang was waving for him to join him and Ceba. Shenlong left his post and quickly caught up with them outside a doorway. Inside was a grizzly scene. There was a pile of bodies, long dead from their ragged appearance and decomposed state. He fought against the urge to explore and stepped past the opening.

All three men walked swiftly with their Type 95 rifles at the low-ready. The only noise besides their footfalls was their heavy breaths. They were spent and running on fumes after their rugged hike and death-defying climb. They needed to rest in the worst way. Food and water would help immensely.

They made it to a large circular opening and slowed. An attack from above was possible. The trained mercs walked with their weapons aimed at the two visible levels. No one sounded the alarm as they passed directly beneath it.

A stairwell greeted them and beckoned them forward.

Up or down? Shenlong thought.

Taking the monastery one floor at a time was the obvious thing to do, but Shenlong wanted nothing to do with the creatures. He doubted there was a viable exit in the lower level, though if there were a clue to where Wu and the American went, it would be down there.

They paused at the juncture while Shenlong decided on the course to take.

Ceba was rambling on about something.

"What is he saying?" Shenlong asked, unable to make out the words.

Gang held up his hand and quieted the shell-shocked Tibetan. "He says he knows what they are."

Shenlong faced Ceba and waited.

"When I was a child, my granduncle told me of them."

"Skip to the end," Shenlong said. "What are they?"

Ceba swallowed and glanced over his shoulder. "My family called them the *mirka*. They are the very embodiment of death. It is said that anyone who sees one dies horrifically." His shoulders drooped. "And we're next."

"Ceba," Shenlong said. The panicked mercenary looked up at him but didn't speak. "Get ahold of yourself, or it won't be the monsters that kill you."

The four remaining Falcon Commandos regrouped in the tree line opposite the cliff. More than half their ammunition was gone, as was most of their teammates. Fan was bleeding heavily from a wound to the shoulder but had fared better than most. In a matter of minutes, six of China's finest had been killed, whether by sniper fire or primal fury.

Shenlong had lied to him. He had known about their pursuer. Fan was also curious whether Shenlong had known about the mountain creatures too.

No, he thought, *I don't think so.*

One of his men had fallen here. If Shenlong had truly known what to expect outside the monastery, he would've immediately moved his people inside. The beasts were a variable that even Shenlong hadn't been aware of.

Fan wanted to know what they were. He and his men had injured several of them with their salvo. Unfortunately, the wounded had been carried off before Fan could identify them. The soldiers had been backed up to the cliff edge before their attackers gave up and disappeared. Still, they had succeeded in reducing the commandos' numbers down to four.

Only one more than Shenlong.

Fan was changing tactics. It was time for him to take over. Too many of his men had died in such a brief timeframe, regardless of who was at fault. He produced a satellite phone but had no signal. So, instead of verbally calling in for backup, he removed a baseball-sized, cylindrical object from his coat pocket and twisted its top clockwise. The beacon would do its job once an orbital satellite drifted into position. Then, another twelve men would be flown in and dropped down on top of them. They were close too. The other team was roughly eighty miles northwest of their current position, on the northern end of Peikucuo Lake in Tibet.

For now, Fan and his three commandos would find cover and sit tight.

The hunt was not over. It was just merely delayed.

42

Valley of Petals

The meal had been fresh and delicious, and his appetite was satisfied. Now, he needed sleep. But he couldn't. There was still too much to absorb, and every minute he got to spend here was precious. Families walked by, giving the three strangers odd looks. Veer was evidence enough that other people had been brought here in the last century. Most of them were from an Asian background, however, there were several people from Africa, Europe, and the Caribbean.

"Hold on, who's this?"

A white male briskly walked toward them. He was dressed like everyone else. Flowing robes seemed to be the dominant fashion here. Whoever he was, he had not been born here and had come from somewhere else.

Veer sighed. "Jack Reilly, this is Gareth O'Connell. He's—"

"A real charmer," Gareth finished, smiling wide. The first hand he shook belonged to May, not Jack. He lifted her hand and kissed the back of it. "It's a pleasure to meet you."

Jack glanced back at Veer. The man did nothing but shrug.

"You're English?" Jack asked, sidestepping closer to May.

"How can you tell?"

Jack didn't know if this guy was for real, or some sort of strategic bioweapon meant to annoy him to death. Whenever he arrived, and wherever he arrived from, Gareth must have thought of himself as quite the smooth talker.

Veer stepped up next to Gareth. "Mr. O'Connell has taken it upon himself to welcome newcomers and guide them along until they get acclimated."

Gareth held his hands out. "I'm a regular welcome wagon!"

"So," Jack said, "what's your story?"

"Oh, me? Well, my tale is similar to Veer's, only with much less agony and dismemberment." Veer gave him a sideways glance. "Anywho," Gareth took a giant step away from Veer, "one day, I'm on a beautiful holiday in the mountains. Next thing you know, a storm hits, and I wake up, and I've been Bibbidi-Bobbidi-Booed here!" He snorted out a laugh. "Thought I was in heaven, at first. But then, I remembered the tasty misdeeds of my past, and no, I knew I must've still been alive." He playfully winked at Veer. "Blokes like us don't see the pearly gates, do we?"

Veer shrugged. "I'm Hindi, so no. What's your excuse?"

Gareth attempted to adjust a collar that wasn't there. "I was quite the womanizer before I was saved and brought here."

"You were saved?" May asked.

Gareth nodded. "A few days after my arrival, I came to find out that an earthquake, a real corker, had hit the Himalayas while I was on top of one of 'em. Just my luck, huh? Maybe it had been divine intervention?" He pointed at the trio. "What about you three?"

"We followed the Sacred Path," Kalsang said.

Gareth's eyes opened wide. "Really? Bloody hell, real Pathers as I live and breathe! We don't get many of you anymore—like ever. Not since that tosser-of-a-Keeper quit."

"That *tosser* was my great-great-grandfather," Kalsang said, standing tall.

Gareth shrugged. "Sorry, mate, but that doesn't make him any less of a tosser."

Veer stepped in between the two glaring men. "Regardless of what we may think of Dhonu Thapa, we can still honor him for his decades of servitude," he looked at the Brit, "and drop it."

Gareth looked back and forth between Veer and Kalsang. His posture changed, and he smiled. "Fine. I guess all our families are full of miscreants, right?" He motioned to May. "I bet Ms. 'Silent-But-Deadly' has a couple of less-reputable people in her family tree."

May crossed her arms. "There are a few."

Jack rolled his eyes. But Gareth wasn't wrong. Every family had a *tosser* in them, and if a family member ever denied that there was one, then it was usually the person rejecting the notion that was the aforementioned *tosser*.

Veer cleared his throat. "With that settled, Gareth, would you please show them the tree."

The Brit nodded. "Of course. Please, follow me. This is going to blow your minds."

Jack scratched his head and leaned in close to May. "Figuratively, I hope."

Petals danced all around them. A couple of them even hit Jack in the face with the softness of what a cloud must feel like. He caught one and confirmed that it was the same type of petal as the one he had examined up on the entrance ridge.

"Incredible, right?" Gareth said. "I guarantee you've never felt anything so soft."

Jack begged to differ. He glanced at May but decided not to enter that mental rabbit hole.

Six of the ten swordsmen followed Gareth's guided tour. They stayed silent and kept their distance but kept within earshot. Unless they could block bullets like Deadpool, they'd be no match for Jack, May, and Kalsang if things got out of hand. Jack didn't see things going the way of Wade Wilson, though. The Petalians had no reason to fear them.

Jack looked around. *But that doesn't mean we aren't being led into a trap.* He was uneasy about no longer being armed. Their guns had been confiscated during their *cleaning*.

It wouldn't have surprised him if the leaders here were even a pinch paranoid about outsiders appearing out of nowhere. So far as he could understand, the only outsiders that lived here had come because they'd been trapped in the mountains by a storm or had gotten caught up in an avalanche. "Pathers," as Gareth called them, weren't all that common anymore. If Jack were in Veer's shoes, he'd be suspicious of this crew.

So, he'd stay on his guard, as would May. She was *always* on her guard. It was a character flaw in her that had come from years of working under her father as a spy. There was a bit of that in Jack as well.

"Impressive," Kalsang muttered as they entered a walkthrough similar to something Jack remembered from Disney World, of all places.

"Yes, we call this the Gallery."

Jack thought back to walking through Cinderella's castle, though this wasn't a castle at all. The high-ceilinged building was like the other flat-roofed Chinese-Cambodian structures from earlier and had been constructed directly over the main road. Cinderella's castle featured mosaic murals depicting specific scenes from the popular fairytale. In this case, it highlighted what must've been notable events within the Valley of Petals. Jack didn't understand what he was seeing, and they weren't given a chance to stop and take it in.

The one constant in all the artwork was a tree.

The city kept to the lowest point of the turkey baster-shaped Beyul—the heavenly valley. Jack slowed as they walked into an intersection of wide footpaths that passed for streets. He looked left and saw that the flat stone pathway ended at a green field. Small huts dotted the *Sound of Music-esque* hills outside the "downtown" area. The residences were simple, and if there was time, Jack wanted to check them out. There were vibrant farms mixed in between the homes. Jack looked right and saw much of the same thing on the other side of the valley. Veer had said their diets were based only on what they could produce here, so the number of farms made sense. The soft breeze even carried some of the petals out into the countryside.

"Veer said something about a tree?" May asked.

"Yes," Gareth replied, "he did. We're headed there now."

It was then that Jack realized that they had been slowly traveling uphill. He couldn't see the end of the road from here. Whatever lay beyond this point was out of sight further ahead and below them. As of now, Jack could only see the tops of a group of trees. *The park from earlier?* Every single one was shedding beautiful pink petals.

As far as the location of their destination…

They crested the rise and enjoyed the scene. The valley opened up and dropped. The main walkway forked up ahead and banked left and right around the main area that Jack had expected to see. Only this wasn't at all what he had pictured.

"Oh."

Gareth stepped up next to Jack. "That was my reaction too."

First, the Valley of Petals was much bigger than Jack had initially thought. The entire city dipped softly and rolled with what nature provided. The one consistency was that everything led to the center of town.

And to the single largest fruit tree Jack had ever seen.

The multitude of treetops didn't belong to a cluster of growths. They belonged to one colossal growth. Jack dug into his coat pocket and removed May's monocular. The only visible portion of the tree was the canopy. The rest of it was hidden from view, disappearing into the earth. To Jack, the depression looked like a gigantic stone well. The circular cutout had been intentional. He lifted the monocular to his eye and looked over one of the thickest branches. Jack saw a color that wasn't green or brown.

"Are those peaches?" he asked, spotting the fruit.

"They are," Gareth replied.

May looked confused. "Your big secret is peaches?"

The Brit smiled. "They're a piece of it." He cleared his throat and faced the tree. "Does anyone know what the height of an average peach tree is?"

No one answered him.

"Well," Gareth continued, "the biggest ones can grow to roughly twenty-five feet."

Jack inspected the tree through May's monocular again, trying to estimate its height based solely on its canopy and the surrounding buildings. His best guess was around a hundred feet tall, which would be insane based on what Gareth had just told them.

"How tall is this one?" May asked.

Gareth stepped forward and faced them. "Two hundred and eleven feet."

Jack stared him down. "But, how?"

A sly grin formed on Gareth's face. "I'll show you."

Triratna Monastery
Forbidden Valley, Tibet

Gang and Ceba guarded the doorway while Shenlong caught his breath and contemplated their next move. The smartest thing to do was to abandon ship and return to Lamabagar. If they were lucky, their vehicles would still be parked where they had left them. If they weren't still there, then, well, Shenlong would have to find another way home.

This had been the single most devastating mission of his career. Shenlong had never had to cope with so much loss and defeat at once. It weighed him down, making him doubt himself. And why wouldn't he lose faith in himself after what he had led his men into? Seven deaths in two days. Seven! Shenlong was flabbergasted that it had gotten out of control so fast.

He sat against the far wall, beneath a table with his head in his knees, staring at the floor between his feet. "Now, what?"

While turning back would be the correct choice, it wasn't something Shenlong had ever considered. He didn't turn tail and run. Shenlong always finished the damn mission. It wasn't even about the money now. David Cho had proved to be the snake Shenlong had always thought him to be. Even after the countless jobs he had done for the man, Shenlong knew deep down that the man was a treacherous worm.

"Shenlong?"

He looked up and found Gang and Ceba staring at him.

Gang stepped toward him. "What do we do?"

Shenlong climbed out from beneath his refuge and retrieved his rifle from the tabletop. He let out a long breath, knowing exactly what needed to be done.

"We find Shangri-La."

"What about the commandos?" Ceba asked.

Shenlong felt a little of his resolve return at the mention of Fan and his team. "If we see them again, we'll be ready. We will give them to the mountain."

43

Valley of Petals

Jack, May, and Kalsang were led down to the 211-foot-tall peach tree. The closer they got the more Jack was in awe of it. It just kept getting bigger and more magnificent with each step he took. He was intrigued by the funneling terrain. It all ended at the tree.

Or was the glass half full, and the terrain begins here?

The Valley of Petals' layout reminded Jack of the Arc de Triomphe in Paris where the city streets radiate outward from that exact spot. The overhead shots of the triumphal arch were breathtaking and something everyone should stop to look up at. Movement within the tree caught Jack's eye. The canopy was too thick to determine what it was, though. They'd have to get closer.

"There must be hundreds of peaches," May said.

Gareth nodded. "More, and they grow year-round. As I'm sure you can see, there is no season change here."

"How does it sustain such growth?" Kalsang asked.

Gareth smiled. "Ah, now that's the real secret of this place."

"What is it?" Jack asked.

"Ah-ah-ah," Gareth waggled his finger as he walked, "not yet. If I tell you, it'll ruin the dramatic reveal."

"Jack," May said, pointing at the tree," look."

They were halfway there and Jack, once again, saw movement within the tree's limbs. He peered through the monocular. What he saw made him stumble and stop.

"Snow leopards?" he asked. "You've domesticated snow leopards?"

Gareth shrugged. "We didn't, no. They were here long before any of us. They've been guardians of the Peaches of Immortality for generations."

May stared at Gareth. "What did you say?"

Gareth looked at her quizzically. "What about? The snow leopards?"

She shook her head. "The peaches. What did you call them?"

The Brit smiled. He knew exactly what she had meant. "The Peaches of Immortality. And yes, they are the same ones from Chinese mythology—the ones the Jade Emperor himself dined on. Similar to the mystic peaches from yesteryear, our variety also extends the lives of those who consume their sweet, sweet nectar. The Greeks have a similar story."

Jack nodded. "Yeah, the Nectar of the Gods."

Nectar.

"Hang on," he said, getting everyone's attention, "Thapa said something about nectar before he died, right, May?"

She nodded. "He did. He also said that it was the lack of nectar that was responsible for his poor health, and the death of his beloved."

"Celia," Gareth said. The man's voice was uncharacteristically laced with venom.

Jack needed to know. "Thapa said that you were all responsible for her demise. Care to explain?"

Gareth took a deep breath. "We are. Well, not me, per se. That happened before my time." Jack, May, and Kalsang all glanced at one another. Gareth must've seen their expressions. "Don't worry, it's not what it seems." He waved them forward. "I will explain as we walk."

Jack eyed the dozen or so lounging snow leopards. They were beautiful, but no doubt, fierce.

"Celia Meier was tried and found guilty of attempting to smuggle nectar to the outside world."

May and Kalsang's expressions matched Jack's. They were stunned.

"She said that everyone deserved to experience what we have." Gareth didn't give anyone time to respond. "I would've agreed with her when I first arrived, but not now. I understand what it is now."

"Thapa said it was a curse."

Gareth stopped and stared at May.

He thought over her words carefully. The Brit turned and said, "And he isn't far from the truth. Those who consume the nectar—even once—are bound to this place forever. If the peaches make it out, it's a death sentence to anyone who consumes them. You must eat them regularly. If not, your body's age catches up with you quickly. Celia never found peace with her decision to stay, but it was *her* decision. She didn't have to eat the peaches."

"What about you?" Jack asked.

Gareth shrugged. "I didn't exactly have a good life before coming here. For me, it was an easy choice. I accepted it as soon as the nectar touched my lips."

He held both of his hands out wide and turned in a circle. "Not the worst place to be *trapped*, is it?"

"A paradise on earth, huh?" Jack asked, not feeling as in love with the idea.

"To some, yes. Everyone has a different concept of what paradise is. The real doozy is whether you choose to acknowledge it as a paradise, or not."

"And Celia didn't," May said.

Gareth shrugged. "I can't speak for her, but from what I've been told, she felt differently in the beginning."

"And my great-great-grandfather?" Kalsang asked.

"You want the prevailing theory?" The Sherpa nodded. "Dhonu Thapa was lonely, and she tainted an honorable man's heart. She used him and transformed him into a disgrace. That woman was the very embodiment of Lilith."

Kalsang looked to Jack for answers.

"In Jewish mythology, Lilith is a demon who preys upon unsuspecting men."

Gareth touched his nose and then pointed at Jack, but he gazed hard at Kalsang. Jack mentally translated the gesture.

You are correct.

"He lied," Kalsang muttered. He looked at Jack. "He lied."

They slowed as they neared the edge of the immense cylindrical well. It was guarded by a ring of archers, as well as swordsmen. They stood fifty feet from one another.

Man, these guys don't mess around.

Jack and the others were given access to it without any verbal exchange.

Jack leaned out and looked down. More than half of the tree was in the hole. The stone reinforced depression gobbled up the lower portion of the tree, showing off its incredible size. It was just another marvelous feat of construction being shown off by the city's original design team.

"Come," Gareth said, stepping down onto a platform.

A stairway, much like the one at the valley entrance, led them down to ground level. Jack watched as old-school pulley systems brought baskets up and down the tree on all four sides. There were also a couple of larger ones connected to platforms. It was how they harvested the miracle fruit. People and leopard seemed to coexist in the tree just fine.

"You said the snow leopards protect the tree?" Jack asked.

"They do, and I know it doesn't look like they're doing much, but the pickers are also their handlers, and only they are allowed in the tree."

"What happens when someone else decides to venture in?" May asked.

Gareth adjusted his robe. "Things get unpleasant in a hurry."

They nearly rounded the entire well before reaching bottom. When they did, Jack was taken aback by the girth of the peach tree's trunk. It was twice as thick as any redwood he had ever seen. He also spotted a heavy looking door built into the side of the well on the other side of the tree. A pair of swordsmen guarded it.

Hmmm.

When his foot struck the ground, he felt something odd. The earth included large chunks of gray granular soil.

"Is this rock mixed in?" Jack asked, kneeling. He inspected a triangular piece with his hand.

"It is," Gareth replied.

May knelt beside Jack. "Your tree sprouted from this?" She picked up a stone, inspected it, then tossed it aside.

Jack gazed up at the Brit when he didn't answer. His face said everything.

"Gareth, what?"

"It is the reason for everything you see." He got down on one knee and caressed the ground. "This, my friends, is a meteorite." Jack's eyes opened wide. "And it's had a profound influence on our peach tree, to say the least."

Jack looked up at the canopy high overhead. "That's," he struggled to find the right words, "amazing!"

Gareth eyed the tree as if it were a family member. "Yes, it is."

Forbidden Valley, Tibet

The brutal display that Yana had witnessed had rendered her muscles useless. She was locked in fear, even after thirty minutes. Yana was still trying to process everything she had seen through her scope. Her eye was still glued to the cliff's edge even though there was nothing to see there, besides a trail of freezing blood running down the rockface.

She traced the crimson back up to the battleground and could just barely see a man's booted foot. Whether it was still connected to the owner, Yana had no idea. Finally, she blinked, and dipped her head. Her face melted into the snow and she left it there until it burned. The sting reinvigorated her, and she climbed to her knees, spun, and plopped down behind a thick pine. Yana took another moment to regain her composure.

She stood.

The way was more than likely clear, but she'd still give it a stealthy treatment, just in case. At this point, she was more worried about being found out by the creatures than any of the soldiers or mercenaries. Yana was pretty sure she knew what the beasts were.

"*Chuchuna*," she whispered, her voice shaky.

Back in Russia, when she was young, her grandmother used to tell her stories of the thick furred Neanderthal-like mountain men. They closely resembled their cousins across the globe, Bigfoot, and the Yeti.

Yana stepped around the tree and headed out. She kept a tree trunk between herself and the ledge at all times. It made her trek slower, but it was the best course of action until she could confirm there weren't any living threats up top. At no point did Yana believe that all of Shenlong's men or the commandos had been wiped out. The Chuchuna were savage and seemed unstoppable, but the men up there were some of the best in the world at what they did.

The hike to the base of the rockface was uneventful. It was precisely what Yana had needed. She wasn't in fighting shape right now. Her mind was still too fractured—still fixated on the battle between man and monster. She headed left, just as the men had done earlier. Yana made it to the obstructed stairway in no time. She slung her rifle onto her back, tightened it down, and immediately mounted the massive boulder blocking the way. She made it to the top, stood, and stretched her back while planning her next move.

She clearly recalled the path Shenlong's people had taken and decided to duplicate it. No one had fallen to their deaths besides the man Yana had dislodged with a bullet. Then again, he was more than likely dead before he had hit the ground. There was a free climb coming, and she'd have help. The Falcon Commandos had attached lines to the rock wall.

Yana flipped herself up and over onto a rocky, tree and snow-packed staircase. She didn't stop. She got to her feet and followed the cut path until she couldn't anymore. The stairs ended at a second broken section, where she found another rope. She also found the man she had shot while he had been climbing. His possessions had been picked through, but a valuable tool had been left behind: The commando's ice axe.

Yana made it halfway up the wall before an odd sound invaded the valley's airspace. She looked over her shoulder, and couldn't identify the origin of this new noise, but she knew what it was. Yana looked around and saw an alcove directly to her right. It looked manmade. She peered straight down at her climbing harness and bit her lip, knowing what she had to do. Yana unclipped herself from the line and ventured off course. Her camouflage would do its job until the inbound aircraft closed in. When it did, she'd need to be somewhere else, or risk succumbing to the same demise as the dead commando she had killed on this mountain.

She checked the time. It had been over an hour since the creatures had attacked Shenlong and the Falcon Commandos. If this was who she thought it was, then they had planned on being needed and had been close by, lying in wait.

Yana clunked right, jamming her ice axe into the rocky crevasses. She was nearly to the circular alcove when the whirling of helicopter blades grew louder. So, Yana rushed and was nearly plucked free by a strong, swirling gust of frigid air. She pressed her chest up to the cliff and rode out the breeze, shutting her eyes as she was battered by it.

When it finally let up, Yana was off again. She swung her axe and found nothing but air. She had arrived at the alcove but hadn't noticed it until now. Just then, the aircraft came into view. Yana threw herself into what she now saw was a drainage shaft. It was wholly impassable but would work as a place to hide, both from the weather and the inbound enemy. She ducked behind a pile of rubble and waited. Once the combined wind and rotor wash dissipated, she popped her head up to see if the coast was clear.

Yana crawled over to the edge and peeked out and up. She was just in time to see the tail of a black helicopter disappear above her head. She waited for it to land, and when it did, she got a crazy idea. If things went further south than they had already, she'd commandeer the aircraft and leave that way. Regardless of what she decided, Yana would have to be careful. The helicopter wouldn't be left unattended. The pilots were going to have to be dealt with. Luckily, she had enough flight training to get the bird in the air.

Landing, on the other hand...

As of now, she was stuck. Yana would need to stay put and wait for the new arrivals to disembark and head inside. Then, she would climb topside to have a chat with the pilot.

44

Valley of Petals

The trio was led into a three-story structure on the outskirts of the stone well. Veer rejoined them and he and Gareth both entered the building and headed for the stairs in the rear. Jack followed with May close behind. Kalsang hung back a little, but ultimately ascended the stairs too.

Once they were all present on the third floor, Gareth announced that they had arrived at their destination, being the good guide that he was. "Welcome to the library." The room was one giant space divided by wooden bookcases, and they were overflowing with aged tomes. "Since the dawn of the Valley of Petals, every one of these books has been penned by someone here. This is our story."

Jack's mouth hung open. The written history of the mythic Shangri-La was right here in front of him.

"The beginning," he said. "Show me the beginning."

Gareth looked to Veer. The Hindi nodded once, and Gareth turned and disappeared into the collection. Veer didn't follow. He motioned for the group to continue into the middle of the room. A large rectangular banquet table greeted them. Veer assumed a position at its center. Jack stood directly across from him with May on his left and Kalsang on his right.

A few seconds later, Gareth returned with two objects. In one hand was a newer, hardback. His other hand carefully clutched a scroll. The latter item looked ancient. The Brit handed both to Veer, who set them down in the middle of the table. The scroll wasn't opened, but the book was.

"This," Veer explained, tapping the book, "is a direct translation of this." He opened his hand and turned it over, hovering it over the rolled parchment. "The scroll is too far-gone to be opened anymore."

No one except Veer spoke.

"Our history, unfortunately, is incomplete. Our ancestors did not record everything. Some accounts have been lost to time. Sadly, they were not backed up like this one was." Veer looked at Kalsang. "It was the doing of a monk who had also helped found Shigatse Dzong. Together, with a select few, he set up this library so we may show newcomers our story."

"When was this put together?" Jack asked, looking around.

"Five hundred years ago."

Jack eyed the newer looking book. "That book is five hundred years old?"

Veer shook his head. "No, this is a seventh edition copy. We've been here a long time, Jack. Eventually, even our copies needed to be copied. There are no computer backups here."

Jack now understood.

Veer took his silence as a signal to continue. "This scroll describes the very first tertons, the ones pictured on the entry stairs. I'm sure you noticed them."

All three explorers nodded.

"One of the weary travelers was a young girl who was fond of her family's peaches." Veer smiled. "She took it upon herself to carry seeds in her pocket, planting them all over the valley, before any of this was built." He gazed out a window.

"What was her name?" May asked.

Veer's face saddened. "We do not know. The scroll was too damaged to read it. But we have come to call her 'Mother.'"

"Mother?" Jack asked.

"Yes, Mother, as she was responsible for everything we are. She birthed this place with a single seed."

"Planted in the pulverized remains of a meteorite," Jack added.

"Correct, though, she didn't know that at the time. Mother descended the sloping crater. She was curious—an adventurer at heart. She planted a seed at the center of a powdered section of the meteorite. Every day, she'd come by and water it. Unless it rained, of course."

"It rains here?" May asked.

"It does, though rarely, and never a downpour. Now, the roots go so deep that we believe the tree uses a subterranean water source to continue to feed itself and thrive."

"And the meteorite soil?" Jack asked.

"We do not fully understand it. No tests have ever been done, but we think it enriched the tree beyond our comprehension." A twinkle formed in his eye. "It is, as you could say, out of this world."

Jack's right eyebrow raised. "Was that a joke?"

Veer's face re-hardened.

"So, the real secret of this place isn't the peaches," May said, "it's the meteorite-enriched soil."

Veer shrugged. "Yes, but we've never tested anything else in it. Mother's peaches are all we need. They were the first, and they will be the last."

"Incredible," Jack said, eyeing the scroll. He looked up at Veer. "May I?"

Veer nodded once. Jack carefully picked up the priceless relic. He glanced at May and Kalsang and held up the scroll in his open hands. His cheeks hurt from smiling so wide. Jack was beyond excited.

"The real-life origin story of Shangri-La. Can you believe it?"

Both smiled.

"So, Jack Reilly," Veer said, "what will you do with this information?"

Jack returned the scroll to the table. "Protect it, and you."

"You are truly worthy of being here then." Veer held out his hand. Jack clasped it. "Now, tell me more about these men who are coming."

Triratna Monastery
Forbidden Valley, Tibet

The three remaining mercenaries hustled to the eastern exit. It had taken some time, but they had finally made it back to the second floor. But this is where they had initially spotted one of the creatures. It had been lingering just outside the doorway. As of now, Shenlong didn't see anything.

He shouldered his Type 95 rifle and slowly walked in a half-moon arc just inside the opening. He absorbed everything outside, minus the area to the immediate left or right of the doorway. Shenlong reached the right-hand side of the exit and nodded at Gang. His man took up position on the left side. Ceba crept up to the center. He glanced at his boss. Shenlong nodded for him to move out.

He did, and nothing happened.

Ceba stepped outside and swiftly cleared the remaining area. Shenlong followed him out and then down a set of icy, stone steps. Gang brought up the rear and paused. So did Shenlong and Ceba. The telltale sound of an incoming helicopter both confused and scared the mercenaries. Fan must've called in support.

"Go," Shenlong ordered, keeping his voice low.

Ceba started up again and in no time the trio was back on ground level. A path led into the trees, and with nowhere else to go within the snowy courtyard, Shenlong hurried into cover. A black Harbin Z-20 transport helicopter appeared from within the fog, sending Shenlong, Gang, and Ceba running down the tree-lined passage.

Shenlong knew the game. He and his men were now on Fan's list, and there was only one way for them to survive.

They'd request help from a very unlikely source.

Twelve black-clad soldiers disembarked the aircraft and stood at attention before their commander, Fan. He was still in charge, even though the man across from him held the same rank. But this was Fan's operation. If the roles had been reversed, Fan would've respected it and done as he was asked. This man should be no different.

"Medic!" the other team leader, Park, shouted. A second man rushed over and quickly went about wrapping wounds and administering pain killers. "What did this?"

Fan looked over the battlefield while the medic tended to his arm.

"In a word, evil."

What was he going to say? He couldn't just come out and tell the man that a pack of Yetis had attacked and killed three Falcon Commandos in seconds. That would only make Fan look incompetent.

"Evil?"

Fan nodded and left it at that. But there was something else he needed to tell him.

"There is also a sniper in the area."

Park relayed the facts then returned to Fan.

"There's one more thing you need to know," Park said.

"Yes?" Fan asked, cringing as the medic tightened another bandage down.

"Minister Zhao has given us additional orders. We are to bring him back viable samples of DNA—any way possible."

Park bore holes in Fan, making sure the message had been received. Unfortunately, it had, and Fan, an honorable soldier, didn't like it one bit.

As soon as the aircraft had touched down, Yana had begun her climb. She moved slow and hung close to the cliff face. She hoped the uneven topography would conceal her as she ascended. If she was spotted, she'd be an easy kill. The thought made her angry.

The Blood Dragon is never an easy kill.

She was tired, though. In fact, Yana couldn't remember a job that had taxed her this much.

"Should've asked for more money."

She climbed up and left, moving away from the monastery. Her plan was to come up directly underneath the military transport. She dug in the ice axe, pulled herself up, and sidestepped left. She repeated the trajectory every chance she got and eventually found herself only feet from the edge. She didn't hear a single voice. Yana would need to expose herself for a brief moment, but there was no other way.

Or is there?

She reached behind her back and unsheathed her knife. The blade tip was a mess from it being used as a climbing tool for a short time. But most of it was still clean and reflective. Yana held it up and angled it in such a way that she could see the grounds outside the monastery doors.

The area was a gruesome disaster.

There were bodies everywhere, and wherever the dead wasn't, the ground was covered in blood. Nothing moved. Yana was alone with her helicopter.

And the pilot.

She sheathed her knife and hauled herself up onto ground level, and army-crawled beneath the tail of the aircraft. Yana gave herself a moment to rest and regain her air. The climb had been just one of several things that had sapped her strength.

After a few minutes, she got moving, feeling good, all things considered. She made it further up the underside of the Harbin Z-20 when a pair of boots appeared off to her left. The sudden appearance of the pilot's feet startled her, and she lifted her head and clunked it back against the helicopter's belly. She silently cursed herself and reached down to her hip and drew her PPQ. Yana rolled onto her right side and aimed the pistol at the man's legs and waited. Somehow, he made no attempt to check beneath his aircraft.

Did he not hear me?

Yana didn't question the man's aptitude. Instead, she took the opportunity to crawl to the right and climb out from beneath the helicopter. Yana stood and holstered her pistol, opting for a quieter option. She loosened her rifle's sling and brought it around. She quickly checked it over and was satisfied in its condition. Yana flicked off the safety and stayed low. Before she stalked around the Harbin, she knelt and confirmed her target's position.

Okay.

She needed to be careful. Even the Falcon Commando pilots were dangerous and well-trained in traditional combat. Best case, he'd only be armed with a sidearm. Also, he wasn't Yana.

Because she was a right-handed shot, Yana headed around the front of the helicopter. The angle would be much better that way. She kept her head down and moved at a snail's pace. She could've just as easily shot the pilot's legs out, but that wouldn't have guaranteed death. He'd still be able to warn his comrades. *That* was what Yana was attempting to prevent. The commandos needed to think everything was fine here.

What is it called? Oh, yes, hunky-dory.

"Hands up!"

Yana looked over her shoulder. She hadn't thought of the possibility of there being *two* pilots.

She lowered her RSASS and raised her hands. "Shit."

The second pilot came closer, and he reached to her hip and relieved her of her PPQ as the first pilot zoomed around the front of the aircraft. He had his own pistol drawn. With no one coming to her rescue, the Blood Dragon acted.

Yana spun nonchalantly and clipped the tip of the second pilot's sidearm with her rifle as it came swinging around. With the barrel pointed in a safe direction, Yana dove forward and grabbed the man's wrist and drove the weapon skyward. They fought for a moment, but the pilot was well built and was stronger than Yana was.

So, she did what she had to, and she kneed the soldier in the crotch. The shot loosened his grip on the pistol, and it made his legs wobbly. Yana spun into his chest and wrapped her finger around his and squeezed. The bullet struck the first pilot in the shoulder and sent him sprawling to the ground.

Yana snapped an elbow up into the second pilot's chin, rocking him backward. She ripped the gun out of his hand but couldn't hang onto it. Before he could recover, Yana jumped forward and kicked him in the chest. He stumbled back toward the cliff but got his footing before going over. Yana heard movement behind her and threw herself at the aircraft. A bullet whizzed by and struck the second pilot in the chest. He looked down at the gunshot wound, stunned that his partner had just shot him. He took a step back and fell to his death.

The stock of Yana's rifle had somehow become jammed in the aircraft's front wheel mount. So, she quickly unsheathed her knife and hurled it at the seated gunman. It found its mark. Plunging deep into his stomach. He reflexively dropped his weapon and clutched the knife's handle. Yana let him be as he fell over on his side and bled out.

She had her helicopter.

Yana stepped around the aircraft and looked out over the valley. She could easily climb inside and take off and leave this dreadful mission behind.

Yana rolled her eyes and faced the monastery.

She just hoped she could get to May and Jack before it was too late. Yana stepped toward the monastery but stopped and looked over her shoulder at the Harbin Z-20. First, she'd search it for supplies. Maybe there would be something useful aboard.

45

Valley of Petals

Gareth had left and returned with three other people, one female and two men. Jack had asked to discuss the incoming force in the privacy of the upstairs library. Veer did not reject the request. He understood the subject of the conversation. If the public found out too soon, it would cause mayhem. Jack wanted Veer to be as prepared to answer any of the citizens' questions as possible.

The three newcomers were introduced as Batu, Ram, and Ella.

The first man was a thick Mongolian with eyes more intense than Bull's, a feat Jack didn't know was possible. He was in charge of the peach tree harvest and its security. The second man's name was Ram, and he was a former Nepali military man. He specifically oversaw the khukuri-wielding swordsmen. That made sense since the curved blade was in regular use within Nepal's armed forces. Interestingly, the third of Veer's captains was an American. And wouldn't you know it, Jack recognized her.

"Ella Presley?"

The athletic, ponytailed brunette turned her stern gaze upon Jack.

"You know her?" May asked, shocked.

"Yeah, well, I know *of* her. Ella was an Olympic champion archer for Team USA." Jack faced the bowwoman. "You disappeared following the 2008 Beijing games. It made headlines." His enthusiasm shrank back. She wasn't pleased with the attention. "What happened to you?"

"Nothing I wish to relive. Can we please focus on the issue at hand?"

Ella was no-nonsense, and Jack was pretty sure he knew why. Whatever she had gone through to get here must've been deeply scarring. Jack faintly recalled rumors of it involving human traffickers kidnapping several Americans, including Ella. If that were true, then Jack would happily leave it alone. It was plain to see that she was now using her expertise here. If the other archers were even half as good as Ella was, they would be formidable.

"Everyone, this is Jack Reilly. He brings us trying news from the outside world."

Jack stepped forward and laid his closed fists on the heavy wood table. He cleared his throat. "There is a heavily armed Chinese force inbound. Their numbers are unknown. Their goal is to confirm your existence and report back to the government."

"The Ministry of State Security," May added. "They want your secrets for themselves."

"And that makes them incredibly dangerous," Jack said, taking back control of the briefing. It was an emotional topic for May, and for good reason, and he wanted to keep emotion out of this powwow. He leaned in closer. "Imagine what China would become with the Peaches of Immortality?"

"It's not a superpower, Mr. Reilly," Ella said. "We can die, same as you."

"True, and it's Jack, but there's also a biotech company involved. Give them a little time to tinker, and well, you do the math."

That softened Ella's stony eyes, worrying her as it should have.

Jack faced Veer. "I'm sure your people are top-notch, but we need a more modern response. Do you have anything harder hitting than swords and arrows," he glanced at Ram and Ella, "no offense."

Veer nodded. "We have a small collection of munitions, but we've never had a reason to gather more—or even a desire to do so."

"Completely understandable." Jack motioned to himself, May, and Kalsang. "Return the pistols we arrived with, and our clothes, and give us access to your armory. We'll do everything we can to help."

Veer nodded. "Our outer wall is strong," he said, "but it's never been tested like this."

Jack shrugged. "I wish we had another option."

"Maybe we do," Kalsang said, getting everyone's attention, "but for it to work, I'll need time to go ask them."

Gareth laughed. "Bloody hell, you're thinking of asking the Dharmapala for help, aren't you?"

"I am."

"It won't work," Veer stated flatly. "They take care of themselves first. Open conflict is not their way."

Jack shook his head. "No, there's more to them than you think. I saw it back at the monastery first-hand. They care what happens around here. This is their home too. If pursued properly, I think it might work."

"Says the man who just arrived," Ella jabbed. "Excuse me, but you know nothing of our ways."

"That may be, but I do know war, and it's coming, regardless of what Dorje and his tribe may think." He looked at Veer. "It would be foolish not to try."

Veer eyed Gareth and his captains.

"It's your call, Veer," Gareth said, stepping away and looking out a window.

The Hindi sighed, then repeated the last thing Jack had just said.

"It would be foolish not to try." He locked eyes with Kalsang. "I'll give you two men. Head for Desolation and see what you can do, but under no circumstances are you to enter that godforsaken place. Gareth," the Brit returned to the table, "get them a key. They're going to need it."

Gareth was clearly against the plan, but he did as Veer asked of him. He may not respect Jack or Kalsang, but he did respect his superior.

"Well, come on, then," Gareth said, waving Kalsang onward, "let's get this over with."

Jack placed his hand on the Sherpa's shoulder as he passed. "Be careful."

Kalsang nodded to him and May and then left.

Veer stepped away from the table. "Make your preparations."

Batu, Ram, and Ella snapped to attention, stomping a foot down as they did. It must've been their version of a salute. Veer returned the gesture, and then the captains were gone.

"So," Jack said, "the armory?"

Veer gazed out the same window that Gareth had. "Yes. Follow me."

He led May out, but Jack hung back and ventured over to the window. It framed their majestic peach tree perfectly. The tree meant everything to these people. Without it, they'd all die.

And Jack would be responsible for the atrocity if it came to be.

Triratna Monastery
Forbidden Valley, Tibet

The newly arrived Falcon Commandos didn't leave much behind. Besides what Yana pilfered off the first pilot's body, including retrieving her knife from his gut, there wasn't much of anything useful for her besides a radio, medical kit, and a flare gun with three flares. She took everything, just in case.

The pilots had awarded her efforts with comms in the way of a short-range radio. It wouldn't do very much of anything in the mountains, but once they got into a more open area, she'd be able to listen in on their conversations. They had also given her a gift in the way of a select-fire, suppressed submachine gun. The QCW-05 came complete with two extra fifty round box magazines. Yana had never seen one up close. It was chambered in 5.8x21 millimeter AP rounds and was of the bullpup variety. The ultra-compact weapon sported a carry handle and iron sights and was presently slung around her back. Yana opted to carry her much larger RSASS than go at it with a firearm she was unfamiliar with.

She made it through the main level of the monastery unseen and stepped back out into the elements via the eastern exit. Yana was curious as to how the door had been ripped free of its hinges. She stepped outside and was bowled into by something massive and furry.

Both of her rifles went clattering to the floor, sliding out of reach. A monster stepped inside, barely fitting through the doorway. It was one of the creatures that had decimated the Chinese team.

And it was pissed.

It snarled and growled like a wild animal but was built like a human being. It resembled her grandmother's Chuchuna in every way. It took a step forward and sniffed the air. Yana went for her sidearm, but paused when the thing emitted a low, guttural growl. It was a warning.

Do that, and you die.

"Easy," she said, speaking in her native language.

Yana removed her hand from her hip and raised it. She slowly sat up and tried to look as meek as possible—which wasn't hard. She was terrified. Yana recalled what they had done to the commandos an hour ago. It was easy to guess what it could do to just one person. But this one was alone. Shenlong's people had been attacked by a pack of these monsters.

It took a second deep breath in, and then another. If Yana had to wager a guess, she'd say it was scenting the air like a wolf. It came closer, its breathing intensifying as it neared. Yana let it too. For some reason, this one hadn't killed her on sight. The Chuchuna was nearly seven feet tall, and its shoulders were broad—a truly hulking form.

Yana shook with terror when it knelt in front of her. It leaned in and took one last breath before doing something she would have never thought possible.

It removed its hood, looked into Yana's eyes, and said, "Jahk."

A woman?

Yana bobbed her head up and down. "Yes, Jack." She put a hand on her chest. "Jack. Friend." Yana repeated the word in English and Chinese, hoping to get through to her. "Friend."

Yana had no idea if the huntress understood her. The fact she was still alive told Yana that this larger-than-life woman knew she was here to help and not harm.

A squeak echoed from behind them.

Yana rolled onto her stomach and dove for her RSASS. She landed next to it and scooped it up, aiming it at the noise's origin. It was the pilot that she had just knifed. Yana had thought he had died, yet here he was. He tried to draw his own sidearm but was too weak to do so.

The mountainous woman snarled, then stopped when Yana pulled the trigger, dropping the pilot where he stood. This time, he was most definitely dead. The detonation of brain matter had confirmed it.

Yana slowly turned over, leaving her weapon where she had found it. She raised her hands only to find that a larger one had been lowered down to her level. The local pointed at the nearby doorway and muttered something in a language Yana had never heard before. But there was one word she did understand.

Jack.

Valley of Petals

The climb up to the mountain pass gave Kalsang the time to come up with the next part of the plan. What was he going to say to convince the Dharmapala to come to the aid of their neighbors? Was there really anything he could say? Needless to say, Kalsang was coming up with nothing. It looked like he was going to have to wing it—like a certain American he knew.

He was given two men, as Veer had promised. Neither were locals as far as their ethnicity. They looked young too, though that meant very little around here. They could've been in their fifties for all Kalsang knew, even if they looked twenty years younger.

The archer was an Arab named Abbud, and his swordsman partner was from somewhere in Eastern Europe. His name was Bohdan. Kalsang guessed he was either Ukrainian or Czech, but it was just that, a guess. And, ultimately, it didn't matter. They were Petalians, through and through.

Kalsang adjusted his ski cap, delighted to be back in his original clothing. He was also happy for his clothes to be clean. His USP pistol was also tucked back on his belt. He gazed out over the sacred Beyul before heading into the high-walled passage. His entourage kept their distance from him but stayed within speaking distance. Kalsang also had their travel permit—their golden key—in his coat pocket.

The only possession he didn't have was his backpack, not that it was needed. This wasn't anything but a cry for help. He doubted there was a circumstance where he'd need the rest of his gear. The only other equipment he had with him were his ice axe and flashlight. The axe hung from his belt, bouncing around against his left thigh.

The trek back through the mountain, the Shang Mountain Pass, took some time, time they didn't really have. Kalsang didn't say a word. He took in the pathway, recalling everything he had learned, finally having the time to delve deeper into it. They had found Shangri-La—the real one and the false one. He had lived inside the embrace of the myth for so long. Every tourist that would come through Padmaarga would ask about it.

Every single one.

The saturation had becoming maddening and had tainted the beautiful *what if* of it. Years ago, he had begun to see the subject as a nuisance—an inconvenience. But as he grew older, and wiser, he realized it was just another art of his culture. Kalsang had once met a Scotsman who had similar feelings about the Loch Ness Monster. He would routinely tell people that Scotland had more to offer than that "foul beast."

And he was right.

The Scottish Highlands were as picturesque a landscape as Kalsang had ever seen. He had been fortunate enough to visit the country once, years ago.

Kalsang had become so lost in his own head that he hadn't felt the temperature change. A brisk breeze had forced itself into the mountain pass. They were close to their destination. They were close to Desolation.

He heard chatter behind him and stopped. Kalsang turned to find his escort cowering back a little.

"Have you never been here before?" he asked, speaking the Petalian language.

The Arab spoke. "No, this is the furthest either of us has ever ventured."

Desolation

Great.

It had taken him this long to realize that he'd been given two novices—two kids. They were as young as he had originally made them out to be.

As he neared the exit, the cold stung his flesh and his eyes. He was forced to hold out his hands to block it. The first step out into Desolation was a hard one to accomplish. His body and his mind had initially balked at the movement. Both had been charmed by the milder climate of Valley of Petals.

Kalsang pushed through the discomfort and was hit with a sharp, icy gust. The young duo did the same, which impressed him. Kalsang could tell they had followed him outside, more out of curiosity than necessity. This was all new to them. Unfortunately, the Sherpa had seen plenty of freezing days like this in his life.

But never under this kind of pressure.

An entire civilization was counting on him.

The archer and swordsman hung back by the exit while Kalsang edged closer to the maelstrom ahead. The nearer he got, the more it hurt.

He was now close enough to touch the wind as it whipped by. It was a sight to see. He looked down at his feet. Most of the grim storm didn't reach out here because of the rocky area surrounding him.

Now what?

Kalsang had no idea what to do next.

So, he took a deep breath and shouted into the wind. "I call upon the Protectors!"

46

Valley of Petals

Jack and May were led into, seemingly, another random building surrounding the massive peach tree. Instead of going upstairs as they had in the library, Veer led them down to a basement that extended well past the boundary of the aboveground structure on all sides.

They came to a solid stone door with a handmade vault locking system. The door even had a spinning, circular handle. Veer removed a key from his pocket and inserted it into the center of the handle. He turned it clockwise ninety degrees, then spun the handle to the left ninety degrees. The custom locking bolt disengaged, and Veer pulled the door toward them.

"Impressive," Jack said, inspecting the door. A single metal bolt had retracted from the non-hinged side of the door. The exposed gear on the back of the door was crudely, yet efficiently, constructed out of stone and steel.

Veer smiled. "We've had a lot of time to perfect the design."

He stepped in first with Jack and May closely in tow. The room wasn't huge, but it housed quite a bit of weaponry. Unfortunately, most of it was of the blade and bow varieties.

"What you seek is in the rear of this room," Veer explained. He stepped aside and allowed Jack and May to continue on without him. "Send for me when you are finished. I will have men stationed upstairs."

"Will do," Jack said. "Thanks again."

Veer turned and left.

May was already deeper into the vault. To Jack's left was a rack filled with bows and loaded quivers. To his right, and spanning the middle of the space, was a similar rack lined with well-maintained and beautifully polished khukuri swords. Jack found May standing in front of a workbench with two shelves attached to the wall above it at the back of the armory.

He joined her and went over its contents.

"Okay. We have three AKMs, one of which looks past its prime. There's also a barebones M-16 Nepali Army service rifle, complete with signature carry handle, and an MP5 submachine gun." He examined the uppermost shelf next. "I see ammo for all of them, but mainly for the AKMs. No shocker there since 7.62x39 is the world's most commonly used rifle cartridge."

"There's a couple of pistols down here too," May said, kneeling.

Jack joined her and saw a foursome of FN P-35 handguns resting atop a vegetable crate beneath the shelving. The P-35 was a Belgian pistol based on revolutionary American firearms inventor John Moses Browning's original design, though he died before it could be completed. Browning had also been responsible for the legendary Colt M1911. It had functioned as the United States Armed Forces service pistol for over seventy years.

Enter gun manufacturer Fabrique Nationale.

The company was forced to move its production from Herstal, Belgium, to

Canada during World War II after the Nazis occupied the country. It was there that the name was changed to "Hi-Power."

Two were in rough shape. The other two looked to be serviceable. And there was plenty of ammo to go around for them. But would they fire? Jack wasn't about to put his life on the line to find out. The rifles were fairly old, but the Hi-Powers were at least a decade or two older.

Jack and May each selected one of the Soviet-produced AKMs and checked them over.

"Gotta love the furniture," Jack said, eyeing the wooden handguard, pistol grip, and stock.

Both added two additional thirty-round banana-shaped magazines each and loaded them in silence. Jack hoped the firearms had been properly taken care of.

"Eh, screw it," he said, quickly disassembling the AKM. He was both happy and confused to see it in great shape.

Must've been Veer, Jack guessed. Then again, there were hundreds of people living here that could've been more than capable of doing the job.

Desolation

Kalsang repeated the same words for fifteen minutes. It had become a mantra. His eyes were shut, his voice was hoarse, and his throat raw from the strain and the constant inhalation of the icy air berating his esophagus and lungs. He couldn't feel his nose and feared his left ear had frozen solid.

"Sherpa!"

Kalsang looked back. Bohdan, the light-skinned European, was shouting at him and waving for him to join Abbud and him. Kalsang wanted to, but he needed to keep trying. Entering Desolation would be a death sentence without the help of the Dharmapala, a tribe he hadn't been able to reach, so going to find them was out of the question. This was all he could do.

One more time.

He dug down deep and roared. "I call upon the Protectors!"

His words were ripped from his lips and thrown into the storm. Kalsang stumbled back and nearly fell but caught himself. He edged away and turned. He immediately locked onto Abbud and Bohdan's faces. They were both wide-eyed with their mouths agape, staring past Kalsang.

The Sherpa faced the onslaught, discovering three shadowy figures moving toward him. He took several steps back and allowed them a wide berth as they exited the storm.

The three tribesmen were enormous, each being over seven feet tall. Kalsang struggled with his icy fingers but was finally able to remove the key from his coat.

He held it up for the trio to see and once more said, "I, Kalsang Thapa, call upon the Protectors." He lowered the artifact and stepped closer to the tribesmen. "Please, we need your help."

The storm was something to behold, but they had no choice but to attempt to cross it. Shenlong linked arms with Gang and Ceba, and the three men ducked into the buffeting winds. Shenlong checked the compass on his rugged watch every thirty seconds to confirm that they were continuing in the right direction.

The going was slow. They were forced to maneuver around large obstacles, including boulders and the remains of primitive structures. Shenlong had no idea what could survive out here. However, the same could be said for the animals of the Sahara Desert or the frozen wastes of Siberia.

Unless it didn't always look like this? He tried to picture the barren landscape as anything but.

Ceba yanked on his right arm. Shenlong stopped, as did Gang. There, barely visible to their left, was a shapeless form in motion. It moved as slow as they did and, thankfully, didn't seem to notice the three humans.

"Come on," Shenlong said, unsure if his words were even audible.

He pulled his men further away from the roaming creature, spotting a significant lump in the terrain to hide behind. The rubble was mostly buried in snow, though the side that was not exposed to the sideward sweeping wind had remained untouched. The mercenaries knelt behind it and caught their breath, happy for the break from the constant wail of the elements.

Shenlong looked at both of his men, the only ones remaining from his original ten-man team. The utter failure of this job had given something for him to ponder. Yes, he had made the choice to accept the job, and yes, he would have turned it down if he had known what the outcome could have been.

"Let's move out," he said, but Gang and Ceba didn't get up immediately. They were spent. They also knew their odds of surviving were low and that they were moving toward an enemy that had proven themselves capable. Why would they listen to him now?

"We will make it home. I promise you."

Shenlong never connected with his men on an emotional level. It made their loss easier to handle. At the end of the day, they were hired contractors and were expendable. But he needed them now more than ever. If Shenlong went on alone, he would certainly die.

Gang stood first.

Ceba didn't look thrilled to join them, but he did. The prospect of being left alone in the storm was so much worse.

The trio re-linked arms and marched back into the open. They came across two more of the wandering sentries. One was so close that they were forced to dive to the bitterly cold ground and wait for it to pass. Shenlong had no doubt it could track them like a predator did its prey.

Whether it was because of the concealing gusts or sheer luck, Shenlong, Gang, and Ceba made it to the other side alive. They crawled up onto an embankment and rushed for cover. Safety was a natural fissure in a tall stone wall here. Shenlong shined his flashlight into it and discovered a worn pathway. He didn't investigate it any further. He quickly stepped inside, as did his companions.

As soon as all sixteen Falcon Commandos entered the turbulent plain, they made contact. The team stood out against the stark white backdrop, making it that much easier to see them. The enemy, the same creatures from before, were quite the opposite. They melded perfectly with the landscape. And they moved impossibly fast, considering how poor the footing was.

Poor for us, Fan thought. *These things live here.*

They formed a tight circle and kept the muzzles of their weapons pointed outward. The rearmost men didn't, though. They were forced to hold theirs at the low-ready and kept their head on a swivel. Walking backward would've been an idiotic thing to do. Fan had given the others the order to engage freely. He and Park kept the combined teams moving, positioning themselves at the front of the group. Every few minutes, one of the commandos, if not several of them, let off streams of gunfire.

But hits couldn't be confirmed. The shapeless blurs disappeared as soon as they arrived. But Fan didn't know what else to do. Ammunition was finite. But if they stopped firing, the beasts would close in and attack as furiously as they had before.

Worse, even. Fan swallowed. After injuring several of the creatures outside of the monastery, they had given them a reason to be more savage than before.

A murmur traveled through the commandos. When it reached Fan and Park, the leaders stopped their advance and looked back. One of the soldiers from the rear was gone.

"Where is Daoming?" Park shouted.

The men positioned on either side of the missing commando could only shrug. Neither of them had witnessed his disappearance.

"They're ghosts," Park said.

Fan shook his head. "They may move like it, but believe me, they are not of the supernatural realm."

"What are they? Can they be killed?"

Fan didn't have an answer to either question. The handful they had shot up earlier should've died during the battle, but he had witnessed their retreat into the trees, moving primarily on their own. He didn't know if their hide was like a rhino's thick, rubbery skin or if they just had a herculean threshold for pain.

Or both.

"Spread out!" Fan yelled. "Stay within shouting distance!"

47

Desolation

"What in God's name?"

That's all Yana could come up with when the inhospitable terrain appeared before her. The tribeswoman didn't look bothered, though. She led Yana up to the edge but did not enter the storm. She just stood tall and waited. Yana hung back ten feet. The intense, bitter air stung her eyes.

"What are you doing?" Yana asked, knowing full well that her words wouldn't be understood. Still, maybe the questioning tone in her voice would be enough to convey the message.

The local replied by lifting her left hand and pointing into the storm. That was the only explanation Yana was offered. They waited a few more minutes until Yana saw movement within the wintery deluge. Another of her kind stepped out onto the large, flat expanse of stone that Yana and her new friend now shared.

And it was bleeding.

Crimson dripped down the fingertips of its right hand. Yana could see two splotches of red beneath its heavy, furred sleeve up near its shoulder. The large woman looked down at the injury. The sight caused her to gaze into the storm and growl.

Just then, the wind died down enough to spot tiny specks of light bursting in uncoordinated sequences. Yana knew what it was.

"Falcon Commandos."

The tribeswoman looked at Yana. The sniper mimicked the action of firing a rifle. She even yelled, "Bang! Bang! Bang!" while doing it.

The message was loud and clear. The tribeswoman said something to her counterpart, someone Yana now realized was a man. He sauntered close enough for her to see his face within his hood. He grunted, stepped around her, and headed back toward the trees. Yana guessed she had told him to get some rest and heal up.

The huntress stepped toward the storm, but Yana stopped her by grabbing her arm.

"Woah, woah, woah!" The tribeswoman bore holes into her. "Easy there." Yana held up her hands. "There are a lot of them, and they all have guns. Sixteen men." She slowly counted them off from one to sixteen using her fingers. Her guide followed along, silently mouthing the numbers in her own language.

The odds didn't seem to bother her. She tapped her chest and then pointed forward. Then, like Yana, she counted off, telling Yana there was more of her kind out there fighting.

She needs to help them.

Yana knew she needed to help, especially if she wanted her guide to continue to help her in return.

"Fine, okay, let's see."

Yana studied the winds and knew immediately that her rifle and scope would be useless. So, she slipped out of her pack, tightened the sling as far as it could go, and positioned it across her back. It was incredibly uncomfortable since the Chinese submachine gun she had pilfered from the helicopter earlier was already there. She made it even worse by putting the pack back on over both weapons. She loosened the straps to make it fit more comfortably.

"How do you want to do this?" Yana exaggerated the shrug of her shoulders.

The woman pulled back the furs from around her waist to reveal her rock-hard midriff and her preferred method of killing. She was a hunter and did so with a pair of clawed brass knuckles made from what Yana recognized as sharpened bear claws and wood. She slid them into place and held them up for Yana to see.

"Holy shit."

The huntress moved to leave but was stopped by Yana, once more.

"Hang on," Yana said, slipping out of her backpack again.

The sniper dropped to one knee and dug through her bag, removing a coil of rope. She unfurled about twenty feet of it. Yana unsheathed her knife and sliced through the rope with a flick of her wrist. Next, she tied off an end to her belt, offering the opposite end to the tribeswoman. Thankfully, she understood what to do.

Once they were attached to one another, Yana lifted her own blade and gave the primal hunter a wink. She was ready.

"Oh, by the way, I'm Yana." She put a hand on her chest and repeated. "Ya-na."

The huntress placed her hand on her chest and said, "Drilha."

Without another word, they stepped into the storm.

It was the closest thing to blindness that Yana had ever experienced. She couldn't see a thing except when the wind died down intermittently. Drilha, on the other hand, seemed to know exactly where she was going. She leaned forward, darting her head back and forth like a scent hound. And that's what she was doing. It amazed Yana to watch the professional in action.

Suddenly, Yana was pulled diagonally left. Drilha sped up, making Yana break out into a light jog. The terrain was rough, and Yana nearly fell twice. Drilha must've sensed her struggling behind her because she slowed enough for Yana to get her feet back under her.

And just in time too.

A blob materialized within the chaotic surge of snow flurries. Drilha slowed to a crawl and got low, but she was so much larger than her human colleague that Yana didn't have to match her stance. Yana equaled the huntress' speed and waited for her to make the first move.

The commando turned, bringing his weapon light around. Yana recognized what was about to happen and shoved Drilha to the ground with all her might. Both women landed on their stomachs, making little to no noise. The snow cushioned their fall, and the wind masked any of the sounds they had made.

Drilha gave Yana a venomous glare but soon realized what Yana had done for her. The light's beam passed over their prone bodies without stopping and without them being noticed.

"Go!" Yana hissed, getting to her feet.

Drilha followed suit and rushed the gunman from behind. Without remorse, she roared and jammed her clawed right fist into his lower back. Yana put the exclamation point on the attack by slitting the man's throat before he could warn anyone.

A second light whipped their way. This time, it was Drilha that hit the ground first. Yana flattened herself next to her, and they waited for it to pass. Yana could tell that Drilha wanted nothing more than to slaughter every one of the Falcon Commandos, but she needed to get to Jack and May. Plus, Yana knew the soldiers would eventually get off a clean shot. Drilha may have been able to withstand multiple gunshot wounds, but Yana couldn't.

Yana tapped the huntress' shoulder and pointed toward their original destination. "Jack!" she said. "I need Jack!"

Drilha looked up at the next closest soldier and sneered, but she returned her attention to Yana and nodded. "Jack."

Valley of Petals

Veer was called to the front gates after meeting with a few of the village's elders. The seniors held no "office" but were respected by everyone and were kept in the loop on all major decisions—advisors of sorts. The oldest resident in the Valley of Petals had recently celebrated his 165th birthday, though Veer wasn't sure how many more he had left in him. The oldest recorded citizen had lived until he was 184, though anything past 170 was rare.

It took Veer some time to get back to the gates, but when he did, he could see guards had already allowed the weary travelers entrance. Typically, Veer—and Veer alone—granted people entry, but this was different. These three didn't need permission. They had all been granted access at one time or another.

The Sherpa, Kalsang Thapa, led the way. He stomped down the main road, separating the gathered crowd of Petalians. Abbud and Bohdan weren't far behind him. They matched the Sherpa's look of disappointment. Veer didn't even have to ask him what the Dharmapala had said. Their expressions spoke loud and clear.

"Welcome back," he said. His men snapped to attention, then relaxed. Veer returned their salute.

Kalsang stopped in front of Veer but gazed further into the city. "Where's Jack and May?"

Veer gave his people a nervous look before tipping his head back the way he had come. "Follow me." He glanced at Abbud and Bohdan. "Leave us. Return to your duties here."

Veer headed off with a disappointed Kalsang not too far behind.

Jack had successfully disassembled all the rifles and checked them over. As he had originally thought, a few of the weapons were entirely unusable. He had discarded them, tossing them into a "dead pile" on the floor. May had taken up the arduous task of loading every magazine she could find. Jack had prayed for her thumbs, hoping they wouldn't get chewed up too badly.

Never once did she complain.

He heard footsteps coming up from behind—multiple sets of them. One of them was much heavier than the other. Jack racked the charging handle on what was to be his AKM and set it down on the workbench. He turned and wiped his oily hands on his pants, seeing Veer step over the threshold into the vault with a familiar face behind him. May paused what she was doing, giving the two men her undivided attention.

"Kalsang," Jack said, seeing the solemn look on his face. "They aren't coming, are they?"

He shrugged. "I spoke with a scout. He said he'd convey our message to Dorje and Drilha." He looked over the khukuris as he spoke. "But based on his demeanor, I think it's safe to say they will be sitting this one out."

May's only response was to turn and continue loading magazines.

Jack stepped up to his Sherpa friend and placed a reassuring hand on his shoulder. "You tried. That's all we could ask for." Jack looked past him and noticed a thick, coiled rope on the wall. He edged around Kalsang, retrieved it, and returned to his workbench. He estimated lengths and cut apart the rope.

Then, he tied them onto the rifles to use as slings.

Good enough.

He turned and tossed the M-16 to Kalsang. May lobbed him a second, curved thirty-round magazine.

"We've got a lot of preparations to make. I need you, Veer, and Gareth, wherever he is, to bridge the language gap and start moving people indoors or out to the farms. If Shenlong gets through the front gate, we must keep the fight away from the tree. Use the buildings." He glanced at May, then back to Kalsang and Veer. "Our enemy is bound to be wearing body armor, so aim low unless you have a clear headshot."

Veer didn't argue as Jack took command. "I will relay this to Ella and her archers. What about Ram's people?"

"If they can get close enough, go for the neck, arms, and legs. Tell them to chop some wood. You—"

A third set of footfalls brought Jack's intense briefing to a screeching halt. It was Gareth, and he was breathing hard. He stopped within the doorway, leaning against it while he gasped for air.

"What's wrong?" Veer asked, back in control.

"We have…more…visitors."

Veer glanced at Jack. "Chinese commandos?" Jack asked.

Gareth shook his head. "No—maybe?"

"Who—?" Veer started.

"Their leader requested an audience with them," Gareth pointed toward Jack and May, "Wu and the American spy."

Jack met eyes with May.

He faced Gareth. "Take us to them."

Marching down the main road of the Valley of Petals, while armed to the teeth, turned quite a few heads. Jack figured that most of the people here had never seen anything like it, especially with modern-ish firearms involved. The newest rifle was the M-16 Jack had given Kalsang, and even it was decades old.

"Do we have you to thank for the condition of these?" Jack asked Veer, holding up his AKM.

Veer nodded. "It helped with the transition of being here. It was quite the culture shock coming from where I did."

"I get it," Jack said. "My first couple of years living on the outside of the military was rough. I had no purpose."

"We all have a purpose, Jack," Veer countered. "Sometimes it just takes a while to figure out what it is."

When they reached the gate, Jack, May, and Kalsang were led up a corkscrewing set of steel and wood steps to the lookout post. It's where they had spotted the archers when they had first approached the gate. Four of them vacated a spot directly above the gates to make room for Veer and the others as they approached. The bald Hindi started forward first but was stopped.

"Let me," Jack said. "It's better they don't know who you are yet."

Veer nodded and stepped aside. Jack shouldered his AKM and aimed it over the edge and down. He spotted three men standing with their hands up and their weapons on the ground.

"These are the men that asked for you," Gareth reiterated. "I believe the one in the middle is their leader."

May leaned in close to Jack. "That's him."

"Him who?" Jack asked, never taking his eyes off the newcomers.

"The one in the middle...that's Shenlong."

48

Desolation

The killer and the huntress skirted around the action and made their way to the other side of the white expanse. They could see the war waging off to their left the entire way across. It pained Yana to hear the cries of injured members of Drilha's tribe. She knew the woman wanted nothing more than to get back out there and slay more foes.

They moved as fast as they could, and as they neared the end, the gunfire ceased. Yana didn't know if the battle had ended or if they were too far away from it now. She hoped all the commandos were dead, of course, but did not think that was the case.

The storm dissipated. An incline similar to the one they had trekked through at the beginning of this hunt came into view. This one, however, sported the bones of hundreds of bodies.

Yana was too exhausted to care. She fell onto it, out of breath. Her hands shook. At least, she thought they shook. She couldn't feel them or the knife she still clutched. She took a second, happy to feel her fingers slowly returning to her.

Drilha paid her recovery no attention. She was turned, facing the storm. The huntress wanted to leap back into action.

"Come with me," Yana urged, pointing toward a hole in the rock wall.

Drilha turned and gazed up at the opening. She shook her head, tapped her chest, and pointed at the battlefield.

Her people need her.

Yana frowned but nodded. "Go."

Drilha didn't verbally respond or give her a wave goodbye. The tribal warrior simply re-entered the blizzard and disappeared. Yana was, once again, alone. But she was infinitely closer to her destination than before. There had been no possible way she would've made it across this storm without Drilha's help. Yana felt terrible for abandoning an ally in need and not helping her more, but she had made a promise to May and Jack.

And to herself.

Yuck. Emotions.

She made her way up the incline and edged herself inside the entrance. Nothing attacked her. Yana stopped, removed her pack, and loosened the sling on the smaller submachine gun. She felt that this was a better option in the tight confines of the tunnel. It also featured a similar suppressor to her RSASS, so she wouldn't be blowing out her eardrums if she was forced to use it while moving within the earth. It would still hurt, but it wouldn't deafen her.

She flicked on its barrel-mounted light and took off at a brisk walk, deeper into the mountain pass.

Valley of Petals

Jack was confused, now more than ever. Shenlong, the man who had been trying to kill him since he first set foot in Nepal, was standing before him in a posture of surrender. He didn't like it one bit. If Jack were as heartless as the mercenary, he would've shot Shenlong, there and now.

But Jack wasn't without heart.

"Why are you here?" he asked.

Shenlong stepped away from his men and lowered his hands down to his side. The archers had their arrows nocked, but they had yet to draw back their bowstrings. The three men below them were unarmed and not an immediate threat. Jack wasn't taking that chance, though. Neither was May. Both aimed their AKMs at the merc. Kalsang gripped his M-16 hard but wasn't actively pointing it at anyone.

"As much as it pains me to admit it, we need your help."

Jack and May laughed so much so that Jack's eyes watered. He hadn't laughed this hard in quite a while. Shenlong didn't appreciate the reaction. Then again, Jack didn't care what the asshole thought.

"I'm inclined to say no," Jack replied. "Give me one reason why we should help you?"

Shenlong stepped even closer. "If you do, I'll give you all the information you want concerning David Cho and Minister Zhao." He bore holes into Jack. "All of it."

"Won't that ruin you?" May asked.

Shenlong shrugged. "For a time, maybe, but Cho turned on us. We have no loyalty to him, not anymore." He smiled. "Oh, and there's also a team of Falcon Commandos beating down this beautiful place's door."

May's eyes darted to Jack, but he didn't need any explanation. He knew who they were and what their capabilities were.

"They were a gift from your father, Ms. Wu." Shenlong stepped back in line with his men. "Safe to say he no longer wants you back alive."

"This is bad, Jack," May said, voice low.

"I know."

She faced him, not caring at all if it gave Shenlong any kind of satisfaction. "China is about to find this place."

"I know!" he shouted, frustrated.

The outburst caused everyone around them to flinch. Everyone except May. She held her ground and rode Jack's emotional wave. It was plain to see that she knew he wasn't directing it toward her. He apologized with his eyes and a nod and turned back to Shenlong.

"Give me a minute to confer with the leader."

Jack, May, and Kalsang stepped away with Veer and Gareth close behind them. They stayed atop the lookout post but out of sight from the men below. This was very bad, indeed.

"They cannot be allowed entry," Gareth said.

Veer held up his hand and waited for Jack to speak.

"I would normally agree with you," Jack said, "but—"

"But nothing!"

Veer shot Gareth a look that shut him up. "Can we trust these men?"

"Absolutely not," Jack replied.

May sighed. "But we don't have a choice."

All eyes turned to her.

"They have invaluable information, and they know where we are. If even one of them escapes, the location of the Valley of Petals will become known to the world."

Veer turned and looked out over the village and thought to himself. After a few moments of peace, he spoke.

"We have a small prison cell."

Gareth seethed. "Veer, no."

Veer turned to Jack. "Give them the option to be led to it or die where they stand."

Veer's morality was identical to Jack's.

Jack returned to the front of the lookout post. "You will step away from your weapons and keep your hands where we can see them. Then, you will be escorted to a holding cell until further notice. We will come to have our chat soon after."

Shenlong conversed with his two remaining men. "We agree to your terms."

"I don't like this," Gareth said.

"Nor do I," Kalsang agreed.

Jack turned to them. "No one likes this, but we need what they have."

Veer eyed Jack, then raised his hand. The archers drew back their bowstrings and took aim. Veer shouted a quick command, and the gates beneath their feet rumbled open. Jack made his way to the rear of the lookout post, leaned over the edge, and watched as four burly men spun two giant wheels attached to chains. When the gates were ten feet apart, the same team of swordsmen from before marched out, dual blades at the ready.

Shenlong and his men were instantly surrounded. The ten white-clad men closed in on the three prisoners and ushered them forward towards the gates. Shenlong motioned for his people to put their hands on their heads, and they did. Another six swordsmen greeted the trio and took up formation in front of them. Jack stepped into view above their heads.

"Too bad they don't have to strip down," Jack mumbled.

May and Veer gave Jack a sideways glance.

Jack shrugged. "Humiliating bad guys is kinda my thing. You should've seen what I did to this guy in Poland."

"Sorry, Jack," Veer said, "but things change in times of war."

That Jack agreed with.

Shenlong looked up at him. "Impressive, Mister—"

"My name is not important, but if you want to call me something, you can call me," Jack smiled, "Uncle Sam."

"Okay, *Uncle Sam*, as I was saying, this is all very impressive, but as I'm sure you have figured out, it won't be enough. What's coming is a hurricane."

Jack heard the rumbles of the locals talking under their breath. While Shenlong spoke mostly the truth, Jack needed to deflect the people's worry.

"That may be so, but the warriors here are far greater than even the might of Desolation!"

The crowd cheered, making Jack feel like he was a medieval king giving his troops a pep talk before their eventual massacre. If a Falcon Commandos team was genuinely inbound, the battle here would be short and anything but sweet.

Jack's knees shook. His legs were about to give out. Luckily, Shenlong and the two other mercs were led away before they could see Jack's confidence falter. He leaned against the guardrail and put his head in his hands. May's hand found his shoulder and she squeezed. Veer leaned along with him.

"What now?" he asked.

Jack stood upright. "We see what they know and pray that the Dharmapala answer our call. Regardless," he looked at Veer, "you might want to start moving your people."

Veer bit his lip but agreed. "We have a sacred place beneath the valley. It will make an adequate shelter. I'll talk with my captains."

Jack's face said it all. He was curious.

"The door near the base of the tree, the one with two men stationed there day and night, you saw it, yes?" Jack nodded. "It leads to Mother's tomb."

Desolation

By the time Drilha made it back to the battle between her tribe and the intruders, the battle had ended. She found five of her own gathered around a lump in the snow-covered ground. She couldn't see what it was, but she could smell *who* it was. She quickened her pace, taking in scents as she moved. No one else had her ability to pick up scents in Desolation.

Sonam!

Drilha rushed over. Her people separated and allowed her to come nearer. As she did, they backed off and gave her room. Not only was she the best hunter, but she was also her tribe's best healer. But as soon as she reached Sonam, Drilha already knew she was too late. There was too much blood on the ground already.

The young scout was hemorrhaging heavily from a wound to his neck. She could see a ragged wound in the side of it, as well as the tool that was responsible: A knife. His life pulsed from the injury as fast as the mighty river to the east.

Drilha knelt beside her kin and wept for him. He was already too far gone to see her tears. She didn't care as they froze on her cheeks. No one in their tribe had died at the hands of an enemy in ages. Sonam's death would be honored. It would be celebrated. A warrior's death.

He lifted a shaky hand up to Drilha, but it fell back to earth before she could clasp it. Sonam was dead.

Drilha roared into the sky, as did the others. Their combined bellows could be heard for miles, carried by the harsh winds of Desolation. She wiped her nose and stood, but not before retrieving the instrument of Sonam's destruction. She brought the blade up to her face, ignored Sonam's scent, and found what she was searching for. She seared the second scent into her memory. If Drilha ever came across it again, she would know who it belonged to.

"Bring him," she said, heading back toward the monastery. As much as she wanted to avenge his murder, and rip his killer to pieces limb by limb, there was an important tradition to uphold.

Two of her largest tribesmen picked Sonam off the ground and carried him. She led them, mumbling her people's prayer of everlasting rest to herself.

"May your spirit soar with the mountain winds. May your body feed the earth beneath our feet. Rest, fearless warrior, rest."

The other members of her tribe were, no doubt, repeating the same prayer.

49

Valley of Petals

Jack stood six feet away from the iron bars. There really was a prison here. It was a single eight-by-eight cell and was more than enough for a place like the Valley of Petals.

"So, you're Shenlong, huh?" Jack asked, looking the mercenary up and down. He had since removed his heavy winter coat to reveal a thick yet chiseled upper body beneath a long-sleeve thermal. The blue dragon scales tattoos were visible along his forearms, thanks to his rolled-up sleeves.

"And you're, what, Agent Wu's new pet?" he replied, coming closer to the locked door.

Jack didn't answer. He shrugged and allowed May to take over. She stepped up next to Jack.

"You said you possessed information about David Cho and a team of commandos that we needed to hear. Start talking, or we'll hand you over to the creatures on a platter made of their bones." May pointed at the two men behind Shenlong.

Jack liked the fact that May had kept up the monster charade. It would serve them better if the prisoners were kept in the dark about who the Dharmapala really were.

She crossed her arms across her chest, trying desperately to relax her jaw. Saying she was tense was woefully underselling it. After all, this man had been ordered to kill her. Jack too.

Shenlong's stony expression faltered. Just the mention of the Dharmapala made the hardened killer uncomfortable.

"Yes," Shenlong said, finding his words, "well, how did you get past them alive?"

"Sorry, buddy," Jack said, "but that's a need-to-know. Answer her question."

"And you, the American enigma. You were obviously a soldier at one time, and now, you're what?"

"Losing my patience."

Veer shouted something in Petalian, and an archer stepped up next to Jack and another one next to May. They drew back their bows, aiming for Shenlong's men. The message was clear: Continue to waste time, and it will be your teammates that die, not you.

Shenlong held up his hands. "Fair enough." Veer ordered the archers to standdown. When they did, Shenlong proceeded with his briefing. "Cho contracted me to hunt down Ms. Wu and the old Sherpa's DNA and deliver both back to him and Zhao, respectively. The mission changed once *he* showed up." Shenlong tipped his chin at Jack.

"You bombed a hospital, you monster!" May shouted.

Shenlong stared at her. "I've done worse. Unfortunately, the Sherpa's blood came back negative, which forced Cho to alter course and—"

"And send you here," Jack finished.

Shenlong nodded. "Yes. We tracked you to Langtang after we stumbled upon an article that detailed a tomb that was found in the valley."

"Hang on," Jack said, "how did you know what to look for, you didn't have—" Jack rubbed his forehead, and groaned. "Binsa."

"Binsa?" May asked. "Who—" It hit her like a ton of bricks. How could May forget Thapa's nurse? "You son of a bitch! What did you do to her?"

The smug prick said, "She was, what you would say, collateral damage."

May rushed forward and reached through the bars and grabbed Shenlong by the throat. "You bastard!"

Shenlong didn't fight her off. He stood still and took her ineffective assault in stride. Jack placed a hand on May's shoulder, calming her enough to get her to release the killer and step away.

"We then came under sniper fire and lost six men."

May laughed, wiping her face dry with her sleeve. "Serves you right. It's good to know our plan worked."

Shenlong's eyes darkened. "That was your doing?"

Jack snorted out a laugh. "What? You can dish it out, but you can't take it?" Shenlong sneered. "I believe it's called 'collateral damage,' right?"

God, that felt good!

Jack reveled in the mercenary's torment. He seldomly tolerated this type of behavior, or enjoyed it, but this guy had hurt so many people.

"Continue," Veer said, standing still as a statue. He, once again, ordered the archers forward.

Shenlong held up a hand, and the archers stood down.

"We followed you to Lamabagar and discovered the beautiful lake beneath the monastery." Jack was about to ask him who he killed there but left the subject alone. If he did admit to murdering someone, Jack was pretty sure he'd shoot him, here and now. That, or May would. "We were met outside by a team of Falcon Commandos."

"Your old outfit, right?" Jack asked.

Shenlong shot him a look, which meant that he had been correct. "They were a gift from Minister Zhao." He gazed at May. "They came with your kill order, and to aid with my mission." He actually smiled. "Your sniper friend killed five of them with five shots to the north of Lamabagar."

His demeanor did a one-eighty. "Then, the creatures showed up. They were—"

"Terrifying?" Jack asked.

Shenlong nodded. "They tore through us as if we were nothing. Our bullets did nothing to them except make them angrier, and lust for our blood more. They whittled the commandos down to four in seconds. One of my men also fell."

But then the asshole had to go and smile.

"What's so funny?" Jack asked.

"It was shortly after the attack that twelve more Falcon Commandos arrived in a helicopter. I'm not sure what happened after that. We vacated the cliffside monastery and came here. I have a feeling they want us gone too."

"I can't imagine why," May jabbed.

"How did you cross Desolation?" Veer asked from the back of the room.

Shenlong looked past Jack and May. "And you are?"

"The man responsible for the safety of this community. Now, tell me, how did you cross that frozen wasteland?"

The merc shrugged. "It wasn't easy, but nor was it all that difficult. If that's all you have as far as security, I'm surprised this place hasn't been found before now."

It was easy to see that they weren't getting a straight explanation out of the guy.

Jack closed in on the jail cell. "And now you beg for our help. How humiliating."

Shenlong met Jack stride for stride until the two men were only a foot apart. "I do what I must. Survival is all that matters, not how you achieve it. Regrettably, I don't think this beautiful place will see tomorrow morning." He turned and stepped away. "Not without our help."

"Sorry, pal, but there's nothing you can say that—"

Once more, Gareth came rushing in. "We have another traveler at the gate!"

Jack let the prisoners be and joined the others in quiet conversation by the doorway. Gareth looked at Jack and spoke, keeping his voice low. "It's another friend of yours."

Jack's eyebrow raised.

Veer faced him. "How many *acquaintances* do you have out here?"

Jack had no idea what was going on. "At this point, too many."

Triratna Monastery
Forbidden Valley, Tibet

They carried Sonam's remains back to the monastery where Dorje was already waiting for them. He stood tall, alone in the courtyard at the base of the icy steps. Sonam was set before his chief. Dorje knelt and said his own prayer, placing his hand across the fallen warrior's closed eyes. When he was finished, he stood and nodded.

"Prepare him."

The same two tribesmen recollected Sonam and carried him up the steps and into the monastery. Drilha was beside herself. Once more, she roared into the air, causing every living creature within a mile to hurry away. Dorje attempted to comfort her, but she shoved him away and ripped a pine tree from the ground, roots, and all. Then, in a display of remarkable strength, she heaved the twenty-foot-tall growth over the low wall as if it were only a twig.

"Calm yourself!"

She snarled and turned on her husband. He growled back, not backing down from her. Drilha didn't back down either. The two were meant for one another.

Drilha's eyes burned. "I. Want. Blood."

The chief relaxed and smiled wide, proud of his huntress wife. "And you will get it. But first, we need to tend to Sonam, and then, gather the other tribes." He stroked her cheek. "We will have our vengeance."

Desolation

The twelve surviving Falcon Commandos took up refuge just inside the entrance to what looked like a tunnel passage through the rock. Both Fan and Park had lost a man during the chaotic ambush. One of them had simply vanished. Park's man had been impaled from behind and then had his throat cut.

Fan couldn't believe it. Since he and his men had landed in Nepal, an entire team's worth of top-notch soldiers had been killed, swiftly. Their intelligence on the matter was slim, to begin with. But no one could've adequately prepared for what they had encountered so far, even the great Sun Tzu. Sniper fire from behind, hostile mountain beasts at the forefront, and freezing temperatures from above.

Park was missing his M95 combat knife. He was sure he had mortally injured one of the creatures, though Fan wasn't convinced that was even possible. Fan was impressed with Park's decision to not fire upon the monster, and instead, had gotten in close and undetected.

"Five minutes!" Fan shouted, aiming his voice down the passage.

Everyone who had been sitting or lying down stood on cue. Each man quickly double-checked their weapons and ammo. A few even stretched while waiting to move out. It was easy for joints to stiffen in weather such as this. Fan was one of them. His back was killing him. Other than that, he felt okay. He was tired, but not exhausted. Working in cold climates did have its benefits sometimes. Sweating to the point of dehydration wouldn't be a problem.

But getting eaten alive is.

Fan started through the mountain pass and met up with the forwardmost commando, Park. He was kneeling and peering deeply into the darkness ahead of them. His eyes were closed. He was concentrating—listening.

"Anything?" Fan asked, partially shielding his weapon light with his left hand.

Park stood and shook his head. "All is quiet."

Fan glanced behind him. "Unless those things are sitting and waiting."

"Yes, that is a possibility, but I don't think so."

Fan looked at Park and waited for elaboration.

"The rest of the creatures did not follow us after we injured the one." Park clicked on his rifle light. "I believe the only resistance we will see from here on will be of the human variety."

Fan sighed. *Let's hope.*

50

Valley of Petals

Four men were left to watch over the prisoners, two archers and two swordsmen. Gareth rushed ahead of Jack, May, Kalsang, and Veer, as well as a plethora of armed guards. They had very little information to go on. Gareth had only been sent for the others and had been given no additional information about their most recent visitor.

As they neared the front gate, Jack picked up on pieces of the crowd's conversations.

"Heavily armed."

"Dangerous looking."

"Fearless eyes."

Gareth and Veer made it to the corkscrewing stairs first with May hot on their heels. Jack had fallen behind a little, as had Kalsang.

"Won't put down!" a man yelled in broken English.

"What?" Veer shouted, looking up.

An archer leaned out over the rail of the lookout post and repeated. "She won't put down weapon!"

"Do not engage!" May shouted, pushing past Veer and Gareth with a burst Jack didn't think she had. "Do not engage!" She made it to the top and waved her hands.

Veer reiterated the order to his men in their language. They all stood down, relaxing their bowstrings. They did not, however, replace their arrows in their quivers.

Jack and Kalsang approached the lookout post shortly after Veer and Gareth. He had figured out why May had gone nuts a moment before. Jack stepped up next to her and looked down at the lone figure standing before them.

"So, you must be Yana?"

The heavily armed blonde gave Jack a quick wave. "And you must be Jack?" She looked at May. "He's cute, good work!"

May looked mortified. She cleared her throat. "It's good to see you too."

Yana took in the archers. "I don't suppose you can tell them I come in peace, yes?"

Veer joined Jack and May, now standing between them.

"Please," May begged. "She's a friend—a real friend."

Jack added, "She's okay, she's been keeping the Chinese off our butts with that big rifle."

"You mean the one she has refused to put down?"

Jack scratched the top of his head and avoided Veer's glare. "Yeah, that one."

Veer wiped the sleep from his face and shouted something in Petalian.

As they had done with Shenlong, the foursome of burley men began to open the gate.

"Keep your hands where we can see them!" Veer shouted. "You will be escorted through!"

Yana looked up at her raised hands and held them higher. "Yes, okay, I am already doing this, see?" She waved them around wildly. "Look, for the people in the back, hands are up!"

Kalsang leaned in close to Jack. "She reminds me of you."

May must've heard the Sherpa's comment because the corner of her mouth curled upward as she headed for the spiraling stairs. Jack, once more, followed May down the steps. He hoped it would be the last time, but he knew it was a fool's wish. There were still plenty of variables out there, namely the Falcon Commandos, and hopefully, the Dharmapala.

When they reached the bottom, a very exhausted looking Russian sniper was led in by the same ten swordsmen that had ushered in Jack's group as well as Shenlong and his men. This had to have been the busiest day ever for them. Then again, Jack knew very little about their past "visitors."

The Blood Dragon was tall. She was somewhere between Jack and May in height, but built similarly to May, toned and lean. She sported white and gray camouflaged winterwear, a backpack, and a bevy of weapons. Yana had been prepared for serious combat.

The first words she spoke when she stepped into the mythic mountain paradise was, "Is there a toilet nearby?" No one answered her. "Fine, I can hold it."

May rushed up to her and embraced the sniper. They parted and faced Jack and the others. She held out her hand to Jack. He joined them and shook Yana's hand. Her grip was strong.

"RSASS," he said, admiring the rifle, "rare in these parts." Jack released her hand. "What can you tell us?"

Yana smiled. "Straight to the point."

"Not always," May added.

Before Jack could reply with a comment, Yana gave them a quick rundown on her last few days. It was great to hear that she had dwindled down the numbers of Shenlong's team and the commandos so effectively, and by herself. Then, she described the bloody massacre outside Triratna Monastery. Everything she was telling them coincided with Shenlong's debriefing.

"The Dharmapala are fierce," May said.

"Dharmapala?" Yana asked.

Jack nodded. "That's what the mountain tribe is called."

"How did you get here?"

The group separated to allow Veer entrance into the circle. His presence changed Yana's demeanor. She instantly became serious and guarded.

"Easy," May whispered. "He's in charge here."

"Veer Burman, this is Yana Fedorov."

"She's Russian," the Indian said.

"And?" Yana replied, taking offense.

Veer gazed at her. "I don't trust Russian military-types."

Yana grinned. "Neither do I. I'm what you would call 'freelance.'"

Gareth pushed his way through. "You're a mercenary?"

"And a damn good one!" she countered.

The Brit rubbed his face hard. "Great, another killer in our midst."

Yana faced him. "Another? Who else is here?"

Jack glanced at May. Yana must've sensed the tension between them. Jack was hoping to avoid this exact situation. The man she had been tasked with hunting was currently sitting idle in a prison cell.

Yana's fire returned. "He's here, isn't he?"

May raised her hands, attempting to keep the sniper calm. "Yes, Shenlong is here, but he has been captured, and—"

"You allowed him to live?" Yana shouted, appalled.

"And he's going to stay that way," Jack said. "Cold-blooded murder is not the way here, and we *will* respect that."

"It will be the way if Shenlong gets free."

"You don't know that," May argued.

"I agree with her," Gareth added, pointing at Yana, "he should be taken care of before—"

Jack stepped forward, commanding the group. "All of you, stop!"

Gareth opened his mouth but was silenced by Jack. "Say something, and she removes your tongue." He pointed at Yana.

The Russian smiled.

"No, someone of Yana's profession is not typically the most ideal of allies," he glanced at her, "no offense." She shrugged. "But I trust her to help us the best way she knows how, and that is a talent we desperately need on our side." He faced the Russian. "And no, none of us will be 'taking care of' Shenlong."

Yana was plainly displeased, but she didn't openly dispute Jack.

"She still hasn't answered my question," Veer said. He gazed at Yana. "How did you get here?"

"The Dharmapala. I made friends with one called Drilha." Yana sunk deep into thought. "I think she knew I was coming."

May smiled. "I asked her to watch for you."

Jack looked up to see that the sky was darkening. A flurry of possibilities flashed across his mind. Few of them were good.

"The soldiers will attack at night. That's when we'll be at our most vulnerable." He turned to Veer. "I'm guessing this place gets very dark after the sun sets."

He nodded. "It does, but we keep oil lamps lit along the main paths, just in case."

Jack looked for them. Four lamps sat atop iron poles at each corner of the nearby intersection.

"Light them accordingly. Give the commandos a false sense of success. They'll think they've got us, but we'll know they're here." Jack faced Gareth. "Start moving your people to Mother's tomb, now."

He didn't budge until Veer echoed the command. "Do it. Batu, Ram, Ella." The three captains emerged from the crowd. Thankfully, Veer continued in English. "Help Gareth. The only ones left topside are those willing to fight."

The captains saluted their leader and went about clearing the immediate area, parroting what Veer wanted done. None of the villagers voiced any argument. They already understood the stakes.

"Veer."

The Petalian leader was lost in the commotion. Even he was having trouble focusing on the issue while his people's lives were being uprooted. Jack gave him a second, before repeating his name.

"Veer."

The Hindi turned and faced Jack.

Jack waved for Yana to join them. "Get her in the highest, most centralized point. We need her to see everything."

He gave the Russian an untrusting stare.

For her part, Yana shouldered her RSASS rifle and gave Veer a wink. "Time to kill some bad guys, yes?" Veer gave Jack one last look. "Go," Yana beckoned, "I will be your guardian angel."

Finally, Veer turned away and headed off, but not before Yana skidded to a halt and shrugged out of her pack.

"Oh, Jack, I have a gift."

"A gift?" he asked.

She nodded. "Yes, from one of the Falcon Commandos. Here." She unslung a second rifle from her back and dug out two large magazines from her pack. "I figured a man of your *background* will see that it gets proper use."

Yana handed Jack a Chinese-made bullpup submachine gun. Jack hated bullpups—chiefly, the ejection port and its proximity to the shooter's neck and the all-important carotid artery. Still, it was a modern weapon and easily the newest one in the Valley of Petals. Jack checked it over, getting a feel for what the compact, select-fire firearm offered. He especially appreciated the can on the end. Having something suppressed would prove invaluable knowing what was coming down the pike.

"Hello, gorgeous!"

"Yes, well…"

Jack looked up from the weapon. "I was talking to her," he said, holding up the SMG. Yana smiled at the humor, then left.

"Should I be worried?"

Jack looked over his shoulder and found May staring at him.

He faced her but didn't make eye contact. Jack continued to fiddle with his new present.

"Nah, she's not my type."

"What type?"

He shrugged. "You know, tall, blonde, beautiful."

"How terrible."

He threw the rifle over his shoulder, unsure of what to do with the much older AKM. So, he kept it, slinging it tightly around his back.

"She's not bad, but I prefer women a little shorter." He stepped closer to May. "Dark hair, dark eyes…" He was only a few feet from her now. "Someone who can take care of herself, but someone who still has a conscience…" His last step put him within mere inches from May. "But most of all, I love a woman who is an emotional disaster."

May rolled her eyes and thumped her forehead into Jack's chest. "You're such a jerk." She lifted her head away and looked into his eyes. "But thanks."

"Are you love birds 'bout done?"

They found Gareth staring at them from ten feet away. Jack realized that he and May were the only ones not moving.

Gareth marched up to them and kept his voice low. "Look, as much as it pains me to admit, we do, in fact, need your help. But we need you both at your best, not getting lost in each other's eyes at the drop of a hat."

Jack was going to argue with him but didn't. The Brit was right.

"How's the evacuation going?"

Gareth looked around. "Fine, you know, considering we've never done something like this before—to this scale, anyways."

"And Mother's tomb?"

He nodded. "Open and already accepting refugees." Gareth looked grim.

"What's wrong?" May asked.

"The tomb. There is no exit down there. If our resistance fails up here, everyone down there is—"

"Then," Jack interrupted, "we don't fail. We *won't* fail."

51

"So, why are we doing this again?" Jack asked, slightly confused. He was currently rubbing a sliced open peach on his clothes and exposed skin. If he didn't know any better, he would've thought he was preparing himself for a man-eating cyclops' dinner.

Kalsang translated the Mongol captain's next words. "He says it's so the snow leopards don't eat you."

Jack and May stopped slathering themselves in peach juice and gave Kalsang a "huh?" look. Kalsang quickly conversed with Batu.

"Evidently, the leopards have been trained to not attack anyone who smells of the valley's sacred peaches. He says, the villagers smell faintly of nectar."

"They sweat peach juice?" Jack asked.

"Something like that," Kalsang replied, closely looking over the peach in his hand. He had yet to join in on the fruit bath.

"Wait. Hang on," May said, tossing her peach aside, "are they going to release the snow leopards into the streets?"

Kalsang looked behind him, then back to Jack and May. "They already did. They roam the streets every night."

Jack pictured it in his mind. He couldn't help but think how awesome that was.

"Does Yana know?" May asked, worried.

Kalsang nodded. "She is already being prepared."

"Man, what I would give to see the look on her face," Jack said, grinning.

"Why?" May asked.

Jack slapped the mangled peach on his thigh and rubbed. "Because she doesn't seem like a fruit bath kind of girl."

"What about Shenlong and his men?" May asked.

"I'm not sure," Kalsang replied. "I didn't ask Batu that. If not, it would be an even better reason for them to stay put."

Jack, May, and Kalsang had been helping to prepare the village for invasion for the last few hours. Yana was watching the entrance from her perch atop the Gallery. It was the tallest structure at nearly sixty feet in height and situated directly over the central footpath. Unfortunately, no one on this side of the front gate was equipped with night vision. Yana was going to struggle to see anything outside the gate until the enemy was right on them.

Before she had headed out, Yana had shown Jack something that would be of great use to them: A radio. If Jack could get another one, they would have a sizeable advantage and would be able to coordinate with Yana, their "guardian angel." Once the conflict began it would be Jack's top priority and he made everyone aware of his plan.

Most of the residents were trudging along to the tree and Mother's tomb. The forward half of the village was deserted of anyone without a weapon. Streetlamps bloomed to life all over the place. Their sporadic placement would create deep shadows and keep most of the village in a state of duskiness. Because of the natural, low-set cloud cover, there were no stars to help light the way. Jack could see a handful of them every now and again, but nothing bright enough to see by.

It just hit Jack that the people living within the Valley of Petals didn't see the stars with any regularity. That saddened him. That had been one of the perks of being a Yellowstone ranger. The starlit sky dominated everything. Camping beneath them was a treat.

Jack adjusted his AKM. Over the last few hours, its rope sling had dug into the meat of his shoulder. Jack could feel the skin beneath his coat and shirt being rubbed raw. He stood erect and found Batu, the head of tree security, standing in front of the locked gates. He was unarmed, except for a single khukuri, and was sporting a deep, scowled face. Batu's posture screamed military.

"Hmmm," Jack said, slipping out of the Soviet rifle. "I'll be right back."

He left May and Kalsang and hustled over to the captain. The thickly built Mongol regarded Jack with nothing more than a curt nod of his head. He didn't speak. Jack wasn't even sure if the man understood English. Jack returned the nod with one of his own, then he held up the AKM, offering it to the man.

Batu didn't take it, at first. But then, he slowly lifted his hands and accepted the armament. He looked it over, seemingly comfortable with the weapon platform. The Kalashnikov wasn't known to be terribly ergonomic, but that didn't stop Batu from swiftly ejecting the banana mag. Satisfied, he slammed it home and racked the charging handle.

Then, Jack handed Batu two extra thirty-round magazines.

That got a full-fledged, mostly toothless smile out of the beastly man.

"Thank you," he said. His accent was heavy.

Jack gave him a thumbs up and walked away. "Good luck."

Batu replied with a second curt nod of his head. He didn't throw the rifle over his shoulder, instead he held it at the low-ready with his index finger visibly off the trigger. Jack felt good about his decision to give up the weapon. They all needed another gun in the fight. Jack still had his suppressed SMG, and 150 rounds of ammo. He'd be fine.

Jack spotted multiple pairs of archers climbing up to the roofs of the structures. Ella had ordered them to do so. Ram's swordsmen were, likewise, spread throughout the village, hiding anywhere they could. They'd be most useful coming up from behind someone or finishing off an injured foe. Regrettably, they'd be useless in open conflict. But that's where the locals had the advantage. They'd be able to move quickly throughout their home. That would especially help during a retreat.

Everyone with a firearm would be set up either on the main path, or around the tree, and waiting and praying for the commandos' numbers to be thinned out before they made it to them. But until then, Jack wanted to check on the evacuation, and make sure Veer and Gareth didn't need anything from him.

Kalsang offered to stay behind and help at the gate. He and Batu quietly went over their plan to keep the entrance sealed for as long as possible. The commandos would be looking to blast it open.

It was nearly dark when Jack and May made it down to the tree. The encompassing guards had doubled in number since their last visit, including more archers than before. There were also fortifications being set into place around it. They were simple, but the large rectangular cut stones would act as protection for the men stationed here. They were around four feet in height and another foot thick.

They were being maneuvered into place by reinforced carts and donkeys. The barricades were ten feet apart from one another and they were multiplying fast. Jack was amazed by how fast these people worked. He received an answer as soon as the thought had come to him.

"It's the nectar that gives them their strength," Ella said, stepping up next to Jack. May was over at the well, looking down into it.

"Really?"

She nodded. "Yes, though it doesn't increase our strength, it does helps us from becoming tired so easily. They can work for half a day at their current pace."

Jack's eyes opened. "At the current pace, they'll have a dome built around the canopy!"

Ella smiled. "Hmmm, that's actually an interesting design idea. I'll pass it off to Batu."

Jack couldn't tell if she was joking, or not, and he decided it would be better to let the comment go.

"How's it going down there?" Jack asked, tipping his chin at the well.

"Follow me."

The archer captain led Jack around to the other side of the tree so they could now see the open door into Mother's tomb. May caught up with them, as well.

"What's...in there?" May asked, her voice catching.

Jack saw what had caught May's voice.

There was a column of children being ushered into the open door of Mother's tomb.

"Their parents are up here with us," Ella explained. "Hopefully, they'll be reunited soon."

Jack nodded. "That's the plan."

"Have you seen combat, Jack?"

"Too much," he faced Ella, "and no, not everyone always makes it home." Jack stomped off, feeling the guilt of everything clawing its way up his spine.

"Hey!"

He slowed, then stopped, but didn't turn. "What?"

May slipped around in front of him and made him look at her. "This isn't your fault."

"If you're about to do the *Good Will Hunting* thing, you can stop right there. And yes, this is my fault."

"No, Jack, it's not." It was then that Jack noticed the tears welling in May's eyes. "It's mine. All of this is my doing." Jack opened his mouth, but nothing came out. "See, even you can't argue with me. I took this too far. If I had left Nepal before being captured, then none of this would've happened."

He knew she was right, but...

"We wouldn't have met." The corner of his mouth turned up. "I kinda like the part where we met." He poked at his sternum, faking still being hurt. "I didn't particularly enjoy the way we met, you know, you kicking my ass and all."

May lightly punched his chest. "Shut up."

"At this point, I think it's safe to say that the MSS or BIOfinity Genetics—or whoever—would've found this place regardless, thanks to Thapa's unexpected appearance."

"It's also safe to say that we didn't help the situation much."

Jack couldn't argue that. "No, we undeniably screwed the pooch here. This is definitely not my finest hour."

May laughed softly. "Same." She sighed. "Now, what?"

"We save as many as we can." Jack and May faced the tree. Ella stood tall. Her eyes were stone-cold. "I didn't ask to be kidnapped and sold to the highest bidder, then have dozens of men—" She stopped and composed herself. "I didn't ask for terrible things to happen, and neither did you, yet here we are." She stepped over to them. "But you can do some good—a lot of good, from what I've seen." She let out a long breath and looked at the tree. "I think you were brought to us for a very specific reason. You too, Ms. Wu." She looked over her shoulder at the shocked duo. "Prove it."

"Prove it?" Jack asked.

She eyed him. "Yes, prove it. Prove it to yourself, and to us." She motioned to the people winding down to Mother's tomb. "Prove it to them."

Jack stared down at the sobering scene.

"Another thing."

He sighed. "Something else to darken the mood?"

Ella didn't laugh. "Veer would like Kalsang to join him in Mother's tomb and help coordinate its defense."

Jack wasn't sure why they wanted the Sherpa, but who was he to argue. "Yeah, okay, sure. I'm sure he'd be more than happy to help."

Ella nodded her goodbye and stepped away. "I'll let Veer know."

Jack glanced at May, then watched the archer march away. "That was—"

"Weird?" May asked.

Jack nodded. "Yeah, very weird."

Fan and Park edged out into the darkness beyond the mountain pass' exit. They had hung just inside of it until the sun had fully set. The plan was to wait a little longer.

Fan reached into a pocket on the front of his plate carrier. Inside was a second metallic sphere. He happily twisted the top of it. Next, he rolled it forward with just enough oomph to clear the passage's tall rocky side. As soon as it reached open air, it began transmitting to a military satellite high in orbit. With any luck, the signal would be picked up within the next few minutes.

Now, even more reinforcements would be inbound. He looked up and pictured it. Fan couldn't wait to see, yet another, Harbin Z-20 arrive and drop in overhead. In a few hours' time, the secrets of Shangri-La would belong to China.

Triratna Monastery
Forbidden Valley, Tibet

The fourth floor of the monastery had been reserved for the Dharmapala's dead, and it had been years since they entombed someone there. Years longer since one of their own had died in combat. And Drilha, Goddess of the Hunt, Queen of the Protectors, was angry. She wanted blood. She wanted vengeance. She wanted the man responsible for his death.

She wanted to feast on his soul.

Drilha reached down to her hip and placed her hand on the blade belonging to Sonam's murderer. His scent was one she'd never forget, not until he was buried deep in the earth. The rest of her tribe knew to give her space, not that she would ever react violently toward them. Drilha loved her people dearly, but her intensity was legendary. Few had the courage to cross her when she was lost in her hunter's mindset.

Like she was now.

But there was one man who never feared her, and his footsteps boomed behind her as he approached. Dorje didn't say a word—he didn't have to. Drilha knew what he would say His presence alone calmed her some. The two had been bonded together for decades now.

The fastest of their tribe, the scouts, were already on their way to the other families. They had been tasked with bringing the strongest to Desolation by way of secondary veins within the mountain. The Triratna Monastery was Dorje's people's access point. The other tribes each had their own. Then, as one formidable force, they would march on the Valley of Petals to rid it of their pest problem.

She looked up from the floor and back to Sonam's covered body.

The soldiers must die—every one of them.

And they would die brutally.

"Come," Dorje said, speaking up for the first time since Sonam had been laid to rest. "It's time."

Drilha's fanged mouth morphed into a smile.

52

Valley of Petals

It was eerily quiet in the village. Yana was focusing on the bridge that spanned the rapidly flowing stream just outside the gate. It was the furthest she could see beyond the entry point. Jack and May were positioned directly beneath her perch Yana was relaying what she saw to them, which was currently nothing. The commandos had yet to move in. Yana's throat was sore from having to shout six stories down to them.

Why? Jack thought, contemplating the reason why nothing was happening yet.

He had figured they would attack shortly after sundown, and not waste a single extra minute doing so. Another option for a delay might be that the soldiers were trying to tire out their opponent. Well, it was working on the normal humans. Jack, May, and Kalsang were already exhausted. The Petalians weren't thanks to their magical go-go juice. They looked as awake and refreshed as ever.

Bastards. He couldn't help but be jealous. *I wonder what just a drop of nectar could do for me?*

Jack shook away the idea. From what he understood, that drop would imprison him here forever. Not that this place was a prison in the normal sense of the word. On the other hand, anywhere could be a prison if it was a place that you were unwillingly chained to.

"Come on," he muttered.

This was the worst thing that could happen to a troop. The delay in action could drive a soldier crazy. Jack was feeling it now. His adrenaline had spiked several times. It bombed as quickly as it spiked. His anxiousness was getting the better of him, and his mind was starting to take over. For him, *thinking* was good during conflict, to a degree. But the thoughts your brain let you have could also get in the way and slow you down.

"You okay?" May asked, seeing him fidget. Jack shrugged, then he yawned. He caught May smiling at him. "I'll take that as a 'no.'"

"This will help."

Veer stepped into view with a swordsman following closely behind him. Instead of carrying his dual khukuri blades in his hands, the soldier was carrying a wooden tray filled with small stone cups the size of a sake choko. The swordsman walked up to Jack and May and held out the tray. Jack glanced at May and shrugged. They each took one of the tiny cups and sniffed.

"Smells sweet," Jack said.

"It is," Veer agreed, "but it will help with your dreariness."

Jack met May's eyes again, and they each downed the warm liquid. It was as sweet as it smelled, and it wasn't a fake, syrupy flavor. This tasted like a very condensed, concentrated sweetness. Jack also picked up on a subtle spiciness on the finish as he swallowed it down.

"Wow," he said. "That's really good. What is it?"

"The base component is that of our peach nectar."

Jack nearly vomited it back up. "What?"

May looked horrified.

Veer looked pleased. He grinned. "Do not worry. The effects of the nectar have been boiled out. Only the caffeine-like 'pick me up' remains. You are fine."

Jack's racing heart settled. Then, it didn't. His eyesight narrowed and focused. He instantly felt overstimulated, and he was no longer tired.

"Woah. This is kinda trippy." He raised his hands and looked at them. His eyes snapped back and forth from one to the next.

"You will get used to it," Veer explained. "The initial reaction is, as you described it, trippy." He smiled. "It will last for a few hours and—"

"I have movement!" Yana shouted from directly above them.

"And just in time," Veer finished, heading off.

Jack stepped into the middle of the road leading to the gate. "How far away?" he shouted, looking straight up.

"Not there!" Yana replied, blinking her flashlight on and off like a strobe. "There!"

Jack had looked away from the sniper's perch to check the gate. He returned his gaze up to the Gallery roof and found Yana waving and pointing her light up at the sky. Jack followed it to where the clouds would be, though it was too dark to see anything. He waited and saw something—a faint light. Everyone near the Gallery moved out in the open to watch as a small portion of sky grew brighter and brighter. Moments later, the light pierced the valley's natural ceiling.

And it belonged to a helicopter.

"Oh, crap," Jack said.

"Jack?" Yana shouted, sounding very unsure.

"What do we do, Jack?" May asked. "We don't have the capabilities to fight that."

"Movement outside the gate!" Yana shouted, letting a round rip.

A second after, her position was engulfed with automatic fire from above. Yana screamed and disappeared from view. Jack dove for cover within the Gallery as the ground was also peppered with rounds. Shouts grew over at the gate and everywhere else, for that matter.

"Jack!" May rushed to him.

He was stunned but fine. Jack got to his feet and looked around outside. He unconsciously bit his lip, deep in thought. Jack desperately tried to come up with a response.

Veer came running inside, breathing hard.

"They're going to give the commandos cover until they make it inside," Jack said, thinking it through. "Once they do make it in, the chopper will drop another team, probably in the center of town." His eyes lit up. "And right on the tree!"

"So," Veer said, "we don't let them in. We delay them for as long as possible—make them alter their plan. Can Yana do anything with the helicopter?"

May shrugged. "If she's still alive."

"It might be too high," Jack added.

They stood in silence, contemplating what to do next.

"What the hell was that?" Everyone spun to find an exhausted, very irate Russian gunner standing behind them. "I get one shot off and nearly get turned to Swiss cheese!" She stomped toward Jack. "No one said anything about another team!"

"How the hell could we've known?" Jack replied, throwing his hands up.

"Doesn't matter," May said. "The plan has changed. So must we."

She was right.

"Yana," Jack said. "Can you snake through the village and find an angle to engage the chopper?"

She shrugged. "If they get low enough, sure."

Jack nodded. "Let's hope they do."

She gave May a worried look before heading off and disappearing into the shadows to their left. With any luck, Yana could at least distract the helicopter for a while until Jack and Co. could come up with something else.

"We should head for the gate and do what we can from the lookout point."

May and Veer nodded and the three of them took off running. Jack was thrilled to hear the *thwap* of a precision rifle expelling a bullet. It meant that Yana was confident she could hit the descending aircraft.

Suddenly, a building behind Jack was decimated by mini-gun fire.

"Dammit," Jack said, watching the black wraith rain down destruction. He'd have to trust that Yana had moved shortly after firing the shot, and that she was already lining up another one somewhere else.

The boost from the peach drink was already doing its job. As soon as Jack felt the lactic acid buildup in his legs, it quickly disappeared. He wasn't sweating either. May also looked as if the drink's effects had worked on her too. The one thing Jack was having an issue with was his eyes. The ultra-focus of his vision was proving difficult to get used to. It was as if everything had been sharpened and slightly magnified, like a really powerful pair of glasses, or reverse beer goggles.

They made it to the front gate in record time, and it was just in time to watch the archers do something right out of the *Lord of the Rings*. Every person with a bow lit an arrow on fire and sent it sailing into the land beyond. Jack didn't get to see where any of them landed due to his low line of sight, but the spectacle had been a delightful one, nonetheless. This was a battle he had never thought possible: Guns versus bows and arrows. But not everyone on this side of the wall only had bows and arrows.

Jack heard a *tink* from behind and turned just in time to see a man fall from the gunner's door of the incoming helicopter. The first shot had impacted the side of the aircraft. The second one had found its mark. Then, the helicopter laid into the area where they thought the shot had originated.

A rumbling sound took Jack by surprise, and he wheeled around and shouldered his submachine gun. To his left, a large garage door lifted, grinding to an open, and out rolled something Jack couldn't wait to see in action. Six men pushed the biggest crossbow Jack had ever seen onto the main path.

The "bolt thrower" was already loaded and ready to rock. It was maneuvered into position and then two men yanked on levers, and another spun a knob around. With each adjustment, the four-foot-long steel arrow was progressively angled skyward.

"Please, light it," Jack begged. "Please, oh, please, light that sucker."

Once it was aimed where the boltmen wanted it to go, the guy who had manned the crank painted a black substance onto its massive, jagged head and then quickly lit it with nothing more than a blade and a flat rock. It burst into flames and was sent flying through the air like a metal, fire-breathing dragon.

The projectile slammed into the front nose of the aircraft, burying itself deep. The chopper instantly diverged off its attack on Yana and dropped, but it didn't explode midair or crash. What it did accomplish, was bring its attention onto the front gate. Smoke billowed from the cockpit area, which was good. Hopefully, with a little time, something vital would fail and bring it down.

"Everybody move!" Jack shouted, hurrying away from the open area in front of the gates.

Archers stationed atop it did the same thing and ran for cover. The aircraft zoomed into position overhead before they could all get to safety. The Harbin Z-20 slowed and turned, showing Jack the gunner door. It opened up on the lookout post, obliterating it, and anyone standing atop it, with ease. Depending on the model of minigun, they could be firing from two-to-six thousands rounds per minute. The tracer fire was frightening to witness at night.

They were outgunned, and soon to be outmanned, if this thing stayed in the air.

Jack spied a spark flash off the pilot's door. He couldn't see her, but Jack knew it had been Yana taking another shot. The Z-20 turned upon impact and hovered directly above Jack. He spun away from the punishing wash created by the rotors, and in doing so, found himself staring at the bolt thrower.

He ran to it and waved his arm. "Help me!"

May and three men came hustling over. Jack followed the other men's lead and helped load a second giant steel arrow into the ancient missile launcher. Together, he and one of the locals yanked back on the thick bowstring while May and another Petalian cranked the device higher. The third boltman held a small bucket of the black fluid and the knife and stone.

The bolt thrower maxed out its elevation without the hovering aircraft being in its crosshairs. If they fired now, they'd miss. They needed the thing to move back the other way a little. As of now, it was too close to the gate.

Another impact along its flank got it moving. Jack and the others hurried to get everything in order. The Petalian with the blade and stone rushed to the front of the armament and began slathering it with the flammable goop. Next was the flame. It lit as swiftly as before, but unlike last time, they couldn't get a shot off.

A bullet pierced the local from behind and punched straight through his chest, hitting the pail of lighter fluid. It burst, coating everything in the stuff, including himself and the bolt thrower. The whole area erupted into flames—the villager included. His cries were cut short by the damage of the initial gunshot wound or possibly the fire itself. Regardless, the bolt thrower was toast. Literally. It was at the center of the inferno.

Standing at the fringe of the flames, Jack put the Z-20 in the middle of his submachine gun's iron sights and pulled the trigger, emptying half the fifty-round box mag into it. As Yana had done, he aimed for the open gunner door. Then, as Yana had done, he moved, running deeper into the village, directly beneath the floating beast. At this point, it was the safest place to be.

Shouts ignited from what remained of the lookout point above the gate. Several archers aimed and let their arrows fly. Three of them were taken down by return fire. Four more ducked and hastily began their crawling retreat.

"Jack, this isn't working!"

He found May and gave her a worried look. They weren't going to be able to hold the gate for much longer. Even with it locked down tight, the commandos were bound to force their way in eventually. Veer appeared from the shadows. Jack faced him.

"Abandon the gate! We fight in the streets!"

Veer didn't react. He resembled a fractured man, a defeated leader. His work over the last two decades had been all for naught. Watching it all come undone in seconds had broken him. His defenses were simply too flimsy to stand against a modern tornado such as this. But Jack couldn't say that. What could he say.

"We can still beat them, Veer. Have faith."

"Faith?"

Jack nodded. "Believe, Veer. Believe we can win. Believe in your people and this place."

That reignited something within him. He shouted at his people several times until the message had been delivered. The remaining archers descended their posts above the gate and rushed into the streets, disappearing inside buildings and into the unlit passages.

Jack and May joined them, sprinting into the darkness.

53

Eleven Falcon Commandos watched from afar. One of Park's men moved off, keeping his head low. He had been given a very important task to complete. The combined teams took up position behind the bevy of cover that the rocky gorge provided. The first obstacle was the bridge gaping a swiftly flowing river. The second obstacle, perhaps the most important one yet, was the front gate to what they believed was the real-life Shangri-La.

Fan was still trying to take it all in. They had discovered the fabled Himalayan kingdom. His gut reaction was to want to preserve everything he saw, but Fan knew his orders, and he'd carry them out without fail. His leadership was already under scrutiny. His team's numerous losses would be blamed on him, not his lack of serviceable intel. Fan had gone in blind, and his men had paid for it.

With their lives.

The soldier crested the bridge and used the descending grade on the other side to quicken his feet. Fan was relieved when he made it to the gate without deterrence. The other commandos, as well as the aircraft, had scattered the archers, leaving the gate defenseless. Not that the archers were a viable defense. The only thing that they did have going for them was having higher ground. And having the higher ground wasn't going to make a difference today.

Park's man finished his task in no time, then shouldered his rifle and backed away to a safe distance. Fan could barely see him now. The visibility was nearly zero. The only thing they could do was wait for the signal.

And it came.

The demolition man's flashlight pulsed twice. Fan counted down mentally.

3, 2, 1.

The lower half of the ancient entry point burst into flames, engulfed by a fireball. Within the explosive illumination, Fan could see that it had been enough to gain access into Shangri-La, and to its secrets.

Jack was making good on part of his plan. He and May roamed the pathways between buildings in search of the dead door gunner. Not only would he have another, better weapon to add to the arsenal, but he would also, undoubtedly, have a radio. If he and Yana could communicate with one another, their chances of survival would skyrocket exponentially.

Jack would switch to the channel Yana had told him to use.

Six.

But they would also listen in on the chatter going on between the commandos. Well, May would. Jack would just do what she said. If they could avoid the soldiers, or at the very least, attack their flank, Jack was confident they could put a dent in their numbers and make them think twice about who they were going up against.

He looked up. *Until the chopper lands.* Once another ground force got added to the mix, the game would be over. He needed to figure out a way to bring it down less gently. They had tried valiantly with the bolt thrower. The Z-20 was still smoking from the hit. Barely.

"Come on," Jack said. "Come to Papa." They rounded another corner. "Bingo."

A mangled body lay in a heap at the center of a well-lit intersection. The gunner had fallen into the worst place possible.

"Damn."

And he wasn't alone.

"Jack, look."

From behind the body emerged a truly frightening sight. The creature stalked forward on all fours, head low, tail twitching. It was the first time Jack had seen one of the snow leopards since they had been released into the village. He thought back to the bath he took with the peach nectar. It was supposed to be some kind of deterrent.

The alpine predators weren't as large as other big cats around the world. A large male could reach 165 pounds, whereas a male jaguar could easily weigh double that. What they lacked in size, they more than made up for with agility and cunningness. They were the ultimate mountainous predator, perfectly built for the rough terrain of places like the Himalayas. Jack had extensively researched big cats since he knew he'd have to work around them in Yellowstone.

These look bigger than 165 pounds, though.

"Jack?" May asked, unsure.

He held up his hand and didn't break eye contact with the cat. He needed to trust the Petalian ways. If they said it wouldn't attack them, then it wouldn't. Jack really didn't want to have to shoot such a beautiful animal.

They were a hundred feet from it when it entered the intersection. It cautiously walked up to the body and took in its scent. Then, it lifted its head and smelled the air beyond.

It looked directly at Jack and May.

For a moment, they all had a staring contest. Then, the helicopter's minigun whirled to life, and the cat was gone, returning to the darkness. Jack's body was enveloped in goosebumps. May was lost in her own mind. Her mouth hung open like a fish, and she just stared forward.

"Come on," Jack said, gently grabbing her arm.

She blinked and nodded, moving along beside him.

"That was incredible," she said.

It was. The experience floored Jack. They edged closer to the lit intersection. Jack looked up and couldn't see the aircraft anywhere.

"Cover me," he whispered.

May shouldered her AKM while Jack darted out into the open. He went into a baseball slide and promptly stripped the dead man of most of his belongings. Jack focused mainly on the soldier's Kevlar vest and the gear it held, radio included. Unfortunately, the gunner had no weapon. He did, however, have ammo for one. And wouldn't you know it, the two fifty-round box magazines looked awfully similar to the three Jack already had in his possession.

Jackpot!

The *whup-whup-whup* of an incoming helicopter got Jack moving again. He sprang to his feet and dove into the cover of a two-story structure just as the Z-20 slid in overhead. He and May ducked inside an ajar door and quickly shut and locked it as a powerful spotlight swung around and ignited it. However, Jack didn't sit still and wait for it to pass. There was no reason to fear it yet. He stood, threw the vest on top of a table, and searched it. He activated the radio and heard people shouting in Chinese on channel two. May joined him and translated the rapid-fire chatter.

"They're sending a man to blow open the gate!"

Jack bit his lip, and his eyes lit up. He spun the dial until it connected to channel six.

"Mayday, Mayday, Mayday! Blood Dragon, you there?"

Yana was swift to reply. "Yes, Uncle Sam, I am here."

Using callsigns was very a "cringe" thing to Jack, but considering who they were going up against, it was necessary. Protecting their identities was vital. Regrettably, May's life would be at risk long after this was finished—if she got away. Jack's name was only known to a few in this part of the world. Raegor had also erased most of his past. Unless you met Jack personally or were with Delta or the Yellowstone NPS, no one would be able to correctly identify him.

"They're setting charges on the gate. Can you get over there?"

"I can try. I am near the Gallery right now. I'll see what I can do."

May was worried. "We need to help."

As was Jack. "I know, but first…" He removed his coat and slid into the vest. "Unless you want it?" he asked, stopping halfway.

May shook her head. "No, you go ahead. I had planned on hiding behind you if we get shot at."

Jack stopped and stared at her. "Did you decide that before or after we got the vest?"

She didn't reply and turned and headed for the door as the spotlight moved off. She placed her ear against it to listen as Jack adjusted the fit of the armored rig. When it was secured to his body, he replaced his coat and zipped it up, testing his flexibility and bending in several directions.

"Wow, these things are dogshit."

May shrugged. "Better than nothing, I suppose."

"True enough." He picked up his SMG. "You ready?"

"Yes." May gripped the door handle with one hand and the lock with the other.

Jack nodded for her to proceed. She snapped the bolt free and peeked through a tiny vertical opening as the entire village shook. They both went sprinting outside and gazed in the direction of the gate. The sky was glowing in a hellish red color.

Yana had nearly been killed twice since the helicopter appeared directly above her head.

The first attempt on her life had been when she was positioned atop what the locals called the Gallery. No one, not even her, could have guessed the Chinese would drop a helicopter on their heads. If it had even been a remote option, Yana would've decided against putting herself directly in its path.

The second time she had almost died was as soon as she had taken her first shot. The round had ricocheted off the chopper's flank, barely missing the minigun operator by inches. Yana was shocked by how fast they had acquired her position. She guessed they had thermal tech on board. It had to be the only explanation. Yana was moving with no light, and there wasn't enough light to reflect off her scope's front glass. Maybe they had seen a speck of muzzle flash, but that should've been nearly impossible due to the suppressor on her weapon and the angle from which she had attacked. Now, she moved before her next round hit, hoping for the best.

So far, she had killed one of the men above her. He had landed with a resounding splat. Yana couldn't lie. She had enjoyed the sound of the impact.

Movement caught her ear back towards the Gallery. Yana was sure it wasn't a commando, but she needed to be certain. She stalked around toward the rear of the structure, let out a breath, and spun inside. The tip of her RSASS' suppressor nearly punched a very frightened Petalian in the chest.

The Brit fell on his ass, cowering at the sudden sight of the weapon.

"Gareth?"

He uncovered his face and looked up at her. "Yana?"

The front of the village was immersed in flames as the gate was annihilated. Yana knew exactly what was happening. Gareth scuttled backward like an uncoordinated crustation. Yana did what she always did. She looked for an opportunity to shoot someone.

She dropped to the ground and laid down on her stomach, snapping open the weapon's bipod as she did. Yana kicked both feet out wide, balancing herself well. She breathed and peered through her scope and waited.

Yana glanced at the frightened Brit, barely seeing him in her periphery. "Watch my butt, yes?" She grinned. "Just do me a favor, and don't stare for too long."

Gareth didn't react to either of the things she said.

"Hey!" she shouted, peeling away from the scope and staring daggers into him.

Gareth pushed away from her and smacked the back of his head against the mosaic tile wall. He resembled a deer caught in headlights, with Yana taking the place of the onrushing semi-truck.

"Make sure no one sneaks up behind me and shoots me in the back, okay?"

He nodded emphatically but did not verbally answer her. Gareth was in shock, unable to process everything that was happening around him.

Yana rolled her eyes and took another deep breath. "How did I get stuck with babysitter duties?"

She locked in the flaming doorway, specifically the smoking hole in its lower half. Yana planned on shooting the first thing that moved through the billowing miasma.

It didn't take long.

An aberration appeared with the haze. It was a solid enough target for Yana to act. She gently squeezed the trigger. The RSASS coughed a round and struck the smoky anomaly, knocking it down. Yana rolled left, leaped to her feet, and yanked Gareth to his.

"Move!"

Bullets zinged past them as the intruders blindly returned fire. Yana wasn't concerned about them, not yet. She was mostly concerned about the helicopter and its minigun reacquiring her.

She and Gareth snaked through the surrounding buildings until they reached a dark alleyway. Even though Yana had only used a single round, she knelt and instinctively checked the magazine's ammo count.

"That's sixteen," she said softly.

"Sixteen?" Gareth replied. "You've killed sixteen of these blokes?"

Yana recounted her kills in her head. "Yes, sixteen. It's been a productive couple of days. Not all of them were Falcon Commandos, though. Six were Shenlong's men back in Langtang. And technically, it's fifteen and a half. Drilha and I teamed up on one back in the blizzard outside the mountain passage." She caught Gareth staring at her. His face was caked in disgust. "What?"

"How do you sleep at night?"

Without skipping a beat, Yana said, "Soundly." She winked at him. "And in the nude."

He shook his head. "Out of all the people to be stuck with, why you?"

Yana stood and leaned around the building. "Believe me. I keep asking myself the same thing about you."

Gareth looked toward the remains of the front gate and sighed. "Bloody hell. Fine, look, if you want to take care of more of these wankers, I can show you a proper spot. But we'll need to hurry."

Yana smiled. "Show me."

54

With no immediate follow-up shot, Fan ordered the incursion into Shangri-La to continue. Another of Park's men had been killed, but this time by sniper fire. Now, three commandos entered together, guns up, eyes forward. If one went down, the other two would respond. But the trio made it without further conflict. They disappeared through the smoking husk of the once mighty gate.

Fan entered next alongside two others. They, too, made it through safely. He stepped around glowing embers and splintered shrapnel. Several bodies greeted them, as did the remains of what looked like an ancient ballista, a bolt thrower.

So, that's what almost took down the helicopter?

Fan had only witnessed the scene from outside of the gate but had been impressed with the ingenuity. Based on what he heard over the airwaves, the Z-20 had nearly been knocked out of the sky. Fan was confident the aircraft would've crashed if the projectile struck a little higher.

Park came through with the rest of the men, and they all spread out and took up positions behind the first cover they could find. This was the most important stage of the assault. Once they were successfully inside, they would call down the third team and sweep the village like a tidal wave.

Much smaller arrows whizzed by, originating from somewhere ahead and above.

"Contact!" one man shouted, returning fire.

A scream quickly responded to the burst of gunfire. Fan spied a body fall from the roof of a two-story, rectangular building and impact the road further ahead.

"Shen!" Park shouted, looking past Fan.

Fan turned to see why Park was voicing a concern for Shen. One of the arrows had hit his man, Shen, square in the chest. The commando gazed down at the projectile and shrugged. He nonchalantly ripped the arrow from his Kevlar vest and tossed it aside.

"Be careful," Fan warned the team.

"Why?" Shen asked, scoffing at the notion. "They attack us with bows and arrows."

Fan gazed back at him. "Two inches higher, and you'd be a dead man. That wasn't a lucky shot." Fan faced the street again. "Until further notice, we proceed with caution, understood?"

Shen stood tall. "Yes, sir."

Fan wasn't about to lose another team.

"Remember," he reminded them, "we need survivors! Round up the able-bodied and the youngest. Everyone else is expendable." He looked at Park. "Do it."

Park nodded and contacted the pilot to find an open area to drop the third team.

"Copy that," the pilot replied. "We need to land for repairs too."

The chop of the aircraft's rotors moved away.

"Move out," Fan ordered, leading the way.

Yana hurried along behind Gareth. He moved much faster than she thought possible. She also carried quite a bit of weight between her rifle and her pack. Plus, she was tired. Yana had been offered the tea made from the valley's peaches, but she turned it away once she was told of the effects it would have on her. As a sniper, Yana's eyes and steady heart rate were her most valuable assets. She didn't like the idea of ingesting something that could disrupt one, or both, of them.

The Brit led her down the sloping path leading to the tree. She didn't question why he was bringing her here, not that he had given her the opportunity. They were off as soon as she told him to show her the "proper spot," as he called it.

The grade flattened out around the tree's deep stone well. Dozens of guards armed with either sword or bow allowed them to continue past without a second look. Gareth slowed as he approached the top of the stairs leading down to the tree's base. Yana finally caught up with him when he stopped.

She limped up to him, feeling a twinge of discomfort in her left hip. Yana kneaded the spot with her closed fist, grunting as she pressed and twisted her knuckles in deeper.

"So," she said, "are you going to show me this spot, or what?"

Gareth lifted his hand and pointed out over the well and up. "There."

Yana craned her neck back. "In the tree? You must be joking?"

He faced her. "Haven't you heard? I'm British. I don't have a sense of humor." A small smile formed on the Russian's face. "You can see the entire village from up there, and there is easy access using the pulley system."

"Pulley system?"

"Oh, right, you missed the tour."

Yana was confused. "There was a tour?"

"Follow me."

Gareth descended to the bottom with Yana close behind. Once they reached the rocky floor, Gareth hooked an immediate right and headed to the front of the tree rather than the rear, where the door to Mother's tomb was located. It had been locked again from the inside and was undoubtedly being guarded fiercely. Yana spotted a heavy-duty wood platform with thick, braided ropes and a giant wheel that belonged to a pirate ship.

"Get on," he said, stepping up to the wheel.

Yana tapped the platform's edge with her foot and then looked straight up. "Woah."

The ropes disappeared into the tree directly above her head.

"Yes, it's a bit of an ascent, but it's the best place for you to do what you do." She nervously nodded and stepped on.

"Up we go."

"Wait!"

Gareth paused and eyed the sniper.

"Tell your men to wait on my signal to engage the enemy."

Gareth nodded, turned, and regripped the wheel but stopped. He, once more, released it and looked at Yana. "What's the signal?"

She smiled like a shark. "They'll know."

His eyes opened wide. He understood. "Right, well, good luck."

Gareth spun the wheel slowly, and Yana rose into the air. The platform rumbled the entire way up. Yana did her best not to look down. She wasn't afraid of heights in the least. Her real fear was falling.

It took nearly five minutes to reach the top of the trunk. The thickest limbs grew from here, and within their bases was a cozy-looking spot to hide. Yana stepped off the uneven platform and onto another one that had been fastened to the tree with rope. There were no nails present. Damaging the tree was, apparently, strictly forbidden.

Yana turned and leaned over the edge and waved. Gareth waved back, then stepped away from the wheel. He cupped his hands around his mouth and shouted several times up toward the men guarding the tree perimeter. Yana heard several of them answer back. A few of the archers even looked up toward her. Gareth gave her another wave and headed off toward the backside of the tree, no doubt going to join his fellow villagers.

Yana inspected her new surroundings and climbed higher. She scaled the limb juncture and knelt. She could see the Gallery from here. Beyond it was the ruined front gate.

Perfect.

She made herself at home. She dropped her pack and unfolded her RSASS' bipod. From here, only her head and shoulders would be visible, if anything at all. The entire upper half of the tree was cast in utter darkness. There was no way anyone would see her up here. Also, there wasn't a rifle caliber in existence that could penetrate her cover. She only needed to be wary of the helicopter and whether or not the commandos carried an RPG.

The second Harbin Z-20 buzzed somewhere off to her right. She angled her rifle towards it and looked through her scope in time to see rappelling lines getting tossed from the open side door. They were too far away for Yana to do anything, though. Eleven men swiftly descended.

She pulled her radio free from a pocket on her chest rig and depressed the talk button.

"Uncle Sam? We have a Dharmapala-sized problem."

"What kind of problem?"

Jack and May quickly fell back, as well as most of the locals who had hung around to fight. Hopefully, an archer could sneak in an arrow around the soldiers' armor. The khukuri swordsmen had become all but useless.

"The helicopter just offloaded eleven more men to the west."

"West?" Jack replied, looking around. "Which way is west here?"

The Russian muttered something incoherently. "The gate is south! Look west!"

Jack re-coordinated himself and then looked west. He couldn't see anything from where he was. There were too many buildings in the way. He thought about finding the nearest intersection and then having another look there, but he was also very aware of the real chance of getting shot if he did.

"What's your location, Blood Dragon?"

"I am pretending to be a snow leopard, if you get my drift."

Jack and May stopped and looked north. They could barely see the canopy from their current position.

"You are?" Jack asked, understanding her veiled reply. Someone could be listening that wasn't friendly.

"Yes, I am. I feel like a child again. Very peaceful." Jack heard her moving around as she spoke. "If you come this way, can you do me a favor and bring some commandos? I would very much like to shoot more."

Jack eyed the radio and swallowed. "So, we're going fishing, is that it?"

"Yes, and you are my bait."

He flopped his arm next to his leg and rubbed his face with his free hand.

"It's a good idea," May said.

Jack nodded. "Yeah, I know. Doesn't mean I have to like it, though." He took a long breath and then brought the radio back to his lips. "Okay, Ahab, here comes your white whale."

He handed the radio to May, stepped away, and raised his SMG into the air. Jack squeezed the trigger and unloaded the remainder of the magazine. He swiftly thumbed the mag release and replaced the empty one with a full fifty-rounder. With any luck, the explosion of gunfire would draw in a handful of the commandos.

"Very good," Yana said. "Now, you two fall back to me. When they are out in the open, we'll play a little game I call 'wolf in the chicken coup,' yes?"

May handed the radio back to Jack.

"Roger," he replied, "but remember, we are wolves too, not chickens. Please, don't shoot us."

"Copy, I will do my best."

Jack stared hard at May. "That's not very reassuring."

A soft chuckle arose from the other end of the radio. "I kid, I kid. You will be fine, but the same cannot be said for the commandos."

"Yeah, sure. Happy hunting, Blood Dragon."

"Yes, same to you, Uncle Sam. Over and out."

Jack and May hurried toward the tree. If the soldiers were coming from the south and the west, and the tree was to the north, they needed to find a spot to the east and hunker down. They descended the sloping terrain, entered one of the dark alleyways, and weaved eastward.

They slowed as they neared the open section of land that surrounded the entire tree. They didn't enter the space, however. Jack and May moved into a building through an open back window, shutting and locking it once they were indoors. Jack activated the SMG's weapon light and showed it around the room. This room was some type of woodwork shop. There were half-finished projects everywhere, mostly tables and chairs. It smelled amazing too. Jack loved the scent of fresh sawdust.

Two shuttered windows bordered the front door. Before checking outside, Jack confirmed that the entry was locked. He moved to the left-hand window and unlatched the simple hook and eye lock. He partially unfolded one accordion shutter and looked outside. May mirrored his movements over at the other window.

Each owned an unimpeded view of the courtyard and the dozens of archers kneeling behind their portable stone cover. Between their positioning and Jack, May, and Yana's firepower, the resistance effort didn't feel half-bad.

The first sign of movement came from the south. The team that had blown the front gate had made it to the outskirts of the 211-foot-tall peach tree first. Initially, it was only a single individual. Then, three more joined him. All was quiet too. Jack glanced down at his chest rig and quickly switched on his radio, switching it over to the soldiers' channel. He kept the volume low. He hoped Yana was doing the same. If anything, it would help her zero in on their exact location. May translated quickly without taking her focus away from the window.

"The local populace has fallen back to the tree," one commando said.

"I suggest we all move in immediately," another said.

Jack was kind of hoping that was precisely what they did. The barrage of arrows and Yana's well-placed sniper rounds, combined with Jack and May's crossfire, would decimate their numbers severely. Unfortunately, there was a more cautious *chicken* in the flock.

"No, we do not know where the sniper is."

Another speaker announced the new team that had landed in the west.

"We are in position and awaiting orders."

"Copy."

"Sir," yet another soldier said, "we have movement behind us."

"A local?"

"I'm not sure, sir, but I do not think so. It's too small."

Jack smiled. *No, not small. It's too low to the ground to be a person.*

One of the snow leopards was closing in, which meant there were others too. He remembered counting at least ten of them at first, but there might have been others he had not seen. Jack wasn't sure how effective the big cats would be against the soldiers. He hoped they could be a distraction, at the very least.

"We have movement over here too," the newer arrival said. "Make that two of them, whatever they are."

"I spot three to the south!"

"What the hell are they?"

Then, the screams started.

55

They were being attacked from every direction. The aggressors were quick, unbelievably agile, and they used the shadows to their benefit. Fan spotted the outline of something moving on all fours. Then like the others, it vanished as soon as a light came its way. Whatever the animal was, it was smart. When one man moved to engage, another of the creatures attacked from a different direction.

The buildings and alleys gave the creatures plenty of places to hide and lie in wait. The tight confines also made it impossible for Fan and Park's men to stay together without making themselves too big of a target.

So far, no one had been killed. But plenty of the men had been wounded by slashing claws and tearing fangs. The animals attacked in complete silence. Not a single growl, or grunt, or howl, or hiss. They didn't make a sound of any kind. Even their footfalls were inaudible.

"Keep moving toward the tree!" Fan shouted. "Three men forward, and three men guarding the rear! Move!"

Fan didn't know how much ammo had been used, and all without a single hit.

The first commando stepped out into the vast emptiness that surrounded the tree. Fan had expected them to be engaged, but nothing had greeted them. He doubted the entire populace had evacuated, and if they did leave, what exit did they use? No, these people wouldn't give up so easily, regardless of how outgunned they were.

A shriek echoed through the streets.

"Got one!"

Fan looked back and saw blood on the cobblestone street, but there was no body. The injured animal had limped away before it could be finished off.

"Did you see what it was?"

"A wolf!"

Fan was confused. "A wolf?"

"No," someone corrected, "it's a cat!"

"Yes, a big one!" another commando confirmed.

The only big cats in the Himalayas were snow leopards, but Fan had never heard of them behaving like this. They were typically solitary hunters, but this was a pack—a large one. The brief glimpses that he had gotten suggested to him that they were much bigger than usual.

Something landed atop Fan, tackling him to the ground from above. He fought and rolled with his assailant, gripping, and tearing at a soft, silky pelt. Illuminated by one of his men's light, Fan could see that the creature was, in fact, an oversized snow leopard. He acted decisively, reaching beneath its open maw. He clutched the cat's throat in his left hand and locked his elbow out. He swiftly unsheathed his tactical knife with his opposite hand and plunged the blade tip into the leopard's exposed chest. He repeated the strike twice more until the animal fell limp beside him.

The tumult promptly stopped, and the other cats withdrew, screaming wildly into the air as they melded with the shadows. Fan doubted that one of their packmate's demise would keep them at bay forever. They needed to get moving again.

Park and another man helped Fan up. He was covered in blood, little of it was his. He wiped off his hands on his pants and one of his men returned his discarded rifle. A ring of firepower had formed around them while Fan knelt to get his air back.

"Did we lose any?" Fan asked, looking up at Park.

He shook his head. "Many wounded."

Fan pushed off his left knee and stood on wobbly legs. Between the brawl with the snow leopard and the attacks in the blizzard and at the monastery, he was gassed. But he still had a job to do.

The final member of the southern Falcon Commando squad appeared beneath the lamps of the low-lit piazza. The western team had yet to show themselves. If they entered directly due west of the tree, Jack and May, and maybe even Yana, would have no shot at them. They needed the other soldiers to come at them from the direction the original team had come for this to work.

Unless we can draw them out?

No, Jack didn't like that. That was guaranteed to go sideways. He was hoping the attack on the southern team had done the job for them. If it had been him, he would've brought his team over to check on the others.

But they have radios. They didn't need to see anything in order to check in on the others.

The battle had sounded brutal. Based on the radio chatter, the animals had come up from behind the southern team and launched as a group effort. Not only had the cats been trained to protect the tree and not attack any of the residents, but they had also been taught to work together. Jack didn't think that was possible.

Unless it's the peaches?

No one had mentioned feeding the snow leopards any nectar. Side-effects would be possible, sure, but what type, and are they different depending on the species? If what he was thinking was true, then the nectar would have a lot of potential applications.

That would make the MSS want it even more, and that was terrifying.

That fact must've been driving May nuts.

"Jack, look."

Jack realized he'd been staring off, lost in thought. He returned his attention to the soldiers and saw that their numbers were slowly multiplying. They weren't easy to see, but if you looked at just the right angle, you could see shapes emerging from the darker pathways. They were also staying put. None of the new arrivals had revealed themselves.

"Come on," Jack encouraged, "keep moving." He pressed his radio's call button. "Get ready, here they come."

"Yes, I see, but we need them to get closer."

"I know," Jack said. "Got any ideas?"

Yana didn't answer him. The echoing cries of a dying crow did. The caws sounded strained, as if the animal was gasping for its final breath.

"Is that her?" May asked, leaning away from her window.

"I think so," Jack replied. "It's working too."

Four commandos edged out further. Each one moved slow and in perfect time with the others. Jack eyed them, then shifted focus to the second set of four as they too advanced.

Jack lifted the radio. "Okay, you can stop."

The cawing proceeded. "I said, stop!" Jack hissed, projecting his whispered voice as much as he could.

Yana coughed. "Yes, okay." She cleared her throat. "And you're welcome."

Jack rolled his eyes. "Wait for two more groups to emerge. Then, go to town."

"Copy. What are you going to do?"

Jack leaned away from his window and looked at May, speaking to both women. "We'll direct our attack on the southern team's rearmost line and then focus on preventing the others from retreating. Hopefully, the archers will take the hint and give 'em hell."

"Let me see," Yana said. "Yes, I can see them. They are still ducked behind their cover. They look ready. I had Gareth tell them to wait on my signal to engage."

"Let's hope they understand what that signal is," Jack said. He absolutely knew what it was.

"Okay," Yana said, "have to run."

Jack set the radio down on a table to his left. He had kept his SMG's barrel rested on the windowsill. He regripped its handguard, but also left it in place. The windowsill would work in the same way as Yana's bipod. Accuracy would be an issue from this range for his short-barreled submachine gun. He was counting on its high cyclic rate to spray the entire group with as many bullets as he could get off before receiving any return fire. Then, he and May would have to move, and do it in a hurry.

"Oh, shit," Jack said, watching the western team send out their own line of four men. A second four-man team quickly followed. And another.

Jack let them proceed a little further.

Good enough.

He picked up his radio, pressed the call button, and shouted, "Now!"

But nothing happened.

"Blood Dragon, do you copy?"

He glanced at May. She shrugged.

"Yana?"

The Russian didn't respond.

She examined both advancing groups. The one from the south was nearer to her position than the western team, but the latter was quickly catching up. At their current trajectories, both teams' first lines would intersect halfway between the outlying buildings and the stone blockade and become one eight-man front.

Yana had already placed her reticle in that exact spot. Her idea was to shift her aim back and forth and take out a trooper from each team with every other shot fired. For good measure, she had switched her radio over to channel two and set it down next to her on her improvised rifle bench. She checked on the archers and spotted the thick Mongol kneeling along with them. He was armed with Jack's AKM.

"Just a little bit closer," she said, encouraging her prey.

There weren't many people that could rightfully call two teams of Special Forces soldiers "prey," but Yana liked to believe she was one of them. Her work leading up to this moment supported it.

She numbered the men from left to right. The southern team's first line was one through four, and the western team's front line was five through eight.

"Four and five are first."

Yana got into position, imagining the action. As she unloaded into them, she'd be forced to swing her rifle wider and wider. With every shot taken, she'd have to quickly attain a new target and fire with as little time in between trigger pulls as possible. She estimated one second per round fired. That meant the movements between bullets would need to be lightning fast.

"Let's go."

Yana let out a long breath and took out four and five in a combined subsecond. She swung back to three. He went down easily. It wasn't until she shot six that their return fire hit the tree. But the shots were wild. She kept going until all eight of the frontline men were dead by either her hand, or by that of the archers. Arrows flew as did the bursts of rifles from the east. Even Batu got into the action.

Jack and May.

The commandos responded by spreading out wider. Some concentrated on the unseen eastern force, others on Yana, and the rest on the archers. The bowmen and women were falling quickly.

Yana lined up the next closest soldier but stopped when she heard chatter on the radio. She fumbled with the device and switched over to channel six.

"Hey, Sam, do you copy?"

"Yeah," Jack replied, his voice drowned out by gunfire, "but we're a little busy!"

She swung her rifle all the way around to the west, away from the fight, and peered through its scope. It took her a moment to locate it, and when she did, her heart sank.

"I don't care how busy you are!" she screamed. "You need to get moving!"

She turned and looked down toward Jack and May's position.

"What?"

Yana growled and shouted. "Move your asses, Jack! You have incoming!"

"What are you talking about?"

"The helicopter, Jack! It's airborne!"

"You're shitting me, right?"

Yana craned her neck right and spotted the Z-20's searchlight come into view as it peeked over the outlying buildings. In a few seconds, it and its minigun would be within range of everyone here, including Yana. Not only was her life in danger, but so was that of every Petalian. And it wasn't just the people that mattered, either.

She looked up into the thick canopy, and then down at the massive trunk beneath her feet. If their peach tree was damaged beyond saving, everyone would die here, sooner or later.

Now, how do I get down?

She eyed the platform. It was looking more and more like a slice of Swiss cheese. In doing so, she spotted movement near the base of the tree.

Gareth?

The Brit was waving for her to get moving. So she did. Yana packed up her gear and edged out on the shaky lift. Bullets whizzed by her. Gareth got her moving as soon as she stepped foot onto the antiquated lift, but it was going as slow as it had before.

Yana shouted into her radio. "I need cover fire!"

"What—why?" Jack asked but must've seen her. "Oh, crap. Hang on!"

Yana shouldered her RSASS and took potshots at anyone she could. She didn't hit anybody, but at least it slowed them down a little.

Another bullet sliced through her coat, barely missing her flesh. She looked down at the perforated garb at the same time Gareth raised a khukuri above his head. He aimed it at one of the thick ropes attached to the platform's pulley system.

He swung.

Yana sighed. "This is going to hurt."

56

Jack was still trying to process just how many people Yana had killed in such a short amount of time. Her ability was like nothing he had ever seen, and that was saying something. He had known some of the most "talented" shooters in the world while with Delta.

The workshop was assaulted by gunfire, much of it successfully entering the building through the windows and wooden door. Jack and May were forced to the ground. They crawled deeper into the room, aiming for the rear door. Seconds later, the shooting stopped.

"Go!" Jack shouted, yanking May to her feet.

As soon as they stood, the barrage picked up again. Jack lost his grip on May's arm and was too busy trying not to die to turn and check on her. He reflexively put his hands over his head, as if the flesh, bone, and blood-made armor could stop the rifle calibers being thrown at them. He didn't stop to open the door.

Jack dove through it instead.

The barrier was reduced to kindling as he soared through it, landing atop the shards with gusto. He didn't look himself over. Jack quickly rolled and took cover, pushing himself up against the rear of the building to the left of the doorway. May army crawled across the destroyed threshold, and took up position on the opposite side of the opening.

"What happened to you?" Jack asked, shouting his words.

"I tripped, no thanks to you!"

"Me?"

May snapped at him. "Yes, you! You pulled me right into a pair of chairs! How the hell am I supposed to move through chairs!"

Jack held back a laugh and said, "Like Casper?"

May couldn't hold back her smile.

The gunfire slowed enough for Jack to hear someone screaming over his radio. He pulled it free from his chest rig and heard Yana shouting for help. May leaped across the doorway and leaned in.

"I need cover fire!"

Jack moved along the rear of the building and peeked around the corner, looking up at the tree. "What—why?" But he saw. "Oh, crap. Hang on!"

Jack replaced his radio and pointed up at Yana. May's eyes said it all.

She and Jack rushed forward and took cover behind the northeast corner of the workshop. Jack stood, while May knelt, pushing herself into Jack's legs. The only thing that would be visible to the commandos would be their heads and rifles.

They sent intermittent bursts of lead toward the remaining soldiers. Many lay dead from gunshot wounds or impalement. Some had received both.

May squeezed Jack's leg. He gazed up at Yana in time to see her freefalling to her death. At least, that's what it looked like to Jack.

"No!" May shouted.

Jack smashed down his radio's talk button and shouted, "Yana!"

They watched her disappear beneath the rim of the tree well. Then, their cover was hit with more rounds. Stone shrapnel was shorn off and thrown at them, forcing them to flee. They ran for it, turning north and continuing in that direction for a few hundred feet. They followed the curvature of the path, making their way around to the back of the tree.

"Mother's tomb must be right beneath us," Jack said, breathing hard.

May didn't say anything.

"Hey, are you—"

"No, I'm not okay, Jack!"

They slowed to a brisk walk.

"Look, I'm sure Yana's fine."

"Fine? Come on, Jack, you saw her fall, the same as me. She's dead."

Jack didn't know how to convince her otherwise, mostly because he also believed Yana had died. He couldn't think of a single way that she could have survived a fall like that.

He stopped. "Maybe she was attached to a safety line, or something."

May faced him and leaned in and kissed him on the cheek. She rubbed Jack's shoulder and then headed off. It had been May's way of thanking him for trying to make her feel better.

Jack wasn't done trying.

He lifted the radio to his lips. "Blood Dragon, do you copy?"

The only sound to answer his was static.

"Yana?"

"Yes, yes, I am here."

May spun and rushed back to Jack, yanking the radio from his hand. "Yana? You're alive? How?"

"Yes, I'm alive, but barely. I took a stray round to my shoulder while I was in mid-air. Could've been much worse."

"But—"

"Gareth cut a rope. The platform swung away, and I dropped straight down. These people, May, they really are incredible! After Gareth cut it, he quickly unfolded a large, framed net from beside the tree and it caught me eight feet from the ground. They installed it years ago after one of the harvesters had fallen to his death."

"So, you're okay?"

Yana snickered into the radio. "It will take more than that to kill the Blood Dragon."

May visibly relaxed and laid her forehead on Jack's shoulder. She took a deep breath. "Where are you now?"

"Gareth is bringing me to the tomb. Everyone still alive is coming too. I'm afraid my part in this fight is over."

Jack took the radio from May. "No, it's not, Yana. I need you to protect those people. They will be defenseless."

"Oh, you misunderstand me. I said my part in *this* fight is over, and never said I was going to crawl into a hole and hide. I plan on crawling into a hole while still doing what I can."

Jack smiled. "Thank you, Yana."

"Yes, well, even us killers can have a heart sometimes."

The line went dead. Jack guessed Yana had made it underground where no signal could reach.

"So, we're alone?"

Jack shrugged. "I guess so."

"So, we failed."

He reached out a hand and gripped May's shoulder. "I didn't say that. We can still do something."

"Like what?"

He didn't get to answer. The helicopter slid into place overhead, its spotlight illuminating Jack and May. They blocked out the sudden burst of light with a hand and clutched one another against the wash of the rotors. The Z-20 turned so its gunner door faced toward them.

"Run!"

Jack and May took off deeper into the village as the minigun whirled to life. They darted around the back of a nearby two-story building just as the machine gun hurled hundreds and hundreds of rounds at them. The impacts were deafening, but that didn't stop Jack or May. They quickly changed directions and snaked their way back to the south.

Unfortunately, the aircraft was able to follow them.

"Dammit!" Jack shouted, as the ground in front of him was battered.

He skidded to a halt and pushed May back the way they had come. They turned west and headed underneath the Z-20, safe from its onboard armament. But then it banked away from them and began its attack again.

They hurried south, then west, then south for another two hundred feet before shifting and moving back to the east. The helicopter lost them for a second, which was fantastic. What wasn't fantastic was that they ran into a trio of startled commandos.

Jack and May laid into them, stopping when one went down. The second and third soldiers turned to run. The second one was tackled to the ground by a foursome of snow leopards. The big cats tore into him with zero remorse. Jack and May tracked the survivor around to the left. They each had replaced their magazines while in motion. The Z-20's rotors roared nearby somewhere. It was close.

Jack edged forward and stopped before turning the next corner. He waited and listened. The second commando was now dead quiet. Slowly, Jack leaned left, exposing only half of his face. He saw nothing and heard nothing. Either the third soldier was hiding, or he had taken off and saved himself.

Barrel-first, Jack slinked around the building, hugging close to it as he moved. He took deliberate steps, keeping them noiseless. Jack came up to an open door and stopped. He held up a fist, motioning for May to hang back. She did as Jack signaled and turned and watched their backs. He swiftly ignited his SMG's light and swung across the opening, flashing its interior with blinding lumens. Nothing jumped out or shot him. Satisfied, Jack raised his hand to silently communicate to May to follow him, but was, instead, yanked into the building from behind.

"Ja—!" May shouted. Her voice was cut off by the closing door.

Jack's attacker wrapped his arms around his throat and squeezed. Luckily, Jack was taller and heavier than his opponent, and he easily kept the soldier from bringing him to the ground where Jack's size advantage would mean very little. They danced in a circle and careened back into the door. Jack split the skin beneath the hairline of his temple when they hit. The door rumbled again, but this time, hit hard from the other side. May couldn't get inside. It had somehow locked, keeping her from being able to relieve Jack of his *nuisance.*

"Jack!" came a muffled shout.

Always willing to fight dirty, Jack bit the commando's arm. He dug his teeth in as deeply as he could. The other man squealed in pain and reflexively loosened his grip. But as he did, he snagged the shoulder straps of Jack's Kevlar vest and pulled him down to the ground. Jack spun and met the guy face to face, forehead to mouth. Jack drove his skull into the commando's lower jaw, causing the man to nearly bite his tongue in half. Blood sprayed into the air as the trooper screamed and hacked up the blood.

"Get down!" May yelled.

Jack now heard the helicopter closing in above them.

A single gunshot obliterated the lock. The report made Jack wince as he was yanked in closer to the soldier. The commando used his legs to lock Jack's neck in a triangle choke. He squeezed. But Jack knew not to freak out.

While still on his back, the soldier drew his sidearm and fired shots at May, keeping her at bay.

Jack calmly rolled his weight forward and got his knees under him. His wrestling partner pointed the pistol down, but Jack caught his wrist and forced it back up. Then, with everything he had, he rocked back and performed the world's oddest suplex. This was where Jack's height and weight advantage paid off. Jack lifted his opponent straight up and drove him face-first onto the stone floor.

The pressure around Jack's neck subsided, and he wiggled out from beneath the unconscious man. May darted inside and found Jack on his knees beside the inert commando, gasping for oxygen.

"You good?"

Jack gave her a thumbs up while he retrieved his SMG from the floor. He headed for the door, shouldering the compact rifle. A single gunshot rang out behind him. He turned and found May standing over his combatant with her pistol in her hand. Jack didn't support her cold-bloodedness, but he understood it.

He grumbled under his breath and made sure the coast was clear. Jack heard but didn't see the Z-20. He and May exited and were immediately engulfed by the aircraft's floodlight.

57

An anomaly materialized overhead, blotting out the searchlight entirely. It ascended higher and higher to meet the aircraft head-on. It impacted it and then ensnared the left-hand wheel strut, causing the Z-20 to dip and sway chaotically. The rotors whined in protest to the sudden addition of weight. It took Jack a second to realize that the object wasn't just some inanimate projectile that had been launched from a medieval catapult. *It* was alive, and it was fighting a military helicopter with nothing more than its fists.

"Is that Dorje?" May asked, still shielding her eyes from the shuddering light.

Jack didn't bother trying to block it out. He was too enthralled with the aerial fisticuffs to breathe, let alone move. After the dramatic shift in the Z-20's course, Dorje leaped from the left-hand wheel strut over to the right-hand strut. The movement threw off the helicopter's flight pattern even more.

Dorje then kicked out and got himself swinging like a mountainous child on the monkey bars. He spun, reached out, and grabbed onto the four-foot-long bolt that was still impaled in the aircraft's nose. He was going for the bolt, as removing it would cause more damage than leaving it alone. Dorje placed his feet onto the thick tire, turned upward, and propelled himself away from the helicopter, releasing his death grip on the wheel strut as he did. The Dharmapala chief used his unmatched strength, and his forward momentum, to rip the enormous steel arrow free.

Jack couldn't believe his eyes.

Dorje used the bolt like a javelin and hurled it through the Z-20's windshield. Even from below, Jack could see that the bolt had hit home. The flickering interior lights of the cockpit revealed the projectile had struck the pilot in the chest. The result was instantaneous. The helicopter drifted off to the right and plummeted to earth somewhere out of sight.

Dorje landed with a boom thirty feet away from an equally stunned Jack and May. He stomped up to them and stopped, standing tall. The chief was pleased with his accomplishment—as he should be. Jack was too, for that matter. But he didn't know what to say. So, he brought his hand to his chest in salute of the big man. Dorje returned the gesture just as three more of the Dharmapala leaped across the rooftops above them.

The Protectors of the Sacred Path had answered the call.

Better late than never, I suppose.

Jack led Dorje over to the building that housed the dead commando. Dorje leaned in, saw him, and sniffed, before looking back to Jack for an explanation. Jack simply pointed at Dorje. He pointed at the commando next.

Jack made sure the final part of his non-verbal message had been received, loud and clear. He looked Dorje in the eyes and swiped his extended thumb across his neck.

Kill.

Dorje smiled, crouched down, and sprang into the air, vanishing from view. Jack blew out a long breath and collapsed into the building and rode it down to the ground. He knew the Dharmapalas' hunting skills would take care of the rest. The fight was over for Jack and May. The real muscle had arrived to clean up the streets.

May slid in next to Jack to the tune of echoing gunfire, and the agonized wails of men.

The front half of the prison was demolished by, of all things, a helicopter. Shenlong and Gang were sitting up against the rear wall when it happened. Ceba wasn't so fortunate. He was leaning against the barred door and was crushed by falling debris.

With the dust still settling, the two remaining inmates jumped at the opportunity to escape and climb over the rubble, and their fallen comrade, to do so. They maneuvered over chunks of stone and the mangled cell door. The only way forward from there was through the buzzing aircraft's side door. Together, they slid it open with a shriek of bent metal siding and clambered inside.

Shenlong took in the scene. The pilot had been impaled by an incredibly large arrow. His partner had been flung against the back of the rear hold. He was alive too. Shenlong rushed to his side, shoving the pilot's pleading, bloodied hand away as he searched his body for anything useful.

He found a couple items of note, mainly a radio and a pistol.

The mercenary smiled, stood, and shot the pilot in the head. Next, he and Gang went about working to open the other side door. It had been forced shut as the crash occurred and had damaged the minigun. Gang also obtained a pistol from the speared pilot. Both men were now armed and ready to leave.

They shoved, working the door back and forth until an opening, large enough to allow them passage, was born. Shenlong slipped through first. He kept an eye out for enemies while Gang followed behind him. He saw nothing, but he heard everything. The roars of beasts and the cries of men filled the, otherwise silent, Himalayan night.

It was what hell must've sounded like.

"Come on," he said, keeping his head down and moving off.

Shenlong activated his pilfered radio and flicked through the channels until he heard something that made his blood boil.

"Yana, do you copy? Come in, Yana."

It was the American. He was still alive, which meant Wu probably was too. Shenlong squeezed the device as hard as he could, feeling the casing give under the pressure. He relaxed his grip and grabbed Gang's arm, stopping him mid-stride.

"All of this," he held up the radio, "is because of them."

Gang nodded and stared at the radio.

Shenlong took a deep breath and blew it out. Escaping was of the utmost importance, but so was settling a score.

Shenlong wanted revenge.

"They must die."

Fan was the last man standing from his original twelve-man team. The rest had all met their fates at the hands of the mountain's creatures, by a bullet, or the voracious felines. He had somehow lucked out and found himself still alive.

He needed to warn his superiors of what was up here. There weren't any more men to send in, not in the immediate area. The plan was for three teams to be moved to Peikucuo Lake and wait to be called in, if needed. Had Fan known what would greet them, he would've asked for twice as many teams.

Fan waited for a foursome of archers to pass by, then he made his move. He headed further away from the center of the village, away from the tree they protected so intensely. He knew it must be the key, though he didn't know how or why. Fan didn't care either. Escape was his only option now. Someone else could deal with this place at a later time.

He headed east and successfully made it to the outskirts of town. Since leaving the battlefield, he had heard nothing. Fan moved slowly, and he listened carefully. An empty stone road greeted his boots. He took a moment to collect himself, moving his hands to his hips, and his eyes to the sky. He took several nerve-calming gulps of air, then turned south. Hopefully, the front gate wasn't being watched.

The trek was peaceful, unnervingly so. Echoes of pain-filled screams whispered to him, making him wince. Soon, they died down along with their owners.

But Fan kept moving.

Miraculously, he made it. A pair of swordsmen stood watch in front of the gate, but that was all. Fan still possessed his sidearm, though it only contained half a magazine. He could easily kill these men, but then he'd be nearly out of ammo. Plus, the gunshots would surely bring more men calling. Fan needed to keep his escape between him and no one else.

He waited, kneeling behind the cover of a pair of squat wooden barrels to the east of the entrance's remains. He stayed put for fifteen minutes, constantly looking over his shoulder, waiting to be attacked by one of the monsters, or perhaps one of the giant snow leopards. Regardless, he'd never look at the big cats the same way.

A commotion picked up somewhere out of sight, and it drew the guards away. Fan made his move. He stayed low. He was within ten feet of the gate when one of the swordsmen turned. With his attention taken away from his duty, Fan stepped through and hurried to the darkness beyond.

He didn't stop.

Fan used the minimal natural light, and his good memory to scale the river's bridge, finding the switchback stairs moments later. He scaled them carefully, dragging his hand across the ornately carved wall as he did. He hit the landing in between and picked up his pace, making it to the cliff that overlooked the entire valley.

Fan didn't stop to smell the roses. He rushed into the roofless V-shaped section of the mountain pass and turned on his small handheld flashlight. The tunnel came to view on the edge of his light, and he slowed. He stopped just outside of it and listened.

Nothing.

Fan stepped in and disappeared, leaving Shangri-La, and the nightmarish bloodshed, behind.

Park and his last remaining teammate were being hunted from above. The entire third team was dead, and he wasn't sure about Fan's fate, or the fate of his men. The howls of the beasts filled the sky above them, and their shadows danced in the firelit pathways. Park knew what it looked like to be played with. They were being ping-ponged around the same way a house cat batted around a mouse.

They had exhausted their rifle ammo long ago. The only firepower that the two men had left were their pistols, and they knew from experience that small caliber rounds did little besides upset their hunters more. The only way out of their current situation was to lose them and escape back through the front gate.

Park's man stumbled but caught himself.

The slight deceleration was his doom.

A massive being landed atop him, crushing him to the cobblestone road. Park heard the soldier's bones snap.

Park tripped and fell, but quickly gathered his wits and climbed to his feet. He looked back and saw Death. It was in a low crouch, studying him. He backpedaled and drew his sidearm, aiming it with quaking hands. It stood and he flinched, accidentally pulling the trigger. The bullet punched into the thick tissue of the creature's left shoulder, doing absolutely nothing to it.

The giant stepped toward him, just far enough for one of the streetlamps to illuminate it. It slowly reached up to its furred head and pulled. Park was surprised to see that the pelt was nothing more than a hood. What lay beneath should've intrigued him. It was a woman with Neanderthal features. She disrobed. Her minimal clothing showed off her muscular build, but also her feminine accents. Park wasn't gawking at her for that reason. He was shocked to see her unsheathe a very familiar knife from her loincloth's belt.

It was his knife.

She brought it up to her nose and inhaled. Even from here, Park could see her pupils dilate as if she was lost in some sort of euphoric state. Park knew what she was doing. She had come for revenge. She had intentionally hunted her family member's killer.

Park whimpered, turned, and ran, slamming into a wall of flesh. He went down, quickly looking up to see an even bigger creature, a male. Park crab-walked away from him and struggled to his feet, feeling his bladder release as he moved. Park stumbled back and bumped into another dense barricade. He didn't get the chance to turn and see what it was. He didn't need to either.

It was *her*.

The huntress grabbed both of Park's arms, just below his shoulders, and lifted him off his feet as if he weighed nothing. She leaned in and sniffed the side of his face. She smelled of rotting flesh and filth. The woman took in one long breath, then let out a low guttural roar.

Park screamed.

She pulled.

Shenlong and Gang moved like ghosts. They stuck to haunting the buildings of Shangri-La over the streets and alleys where the real phantoms roamed. So far, they had avoided one of the beasts, as well as a pair of snow leopards. Those two factions were the real challenge. The locals armed with khukuri blades and bows and arrows weren't much of an issue. They ran through the passages in droves, making it easy to hear them coming.

Gang was falling behind quickly. Shenlong was tired too, but he pushed himself harder than most. They were nearly back to the southern side of the tree courtyard. Shenlong tiptoed up to the corner of the square, three-story structure and peeked inside one of the first-floor windows. He saw bottles—wine perhaps. But it appeared as if no one was home.

Perfect.

Shenlong tried the accordion shutters and found that they were unlocked. He climbed inside. He planned to traverse the interior of the building and head for the front door. Gang was slow to follow.

He was startled by an onrush of multiple footfalls. From Shenlong's vantage point, he watched as Gang stole a glance behind him, then took off running past the wine shop. Gang disappeared behind the wall that separated the window that Shenlong had crawled through from the next window further up the road. When Gang did reemerge, he stuttered to a stop with no less than eight arrows protruding from his back.

Shenlong floated into the next room without giving Gang a second look. His entire ten-man team was officially dead. All except for him.

58

Bodies littered the area surrounding the tree well. All of them, Petalian and not, were covered with coats, blankets, or cloaks. The people here regarded the dead, no matter who they were. Jack respected that mindset. A loss of life was always tragic to him, but sometimes, it was the necessary outcome to preserve the lives of others. For that same reason, May had executed the unconscious commando earlier.

You aren't a choirboy either, Jack.

He had killed a good many people in his life, and not just when he had served. Even in his most recent escapades several people had died by his hand. It was a casualty of the job.

Death didn't bother Jack.

Needless death did.

The people on both sides of this conflict had chosen to fight whether forced into it or indoctrinated into it. Some called it training. Others called it brainwashing. Jack felt somewhere right in between. The soldiers that had attacked this peaceful village stood on the ledge overhanging indoctrination. The men he had fought against in Iraq had leaped from that cliff years before Jack had ever stepped foot on the sand.

He and May checked on those in need of help, though the Petalians seemed to be handling the disaster rather well. The Valley of Petals was very used to being on their own and relying entirely on self-sustainment. Jack wasn't sure there was a real medic available.

Everyone, it seemed, was a medic.

Jack and May were given another round of peach tea, and this time, they guzzled it down. How on earth did they brew more so quickly? Jack had no idea. But if it was in regular use for bumps, bruises, cuts, and even broken limbs, then he guessed they must have it ready to go, and in ample supply.

The brew entered his system as swiftly as it had the first time, but its effects weren't as odd. Jack wasn't sure if he was *that* tired, or if his body had gotten used to it. Still, he was feeling infinitely better in seconds. May looked much improved too.

Veer and Gareth appeared, finishing their ascent back up to ground level. Kalsang and Yana weren't with them. The Hindi must've seen the worry on Jack's face.

He held up his hand. "Your friends are fine."

Gareth shrugged. "Well, the Sherpa is. Your Russian friend is, well, something else."

"How is she?" May asked.

Gareth laughed. "Mentally, she's fine, and that's the problem. She needs rest, and she wants nothing to do with it."

May smiled. "Sounds like Yana. I don't think she knows what rest is."

"She also curses a lot." Jack, May, and Veer all stared at the Brit. He shrugged. "What? There are women and children present."

May looked at her feet and kicked at a piece of loose debris. "Yes, that *also* sounds like Yana."

Where's Kalsang?" Jack asked, not seeing the Sherpa anywhere.

"Come," Veer said, "we will take you to him."

Veer and Gareth turned and headed back into the well.

"Where are we going?" Jack asked.

"Mother's tomb," Gareth replied. "Your friend won't leave."

"Why?"

The Brit glanced over his shoulder at Jack. "You'll see."

That made Jack and May suspicious, not that Veer, or Gareth had given them anything to worry about so far. No one in the Valley of Petals had.

They passed Batu and Ram on the way down. Both men were nursing multiple injuries, but nothing too serious. Jack had yet to see Ella. He hoped the archer had survived. He'd really love to buy her a beer someday and shoot the shit.

They rounded the tree and headed for the tomb's entrance. Dozens of people funneled out and paid their respects to Jack and May with their signature straight-backed salute. The attention made Jack uncomfortable. The villagers parted as they exited, allowing Veer, Gareth, May, and Jack inside. The tunnel on the other side of the door was twice as wide and featured the same lamps as the street corners aboveground. The wall-hung lights allowed Jack to see all the way to the rear of the chamber ahead, though he couldn't see the ceiling of the next room because of the lower roof of the entrance passage.

But he could tell that something large stood at the rear of the room.

We're headed under the farmlands. Jack had presumed as much.

He fell in line next to May. Her face was perfectly illuminated by the lamplight. Jack was lost in her eyes, as the flame danced in them. She caught him staring and stared back.

Their attention was torn away from one another when they entered the chamber—the tomb. It was mostly empty, save for a single stone sarcophagus, and the enormous statue of a young woman beyond it. It reminded Jack of the Seven Sisters Monument back in Wyoming.

Only this was just the one girl. And she held a miniature version of the 211-foot-tall peach tree in her cupped hands.

"Mother," Jack said, awestruck.

"Yes," Veer said. "This is the Mother of the Valley of Petals."

Hundreds of people sat on their knees in reverence of the young girl, though to Jack, the forty-foot-tall stone memorial resembled someone older than he had expected.

"How old was she when she died?" Jack asked.

"Nineteen," Veer replied. "She left behind a baby boy who would grow up to govern this place with the same kindness that Mother was known for."

"How did she die?" May asked, her voice low.

Gareth took over. "Our records state that she developed an illness that was incurable. Unfortunately, she never got the chance to see what her creation could do."

"The story says," Veer continued, "that the peaches ripened into what we have today in the season following her death. Those who knew Mother best said it had been a sign from her." They stopped while everyone looked up at the statue. "The tree had needed her spirit to transform."

"What was her real name?" Jack asked.

"Sangpo..." Veer faced Jack. "Sangpo Thapa." May stepped up next to Jack and they both stared at the Hindi. "Yes, she was Kalsang's ancestor."

"What?" Jack was furious. "Why didn't you tell us any of this earlier? Kalsang should've been told, at the very least!"

"He needed to find out for himself," Gareth replied, joining them. "Telling him wouldn't have had the same impact as showing him."

May looked up at Mother, Sangpo, then back down to the local men. "That's why you insisted on having him join you down here instead of staying and fighting up in the village."

Veer nodded. "Correct."

"Sangpo. What does it mean?" May asked.

Veer smiled. "It means, 'to have a good heart.'"

That made May smile.

A question dug at Jack. "How did Kalsang not find out sooner that his ancestor was the birth mother of Shangri-La? His grandfather should've known, right?"

"Not unless he himself didn't know," Veer replied. "We don't know how much Dhonu passed down before he disappeared."

"Perhaps that's why Dhonu finally abandoned his post," May said, getting the guys' attention. "He was, technically, the heir to the undying kingdom and all he had to show for it was, what?"

She didn't need to add anything. The answer was clear.

Dhonu Thapa had nothing.

But that wasn't the fault of anyone here. Jack needed to remember that. No one—not Veer or Gareth—was responsible.

Gareth cleared his throat. "Once Mother's tomb was complete, her remains were exhumed and moved here where they still rest today. Citizens are required to return once a year and pay their respects."

"As will I."

Kalsang looked up at the statue, mumbled something to himself, then stood.

"You will?" Jack asked.

"Actually," Gareth said, "Kalsang has offered to stay behind and learn more about his bloodline."

"So," Jack said, "you gonna eat a peach, or what?"

Kalsang didn't respond. That would be a decision he'd make on his own, in private. Because if he did, he'd become a permanent resident of the Valley of Petals.

Veer left shortly after he had dropped the mind bomb pertaining to Kalsang's family tree. His presence had been requested topside by Batu. Jack, May, Kalsang, and Gareth hung around off to the side and quietly conversed, talking about what they had gone through over the last couple of hours. Upon Gareth's mention of running into Yana by the Gallery, Jack, once again, questioned her whereabouts.

"Where is she?"

"Right here."

They all turned to find the Russian sniper being led to the group by two local women. Her winter coat was peeled back, and her thermal undershirt had been cut apart to reveal a bloodstained left shoulder. May met them halfway to check on her friend. One of the villagers struggled to carry Yana's rifle. Jack happily released her from her burden.

Yana looked them over. "From the looks of it, I'd say we did okay, yes?"

"Yeah," Jack replied, "we did okay. A lot of senseless killing, though."

The Russian stared at Jack. "The taking of innocent lives is senseless, yes, I agree. But the soldiers that came here to harm these people deserved their end." She shrugged out of the helpers' hands and stood slightly hunched, favoring her shoulder. Yana nodded her thanks to the two women who had been watching over her.

"How do you feel?" Jack asked.

"Like I got shot, but the pain is not too bad. They finally convinced me to try their tea. Then, they poured a healthy amount right into the wound." Yana rotated the joint ever so slightly. "That stuff is incredible. At this rate, I'll be good as new by morning."

They left together as a group. The villagers gave them the same attention as before. This time, Jack didn't feel as awkward now that he had learned more about their history. He appreciated their appreciation. But he still felt responsible.

But they aren't pointing fingers, Jack. Even Gareth hadn't brought it up since their initial meeting.

Yana showed off the netting she had mentioned over the radio. Jack was beyond impressed with its design. The frame folded directly into the tree trunk and could be deployed by a single man with one quick pull. It was how Gareth had saved her life.

She thanked him properly by slapping a big wet kiss on him.

Jack stepped onto the first stair and heard something he wasn't expecting. A single pop reverberated around them, bouncing around the stone well. The noise had originated from the surface.

Jack tore off up the stairs as people screamed. He quickly armed himself with Yana's rifle. He confirmed it was loaded as he moved, refamiliarizing himself with the weapon's fire controls. Jack was confident with any modern firearm, and from the sound of it, he'd need to be. He heard feet pursuing him but didn't look back to see who it was. He had no doubt it was May. Kalsang too.

Upon nearing the top, Jack slowed and shouldered the big RSASS. He stopped as soon as he was high enough to aim it over the rim. It wasn't hard to spot the culprit. He was roughly two hundred feet away and an easy shot. But there was too much movement to see exactly who was where or what was happening.

"Has Veer," one woman said in broken English. She was lying on the ground ten feet from Jack, covering her head with her hands.

"Who has Veer?" Jack asked, never looking away from the scope.

She shook her head. "Bad man."

No shit, really?

As the crowd continued to disperse, Jack finally got a look at the shooter. "Shenlong," he said.

"What?" May said, shocked. "He's free? How?"

"Doesn't matter," Jack said. "All that matters is that he *is* free."

"Where is the American?"

Uh, oh.

"You're being summoned," May said. "What's the plan?"

Jack glanced over at her. "I'm going to shoot him."

"From here—with Veer in front of him? You can't take that shot, Jack."

"Yes, he can," Yana said, sliding up next to May. "I believe in him."

"Thanks, but I'm siding with May on this one. It's too risky."

Yana grumbled something in her native language, no doubt a profanity.

Jack sidestepped up the stairs but did not lower the rifle. He carefully felt for solid footing while keeping his eye glued to the scope and his cheek pressed against the stock. Shenlong spotted him as he emerged.

"Drop your weapon!"

Jack snorted a laugh. "How 'bout, no?"

He continued forward, much to the fury of the mercenary. Veer expressed indifference. His calm demeanor helped Jack immensely. If the hostage had been frantically screaming, crying, and wiggling around, it would've made the situation much worse.

Jack paused after fifty feet. A body was on the ground ten feet from Shenlong and Veer. It was Batu, and thankfully, he was still moving. That had been the single gunshot they had heard from below. Shenlong must've taken Veer as his hostage immediately afterwards. Now, everyone present watched the situation unfold.

Including the gathering Dharmapala.

Shenlong looked behind him and spied the tribe closing in. He jammed the pistol's muzzle deeper into Veer's temple. "Tell your apes to standdown, or you die!"

"My life is inconsequential," Veer said. "I will happily trade mine for yours."

Jack couldn't be more impressed with a man than he was with Veer Burman. He was willing to sacrifice his own life for the greater good. The decision was an easy one for Veer because of what the Valley of Petals meant to him.

To everyone.

"That may be true, but what about his?" Shenlong tipped his chin toward the injured Batu. "Once you're dead, there will be nothing to stop me from killing him. Not even your new American friend will get that quick of a shot off, nor will your snow apes be able to make it here in time."

He was right. Even if Jack was on his A game, he doubted he could make the shot with Veer's body still in the way. If Shenlong was as good as Jack knew he was, then he'd easily be able to kill Veer and then snap the pistol down to Batu and finish him before Veer's corpse fell away.

But none of that happened.

An arrow pierced Shenlong's gun hand. It struck with such velocity that it penetrated far enough through to lodge the razor-sharp tip in the merc's throat.

What the hell!

Jack searched for the archer responsible and found her kneeling off to his left. Ella Presley had quickly lined up and taken the shot while Shenlong's attention had been on Jack. Veer dove away, giving Jack the opening he needed. He pulled the trigger while Shenlong gasped for air. The .308 black tip struck Shenlong an inch above where his body armor stopped and knocked him off his feet.

As the mercenary's life faded, Veer crawled over to Batu and shouted for help. Three residents sprinted over, pulling all kinds of bits and pieces out of their bags and pockets. Everyone here was, indeed, a medic in some way.

Jack lowered the rifle and gave Ella a playful wink. The Olympian gave him one back and got to her feet. She was immediately surrounded and congratulated on a job well done, as was Jack.

"Nice shot," Yana said, stepping up next to Jack, "and no, you can't keep it."

Jack rolled his eyes and tossed the RSASS over his right shoulder as May slid herself in under his other arm and embraced him.

59

The Dharmapala were granted refuge and treated like heroes, which they were. Veer extended them the opportunity to stay through the night as his way of thanking them for their service. Dorje initially declined. It wasn't until Drilha stepped in, much to her husband's displeasure, and replied with something to the gist of, "We'd love to, thank you," that they settled in.

An elderly woman applied an ointment to the cut on Jack's head. It was the same stuff that they had used on Yana's shoulder. At first, he declined the creamy agent.

"Relax," Gareth said, "it's like the tea, and will ward off infection."

Jack eyed Yana. She gave him a thumbs up. "Works like a charm."

That's when Jack gave in. And yes, it did work like a charm.

The Dharmapala refused treatment. They had their ways, and they weren't about to change. Besides, Jack suspected there was more to their body chemistry than just being super strong and somewhat invulnerable to injury. He didn't know what made them different or if it was tied to their Neanderthal-like DNA, but their makeup was definitely unique. They possessed several inhuman qualities.

They're truly special.

Once everyone was bandaged and refreshed, they moved to the library and lounged around on the upper floor. Jack found a chair and happily sat, as did everyone except for Veer. The Hindi stood with his hand placed squarely on the conference table, once again reading through the account of Mother, Sangpo Thapa.

Jack and May sat next to one another. She was deep in thought.

"What's wrong?" he asked.

"The jars," she whispered, leaning in close to him.

"What jars?"

"The jars from Langtang. What are the chances they held nectar?"

Jack knew where she was going with this. "Pretty high, I'd say. Remember the solid substance inside of them?"

May nodded. "Yeah. Looks like Celia wasn't the only thief this place has had to deal with."

"Or it's third, fifth, or last," Jack said. "That stuff is just too incredible not to try and sneak some to the outside world. I guarantee it's how the other cultures heard about it."

One of those cultures was the Greeks and their Nectar of Life. Jack had no doubt the nectar had been smuggled to the Mediterranean where it then took on a life, and lore, of its own.

"How 'bout we keep that little nugget to ourselves, okay?"

May nodded. Their discovery in Langtang meant nothing to this place now and could only further tarnish the Thapa name.

Gareth joined them from the back of the room, holding another book similar in size to the one Veer was looking over. He didn't open it. Instead, he handed it to Kalsang without a word.

Kalsang accepted it, unsure of why. But he must've figured it out as soon as he opened the cover.

"What is it?" May asked.

Kalsang stared at the first page and said, "My entire family tree up to Dhonu Thapa."

"You belong here, Kalsang," Gareth said. "We all see that now. You belong where your bloodline began."

"Technically," Yana said, filling the quiet room, "wouldn't it have begun where Mother was born?"

Jack groaned. "Way to ruin the moment, BD."

"BD?" Gareth asked.

Yana tapped her chest with each word. "Blood. Dragon."

"Oh, right."

"So, Jack," Veer said, "what will you tell your people back home? Can we trust you to keep this place a secret?"

Jack stood and walked over to the table. "I'll recommend a few defensive upgrades to this place, but other than that, I don't think we should change a thing." He turned his head and gazed out the window, seeing the tree. "This place really is paradise."

"You could open an Airbnb, and…" Yana halted whatever she was going to say when she realized everyone was staring at her. "Never mind."

Jack turned away from the table but stopped and reapproached it.

Veer looked up from the book and waited for him to speak.

"Your relationship with the Dharmapala."

"What about it?"

Jack leaned on the table with two closed fists. "I suggest you strengthen it. You are bonded to one another. It would benefit you both if you worked together more than just as 'protector' and 'protected.' I think it's safe to say that the old ways are dead. We've all seen what happens when a single cog fails. This system was nearly burned to the ground because of one selfish, lonely man."

Veer opened his mouth to speak, but Jack cut him off. "Imagine what would happen if Dorje and his people suddenly decided not to watch over the bordering lands." Jack stuck out his hand. Veer cautiously clasped it. "You're a great leader, Veer. I'm not taking anything away from you. Based on everything I've seen, you've done an exceptional job. The way you stood your ground with a gun to your head was inspiring. Your people are lucky to have you."

Veer nodded his understanding. "I will speak to my people and convey what you have said." He squeezed tight. "Thank you."

Jack shrugged and released his hand. "No problem, it's kinda what I do. And don't worry about the Chinese finding out about this place. I promise we'll think of something."

Veer eyed the tree through the window. "Yes, let's hope so."

Jack returned to his place next to May. She took his hand in hers and clutched it hard. She laid her head on his shoulder.

"Do you actually think we can hide this place from the MSS?" she asked.

Jack smiled at Gareth as he passed by, then whispered exactly what Veer had said.

"Let's hope so."

Dorje and Drilha led the way through the ruined front gate. Remarkably, measures were already underway to repair the damage. Batu was already healing from the comfort of a padded chair while a crew of fifteen got started. He had refused to stay sidelined.

It was time to go home.

Jack had found Shangri-La, and it was weird, wild, wonderful, and better than anything he could've expected. He had even made a few more friends along the way, though he was sure Veer and Gareth would rather that he never return.

He had caused enough problems.

The Dharmapala leaders had offered to escort Jack, May, and Yana back to the Triratna Monastery as soon as they desired. Jack felt it was time to allow this amazing place to heal, as it had done for centuries.

In secrecy.

They hiked up to the overlook—the place where Jack had first laid eyes upon the beautiful pink Beyul—the heavenly valley. He faced the mountain pass and took a deep breath, knowing he'd most likely not see it again. It saddened him, but he also knew it would be necessary. This place needed to be left alone. It had thrived for centuries, and today, the entire valley had nearly been flattened the one time modern man had intervened.

Whispers between the Petalian guards caught Jack's attention. He turned toward them, Veer, and Gareth.

"What's their problem?" he asked.

Veer went back and forth with his men, then provided a translation.

"They," Veer sighed, "want you to stay. They believe you would be an asset to us." He faced Jack. "Most of the people here have never seen the outside world. The soldiers scared them. It has been a reality check."

Veer turned toward the valley. He dug through his robe and pulled a small, round object out. He held it up and looked over his shoulder.

It was a peach.

"You *could* stay, you know?" Veer faced him. "You've shown yourself to be worthy."

He tossed the peach to Jack.

Jack caught it and looked it over. He brought it up to his nose and sniffed it. It smelled sweet, even with the furry skin still protecting it.

May stepped up close to Jack. He looked at her. "Whattaya say? How would you like to gain another hundred years on your life?"

The corner of her mouth turned up. "I'm not sure I'm ready for that kind of commitment with you."

Jack grinned. "Fair enough."

May stepped away, reaching out her hand.

Jack looked back and forth between her hand and the peach he still held.

He made his decision.

Jack underhanded the peach back to Veer. "Perhaps another time." He winked. "I still have some living to do."

Triratna Monastery
Forbidden Valley, Tibet

Yana had also decided to pass on staying. She still had some living to do too. But that didn't mean she wasn't opposed to rambling on about how amazing it would be to be an immortal super sniper.

"I could be just like Winter Soldier!"

Jack gave her a sideways glance. "Are you trying to convince us or yourself?"

"And you wouldn't be immortal," May corrected.

"Yeah," Jack agreed, "Bucky was a badass, but he wasn't immortal."

Yana scoffed at their reaction. "You know what I mean. And Jack?"

"Yeah?"

She pointed at his forehead. Jack's eyes crossed as he followed her finger. "Your nerd is showing."

Yana entered the monastery first, not letting Jack get another word in. They stepped over the threshold of the busted side door and out of the elements. Jack was instantly warmer just being back indoors, even if there was a horrid draft.

A storm had rolled in a half hour prior, and the weather had gotten nasty. He expected to be stuck here for the night.

"Too bad we can't leave right now," May said, gazing out the nearest window.

Yana shook her head. "Better we stay grounded than risk getting knocked out of the sky."

"Yeah," Jack agreed, "that would be bad. You sure you can pilot that thing?" He looked through the large, open second floor. It was still too dark outside to see the first Harbin Z-20 that Yana had been telling them about on their exodus from the Valley of Petals.

Dorje and Drilha led them in then disappeared down the hall before returning a few minutes later with two large armfuls of dried firewood. Jack helped them get it lit while May assisted in getting Yana settled in for the night. She was doing a hell of a lot better but was still favoring her right shoulder and arm. Jack hoped she'd be in better shape in the morning. She was the only pilot here, after all.

And that was the plan. They'd spend the night here under the watchful eye of the greatest the Dharmapala had to offer: Dorje, their strongest, and Drilha, their finest hunter.

They awoke to a high-pitched shriek and a bellowing roar. Jack leaped to his feet, pistol drawn, as did May. Yana still wasn't moving as fast, but she unavoidably got to her feet, clutching her PPQ in both hands and looking for someone to shoot. It seemed that her left shoulder wasn't bothering her as much as it had the night before.

"What the hell was that?" Yana asked, wiping the sleep from her face.

"No idea, I—"

Jack was cut off by another scream, then the voice's owner appeared beyond the window behind them. All three of Jack, May, and Yana rushed to it and leaned out in time to see a black-clad man disappear into the thick fog of the Forbidden Valley. Jack knew the impact would be nasty.

"Was that a Falcon Commando?" May asked, looking back and forth between Jack and Yana.

Both shrugged.

A snort caused them to look up. They found Drilha standing directly above them, leaning out of a window. Evidently, she had discovered an uninvited guest and tossed him out. Literally.

Drilha disappeared from view, satisfied that she had successfully rid her home of the pest problem. Two minutes later, she joined the others, along with Dorje, who was carrying a necklace. Jack then saw a pair of dog tags dangling from it.

So, it was a Falcon Commando!

Dorje handed it to Jack, who then passed it to May.

"There's a name on it," he said.

May held it up and struggled to read it through the fresh blood. "I think it says, Fan." She looked at Jack. "Who's Fan?"

He had no idea. "Whoever he was, he was no friend of the Dharmapala, that's for sure."

"I don't know about you two," Yana said, "but I believe that is our cue to leave. Storm has let up too."

May nodded. "You won't get an argument out of me."

Jack stretched his sore and tired legs. "Ditto." The peach tea had worn off overnight.

Jack, May, and Yana gave Dorje and Drilha a slight bow, crossing their chests with a fist. The ancient hunters returned their respective gestures.

Jack turned but stopped, remembering the only two words he knew that Dorje and Drilha would understand.

He waved and said, "*Dhan che.*"

"*Dhan che?*" May asked.

Jack nodded. "It means 'thank you.'"

May and Yana followed Jack to the other side of the monastery and then outside. The storm had, indeed, subsided. It was still cold as hell, but it wasn't unbearably frigid.

Yana pushed ahead and climbed inside, plopping down behind the yoke. Jack watched her flick a bunch of switches and punch the dashboard twice, passionately screaming at it.

"She's something else, huh?"

But she didn't hear him. May had wandered off to the edge of what had become a helipad. The rotors came to life slowly as Jack moved to join her, carefully stepping over chunks of what he knew was human flesh, but a substance he told himself was cherry Jell-O.

They stood in silence and watched the fog drift by and change shape with the incoming breeze. It wasn't until something strode up next to them that Jack and May moved again.

Yana appeared. "So, do you want to leave or not?"

All three climbed into the low-roofed rear hold. Yana continued into the cockpit and slid into the pilot's chair, rotating her arm as she prepped for takeoff. Jack and May sat on the left-hand bench seat. Jack laid his head back against the inside wall and closed his eyes.

"Jack," May said, tapping his leg.

He opened his eyes. "Yeah?"

"Look," she replied, pointing out the open door.

Jack obliged and spotted Dorje and Drilha standing outside the monastery doors. He got up and wobbled over and hunched. Yana got them into the air with little difficulty. Jack gave them one last wave before closing the door and returning to his seat.

Emerald Lotus Monastery
Lamabagar, Nepal

The flight back to civilization hadn't taken long. That worried Jack. The Valley of Petals wasn't all that far away from civilization. The bleak weather of Desolation and, of course, the savage Yetis were the only things stopping people from making the discovery themselves. A smirk formed on Jack's face.

"What's so funny?"

With the back of his head against the hull, he rolled it left to face her. "Do you realize that we found Shangri-La *and* proved that Yetis exist?"

"Sounds like a fairytale to me. I don't think anyone will believe us."

Jack sat up. "That's what I'm planning on."

They slowed and hovered in place. The descent wasn't as smooth as Jack would've liked. They bounced around like mad. Jack couldn't hear much over the rumble of the aircraft, but he was pretty sure he could hear the pilot cursing in Russian again. Just when he was about to lose a filling, they evened out and touched down.

Jack and May couldn't get out soon enough.

Jack threw open the rear door and was met with the astonished gaze of nearly three dozen people. He yanked his sock hat on lower and slipped on a pair of sunglasses Yana had found up front. May pulled on her coat's hood and tightened the drawstrings. Both needed to hide their faces.

They jumped out and headed up front. Yana slid open a small side window and tossed something at Jack. He caught it, confused.

They were a set of car keys.

"You aren't coming with us?" he asked, shouting.

Yana patted the outside of the helicopter. "I just traded it in for something a bit more my style!" She gave him a playful wink. "Until next time!" Yana kissed her hand and then blew it at May. She closed the window, powered the Z-20 back up, and lifted the military aircraft into the sky.

As the locals and vacationers watched the hulking black beast take off, Jack and May slipped away.

EPILOGUE

Suri, Nepal

It took a while, but Jack finally got enough of a signal to make a call. He punched in the number of the shadowed Solomon Raegor, just like he had done the last time he'd been in May's safehouse in Kathmandu.

"Jack, finally; you okay?"

"I am, sir, thank you."

He grumbled. "And since you aren't driving, I assume Ms. Wu is there too."

"She is, yes."

Raegor cleared his throat. "Hello again, Ms. Wu."

"Hi," May replied, unsure what to say.

"Jack, the mission."

"A resounding success. Well, sort of."

It took him a bit to explain everything that had happened since they had last talked. But Raegor was so enthralled with the tale that he sat forward, leaning into the call—the story. Jack knew Eddy would be just off camera, probably doing the same thing. Everything Jack was telling them was bonkers.

"That's quite the adventure," Raegor said, sitting back. "And yes, I'll make the necessary arrangements. This valley will be protected at all costs. There's too much at stake considering what you discovered."

"I appreciate that," Jack said. "They are good people." He sighed. "I kinda wish I had never found it, to be perfectly honest. We may have done more bad than good this time."

"I understand, Jack, but this is what we do. Unfortunately, for us to protect something, it must be found first. That's the game."

"It's not a game to them, sir."

"You know what I mean, Jack." He sat forward again. "Let me ask you this, you too, Ms. Wu. Do you believe the Chinese government would've eventually found the Valley of Petals?"

Jack looked at May and answered. "We did, so yeah, I think they would've eventually stumbled upon it."

"Then, you should regret nothing about what you did. I know it's difficult to grasp sometimes, but you are doing something great, Jack."

"Thank you, sir. I appreciate the support."

"Well, you've done nothing to make me think otherwise. I've been glad to have you on board ever since that night in your living room. Good coffee, too."

That made Jack smile. But it also gave him an idea.

"So, speaking of employment…"

May shot him a surprised look.

"Jack, no," Raegor said quickly.

"Seriously, sir, May is perfect."

She smiled.

"Is she now?" Raegor asked. Even though Jack couldn't see his face, he knew the man was smiling wide too.

Jack shifted in his seat, feeling a touch of embarrassment. "Think about it, sir. Imagine someone with her contacts in Southeast Asia, willing to fight the good fight."

"Is she?" Raegor asked. "Is a former MSS spy willing to fight the good fight?"

Jack looked away from the phone and stared at May. She took a breath and said, "Yes, sir, I am."

Jack jumped back in. "She's a whiz with Chinese culture, speaks four languages, and has had a lifetime of experience within global espionage. Plus, she packs a mean punch."

"You have experience with that?" Raegor asked, half-joking.

Jack rubbed his jaw as May pulled off onto a precipitous rest stop and parked. "Uh, yeah, I do. Our introduction didn't go as smoothly as I would've liked."

Raegor went silent for a moment. Then he leaned forward again. His voice was low and in control. "You like her, don't you?"

Jack glanced at May. She was already staring at him.

"I do," Jack replied, still not looking at the phone.

May was grinning ear to ear. She tucked a loose strand of hair behind her ear.

"She'll be a distraction. No offense, Ms. Wu."

"No, she won't, sir," Jack said. "I'm not looking for a partner. May is more than capable enough to do her own thing. I'd expect someone from her professional background could help us a lot."

"Like what, 'global espionage?'"

Jack grinned. "Exactly, and in Asia of all places."

Silence.

Jack's right leg bounced up and down. "Please, sir. She'll do great."

"And how do you know that?"

"Because I've seen it first-hand. I trust her with my life. The least we can do is trust her with a job, especially after everything she's done for us."

"Hmmm." Raegor leaned off camera and mumbled something to someone, undoubtedly Eddy. When he returned to frame, he sat back. "Ms. Wu, I assume you're still listening?"

"Yes, sir, I am."

He dramatically leaned forward again. "Welcome to the Tactical Archaeological Command. You'll be answering to me from now on."

Jack handed her the phone. She took it, unashamed of the tears streaming down her face. "Yes, sir. And thank you. This means the world to me."

"Yes, you are very welcome. As Jack said, your unique skillset will come in handy as long as you're willing to get your hands dirty from time to time."

"Her hands are filthy, sir!" Jack shouted.

"You're not helping, Jack," Eddy added from off camera.

Jack shrank away.

"First thing's first, May." It was the first time Raegor had called her anything besides 'Ms. Wu,' "I need you to do me a favor."

"Anything, sir."

"Keep our boy's head on straight, will you? He gets distracted easily."

Jack's mouth hung open at the jab, funny or not.

"Copy that, sir."

"Jack?" Raegor asked.

"Y—yeah, I'm here."

"What about the Chinese? They know where your valley is. Flight logs, radio signals—they can track all of that. It's only a matter of time before they send in more troops."

That was Jack's number one concern. And he had no answer.

But May did.

"I can help with that, sir."

"You can?" Jack, Raegor, and Eddy said together.

She looked away from the phone, talking to Jack. "I still have friends on the inside, remember?" She looked back at Raegor. "Let me make a call. I'm confident he can help."

"Who?" Raegor asked.

"Sorry, sir, anonymity is king in this line of work."

Raegor didn't like that, but he could appreciate it better than most. He was technically dead, after all. "I...understand." He visibly relaxed. "Huh, I may actually get some decent sleep tonight. Thank you for that. Take a few days leave and see the sights. Enjoy yourselves. You deserve it. And May?"

"Yes, sir?"

"We'll be in touch. Raegor out."

May handed Jack back his phone.

"What now?" she asked. "Where do I go from here?"

"Like Raegor said, let's take a few days and enjoy ourselves. We—"

"And what about after that, Jack? I can't go home!" More tears streaked down her perfect cheeks.

Jack's eyes lit up. "Come home with me!"

"What, no! Look, Jack, I like you, but—"

He grabbed her hand and squeezed. "You'll be safe, I promise. Who in their right mind will come looking for you in Cody, Wyoming? Of all the places in the world to lie low, it's the perfect one. My friends will help too."

"Your friends?"

Jack nodded. "There's no one I trust more than Bull and Hawk." May opened her mouth to speak, and it made him panic. "And you!" That made her eyes roll. "They're loyal to the core. You'll see."

May bit her lip and looked out the driver's side window. Jack understood what he was asking her to do. He was asking her to start her life over and move halfway across the globe.

"Jack, I—"

"Do you trust me?"

May turned and faced Jack. "You know I do." She laughed softly. "Honestly, you're probably the most trustworthy person I know."

"Then," he said, leaning in close, "trust me now." He gave her a quick peck on the lips. "Come home with me, May."

She was still unsure. "What's in Cody?"

Jack snorted. "Not a damn thing."

May's worry melted away. She smiled and said, "I like the sound of that."

She leaned in and kissed Jack deeply.

They parted and just enjoyed each other's company while staring out the windshield at the beautiful landscape. May squeezed Jack's hand, and he realized something.

Tertons were supposed to be gifted a treasure when they needed it most. Jack knew it was sappy to think, and he'd never say it out loud, but he was pretty damn sure that the woman sitting next to him was his treasure.

BIOfinity Genetics Group
Shanghai, China

David Cho was in a lot of trouble. Not only did his men fail miserably, but they did so with his life on the line. Both he and Minister Zhao had gotten nothing out of it except thirty-six dead commandos and ten dead mercenaries. David still couldn't appropriately process the death toll. Technically, the men were still listed as MIA, though David had no idea how the military would investigate their disappearance.

They must know something.

The last he had heard from Shenlong was that they were headed into northern Nepal, deep into the Himalayas. He also knew about a second team being sent in even further north of that. But then, the details had become scarce, whether on purpose or not. It wouldn't have shocked him if the MSS—partnered with the army—wanted to cover up the loss of so many men.

His intercom buzzed. "Sir," Li said, "Minister Zhao is—"

David's office door burst open before his assistant could finish. The man standing in it wasn't just Minister Zhao. It was so much worse.

It was a furious Minister Zhao.

David was going to die, one way or the other, yet he was still terrified of the man. He knew he could say anything he wanted, but at the moment, he couldn't formulate words.

Zhao beat him to it.

"If you're going to say something, don't."

So, David kept his mouth shut, and he slowly reached over to his top right-hand drawer. He pressed his thumb on the concealed fingerprint scanner and unlocked it. Inside was something David had very little practice with.

A gun.

Zhao silently walked over to the large window lining the left-hand side of David's office. He stared out of it for a time.

He sighed. "We lost everything because of you."

What?

"No," David retorted, "this was all your daughter's f—"

He stopped when Zhao's eyes darted over to him within the reflection. He turned, never once taking his gaze off David. He stepped up to the opposite side of David's desk and slammed the base of both fists into it. He leaned across the table.

"What did you say?"

David decided to choose his words carefully. "What I meant was that none of this would've happened if it weren't for Agent Wu's treachery." David relaxed, putting on his salesman persona. But he also decided to add in a touch of blackmail. "As far as I see it, this is no fault of anyone in this room. Wouldn't you agree, Minister?" He laid it on thick. "I believe there is a general somewhere in Beijing to blame for those men's deaths."

A smirk formed on Zhao's face. "You are a piece of work." David wasn't sure if that was a compliment or not. The Minister narrowed his eyes. "BIOfinity Genetics is mine."

David shot to his feet, keeping his fingertips on the unlocked gun drawer. "Over my dead body!"

"Very well."

Minister Zhao reached into his expensive jacket, drew a sound suppressed pistol, and shot David Cho in the forehead. The CEO's lifeless body collapsed in his expensive, leather, soiled chair.

Li Huang, David's loyal assistant, entered the room to a gruesome scene. Blood coated the wall behind his late boss' desk, and David now sported a hole in his skull. Unsurprisingly, Li didn't seem to mind it.

"You've done well for me over these last few years, Agent Huang." Zhao rounded the desk and unscrewed the suppressor from the pistol. He tucked the can into his inner jacket pocket.

Li curtly bowed. "Thank you, Minister."

"BIOfinity Genetics is going to need a new CEO," Zhao looked at Li. "You up to the challenge?" Zhao set his pistol on the table and wrapped David's lifeless hand around it. Now, it looked like a suicide.

Li considered the offer. "Thank you, Minister," he bowed again, "but I must respectfully decline. I believe I am of better use to the ministry at my current station."

Zhao nodded his approval, very impressed with the young man. "Very well." He turned. "I will ensure you are rewarded generously for your work here." Zhao rounded the other side of the desk, sanitizing his hands with a cleansing wipe. "In the meantime, find me a suitable, moldable replacement for that late David Cho."

"No, Minister, I won't be doing that."

Zhao looked up from his hands and was shot in the forehead.

By Li Huang.

Li re-holstered his own suppressed pistol, an exact duplicate of the one he knew Minister Zhao carried. He even knew the ammunition the man used.

Li entered the office, wearing the gloves he had slipped on as soon as Zhao had crossed the threshold. He removed Zhao's gun from David's hand and racked the slide, removing a second round. Li caught it and dropped the handgun on the carpeted floor beneath David's dangling hand. He returned to the door, retrieved the spent casing from his pistol, and tossed it on the ground near David. Now, to the untrained eye, it would look as if David had killed Zhao and then taken his own life. Before he left, Li retrieved Zhao's suppressor from his pocket.

"I'll take this."

Li holstered his duplicate pistol beneath his jacket, exited David's office, and shut the door. He slipped off his gloves and put them in his pocket, removing his phone from another pocket.

Li quickly dialed.

The phone rang once. "It is done."

"Thank you, Li," May said. "I owe you one."

"No, May, it is I who owes you. It was my pleasure to rid the world of him."

"Yes, well, I wish I could tell you how many lives you just saved, but I can't. You understand."

"I do," he said. "People in our profession must keep secrets, even from one another, no matter how much we trust the other. As you have requested, I will have our cyber team wipe the Falcon Commandos' last known location from the MSS database and have my contacts in the army do the same. It will be as if they vanished into thin air. Whoever it is you are trying to protect, they are safe."

"Thank you, Li."

"You are most welcome. If you need anything, you know how to find me, though it may be time for me to join the private sector too."

May chuckled. "Believe me, from my experience, I suggest you do just that. People in our line of work often have a brief shelf life." Li knew many agents who had died young. "But whatever you decide, can you do me a favor?"

"Name it."

"Do it for the right reasons, not for the right amount of money. Goodbye, Li."

The End

ABOUT THE AUTHOR

Hi, my name is Matt. I'm the international bestselling author of the electrifying JACK REILLY ADVENTURES, as well as two dozen other titles, including DARK ISLAND, and the intense UNSEEN action-horror novels. Moreover, I've been fortunate enough to partner with *USA Today* bestselling author Nick Thacker to create the wildly popular ZAHRA KANE archaeological thriller series. I'm also the Managing Editor for Conundrum Publishing, and I host REAL-LIFE FICTION on YouTube, a video podcast that features the book industry's finest talents.

My work is heavily influenced by the likes of Indiana Jones, Uncharted, Tomb Raider, The Mummy (1999), National Treasure, and The Goonies. As you can see, I'm a little obsessed with tales of daring adventure. When I was growing up, other kids went nuts for Star Wars or Star Trek. But not me. I fell in love with the globetrotting antics of Dr. Henry Jones, Jr., and the rest, as they say, was history. From that moment on, I was hooked. Though I dabble in other genres from time to time, my heart will always belong to ADVENTURE.

I live twenty minutes from the beach in sunny South Florida with my amazing wife, our two beautiful daughters, a lovable pitty, and an overly dramatic black cat.

YOU CAN VISIT MATT AT:

Website: MattJamesAuthor.com
Facebook: Facebook.com/MattJamesAuthor
Instagram: MattJames_Author
YouTube: Conundrum Publishing
Podcast: Real-Life Fiction

Printed in Great Britain
by Amazon

25300305R00175